HOT FOR THE HANDYMAN

THE SINGLE MOMS OF SEATTLE, BOOK 3

WHITLEY COX

ISBN: 978-1-989081-39-6

ALSO IN THE SINGLE MOMS OF SEATTLE SERIES

Hot for Teacher
mybook.to/hotforteacher
The Single Moms of Seattle, Book 1
Celeste and Max

Hot for a Cop
Mybook.to/hotforacop
The Single Moms of Seattle, Book 2
Lauren and Isaac

For the husband.
You're my Double H!
xoxo

1

"I DON'T CARE if you don't have matching socks. I am leaving this house in two minutes," Bianca Dixon called up the stairs to her six-year-old twins, Hannah and Hayley. "In other words, get your scrawny asses down here," she muttered under her breath.

"Scawnyass," echoed Charlie, her two-year-old son, sitting on the stairs heading down to the garage, kicking his feet and poking the eyeballs of his dinosaur stuffed animal.

Bianca grabbed her purse, her kids' backpacks for school and day care, and her lunch bag, hoisted Charlie onto her hip and headed down to the door to the garage.

"I mean it, girls. Get your butts down here."

Stomps and growls were followed by thundering size-one youth feet that rumbled the foundation of the house as her bickering twins descended the stairs.

"You can't leave without us, Mom," Hannah said with impatience. "The whole reason we're even leaving is so Hayley and I can go to school." She sat at the top of the stairs and pulled on her running shoes.

Her identical twin sister, just with a shorter haircut,

joined her and pulled on her matching shoes. "Yeah, Mom. We're *only* six. You can't leave us home alone. Otherwise, you'll get in trouble."

Bianca rolled her eyes. "In trouble with whom?"

The girls looked at each other, smiled and turned back to their mother with triumph in their brown eyes.

"Nana," they both said.

Bianca rolled her eyes again, placed Charlie on the ground beside her and opened the door to the garage. "Get your asses down the stairs, or you *won't* be going to Nana's soon."

That was a big ol' lie. No way in hell was Bianca giving up her child-free moments and denying her parents and children time together without her as a referee.

Hannah and Hayley's mouths dropped open.

"Mom said a bad word," Hayley whispered to her sister.

"We can tell Nana when we see her. Just be good so we can see her," Hannah replied.

"Get down here!" Bianca yelled, heading into the garage to load up her Honda Odyssey.

She had just gotten Charlie into his car seat and was closing the sliding door to the van with all her children strapped in with socks, shoes and combed hair when her cell phone began to warble in her purse.

"Fuck," she murmured as she swung in behind the steering wheel.

"Duck," Charlie repeated. "QUACK!"

She dug around in her purse and found her still ringing phone.

Of. Fucking. Course. It was her cheating-ass ex.

She canceled the call, hit the button to open up her garage door, and turned over the ignition. He could wait.

The last thing she wanted was to talk to the lying, cheating, wimpy, small-dicked douche. Particularly with her children within earshot, because then she'd have to remain pleasant with the fucker.

Glancing at the clock on her dash, she took a deep breath. She still needed to run by the property she managed to check in on the handyman before she took the girls to school. Charlie didn't start day care until nine thirty, so she had a bit of leeway there.

A huge delivery of kitchen cabinets was arriving today and Rod—the handyman—hadn't answered the last three of her text messages or the last four of her calls.

She needed somebody at the house to receive the delivery, and she couldn't guarantee that they wouldn't be delivered at nine sharp. She had to make sure Rod—her sixty-plus, round-bellied, chain-smoking, misogynistic handyman —was there and aware and didn't dick off to the hardware store or something.

From the moment she'd met him, she had reservations about the guy. He looked down on her, spoke down to her and smoked like a chimney.

But her last three contractors had left mid-project. One because he hurt his back, another because he got a job with another company across town, and then the last one moved to an entirely different state.

So she took pity on her kids' piano teacher's brother, out from Idaho, down on his luck, and apparently good with tools. Rod had been "working" for her for the past ten days, but so far, the guy wasn't worth the four grand they'd agreed on for him to get the first two units where she needed them to be. The guy hadn't earned five hundred in her opinion.

How long did it take to paint one bedroom?

She painted the kids' room, her room and both upstairs bathrooms in two days. And that was *with* children running around like jammy-hand meth-heads.

"What did you pack us for lunch?" Hannah asked as

Bianca turned out of their townhouse complex and onto the main road. Hannah was her loud, type A alpha-child. She had no problem voicing her opinions, taking charge and ruling any roost she set foot in.

Except Bianca's roost, of course.

Only one hen ruled that house. Only one *queen*. And her children knew it. As hard as Hannah tried to run the show, Bianca pushed back enough that her child was finally—after six *long* years—learning her place.

"I packed all three of you turkey bacon, cheese and pickle sandwiches, a yogurt tube, a banana each, some cucumber and pepper slices and one of those coconut bars you like."

All three kids cheered.

"Yay! Candy bars!" Hannah screamed.

They weren't candy bars. They were coconut- and cocoa-flavored bars made by some local health-food company and geared toward children who were picky eaters. Somehow, the creators had managed to jam spinach, dates, carrots, chia and hemp hearts into the bars without tainting the flavor. Her kids thought they were getting candy, when in truth they were getting two servings of vegetables and two tablespoons of coconut sugar.

In your picky-eating faces, you little crotch demons.

"Thanks for such a great lunch, Mom," Hannah said. "That sounds so good."

Hayley made a noise of agreement. "Yeah, so good, Mom. I love those sandwiches."

She could serve up turkey bacon, cheese and pickle sandwiches for every meal of every day and her kids would devour them. At least it hit all the major food groups—kind of. Pickles were still considered vegetables, right?

"*Shake off*," Charlie called out. "*Shake off*. Pwease."

Rolling her eyes, she turned on the music in the van and

located Taylor Swift's *Shake It Off* in the playlist on her phone.

As soon as the upbeat, peppy tune started, all three kids began to dance in their booster and car seats.

And she had to admit, when Taylor told her to *Shake it off*, her foul mood from earlier did slough off.

"Dance, Mama," Charlie said. "Dance."

They were only about two minutes from the property now and stopped at a red light. If she left the kids in the van with the door open, ran up to the front door, left that open too and spoke quickly to Rod for under two minutes, she could run back to the car and still get the girls to school on time.

"Dance, Mama!" Charlie ordered.

Bianca rolled her eyes again. "Okay, okay." Her torso jostled and twisted, then when the "Shake it off" part started, she batted invisible dirt off her shoulder, only when she glanced beside her, the man on the motorcycle in the adjacent lane was grinning at her. His long nose wrinkled. He bobbed his head and gave her a jolly thumbs-up just before the light turned green and he sped away.

Her face burned with embarrassment, and she turned the volume down.

"Up, Mama. Up," Charlie ordered. "Loud-ah."

"Why'd you turn it down?" Hayley asked. "Was it because that man on the motorcycle was smiling at you?"

Ignoring her children's demands and how astute her six-year-olds could be, she turned down the street where the soon-to-be-affordable off-campus student housing would be.

Two developers up in Canada—James Shaw and Justin Williams—bought up old, run-down houses in university districts, then they renovated them, turned them into multi-unit dwellings and offered them as affordable housing to students. They'd done it several times in the Seattle already —three of their properties Bianca already managed—as well as in Vancouver and Montreal in Canada and Eugene and Portland in Oregon. If the students moved out over the summer, she rented them as Airbnbs or whoever needed short-term housing. So far, it'd been working like a dream.

She slowed down when the van approached the house, and thankfully, Rod's beat-up old Nissan truck was parked out front. At least he was there.

Turning off the ignition, she went to unbuckle her belt when Charlie yelled, "Shake off, again ... pwease."

"Can you leave the music on, Mom?" Hannah asked. "It'll keep him happy."

Nodding, Bianca shoved the key back into the ignition, turned the music back on but kept it low so she could still hear her children if they suddenly started choking on their own spit. She unrolled her window and made her way to the front door of the unit Rod had been assigned to work on.

She went to open the door, thinking Rod wouldn't have locked it if he was working inside, but it was locked.

Odd.

He'd never locked it before when she went there to check on things.

Though she hadn't been by that early in the morning since he started working for her. She usually popped by after she dropped the kids off at school and day care. Maybe he had earmuffs on and was using a power tool and didn't want to worry about anybody breaking in.

It wasn't a *huge* unit. But it was a decent size. Two bedrooms with a small living room, kitchen, dining area and a bathroom. Perfect for two students, or three if they got along. An identical unit was next door, and two one-bedroom basement suites would go in below.

She'd had the job managing the rentals for almost a year, and she vetted tenants hard in order to eliminate the potential for headaches down the road.

So far, no headaches.

Except for Rod. He was proving to be the biggest headache out of everything.

If only she could find a decent handyman. A jack-of-all-trades to get the house ready for school in August. It was early May. They didn't have much time left.

Fishing her property keys out of her purse, she slid the key into the lock and opened the door, only to be greeted immediately by the loud, obnoxious grunts and groans only heard when two people were having sex or moving heavy furniture.

What. The. Fuck?

There was no furniture in the house yet. So that only left one source for noises like that.

With her keys still hanging in the door, she followed the noise.

That's when she found Rod lying on a blow-up mattress in one of the bedrooms, his boxers down to his ankles while a woman with faded pink and blonde hair bounced up and down on his lap. She looked as bored as Bianca was shocked.

"What the *fuck* is going on here?" Bianca yelled, slamming her hand on the wall and turning on the light.

The woman on top of Rod shrieked and spun around. She looked young enough to be his granddaughter.

Rod was pushing seventy—for sure. Though you really can't tell when people smoke several packs a day. He could have been younger than Bianca, who was thirty-seven.

Not fucking likely though.

The little pink-haired thing on his lap still had that baby-faced peachy glow to her skin and wide-eyed innocence. Though Bianca didn't think she had any of that innocence left; she just played the part well. Well enough to get customers.

Pink-hair clambered off Rod and pulled her skirt down over her crotch. She went on the hunt for her top.

Rod didn't even seem embarrassed. He lazily tucked his wrinkly old man sac and condom-covered knob back in his boxers and stood up. "Why are you here so early?"

Blinking hard enough she saw spots and shaking her head, Bianca found herself at a loss for words. "Wh-hy am *I* here so early?" she sputtered. "That's the first thing you have to say to me. Why am *I* here so early?"

He nodded, reached for a pack of smokes from his duffle bag and went to light up.

"No smoking in here, you sick pig."

He reared his head back, jowls wobbling. "What the fuck, bitch? What crawled up your ass this morning?"

"Don't *what the fuck me*. I've texted you three times and called you four times to see what is going on and if you'll be here today to accept a delivery, and you never got back to me. You haven't done *half* the things on the list. You take dozens of smoke breaks. There are burn marks and ashes everywhere because I *know* you're smoking inside, and now I come here and find you with—" She pointed at the pink-haired girl, who had found her shirt and tugged it over her tits. She was now lacing up big combat boots.

Rod shrugged. "What the fuck do you want from me?"

She was in the twilight zone.

This was not happening.

They didn't make people as horribly ignorant, disrespectful and repugnant as this, did they?

"How about a little respect?" she finally said.

He shrugged again. "Fine, you have it. Now can I finish my smoke and go grab a coffee?"

Bianca scoffed. "Dude, you are fired. Get your shit, give me your keys and get the fuck out."

He rolled his eyes and reached into the pocket of his jeans

that were lying on the floor, the movement causing the head of his flaccid cock to poke out the hole of his boxers and the condom to fall off and onto the floor.

She averted her eyes and struggled not to gag.

Pink-haired girl finally got her boots laced, gathered her items, but then stood there like she was waiting for Rod or something.

Bianca turned to her. "Can I help you?"

The girl nibbled on her lip and glanced down at her feet.

"Yes?" Bianca asked with impatience.

"He needs to pay me."

Grunting but not hustling to vacate the premises like any normal person would, Rod grabbed his jeans again, pulled out his wallet and lifted two bills from inside. He held them out for the girl.

Sheepishly, she stepped forward and took it. Her mouth opened when she counted it. "I—it was one hundred for the night."

Rod snorted and closed his wallet. "Yeah, but we were interrupted so I didn't finish this last time. Forty."

This last time.

Bianca was going to be sick.

The girl's sad, pale gray eyes shifted to Bianca. "I—"

As angry as she was, Bianca's heart went out to the girl. She couldn't be more than twenty-five, was clearly down on her luck and had taken to selling her body to feed herself.

The question was, how much of that money would end up in her pocket, and how much went to *someone* else? And if she didn't show up with the full hundred, was she going to pay for it in other ways?

Lunging forward, Bianca grabbed Rod's dingy jeans from the floor where he'd already stowed his wallet. She opened his wallet and found the remaining sixty bucks.

"Don't touch my fucking money." Rod made to take the

wallet back from her, but she shot him a look that should have made him evaporate into the ether or, at the very least, back the fuck off. She spun around, grabbed the money and handed it to the girl. "You need to go."

Relief filled her face, but her gaze shifted to Rod behind Bianca before landing back on Bianca, concern in her eyes. "You'll be okay here?"

Bianca nodded, her sympathy for the young woman growing along with her appreciation that, despite how she looked, the woman held concern for Bianca's well-being. "I will be. You go get something to eat, okay?"

The girl didn't need to be told twice and ran out of the room.

Even through the white-hot fury inside her, it broke her heart. That young woman was somebody's baby. Somebody's daughter. She had parents out there who could be wondering where she was, worried.

She said a silent prayer that she didn't do anything to her children as she raised them that drove them from her arms and to the streets to sell their bodies. No matter how old they were, her babies could always come home to Mama.

She headed over to the corner where Rod's bag was, picked it up and shoved the blankets, pillows and clothes into it haphazardly. "You've been living here?"

He didn't say anything.

She found his laptop in the corner, the video option engaged.

Fuck, he was filming himself with the prostitute.

Damnit. What kind of a monster had she hired?

She closed his laptop and shoved it into his bag, marched through the house and tossed the entire bag out onto the concrete walkway. "Get the fuck out of my house, now!"

Rod, still in his boxers, with a heavy layer of white scruff on his jaw and a holey off-white, stained wife-beater covering his beer belly, stood in his socks on the front stoop. "My computer was in there."

It was becoming clearer every second that this man was a psychopath if not even his computer being ruined phased him.

"I don't care. It shouldn't have been in the house. *You* shouldn't have been in the house unless it was to work. You definitely shouldn't have been fucking a damn prostitute in the house."

He stepped down the walkway and grabbed his bag. He glanced at the open window of her van, where her three children stared at them. "You talk like that in front of your kids? In front of your *daughters?*"

"What the fuck does daughters versus sons have to do with a damn thing?" She planted her hands on her hips and glared at him. The pink-haired girl whizzed by behind him in a seen-better-days brown Chevy Sprint.

Rod snorted. "Teaching some real *class* to those girls. Mother of the Year right here, everyone!" he announced, pointing at Bianca to anybody in the neighborhood that cared. Nobody was around. And she really didn't think they'd balk at her use of profanity over his current state of undress and what he'd just been doing in the house he was supposed to be working in, not *living* in and whoring around in.

"I'm teaching my children to stand up for themselves, you useless waste of skin. Teaching my girls to be warriors. Get out of here, Rod."

He shrugged. He actually shrugged. "Then pay me."

"I'll go through the house, see what's been done and pay you for services rendered. I'll also be deducting damages and if anything is missing. I'll give the money to your sister when I've figured out what your ten days of *work* is worth."

Shaking his head like an arrogant son of a bitch, he lit up

a cigarette from a pack he grabbed from his backpack. "You like who you are? You like your life?"

"I fucking love my life and who I am. You like your life, Rod? Like who you are? Cheating people, lying, damaging property, hiring hookers to get you off?"

Pinching his cigarette between his thumb and forefinger, he took a long, lip-puckering inhale, which caused his eyes to form thin slits. "I like who I am. It's you who needs to calm the fuck down."

Scoffing, she shook her head. "That's fucking sad. If I had your life, I'd have killed myself by now."

With a sneer, his eyes traveled her body. "Ever thought of going on a diet?"

She resisted the urge to laugh. She'd been under a hundred pounds when she arrived in Seattle almost a year ago. She was skeletal after the stress of her divorce and what Ashley put her through. She felt like the only control she had left in her life was what she did or *didn't* put in her mouth. It'd taken her a long time to put the weight back on. And yeah, she had a bit of plush now. A squishy middle and an ass that filled out her jeans and then some, but at least her family didn't look at her like she was going to die of a heart attack at any second.

"Did you just call me fat?" she asked with a laugh.

He shrugged again. "I'm not leaving without my money."

"And I'll call the fucking cops if you don't. You are trespassing. Hand over your keys, now. Or I will call the police and have you arrested." She'd been walked on before by a man, treated like less than she was worth, and although Rod wasn't a romantic partner, he was still a man who thought he could treat her like dirt.

That was the problem with men of a *certain* generation. Her father's generation—not that her dad was anything like Rod—but they had a hard time being *beneath* a woman young enough to be their daughter. To take direction and be given orders by someone of the weaker sex—and a millennial to boot. His fragile ego and his arrogance made him incapable of shutting up and blinded him to the progression of the world. He couldn't just put his head down and do the fucking job he'd been hired to do.

No, he figured with age came wisdom, and with a penis came immunity.

The former wasn't always true, and the latter was never true.

Why was it so difficult for men to understand that a mushy bit of flesh hanging between their legs does not immediately garner them respect, nor does it grant them the license to treat others like crap?

"I'm not leaving. Call the cops then." He pulled on his jeans, reached into the pocket and tossed the keys on the ground in front of her. "I've done nothing wrong."

Bianca thought her head might explode.

Done nothing wrong?

Done nothing wrong!

He was using his place of work as a place to stay and a place to bring hookers. What kind of mental case had she hired?

Fuck Lorene, the piano instructor and her *reference* for her brother. She was either equally fucked in the head as her brother, pulling a fast one on Bianca or had no clue who she was related to.

Either way, Bianca would be giving Lorene an earful when she got the chance.

Pulling her phone free from the back pocket of her denim capris, she glanced at the time before she went to call the non-emergency line for the police.

Damn it.

The girls were going to be late for school.

Fuck. Fuck. Fuck.

Shaking her head, she glared at Rod before turning around to go and lock the house. She'd have to come back and deal with everything once the kids were in school and day care.

She could not catch a damn break.

Not bothering to look at Rod, she climbed back behind the steering wheel of her van, turned on the ignition and backed out, nearly causing the back end to fishtail.

Somehow, by grace and by God, she managed to get mostly green lights and was only eight minutes late dropping the girls off at school.

With Charlie on her hip, she ran behind her twins, murmuring, "Quick, quick like bunnies" through the parking lot.

"We're going as fast as we can, Mom," Hannah said, turning around, fixing her mother with a look Bianca only saw on her friend's sixteen-year-old.

"No time for attitude, Han, just go as fast as you can."

It was early May but already getting warm out. Bianca's dark brown hair that had escaped her messy bun flew around in front of her, only to get plastered to her sweaty face as soon as she stopped in front of the girls' closed classroom door. She set Charlie down on his feet and opened the door, earning herself a lifted eyebrow from Miss Beatrice, the first-grade teacher.

This wasn't the first *look* of displeasure she'd received from her daughters' teacher. She and Miss Beatrice had a bit of tenuous relationship. Miss Beatrice didn't understand how busy Bianca's life was and that she was doing her very best when it came to her children. And Bianca didn't understand why Miss Beatrice needed to start every email she sent Bianca with *Just a friendly reminder, but ...*

Just a friendly reminder, but you forgot to send the girls communication folders with them. It's every OTHER Friday, not EVERY Friday.

Just a friendly reminder, but it was LAST week that we had the bake sale and you didn't send anything. I have a blueberry allergy so I just tossed the muffins you sent today.

Just a friendly reminder, but school starts at 8:35, not 8:37, not 8:45, 8:35 and it is really important that the kids arrive ON TIME. Showing your children how to be on time is a great way to get them prepared for the working world.

Bianca stifled her growl.

Go suck an egg, you childless, judgmental cow. You have no idea the morning I've had or the morning I'm going to continue to have.

Ignoring the teacher that she was glad her daughters were going to be rid of in a few weeks, she ushered them toward the coat closet and cubby area, assisting them in changing into their inside shoes and removing their sweaters. They didn't need sweaters, but when she sent them to school without sweaters last week for A SINGLE DAY—a very warm day—she received a strongly worded, condescending email that evening from Miss Beatrice.

Just a friendly reminder, but children need sweaters in case they get cold at school. Even during the warmer months. Please take the time to take care of your children.

Grrrr.

After a quick kiss to her girls, followed by an "I love you," she patted their butts and sent them toward the carpet, where the rest of their class was listening to Miss Beatrice read a story.

Miss Beatrice gave her another scolding look as Bianca, with Charlie back on her hip, exited the classroom and quietly shut the door behind her. She was halfway to freedom, halfway down the hall to the exit when a shrill "Oh,

Bianca!" made her blood turn icy and her whole face cringe. Her asshole puckered too.

"Oh, Bianca, I'm so glad I caught you. I thought for sure I would see you during drop-off, but it would seem your girls are late today ... again." It was Gwynyth—yes, *two Y's*—Charlemagne, a fellow mom in Hannah and Hayley's class. Her daughter, Duchess, was the same age as the girls, and her son, Duke, was two years ahead of the girls. No need to slag on the woman's name choices. The universe would do that for her.

"Yes, Gwynyth, I had an issue come up at work I had to deal with, which is why we're late. I have to head back there now, actually. After I drop Charlie off at day care." Which she was also going to be late doing.

She only hoped Rod didn't go full psycho and light the house on fire.

"I don't know how you do it, Bianca," Gwynyth said, flipping her blonde hair behind her with her perfectly French-manicured nails. "A *working* single mom to three kids. I feel like I'm losing my mind most days, and I only have two kids, a husband and I don't work. I certainly wouldn't want your life."

Bianca's smile was forced and brittle as she hoisted a hefty, pancake-loving Charlie onto her hip a bit better. She loved his tummy and baby chunk and wouldn't trade an ounce of her little boy for the world, but when she had to hold him for more than five or ten minutes, her biceps started to scream at her. "Everyone's Everest is a different size. I do it because I have to."

Gwynyth pursed her lips. "Well, anyway, I'm glad I caught you. We need somebody to organize the end of school joint class-parent gift for Miss Beatrice, and I figured since you have two children in her class, it would make sense if that was you."

What. The. Fuck?

She fucking hated Miss Beatrice and Miss Beatrice hated her.

Thankfully, the woman seemed to be professional enough not to take her dislike for Bianca out on Hannah and Hayley. Those two raved about their teacher and how wonderful she was.

Gag.

She switched Charlie to her other hip, and he promptly shoved his tiny finger into her ear. She swatted him away. "I'm not sure I'm the best person for the job, Gwynyth. I have a full-time, demanding job and three children. Plus, if you haven't noticed, I'm not exactly Miss Beatrice's favorite parent. Why can't you do it? You just said you don't work and noticed how full *my* life already is. Why are you asking me to do it? Can't you just take the bull by the horns and get it done?"

She had zero patience for this woman—for most of the moms she'd met in the pickup line. So many of them looked down on her because she was a single mother. A few of the women she also knew from way back in high school, and she was pretty sure her brother Scott had scorned at least two of them.

Thanks, Scottie.

Gwynyth's eyes glittered with a mischievous twinkle that made the hair on the back of Bianca's neck stand up. "I'm simply much too busy. And Miss Beatrice loves all the parents; don't be silly. Just like she loves all the students. It's not a big job. Just email the parent list and ask for suggestions on gifts. Take the top ten gift suggestions. Create a poll. Send the poll to all the parents, and then the top choice is the gift. Then get everyone to e-transfer you their child's share of the money. Then go buy the gift. You, of course, will pay two shares as you have two children in the class." Gwynyth's smile was so white, Bianca's eyes hurt.

"Of course," Bianca said blandly. "Easy peasy."

"Exactly. Now, I have to run. These thighs aren't going to spin themselves bikini-season-ready if I don't get them to the gym." She tittered at her own stupid joke and took off in the opposite direction of Bianca—thank God.

Growling, which only caused Charlie to growl too, Bianca stepped up her pace, booked it down the rest of hallway and burst free into the fresh air as if she were a prisoner finally released after a life sentence.

2

As she fastened her little boy into his car seat, her phone began to warble in her purse.

Please don't let it be the fire department saying the house is on fire. Please. Please.

As she swung in behind the steering wheel, she reached for her phone only to see that it was once again her fuck-face ex. She canceled the call, turned on the van and backed out of her stall.

Her phone rang again. This time it wasn't Ashley. It was the cabinetry company.

Carefully, she set her phone in the dash holder before answering it. "Hello?"

"Hey, Bianca, it's Hoyt.

"Oh, hey, Hoyt."

"I just wanted to let you know that we're about ten to fifteen minutes away from the house if you wanted to make sure you or your carpenter are there to let us in."

"Shit!"

"*Sit*," Charlie mimicked.

Hoyt made a noise in his throat. "Sorry?"

"No, no, it's fine. I just fired my handyman today for squatting in the house and entertaining hookers, so it'll have to be me that meets you in ten minutes. I'm en route anyway."

Hoyt was silent for a moment before he breathed, "Damn, that sucks."

"Indeed. I'll see you in ten, Hoyt." She hung up. Hoyt was a good friend of her father's and an excellent cabinetmaker.

She took a deep breath to enjoy the silence of the van. She could see in the mirror that Charlie was deeply engrossed in a book.

But blissful quiet was only fleeting when her fuck-face ex started to call again.

"What?" she answered, growling under her breath as the image of Ashley popped into her head.

"That wasn't very polite," he admonished.

"Neither is sleeping with your twenty-seven-year-old secretary, knocking her up and leaving your wife and three children. Did you call to debate manners, Ashley? Because I really have zero time or patience for it." Now that the girls had been dropped off, she didn't have to worry so much about how *kind* she was to her ex. Charlie didn't understand. Soon he would, so she only had a small window where she could release her rage on her ex-husband when she wasn't completely alone.

"Jesus, Bianca, what crawled up your ass this morn—"

"Bye."

She ended the call and exhaled.

"That Daddy?" Charlie asked.

"Yes, sweetie. That was Daddy."

"My see Nana and Papa soon, okay? My go Nana and Papa house. Sweep over with Hanna and Haywee." She liked that her father had become the number one man in her son's life. He offered Charlie more anyway. More of his time, more of his heart and more of his wisdom.

"Absolutely, kiddo. You got it."

Charlie rarely asked about Ashley anymore, which eased the strain on Bianca's heart. The girls asked about him more, but even their queries seemed to be dwindling. It'd taken some time for the four of them to find their groove without Ashley, but now that they had, Bianca was doing everything in her power not to rock the boat, fuck with her kids' heads or hurt them any more than they'd already been hurt.

Her phone started to ring again. It was Ashley.

"Gonna be nicer to me?" she asked, answering it again.

She could practically hear his eyes roll in his head all the way down in Palm Springs. "I'm calling to see what the plan is for the kids this summer."

"What do you mean, *what is the plan?*"

"Well, are they in any camps? Day care? Do you have any trips or camping planned with them? I know your parents bought that motorhome two years ago. Are they taking the kids anywhere?"

Right, summer vacation was soon. *Crap.*

Here Bianca was just trying to get to the next day. She hadn't even thought as far ahead as next month.

"No plans yet, really. I think my parents are going to help out as much as they can. I have some teen sitters who are looking for cash too. Charlie will stay in day care. It's the girls I need to find a place for. Probably put them in some art or dance camps, maybe soccer. Why?"

"Well, Opal and I were hoping to see the kids for like a week this summer. So they could get to know their brother and sister."

She waited for the inconsiderate demand to come next. There always was one with Ashley.

"You and the kids could fly down here for a week so that they could meet their siblings. Bring the kids by for few hours a day sort of thing."

Annnnnd there it was.

She'd called it.

"Let me get this straight, Ashley. You and Cubic Zirconia want me to pay for my flight and three other flights, then pay for a hotel for a week so that you two can see your children for a *few hours a day* when it's convenient for you? Am I understanding that correctly? What am I supposed to do when the kids are with you? And more importantly, what the hell am I supposed to do with the kids when they're *not* with you?"

Murmuring on the other side of the phone had her seeing red.

"You're being a little unreasonable, here, Bianca," Ashley said. "Emerald and Garnet are Hannah, Hayley and Charlie's siblings. They need to meet them."

"I completely agree, but that's not on me to make it happen. I have a job here. I have a life that I'm trying to rebuild with my children, my friends and my family. I know you love your kids, Ashley—and you *were* a great father—but since we moved up here, you've become a pretty crappy dad. You've seen them twice in the last year."

"Because you took them over twelve hundred miles away from me," he spat back.

"Because there was nothing left for me in Palm Springs. I moved there to be with you. But now that we're not together, nothing was keeping me in that fire pit. This was all handled with the lawyers. You agreed to the terms."

"I had no choice. Your brother and his raptor-taloned wife would have rendered me a eunuch if I'd pushed for you to stay in Palm Springs."

Yeah, they would have. That thought made her smile. Her brother Liam and his wife, Richelle, had represented Bianca in her divorce, and Ashley was left with joint custody and a hefty alimony and child-support payment. If he continued to push her like he was right now, he'd get a second helping of just how *unreasonable* she could be.

She let out a deep sigh. Rarely did she and her ex have a conversation that didn't get heated. She just hated him so much for what he did to her and the kids. "Then fly up here yourself, Ashley. Get the kids, fly back with them, take them for the week, and then fly them home."

"That's four flights for me alone, plus round trips for the kids. I can't—"

"But you expected me to fork out four round trips?"

"You're being ridiculous, Bianca," Ashley said with impatience.

She was being ridiculous? Oh, her ex called her at the wrong time on the wrong fucking day.

"Tell you what, Ashley. I'll make you a compromise, just to show you that I *can* be reasonable. You book a flight for yourself and the kids. Fly up here. I'll even meet you at the airport with them. You take them for a week, and then I'll fly down to Palm Springs, meet you at the airport and pick them up. I'll pay for the kids' flights home. Go halfers with you."

He went to say something, made a strangled noise in this throat instead, and the line went quiet for a moment like he'd put his hand over the receiving end. She could hear faint muffles, then he was back. "We can't take them for a whole week," Ashley said, his words robotic like he was being coached.

"And why not?"

"Because I work, and it'd be too much for Opal during the day. That's five children you're expecting her to be in charge of."

"Then take the week off." It wasn't rocket science.

He made another garbled, choking noise in his throat.

God, he was a selfish prick.

"You really need to accept that I'm with Ashley now, Bianca," Opal's breathy voice came over the line. They'd put her on speakerphone. "You're acting rather petty. It's an unattractive look. Think of how much more beautiful you'd be if you just moved on and put your children first. Put their right and need to see their brother and sister first. *Surely* you understand how difficult it is to raise twins and that us asking you to bring the children down, to make it easier on me with the babies, is not unreasonable."

"*Surely* you're joking. My children's *rights* are the rights to have a roof over their head, clothes on their backs, food in their bellies and an education. They have no *right* to see their love-child half-siblings. A want? Yes, maybe a little, but there is no need or right involved. But we all know you get your wants and rights mixed up, right? You thought you had a *right* to sleep with my husband, when really it was just a want. A want that you acted on."

"There's no reasoning with her, Ashley. She obviously has mental health problems," Opal whispered, though blatantly loud enough for Bianca to hear.

"Nobody asked for your opinion, Pyrite!" Bianca snapped. "Ashley, take me off speakerphone."

"You can't let her speak to me this way," she heard Opal whine.

Bianca would speak to that pretentious little homewrecker any way she damn well pleased. Opal had smiled to Bianca's face for months, all the while fucking Bianca's husband behind her back. Opal could go sit on a rusty fork and spin for all Bianca cared.

Static and muffled voices echoed over the phone just as Bianca pulled up to the house—still standing and not charred to a crisp—but with Rod sitting on the porch with a big smirk on his face. "Listen, when your flights are booked, Ashley, let me know. I'll make sure the kids are all packed up for their week with Dad and stepmommy dearest." She ended the call at the same time the big delivery truck for Grant Cabinetry pulled up to the curb.

Hopping out of the van, she hauled Charlie out of his car seat once again, giving a small thanks to the universe that he too hadn't been twins and he was such an agreeable, good-natured child. She could lug him around pretty much anywhere with her, and as long as he had his five-pack of dinosaur board books, his dinosaur stuffed animal, aptly named Rawr, and a to-go container full of Goldfish crackers, Charlie was a happy camper.

Ignoring Rod on the front porch, she went around to the basement door at the back of the house and unlocked it, greeting Hoyt on her way back toward the curb. "The two smaller sets of cabinets can go in these units here. I'll go and open up the front doors for the larger units when you're ready."

Hoyt's grim smile beneath his bushy salt-and-pepper mustache said he could tell she was at the end of her rope. "You're amazing, Bianca, really. Three kids, this job and putting up with lowlifes like that tool on the steps—I'm assuming that's the *ex*-handyman?"

"You assume right. Thanks, Hoyt. Just trying to pay the bills. I appreciate how quickly you guys were able to get these done." She humorlessly laughed. "You don't moonlight as a handyman, do you? Or know a handyman who *won't* squat where he works and bring in hookers?"

Sadly, he shook his head. "I'm afraid the answer to both of those questions is *no*. I'll ask around, though."

Nodding and thanking Hoyt, she left him and his son, Bill, to unload what she'd bought. She went to the front of the house, set Charlie down on the grass with his fish crackers, his dinosaur and books and approached Rod. "You need to move."

He lifted one shoulder, squinting in the glare of the harsh

morning sun as he raised his gaze to her face. "And you need to pay me."

"I told you I would. I told you I'd pay you when I figured out how much of the *agreed-upon* tasks you actually took care of."

He shook his head. "You promised me four grand."

"And you promised you'd get the job done. You've been working here ten days and have done what took me three days to do in my own home—with three children running around and a full-time job."

"Well la-di-da," he sang. "Aren't you just Little Miss Perfect. Then you won't have a problem getting the rest of the house done by yourself."

"You caught me on the wrong day, Rod." Grinding her molars together, Bianca bunched her fists, took a deep breath and set her shoulders back. "Get. The. Fuck. Off. The. Property. Now. Or. I. Will. Call. The. Cops."

Rod rose to his full height in front of her, stepped into her space. Bianca wasn't tall. She wasn't as short as her sister-in-law Richelle either, who wasn't even five feet. But Rod had a good six inches on Bianca at least. And most definitely a good sixty pounds or more. Ironic how he'd asked her if she ever thought of going on a diet when what looked like a third-trimester baby beneath his shirt sat between them.

"Go ahead and call the cops, little girl. We'll see what happens when I tell them you're refusing to pay me." His cigarette breath and unwashed body odor wafted over her, making her gut churn.

He was an idiot to think the cops would get involved with an issue like him not being paid. Not that she was a lawyer or a cop, but she knew enough facts about the law and the real world that he'd be arrested for trespassing, but if he wanted his money, he'd have to file a civil suit.

She turned her head and took a deep, fortifying breath of

fresh, untainted air before turning back to face him. He didn't scare her, and she needed to show him that. "You're just a sad, old man who can't handle having a *woman* half his age as his boss. A woman who knows what the fuck she's doing and is doing it well. I threaten you. I threaten your *kind*."

His chuckle was grating and downright evil. "Yeah, and what's *my kind*, little girl?"

"A boomer with one foot in the fucking grave, past his prime with nothing left to contribute to society. A waste of skin. Hell, you even have to *pay* for sex because no woman, not even those your own age, will let you stick it in them willingly. You're a sad, old son of a bitch motherfucker whose old man should have pulled out and saved society the plague that is you."

"You fucking bitch."

She wasn't expecting the shove.

The rage, yes. But she didn't expect him to lay his hands on her, so she lost her balance and tumbled to the concrete walkway on her ass. A sharp stab of pain sprinted up from her tailbone, neck and neck with the fear that coursed up the length of her spine.

She'd pushed him too far.

She'd intended to show Rod that he wasn't dealing with some shrinking violet who would let him get away with what he'd done. That she wasn't somebody who could be walked on. She was a fighter and stood up for herself.

But she'd goaded him.

Ran her mouth like the Dixons were known to do.

Her brother, Scott, had ended up with a broken nose at least twice because of his smart mouth, and lord knew Liam was challenged with knowing when to shut up.

Was it her turn for her nose to meet the hard end of a fist because she'd picked the wrong time to engage her warrior-princess trash mouth?

Rod stood over her and lifted his arm, his palm open at least, so he was going for the slap rather than the punch. "Calling me a motherfucker. A son of a bitch."

She covered her face and shielded her head with her elbow but knew it probably wouldn't do much good.

She was sure the noise of a motorcycle had been present earlier than when she finally heard it, but she was too distracted by the shove. But the loud, thunderous holler of "Hey!" had her opening her eyes and pivoting where she sat to find a tall, muscly man with a beard and one of those black skull bucket-style helmets climbing off his shiny Harley.

With long-legged strides, anger in his eyes and fingers curling into fists at his side, he approached a paused and confused Rod.

"The fuck's going on, brother?" the man from the motorcycle asked. "You planning to hit this woman? You a woman beater?"

"She called me a son of a bitch and a motherfucker," Rod said, dropping his arm. Ah, so he had mommy issues. Interesting.

Bianca scrambled across the walkway and grass to Charlie, hugging him close.

"Mama okay?" he asked, cupping her face, his jaw moving as he munched on fish crackers.

"Yeah, baby," she breathed, her pulse racing, tears stinging her eyes. "Mama's okay."

The man from the motorcycle stepped into Rod's space. He had a good three inches on Rod, and even though Rod had a gut and was probably heavier, the man from the motorcycle had breadth to his chest and muscles beneath his short-sleeved T-shirt. A shirt that exposed two full-sleeves of tattoos along his tanned arms, and she noticed tattoos on his chest along the shirt collar as well.

"Are you a son of a bitch and a motherfucker?" Mr. Harley

asked, his face a stiff mask. "I'm leaning toward yes, since you were gearing up to take a swing at her."

Rod's face went the color of a too-ripe tomato. "She owes me money."

"Yeah? For what?"

"She hired me to do work on the house, then she fired me and now she won't pay me."

Mr. Harley swung his gaze back to Bianca. That's when she noticed how blue his eyes were. Such a stark contrast to his dark, tanned skin. It was striking and made a jolt of something flash through her. "You owe him money?"

Clutching Charlie tighter, she nodded. "I came here today to find Mr. Penner, who I hired ten days ago as a handyman to help finish some renovations, having sex with a hooker on a blow-up mattress. He's been living here. Cleans up his stuff before I arrive most mornings, so I think he just arrives early. He also hasn't accomplished half of what I asked him to do in the ten days he's been working here. I made him an extensive list with the agreement that when he finished the list, I would pay him four grand. He painted one bedroom and tiled a quarter of one bathtub in one bathroom."

The blue-eyed bearded man with tattoos, a long, prominent nose and full, luscious lips lifted an eyebrow before turning back to face Rod. "Hookers, really, bro?"

Rod didn't say anything.

"How much will it take for you to get gone and never come back?" Harley man asked. "'Cause you ain't getting four grand for one painted room and a quarter-finished tub—I could do that in a couple fucking hours." He scoffed and shook his head, glancing at Bianca. "Guy's fucking dreaming."

"I said I would go inside and take inventory of what he did, survey any damages, because I *know* he's been smoking inside even though he's not supposed to, so I know there are burn marks on some countertops. And he's not seeing a dime until I can guarantee nothing's been stolen." She glanced at Rod. "You still can't give me a straight answer about where that over-the-range microwave went. I dropped it off the day you started working here, and two days later it's suddenly *missing*."

Rod shifted from foot to foot, pulled his pack of cigarettes out of his pocket and went to light up . "Dunno what happened to it."

Mr. Motorcycle rolled his eyes. "Right, and I bet you also have a ten-inch dick?"

Bianca resisted the urge to snort. Unfortunately, she'd seen Rod's dick. She could now attest that it was a far, far cry from ten inches. She bet the man had a hard time seeing it when he stood in the shower.

Oh fuck, now she was picturing Rod in the shower.

Gross.

She needed to scour that image from her brain, replace it with something else. Like the tattooed man in front of her in the shower.

Ah. Much better.

"How much, bro. I'm losing patience, and I'm sure that nice lady over there lost her patience with you a long time ago."

"Half," Rod finally said. "Two grand."

Bianca snorted. So did the blue-eyed man with the beard.

"Try again."

Rod cleared his throat. "A grand."

The tall man who'd come to her rescue stepped closer to Rod, forcing the white-haired waste of skin to back up. "You licensed? Running a legit company?"

Rod shook his head. "Was a handyman back in Idaho. Had my own company there."

The man on the motorcycle rolled those crystal-blue eyes. "But you don't now. So try. Again."

"Five hundred."

Her savior's plump lips curled into a smile in the middle of his beard and mustache. A big hand slammed down hard on Rod's shoulder and squeezed enough to make the asshole wince. "I had a feeling there was a reasonable bone inside that body of yours, brother. Just had to dig a little through all those layers of douche." He reached into his wallet.

Bianca stood up and plunked Charlie back on her hip. "You don't have to pay him. I'll run to the bank."

He pulled out a bunch of fifties and twenties, counting them out. "I got three-fifty here. Can you come up with the rest?"

She could. She had four emergency fifties stashed between her purse and wallet. Just in case her card was declined or whatever.

But then she'd owe the handsome stranger.

It's better than owing Rod.

Swallowing, she set Charlie back on his feet, turned her back so they couldn't see where she hid the money in her purse or wallet and fished them out. Spinning back around, she held out the two hundred bucks. "I've got two hundred here." Fighting the warm bubbles in her bloodstream from the handsome stranger's gaze, she handed it to him. "I'll run to the bank right away after this and get the money to pay you back."

He simply shrugged. "I live a block away. Get it to me when you can. I'm not hard up." He counted out five hundred bucks and handed it to Rod. Only when the asshole went to take the money from him, the handsome stranger held on. "I don't *ever* want to see your fat face on this property again, ya got it? If I ever see you harassing this nice lady or even looking at her, I'll staple your tongue to your taint so you can watch me kick your ass. You'll be tasting shit and leather for a week. Ya got it?"

He released the money, and Rod took it.

"Now get the fuck outta here." He jerked his head toward the road, the growl unmistakable from his tone.

Rod's eyes shifted toward Bianca, the smoke from the cigarette hanging between his lips curling up around his head like a gray halo.

Charlie looped his arms around her leg, and she cocked her hip, leveling her gaze at Rod. "I will call the cops. I wasn't bluffing."

Rod squinted.

"Get out of here," the handsome stranger barked, stomping his booted foot. That seemed to light a fire under Rod's ass, and he jumped where he stood causing the cigarette to fall to the walkway. With fumbling hands, he leaned forward, picked it up and quickly lumbered toward his pickup truck parked on the road.

At the same time, Hoyt and Bill came around the corner, which reminded Bianca that she needed to unlock the front doors to the two top units. She gently shook Charlie free from where he was hugging her leg and made haste to go unlock the doors. "Sorry, Hoyt," she said apologetically. "Got caught up with—"

Hoyt held up his hand. "Don't sweat it, Bianca. We're all good. You just take care of what you need to, and we'll do the rest."

"You're the best, Hoyt," she said, stepping back down to the walkway where the sexy stranger stood waiting for her.

"Bianca," he said her name slowly. "Bee-yahn-kah. Bee-onnn-kuh. Bee-yank-ah." He rolled her name around on his tongue like it was a gobstopper.

She wanted to be that gobstopper. Have him roll her body around on his tongue and not just her name.

With heat not just from the unrelenting sun coursing through her, she returned to Charlie sitting on the grass and made sure he was okay. She knew he was, but it was the distraction she needed as she was unable to look at the handsome stranger without feeling like she was going to catch fire.

A throat cleared behind her and she was forced to lift her head and turn around. Her temperature skyrocketed as those blue eyes hit her, her breath escaping her lungs on a rattle. "Um ... thank you for your help. For intervening when you did, for putting the fear of your boot in his ass in him, and for loaning me the money." Her fingers knitted in front of her. The look he was giving her was unnerving in the most exhilarating kind of way.

"Bee-yon-kah."

She glanced up at him from beneath her lashes. "Why are you saying my name like that, over and over again?"

Those lips spread into a big, cocky smile. "It's just a beautiful name for a beautiful woman. I like saying it. Wanna tell me the whole story of how you wound up with that winner as an employee?"

"Mot-sick-oh," Charlie cried, beelining from where he clung to Bianca's leg, spinning around it to where the man, whose name she still didn't have, had parked his very shiny, very sexy motorcycle.

"Charlie, don't touch." She chased after him.

"It's okay." The man's deep timbre followed her. His voice reminded her of the hog—did they still call Harleys hogs?—he rode. Deep, dark and rumbly. In other words, panty-soakingly magnificent. He sidled up next to her on the curb, where Charlie was ogling the bike. "He can sit on it, if it's okay with you?"

"My sit, my sit!" Charlie cried, bouncing up and down with his arms in the air.

Nodding, Bianca said okay, and the man picked Charlie

up under the arms, straddled his bike and plopped Charlie in front of him. She didn't remember seeing him do it, but at some point in their altercation with Rod, he'd removed his helmet to reveal dark brown hair, long on top, messy, floppy and something she desperately wanted to run her fingers through.

The thoughts she was having about this total stranger were so unlike her. She normally didn't like beards, tattoos or men who looked so ... *badass*.

Liar. You named your vibrator Jason Momoa. You like beards. You like tattoos. You like bad boys. You've just never dated one.

Her conscience was always ready to call her on her bullshit.

The man oozed danger, and she was drawn to him like a bee to the first blossomed flower of the spring.

"Keep talkin'," he said. "How'd you end up with that world-class citizen?"

"My kids' piano teacher knows I'm a project manager for this affordable student housing renovation and asked if I had any odd jobs that needed to be done. I've lost three carpenters in the last couple of months because of illness, job change and moving, so I said, sure. I thought Lorene was vouching for her brother. She said he used to do a bunch of construction stuff back in Idaho or wherever. I said I'd give him a shot. But I got a weird vibe from him day one."

"Shoulda called it then and kicked his ass to the curb."

Easier said than done. She was on a deadline.

Clucking her tongue, she pushed her sunglasses up into her hair. "Yes, well, hindsight is always twenty-twenty, isn't it?"

He nodded. "Seems that way."

"Besides, I needed someone to work on the house, and I thought since his sister was vouching for him, I'd give him the benefit of the doubt."

"How'd that work out for you?" he asked with a wise-ass grin.

"I think we all know the answer to that. Guy is useless as f —" She glanced at Charlie. "As a fart though. Slow as molasses and undermined everything I said. Questioned it. And not from a *he has construction experience and I don't* but from an *I'm a man and I know everything* perspective. *Obey me because I have a small penis and make up for it by being an enormous dick.*"

Handsome motorcycle man snorted. "You've seen it?"

"Just now." She nodded, making a face that said she wished she hadn't and was disappointed she couldn't bleach her memory clean.

He nodded. "Gotcha. 'Cause he was sleeping here and bringing in whores?"

"I just found out today—which was when I saw his ..." She shuddered. "But I think he's been doing it since day one. I feel like such an idiot."

"You couldn't be further from an idiot," he said, absolutely zero humor in his tone. "Don't talk about yourself like that."

The demand in his tone made butterflies take flight in her belly. His gaze seared her, and a tremor of lust cascaded up her body, originating from between her thighs.

"I caught him off guard today. He thought he was getting away with it because I normally don't show up until after nine thirty, once I've taken the kids to school and day care. But today, I popped in early, as he wasn't answering my texts or calls. I needed to make sure he would be here to let in the cabinet guys. Found him on his back with some twenty-something pink-haired girl bobbing up and down on his baby carrot like he was Casa-fucking-nova."

He snorted again. "Smart, funny and beautiful. You're the whole package, *Bee-yan-kah*."

There he went again, rolling her name around in his mouth like it was a gumball.

What the hell?

"Why do you keep saying my name like that?"

He grinned, turned on the bike with the kick start and let it rumble, all to the complete elation of Charlie. "Because it makes your cheeks turn such a pretty shade of pink," he said, his smile growing. "I think I might be able to help you out."

He let the bike purr for a few minutes, a grinning, bouncy Charlie in front of him, before he finally turned it off and helped Charlie down, setting him gently on the ground.

"Moh mot-sick-oh," Charlie pleaded. "My want moh mot-sick-oh, pwease."

"Sorry, little man," he said. "Gotta ask your mama something."

Bianca picked up Charlie and plopped him on her hip. "You thank the nice man for letting you sit on his bike."

With a giant bottom lip, Charlie turned his face into Bianca's neck. "Tank-koo," he whispered.

"Anytime, little man." He focused back on Bianca. "I might be able to help you. So happens *I've* done a lot of construction. Concrete, drywall, roofing, cabinets, tiling, painting, flooring. You name it, I've probably done it in the last twenty years."

She was skeptical. Why was he available, then, if he was capable of so many different jobs? Shouldn't he be booked solid? She must have appeared wary, because a white smile and gentle eyes met her furrowed brow.

"I don't *need* to work. I own a few properties and do well with those. I'm only here for the summer anyway. Ride down to the Baja mid-August and spend my winter down there working odd jobs and running the bar I own. No need to work here if I don't have to. But if you need someone to help you finish your house, I can do it."

She swallowed. If he had as much experience as he said he did, he probably came with a hefty fee. Not that James or Justin would so much as balk at getting the job done well for a big price tag, but she would prefer to come in under or on budget.

"Tell you what, Bianca, gimme your phone number, and I'll send you a list of references who can vouch for me. They'll tell you I'm not some grifter out to take you to the cleaners and bail halfway through a project."

"My phone number?"

"Yeah, you know, that ten-digit ... never mind, gimme your email instead. I'll head home now and send it to you. If you like what you hear, we can meet back here tomorrow morning, go through what needs to be done, and I can give you a quote on my fee."

"I—"

"I won't be offended if you say no. Just figured you needed help, needed a handyman, and I've been told I'm handy." There went that smile again. She had to stop herself from swooning.

"Okay."

He held out a big, long-fingered hand. "Jack. Jack Savage."

Jack Savage.

Now she wanted to roll him and his name around on her tongue.

She took his hand. It was warm, rough and sent a jolt of something straight to her clit. "Okay, Mr. Savage—"

"Jack, darlin'. Call me Jack, please."

She breathed out slowly through her mouth. "Okay, Jack, say I hire you. All four of these units need work. Can you guarantee me all of them will be done before you leave for the Baja in August? You're not going to leave me high and dry?"

He smiled again. "I can. But only if you promise *me* something."

Bianca's eyes narrowed. "What's that?"

"That no matter what happens, you won't fall in love with me."

3

THERE WENT THOSE CHEEKS AGAIN.

The prettiest shade of fucking pink he ever did see.

On the prettiest—fuck—the most gorgeous woman he'd ever laid eyes on.

This Bianca—damn, he even loved her name—was the epitome of sensuality, sexuality and spunk, all rolled into light brown eyes, glossy brown hair and curves he wanted to sink his teeth into.

He'd been waiting for her to remember him as the man at the intersection who'd given her a thumbs-up when he caught her dancing in the car, but so far, she hadn't made the connection.

Her day was rough. He bet she couldn't remember what she had for breakfast, let alone a man who'd made her cheeks turn that sexy fucking pink as she let loose to Taylor Swift at the red light.

Sputtering, she blinked a bunch of times over those eyes he wanted to see gaze up at him as she fell to her knees and took him in her mouth. "Fall in *love* with you? You want me to promise not to fall in love with you?" She snorted before tossing her head back with a laugh. "Good one, Jack. I needed a laugh like that today. Thank you."

"Just doing my job, darlin'," he said with a big grin he knew was borderline cheesy. "Keeping the boss-lady happy. But seriously, I'm here to work and just for the summer. Try to keep it in your pants when you're around me, okay? I got a job to do." He followed up with an even bigger grin and a wink.

Her smile was natural and carefree, and it took her looks from a ten to a fucking twenty. "You always this cocky?"

"Not cocky, darlin', just funny. Love to make people—women—laugh. Make 'em smile. Too much in this world has you frowning. The patriarchy, wage gap, pants without pockets."

That got her laughing. "It is a plague we all face. Whoever thought pants without pockets was a good idea ..."

"Was probably a man."

"You're probably right." Sighing, she nodded. "I'll do my best to keep it in my pants *with pockets* and not fall in love with you. You have my word. Besides, love, romance or anything in between is so far off my radar, it's invisible to the naked eye." That last bit was said with a twinge of regret in her tone and made him wonder what her deal was. Divorced? Widowed? In a loveless marriage with a limp-dicked moron?

She had no ring on her finger, but that meant very little in this day and age. He'd made his "don't fall in love with me" joke before even asking if she was with someone. Before finding out if she was in love with someone.

Lifting one shoulder, he said, "Good to hear. Don't need to be getting fired mid-project because my boss has gone and fallen head over heels for me and I can't get my work done."

She rolled her eyes, and he had to shove his hands into his pockets to keep himself from grabbing her by the pony-tail. "I think I can agree to those terms, Mr. Savage," she said with a chuckle to her voice, that big, beautiful smile still making the whole sky seem brighter.

"Jack, darlin'. You really gotta call me Jack." He pulled out his phone. "Gimme your email address, and I'll send you some references. Though I can already swear to you I don't intend to squat in an unfinished rental. I got a nice warm bed of my own, and I *definitely* don't need to pay ladies of the evening to suck my stiffy for me."

Her nostrils flared, and fuck if her eyes didn't drift down to his zipper.

He fought back a grin, brought up the contacts app in his phone and prepared for her to rattle off her email address.

But she wasn't paying attention.

She was still staring at his crotch.

Smiling wide, he cleared his throat and watched as her gaze climbed his body slowly, like she was imprinting every damn inch of him on her memory for later.

He'd already done that himself with her body and would *definitely* be thinking about Bianca later.

"Bianca," he said gently. "Email, darlin'. Or your phone number if you're willing to take the risk and give the big bad biker your digits."

"Big bad biker," she breathed quietly, her eyes focusing on his lips.

Her tongue slipped out and slid across the seam of her mouth, coating her lips until they shone bright red and irresistibly kissable.

Jack fought down a groan and cleared his throat again. "Number or email, sweetheart, gotta find a way to reach you. Unless you want to just skip the foreplay and give me your home address?"

That snapped her out of her trance. Her head shook, and she blinked. "Email address, phone number, right. Sorry."

She dug around in her purse, paused and glanced at him curiously. "Foreplay?"

"Just gimme your number, Bianca," he said with a laugh.

Nodding, she quit rummaging through her purse and rattled off her digits, followed by her email address.

"I haven't had a chance to change my email address yet since my divorce. I'm not Bianca Loxton anymore—even though that's what my email address is. I went back to my maiden name. I'm Bianca Dixon again."

She was divorced. And recently so. Interesting.

That explained love, romance or anything in between being invisible to the naked eye. She was jaded. She was hurt.

What limp-dicked fucker would hurt a woman like Bianca?

"Bianca Dixon." He said her name slowly.

He'd heard that last name before.

His brows pinched. "You related to that big lawyer guy in town, Lyle Dixon?"

Her grin hit him hard in the solar plexus. "*Liam* Dixon and yes, he's my big brother. I have another brother, too. Scott Dixon. He runs Dynamic Creative. It's a marketing and advertising company."

He nodded. "Powerful family."

Those lips he wanted to kiss, fuck and take as his own twisted, and she glanced at her van. "They are. I'm just trying to put food on the table for my kids."

"You got more than Charlie here?"

"Twin girls, Hannah and Hayley. They're six and in school right now and—" She smacked her palm to her forehead, her brown eyes growing all panicky. "Shit, fuck, damn. I'm supposed to be getting Charlie to day care. What time is it?"

He checked his phone. "Almost ten."

"Crap!" She hurried to her van and practically tossed poor Charlie inside, though by the giggles he heard from the little boy, Charlie wasn't hurt. He wanted his mother to toss him again.

Jack followed Bianca and stood behind her as she buckled her son into his seat, enjoying the view of her ass as she bent over, the line of her legs, the flare of her hips and the hourglass of her waist. He tucked his bottom lip between his teeth to hold in his smile as she continued to mutter curse words and verbally flagellate herself for getting distracted.

"Stupid fucking Rod."

"Soopid Wod," Charlie repeated. "Duck! Sit! QUACK!"

Jack snorted. She had a mouth on her like a trucker, and if she wasn't careful, her kids would too.

"Freaking Gwynyth. Sure, I'll buy the teacher a present. How about a box of live scorpions?" she murmured. "God-damn Cubic Zirconia better watch her scrawny ass before I kick it into next week. I'll do it through the fucking phone."

Gwynyth? Cubic Zirconia?

Did Bianca have a lot of enemies? Or were there just a lot of people placing unreasonable, unrealistic demands on her and she'd finally reached her breaking point?

She didn't strike him as the type to have a long list of enemies. She struck him as a woman who gave everyone around her one hundred and ten percent but then was scraping the bottom of the barrel and coming up with dust when it came to taking care of herself.

She stood up straight and spun around, surprise flaring in her eyes at seeing him right behind her. She made a little squawk that caused his dick to jump. "Sorry. I have to run. If I intend to get anything done today, I need to get Charlie to day care. Seriously, when it rains, it pours."

He backed up a few steps so she could shut the sliding door of the van and open the driver's side. She turned on the ignition but then shut it off again, her eyes following the two cabinetmakers as they carried cabinets from their truck into the house.

She slammed her forehead onto the steering wheel. "Damn it. I can't leave yet. I'll need to lock the house after they leave."

He had no idea who Gwynyth or Cubic Zirconia were or even half of the problems that Bianca had already faced that morning—and it wasn't even noon—but his heart went out to her. Clearly, she needed the time away from her children not only to get work done but also to just take a deep breath.

The window was down, and he put his hand inside the van. "Give me the house keys, darlin'."

When she lifted her head, tears brimmed her eyes, and it fucking gutted him.

"Gimme the keys, Bianca. It's not a request. I'll lock up."

Her deep frown and sad look of utter loss and confusion had him darting around the front of the van, opening the passenger door and pulling her purse from the seat. He found the keys marked *Arbutus Drive House* and clutched them in his fist.

"Go drop Charlie off at day care. I'll text you my address if you want to come grab the keys later, okay? Better yet, I'll go take a wander through the units here and see what's left to do. Sound good?"

He'd only just met this woman, but he'd already witnessed how strong she could be. She was probably running on fumes.

Her bottom lip and chin wobbled. But the look in her eyes, the genuine gratitude, twisted something inside him he hadn't felt in a long time.

Slowly, she nodded.

"Come back when you're ready. I'm not in any rush."

She was still nodding as she turned the van back on and tossed it into reverse.

"Drive safe, darlin'."

She was still nodding, but the look in her eyes had shifted to something he recognized well—relief.

"Stop and do something for yourself, sweetheart. Even if it's just a fancy coffee," he called after her as she began to back out of the driveway.

Her head was still bobbing.

She gave him one last glance before she sped off down the road, and he could have sworn he heard a high-pitched "Bye, Jack" from Charlie inside the van.

He waved and watched her disappear before heading into the house to survey the damage.

He didn't need the job.

He made enough scratch from his bar in Mexico, doing odd jobs around town all summer for people who knew him, and off his properties that the money from Bianca's project would be just a bonus.

But she needed the help.

Plus, she was hot as fuck, and even if he just got to look at her, he'd be a happy man.

A woman hadn't revved his engine quite like Bianca did in a long fucking time.

Nodding at the cabinetry guys, he stepped over the threshold of one of the units and into the house.

It looked to be a duplex that had been renovated into a fourplex. Two basement suites were added below, accessed from the backyard. A smart move.

He had a couple of duplexes but needed to look into converting them the next time his tenants moved out. He could make more money that way. Four rents a month rather than two.

"You the new handyman?" the older cabinetmaker asked. Jack had heard Bianca call him Hoyt.

Jack nodded, slowing turning around in what he assumed

was going to be the living room. "Might be. Bianca needs to call my references first."

Hoyt's green eyes turned fatherly. "She's a good kid. I'm friends with her father, and all the Dixon kids are good kids. She moved back up here from Palm Springs last year with her kids after her husband cheated on her with his secretary and got her pregnant."

Jack shut his eyes, scratched the back of his neck and shook his head. "Fuck, that's rough."

He opened his eyes to find Hoyt nodding. "She's trying to make her way in the world again, which ain't easy no matter how old you are, but with three kids—six-year-old twin girls and little Charlie, who's two—she's got it harder than most."

"She's got family here though, right? She mentioned her brothers and obviously her parents."

Hoyt nodded again. "She does. But she's got pride too and wants to do as much on her own as she can." Hoyt wiped his hands on his jeans before plunking them on his hips, surveying the kitchen and living room area. "All four units are in the same stage of renovation. It's gonna be a big job. You up for it?"

Jack liked to think of himself as a relatively smart guy. He didn't have a fancy degree hanging on his wall, and his invitation to Mensa hadn't gotten lost in the mail, but he figured he had a pretty good grasp on social cues and nuances, and his street smarts had saved his hide more times than he could count.

Hoyt wasn't *just* implying that the renovation was going to be a big job. And by the way the man's salt-and-pepper brows lifted on his forehead, he was driving that point home.

Bianca was going to be a big job too.

Jack shoved his fingers into his hair, turned his head and smiled. "Just trying to help the lady out, is all."

He wandered into one of the bedrooms, where a

disgusting old blow-up mattress sat in one corner. This must have been where Rod was doing his dirty deeds.

"Sick fucker, huh?" Hoyt said behind him. "Glad you put the run on 'im. Hope for his sake he doesn't come back."

"If he's smart, he won't," Jack said, reaching the blow-up mattress in three strides. He pulled his switchblade out of his jeans pocket and stabbed the mattress. "Ain't nobody gonna wanna sleep on that thing."

"Good call," Hoyt agreed.

Jack grabbed the deflated single mattress, opened the bedroom window and heaved the thing out onto the lawn. There was already an industrial-size garbage bin out back. He'd toss it in there before he left.

He continued on through the rest of the house, out the front door and into the other units. Hoyt followed him.

"Bottom units are one-bedroom, tops are two," Hoyt said. "Bianca wants to put the laundry room here," he added, sweeping his hands in a gathering motion as they stood on a covered concrete patio area beneath the upstairs sundeck. "I'll make the cabinets and shit once the place has been enclosed. You good with framing and drywall?"

Jack nodded. He'd gutted and renovated two duplexes from the studs up. Besides electrical and plumbing, he did everything himself.

"Got tools?" Hoyt asked.

Jack nodded again. They'd have to properly insulate that laundry room, otherwise it'd cost a fortune to heat the place and she'd run the risk of her pipes freezing. He fucking hated dealing with insulation, but he knew how. He just itched like a bitch after.

A man who looked a lot like Hoyt, only younger, came around the corner. "Thought I'd find you here," he said. He held out his hand to Jack. "Bill Grant."

"Jack Savage," Jack said, shaking Bill's hand. "You guys do nice work with them cabinets. Real nice."

Hoyt and Bill both beamed.

"You ever in the need for some cabinets, come to us first," Hoyt said with a chuckle. "We'll hook you up."

Jack nodded. "I will."

"And you look after our Bianca and we'll give you the friends and family discount."

Jack chuckled. Hoyt had no idea how Jack wanted to *look after* Bianca.

The glint of humor in Bill's eye said he caught Jack's wavelength. Jack was also happy to see a wedding band on Bill's left hand. He was a decent-looking guy and around Bianca's age. It kept Jack's need to stake a claim at bay.

"Well, it was nice meeting you, Jack," Hoyt said, sticking out his hand for a shake.

Jack took it. "And you, Hoyt."

"Gotta head out on another delivery. You'll lock up? Bianca gave you the keys?"

He took the keys from her purse, but yes. He pulled them from his pocket, dangled them in the air and smiled. "We're all good, man. You guys have a great day."

Bill and Hoyt waved as they turned the corner. "You too."

Jack went about locking up the bottom units, the sundeck and then finally the two front units. The place certainly had potential, but it would be a lot of work. He could get it ready for when school started in August, though it'd be tight.

A lot of long days.

He was used to his summers being his.

Long rides on his bike.

Days at the beach.

Mornings in his hammock with a good book.

Maybe a beauty in his bed at night riding his dick until his balls were drained.

He'd earned his free time. He'd earned his freedom.

Even though he was only forty-three, he felt a fuck lot older than that.

He'd lived an entire lifetime. Had scars and tattoos, surgeries and demons to prove it.

Climbing back on his bike, he fastened his helmet on his head, tossed on his shades and pulled out his phone. He sent a quick message to Bianca with his home address. When he got home, he'd send her his references.

Not that she needed to call any references. He wasn't some low-life, hooker-buying scumbag who wouldn't follow through on a job.

He turned over the ignition on his bike, checked for traffic and peeled back out onto the road, keeping his eye out for the piece-of-shit truck that belonged to that douche Rod. It'd be just like him to wait until the place was empty only to return and stir up shit. The guy was a waste of fucking skin.

He did a loop around the neighborhood for good measure, then headed home. He only lived a block from the reno house, so it would be easy-peasy to go home for lunch as well as keep an eye on the place.

He'd mowed the lawn last night when it cooled off, and the sprinklers came on while he slept. Unlike the yards around him with their dry looking grass threatening to turn brown before the first day of summer, his yard was green and pristine. He'd spent a shit-ton of time and money landscaping it and putting in the irrigation system, but it was worth it in the end. The place looked like a million bucks.

Located on a corner, it had a driveway out front for the duplex tenants, while he parked his bike and truck in the back off the side road. It was a big lot, big enough for the tenants to have their own yard and for Jack to park his Airstream trailer. He'd bought a camper too, which he put up on blocks, and his twenty-six-year-old son Simon was living in that.

He'd thought about applying with the city to get it rezoned and putting in a carriage house in the back, and maybe one day he still might, but for now it all worked.

Crab walking his Harley backward, he stowed his sled beneath a lean-to he built using two-by-fours and sheet metal roofing to keep his baby out of the sun. He headed to his trailer just as Simon was coming out of his camper.

"Hey, Dad."

"Hey."

"What's the big smile for?"

Was he smiling? He hadn't even noticed. Except when his lips dropped to neutral, his cheeks felt instant relief.

Jack shrugged and unlocked his trailer. "No reason."

Simon followed him into his trailer. "I don't believe you."

"You saying I'm a grumpy fuck normally?" He turned his head toward his son, opening up the fridge in his kitchenette and pouring himself a glass of water. He lifted his brow to ask if Simon wanted one.

His son shook his head. "No. Not at all. But that's a certain smile and usually one accompanied by the impending companionship of a beautiful woman." Simon grinned. He was decked out in his usual dark polo shirt and chinos.

He worked as a freelance software engineer and made enough money that he could set his own hours. He rented a small office space downtown and employed a co-op student.

Jack was hella proud of his kid. Simon had been living down in California for the last few years, though he always returned home to Seattle for the summer—as did Jack to be with his kid. But this summer, Simon announced he was home for good, and Jack wasn't so sure he should be heading back down to the Baja again if his kid was going to be here.

Then again, Simon was an adult, and as much as Jack loved his kid, he couldn't live his life according to his kid's schedule.

"Who is she?" Simon probed, leaning back against the stove and crossing his ankles.

Jack rolled his eyes, finished his glass of water and tugged off his T-shirt. He was surprised Bianca hadn't wrinkled her nose at him. He'd been down on the beach doing a workout and sure as shit figured he smelled like a gym locker.

"It's not like that." The hell it wasn't. "I'm just gonna help a nice lady out with some renos. Her other handyman turned out to be a whore-chasing squatter who was trying to show Bianca who was boss when I intervened."

Simon's blue eyes widened. "Holy shit. She okay?"

Jack nodded. "Yeah. Think so. Stressed as fuck, mom of three, divorced, trying to work. But not physically hurt."

Simon's gaze turned wary, and he whistled. "Three kids. Jeez. You wanna get tangled up in that?"

"Not getting tangled up in nothing, just helping her out, like I said."

Simon's mouth pursed, and he rolled his eyes. "Sure, and I was a planned pregnancy. Just be careful, Dad."

Jack cleared his throat and opened the door to his bathroom. He needed a shower. "Don't worry about me. You heading to work?"

Simon nodded. "Yeah. First wanted to see if you wanted to grab dinner tonight, my treat. There's a new food truck down by the aquarium. Argentinian."

Jack started to unfasten the big buckle on his belt. "Can do. When you back?"

Simon shrugged. "I'm the boss, so whenever I want. But probably six-ish. That work?"

Jack nodded. "Sounds good." He dropped his jeans and the basketball shorts he'd worked out in, leaving him in nothing but his boxer briefs, and turned on the water to let it get warm.

Nodding, Simon opened the door of the Airstream. "See you later then."

Jack nodded. "Have a good day, son." He hopped into the shower when Simon waved goodbye.

It wasn't unlike his kid to ask him to grab dinner, but the way Simon asked made Jack think there was something more to it. Like he had something big to tell him.

Was it finally going to be about that guy Jack saw sneaking out of Simon's camper early in the morning?

He'd only been in his son's life for the past fourteen years, but he'd known Simon was gay for the last twelve. His son had never come out to him though.

Not that Jack gave a flying fuck who his son was attracted to. That didn't change how much he loved his son one iota. He just wished Simon felt comfortable enough to tell his father his truth.

Jack had gone over in his head at least a hundred times how he could bring it up to Simon, but each time he tried, it just didn't feel right.

What if his son wasn't even sure of his own sexuality yet and he was just experimenting? Maybe he was bi? Though Jack had never known his son to bring a girl home once.

He scrubbed his body in the shower, grateful that he had his son in his life at all.

He was fortunate the universe had given him a second chance. That Simon had given him a second chance. When his parents were still alive and his homelife normal and wonderful, he would have laughed in anybody's face who said his world would take the hairpin turn it did after his parents passed.

Grief and a loss of direction will make a person do stupid things. Regrettable things. Illegal things.

Father at seventeen.

Heroin addict.

Prison.

Breaking his back.

Painkiller addict.

And then finally a single dad.

Thank God for his kid finding him. Simon knocking on his door with a black eye and swollen lip smacked the sense into Jack he needed. He got clean, got custody of his kid from Simon's bitch of a mother and her abusive husband, and Jack did right by his kid from then on.

But since they both moved back to Seattle in April, nearly every morning, Jack was woken up by the camper door opening and closing and a man around his son's age leaving quietly to where his Acura was parked up the road.

He hoped his kid knew that Jack would love him no matter what and welcome any boyfriend, girlfriend or *they* he dated with open arms and a big smile. Jack didn't have any beef with the LGBTQ-plus community. Love was love was love.

If you had love in your life, you were all the richer for it.

No need to judge or hate.

Everyone ended up as worm food in the end. Why cause grief and breed hate during our short stint breathing?

His thoughts drifted from his son to Bianca and those hips of hers. That ass wiggling back and forth as she buckled Charlie into his car seat. The woman had an ass on her, for fucking sure. And that ass refused to quit. Her tits were nice too from what he could see in that mom blouse she was wearing. A T-shirt button-up thing in pink and white stripes. Sure, she made it look good, but he bet she had some delicious cleavage hiding behind those buttons. Cleavage she needed to show off in a tight, low-cut tank top.

His cock grew in his palm as the image of burying his face

between those two milky mounds consumed him. Each stroke had him growing harder.

He'd told her she couldn't fall in love with him—and even though he'd said it jokingly, he also meant it. He didn't do commitment. He did flings and fun. It was just easier that way. Nobody got hurt. He never stayed in one place long enough for a relationship beyond the fun and physical to go anywhere anyway. If Bianca wanted to sit on his face all summer while he renovated her fourplex, then by all fucking means, but that was all he could promise her. Orgasms, fun and a finished fourplex.

He was close, envisioning himself holding on to Bianca's hips as he powered into her from behind, her ass cheeks jiggling with every pound, thighs quivering and knees threatening to buckle. He'd only just met the woman, but those soft brown eyes of hers hit him hard and dead center.

His balls tightened up, and his breathing grew erratic. A couple more quick tugs and he'd feel the relief he needed. In his fantasy, she glanced behind her and pulled her ass cheeks apart, welcoming him to take her there.

No chick had ever had to tell him twice.

He slipped out of her hot, tight pussy and pushed his cockhead into her even tighter ass.

Fuck, yes.

Two more harsh, unrelenting slams and he was coming hard in his hand—or in his mind, Bianca's ass—all to the sound of his phone ringing in his jeans beyond the bathroom door.

That was probably her wondering where he was with her keys.

He also had to get her those references. After the Rod debacle, she would call every person on his list, no fucking doubt about it.

He finished, washed it all down the drain and turned off the tap.

He loved his Airstream. It was roomy, fully redone inside, with a huge bedroom in the back and a big bathroom and stand-up shower. None of this shower over the shitter thing that some trailers and campers had. He was too big a guy to deal with that and would probably soak the toilet paper every damn time.

Wrapping a towel around his waist, he opened the shower door and the bathroom door, snatching his phone off the counter.

One missed call.

He immediately called her back.

"Jack?" Her voice was panicky. Shit, was Rod back at the house?

"Bianca, is everything okay?"

She breathed out a sigh. "Yeah, it's fine. I just ... when you didn't answer, I started to think maybe you'd had an accident on your bike or something or Rod found you and hit you in the back of the head with a lead pipe."

She was concerned about him.

Besides his son, it'd been a long fucking time since anyone gave a shit about him, and that made his chest tighten in an unfamiliar way.

"Was just in the shower, darlin'. I'm okay," he said with a forced chuckle in order to hide the sudden flood of emotion in his tone. "You okay?"

"Yeah. Just wanted to come grab the keys from you. Did you have a chance to wander through the house?"

He tightened the towel around his waist and made his way through the trailer to his bedroom, pulling out a pair of shorts and boxers from his dresser. "I did, yup. Gonna be a big job."

"Can you do it in three months?"

"I can, yeah. Be long hours, but I can do it."

Another sigh of relief, followed by a pause.

"Did you go get yourself a coffee, darlin'?" he asked. "One with extra whipped cream?"

Okay, he'd admit it, he was flirting with her. He didn't need to add that whole bit about the whipped cream, but the noise she made on the other end proved it'd been the right decision.

"I did," she whispered. "Even bought myself a brownie."

"Good girl."

"You still need to send me your references."

"Was gonna do that as soon as I put some pants on."

Her sharp inhale had him smiling.

"You picturing me without pants on, Bianca?"

She cleared her throat. "Nope." Her voice croaked like a horny frog. He had to smother his laugh with a hand over his mouth. "My friend's boyfriend is a high school teacher, but he said once school is done, he can help with the renovations during the summer if you need an extra hand. He also rides a motorcycle so you guys can talk handlebars and fuel tanks and mufflers and stuff."

Jack chuckled. "Yeah? You think that's what guys who ride sleds talk about?"

"I have no idea what guys who ride *sleds* talk about."

"Where are you now, Bianca?"

"I'm at another property, meeting with the company who is going to clean the gutters and moss off the roof. Why?"

"I can meet you wherever, darlin.' You can come here, or I can come to you. Whatever you need."

"Whatever I need," she said softly, though he didn't think she was speaking *to* him. "Send me your references first, Jack. That's what I *need*. Then we can meet later so I can get the keys."

"You got it." He opened up his laptop on his kitchen table and waited for it to turn on. "Gonna send it in a minute."

"Okay. It's Friday, so chances are I won't meet you at the house until Monday. Does Monday work for you? *If* your references check out and I offer you the job?"

He grinned and brought up his email. She was cute, playing hardball.

"Monday works great, darlin'."

"If I become your boss, you won't be calling me darling."

"Ma'am, no ma'am. But you're not my boss yet ... darlin'."

"Send me your references, Jack."

"On it."

"And Jack?"

"Hmm?"

"Thank you again for today."

"No thanks necessary, Bianca, but you're welcome."

"Goodbye, Jack."

"See you soon, Bianca."

She disconnected the call, and Jack shot off the email of his references to her, all while sporting the most uncomfortable fucking stiffy under his towel. He'd just rubbed one out in the shower, and here he was ready for more.

It was Bianca and that voice of hers. Those pink cheeks that blushed when he said her name, and he couldn't forget that ass. That ass was impossible to forget. That was an ass wet dreams were made of.

Rolling his eyes, he flung the towel to the floor and headed back to his bedroom, snagging the lube from his nightstand. He had nothing else to do. Why not keep his balls happy? And if images of Bianca's ass happened to float back into his mind as he pumped his fist, then so be it. He had a feeling Bianca was going to be a force to be reckoned with.

Good thing he enjoyed a good reckoning.

4

JACK AND SIMON were just finishing up their dinner down at the new Argentinian food truck when a text message popped up on his phone.

Your references check out. Spent over twenty minutes on the phone with a Mrs. McMurray. She certainly loved that new deck you built her last summer.

Jack snorted. Was there jealousy there in that text? Hidden deep between the lines?

Did Bianca know that Mrs. McMurray was a kindly woman in her late seventies with an arthritic hip and a boyfriend named Fergus who was a scandalous five years her junior?

But he had done a nice job on Mrs. McMurray's deck. He'd put in a koi pond for her too, along with a natural-looking rock water feature.

Smiling as he and Simon walked along the sidewalk, he texted her back. *Glad my references are singing my praises. Do I get the chance to add you to the list of people who love what I can do with my hands?*

Simon glanced down at what Jack was texting and made a guttural laugh. "That the woman you helped earlier today?"

Jack nodded. "Yep."

"Keeping things professional, I see, Dad."

"Utmost professional," Jack replied with a grin. "I'm a gentleman of the highest standards."

Simon only rolled his eyes and shook his head.

Another text from Bianca rolled in. *Mr. Savage, I would like to offer you the job of contractor for the fourplex if you would be interested. However, I still require a quote on your expenses and fee, please. Please get that to me at your convenience.*

Grinning, he texted back. *Ma'am, yes, ma'am. When do you want your keys back?*

I'll be home tonight if you want to bring them by.

Abso-fucking-lutely.

Can do. I can come by whenever.

How about 8:30. The kids will be in bed by then.

See you at 8:30, Bianca.

"Looks like you've got a new job," Simon said, his grin growing. "Grab a beer?"

"Sure." He thought for sure his kid would have said what was on his mind by now, but Simon hadn't. They'd had a killer dinner at the food truck, dodged tourists and watched the boats buzz around the harbor, and all Simon did was talk about work and his upcoming camping trip to Cannon Beach. He hadn't mentioned whether his friend from the camper would be joining him.

They ducked into a pub along the water and found a seat out on the deck.

It wasn't until they both had beers and were tipping the ice-cold brews up to their lips that Simon finally relaxed and his shoulders left his ears. "So, I've been meaning to mention something to you," he started.

Here it was.

Finally, his son was going to trust him enough with his truth.

Jack adjusted how he sat in order to make himself look even more receptive and open. "Yeah?"

"I've been saving for a while now and looking at houses. I think I'm ready to buy."

"A house?" Jack asked, confused.

Simon's brows pinched. "Yeah. What did you think I was going to say? You look surprised."

Jack shook his head. "Uh ... nothing. That's great, kid. Lemme know if you want me to come look at anything with you. What are you thinking? Townhouse? Condo? Fixer-upper?"

Simon shrugged. "Mortgage broker says I'm approved for about six hundred thousand so I could probably afford a decent detached rancher. I just wanted to let you know that I won't be squatting in the camper for much longer. I do appreciate you letting me crash there though."

Jack nodded, impressed with his son and how well he'd done financially. "Anytime, kid. You know that. And good job. I'm proud of you. Don't forget the big backyard so I can park my Airstream," he teased.

Simon nodded, a jocular glint in his eye. "Oh, for sure."

Jack brought the beer to his lips and cast his gaze out to the sparkling bay. Should he bring up the guy with Simon, or was now not the right time?

Silence filled the air between them, but Simon seemed content with it and sipped his beer, watching the boats whiz around on the water.

"I wouldn't be able to be what I am or *who* I am without you, Dad," his son said after some time had passed. "I can afford a house because you *were* the house, the home, the rock I needed when I was a kid. I don't think I'd be the success I am now without you. I would have fallen through the cracks."

If he'd even survived long enough *to* fall through the cracks.

But neither of them said that. They let it hang unsaid in the air.

Fuck if he didn't love his kid more than anything in the goddamn world.

Glad he had shades on, Jack took a long pull of his beer to work through the hardening lump in his throat. He faced his son. "Just hate that I hadn't been around sooner. Making up for it now though, I hope."

Simon's blue gaze softened. "And then some, Dad."

Jack nodded. "Love you, Simon."

Simon's smile was gentle and his eyes damp. "Love you too, Dad."

AT EIGHT THIRTY SHARP, Jack pulled up to the townhouse with the address Bianca had given him. The porch light was on but unneeded. The days were getting longer, and it was still warm out. The white picket fence surrounding a small patch of grass and walkway spoke of perfect families and perfect lives living in a bubble out in perfect suburbia.

He'd had that life once.

Fleetingly.

Felt like a lifetime ago, too.

With his helmet in his hand, he opened the gate and crossed the walkway, where chalk drawings decorated the concrete.

He didn't even have a chance to ring the bell or knock before the door swung open. She stepped out and shut it behind her.

His imagination hadn't been playing tricks on him all day. She was still as fucking hot as ever.

More so than when they first met because she'd ditched that mom blouse and sported a thin-strapped black tank top that showed off *all* the cleavage. He was having a hard time keeping his eyes from drifting to the pillowy, creamy place he'd like to set up camp, call home and die a happy fucking man.

"Sorry. The kids are asleep, and I heard your bike. I didn't want the knock or bell to wake them. It's been a day." Her hair was still up in a topknot, but a lot of it had worked its way out and fell in chunks around her face.

"It was a *day* this morning. I hope it didn't get any worse," he said, reaching over and tucking a strand of hair behind her ear, causing color to flood her cheeks.

She let out a shallow sigh. "Nothing out of the ordinary. Haylee and Hannah dressed their brother up like a girl. He was into it at first, until he wasn't, but the girls were taking pictures of him, and when he bailed midway through the 'summer photo shoot,' they got mad and sat on him."

Jack snorted. "And you were left playing referee?"

"Referee, chef, chauffeur, bug killer, monster chaser, owie kisser—my titles are endless." She blinked up at him, and that's when he noticed the redness of her eyes. But it didn't look like she'd been crying. He inhaled deep through his nose and caught the faintest scent of pot.

Was Bianca toking up?

His lip twitched. "Ma'am, were you indulging in the ganja?"

The pink in her cheeks darkened, but then she straightened up to her full height, tossed her shoulders back and looked him square in the eye. "I'm a better mother because I do."

His brows lifted, but he didn't say anything.

"It's legal in Washington State. I'm not doing anything wrong."

"I never said you were."

Her confidence deflated, and her shoulders dropped. "I smoke a joint once in a while, not every night. I usually wait until they're spending the night at my parents' to do it, but if I've had a particularly rough day—"

"Like today."

Her head bobbed. "Yeah, like today, then I'll have a few puffs. I always text my friend and neighbor to make sure she's home in case there's an emergency, not that I ever get so high I couldn't function. It just takes the edge off of ... life, you know?" Her sigh came out in a deep exhale that he felt on his chest.

He held up his hands. "No need to explain to me, darlin'. You do you. Whatever gets you through to the next day."

But it seemed she *needed* to explain because she did. "I started doing it when I moved back to Seattle after my divorce. It calms me down. It also helped me put on weight after I dipped below one hundred pounds because of the stress. Munchies are a real thing, you know. I love me some brownies." Her eyes gleamed.

Fuck, Hoyt had told him about Bianca's cheating ex. Jack could only imagine that had been a stressful time for Bianca.

"It also helps me sleep, which I feel like I'm *still* catching up on from last year."

"That bad, huh?"

She nodded. "Yeah. That was *not* a good time in my life."

"Listen, the *last* person to judge you enjoying a little Mary Jane is me. So smoke away, sweetheart. Do what makes you feel good. What makes you feel human."

Relief filled her tired brown eyes. "I do feel more human afterward."

"Then keep doing it."

He pulled the keys from his pocket and dangled them in front of her. "I went into the place, got a good look around. Hoyt mentioned you wanted to put in a laundry room where that covered patio is?"

She nodded, taking the keys from him. "Yeah, can you do that?"

"I can."

"But it'll cost me?"

He lifted his shoulder. "I'm not gonna charge you an arm, a leg and your firstborn. Particularly since you have *two* first-borns, and by the sounds of it, they're a handful." He grinned, hoping she knew he was kidding. "I'll do right by you, Bianca. Give you my estimate Monday. Sound fair?"

She nodded.

"You got fixtures, flooring, backsplash and the like picked out yet?"

Her head shook, and she dropped her gaze to her feet. "Not yet. I know I should have done that by now, but with each contractor leaving, it got pushed back."

"We'll go together to pick them out. I've got an account at most home renovation stores and can get you a deal. My buddy at Finlayson Hardware always hooks me up when I need something."

Her head lifted, and she hit him with a look similar to the one earlier today. A look filled with hope and gratitude. Peace of mind and a sense of calm he hadn't seen her have until that moment. Granted, he'd just met the woman, but he'd always considered himself a pretty decent judge of character, and Bianca seemed calmer.

Good ol' Mary Jane and her relaxing ways.

"We'll get the house ready, Bianca, don't worry. And if your friend's man is willing to pitch in, then all the better." As long as Jack didn't have to teach the guy how to do every-thing. That would only slow him down.

A tear sprang into her eye, and she nodded. "Thank you, Jack."

He tipped an imaginary hat. "All in a day's work, ma'am."

That got her to crack a smile and blink away the last of her unshed tears.

He turned to go. "I'll see you Monday, Bianca. Have a good weekend, and don't get *too* stoned." That last bit was said with a smile, his hand on the gate to her picket fence.

She smiled again. "Just enough to take the edge off."

"That's right. Just enough to take the edge off." He closed the gate and headed to his bike parked along the road. She was still standing on her stoop, watching him.

He fastened his helmet and turned over the ignition, letting his bike rumble for a moment. With a final wave and nod, he sped away into the street, but he couldn't stop himself from glancing back in his side mirror to see her standing by the gate, her arms wrapped around her body, watching him go.

Bianca Dixon—he'd known her for less than a day, but he already knew the woman was going to be his undoing. He could just feel it.

BIANCA CLOSED the door behind her and plastered her back against it, her lip wedged between her teeth and a smile on her face.

Who was this Jack Savage guy anyway?

A sexy, bad-boy biker handyman, that was who.

He'd ridden in on his shiny bike when she needed help, only he was anything but a white knight. He was dark, he was dangerous, and he made her body react like she'd just stuck a fork in an electrical socket.

She was pretty sure she'd had a mini climax when he

tucked her hair behind her ear and then another mini when he said, *"Do what makes you feel good. What makes you feel human."*

If only he knew what she wanted to do to feel good. What she wanted to do to feel human.

It'd been over a year since she'd been with a man, and although that wasn't a long time for some, she missed it. And it wasn't just the sex that she missed, though Ashley hadn't even been very good in bed. He'd been okay, but now that they were divorced, she had no problem saying she'd had better before him. The guy had like three moves and he just kept them on repeat. He also wasn't a big fan of reciprocal oral sex—he'd do it, but not for long, and he usually made up every excuse in the book to get out of it.

Was he eating Opal's pie every night?

She didn't think about that for too long though because either way, it just made her mad.

She needed to think more about Jack.

Sexy, tattooed, tanned, bearded, blue-eyed Jack.

His voice was like a Harley come to life, rumbly and deep. The throaty grumble of a male lion as he stalked the savannah in search of a mate or prey he could sink his teeth into.

Her mouth filled with saliva at the thought of getting to sink her teeth into any part of Jack. Feeling the scratchy hair of his beard against her skin as he kissed her. Ashley was always clean-shaven, and even though he was a nice-enough-looking guy, Bianca had to admit, she liked the rough and tumble look.

And Jack didn't just have scruff. He had a proper beard. Like he'd been growing that thing for a while now.

Her nipples beaded to hard points beneath her tank top, and she cupped her breasts, running her thumbs over the tips. She'd ditched her bra after she put the kids to bed. She always did. No bra, a glass of wine and once in a while, a joint. It was how she finished off the day. It was how she stayed sane. It was how she had the energy, the drive, the will to wake up and do the whole shitshow of life all over again. She gave herself two hours in the evening, from eight until ten. Those were her hours. She didn't clean, she didn't fold laundry, she didn't do a damn thing that would benefit another soul besides her.

Sometimes she read a book. Other days she watched television or played on her phone. And then some nights, like tonight, she went upstairs to her bedroom, locked the door, turned off the lights, shed her shorts and underwear, climbed into bed and closed her eyes.

Jason Momoa, her vibrator, was plugged in and ready to go in her nightstand. She reached for him, slid him inside her pussy, turned on the vibration mode to level four, the suction mode to level two, put her head back on the pillow and imagined Jack's mouth tracing a path across her body.

She strummed her thumbs over her nipples, plucking and tugging. Jack's lips traveled farther south, his beard tickling her skin, which had already grown sensitive from his kisses.

She was close—it didn't take much with Jason Momoa between her thighs and thoughts of Jack in her head—but a gentle *knock knock* on her bedroom door had her eyes flying open and Bianca tumbling down that orgasm mountain backward.

"Mama?" It was Charlie.

He'd been waking a few times over the last week and a half. He kept saying his mouth hurt. He was also having an impossible time keeping his fingers out of there, which for a little boy who loved to play in the dirt meant his immune system was going to be top-notch when he was an adult.

She pulled out Jason Momoa, turned him off and slid

from beneath the covers, tugging back on her panties and shorts.

Knock knock. "Mama?" Charlie's voice was more frantic this time and his knock harder. She unlocked and opened the door to find her sleepy-eyed little man with wild bed head looking like he was lost and on the verge of tears.

Scooping him up, she carried him into her room and sat on the edge of the bed with him in her lap. She felt his forehead—he wasn't warm.

"What's the matter, bud?" she asked.

"My mowf hurts," he said, pointing to his lips. "Teef."

Yeah, she suspected he was cutting some molars. He'd been hit or miss with food for the last ten days as well. Though he never seemed to be in too much pain for those damn Goldfish crackers.

"Sweep wiff you, Mama," he said, nuzzling his face against her collarbone.

Nodding, she pulled back the covers on the opposite side of the bed from where she'd been, and he crawled out of her lap and snuggled down deep. "I'll go get you some Tylenol," she said, sitting up from the bed and heading to her bathroom. But by the time she returned, Charlie was already asleep again, his thumb in his mouth, eyes shut, his brown hair wildly strewn across the pillow.

Rolling her eyes, she put the Tylenol back in the bathroom, gently pried Jason Momoa out from under the sheets and went to wash him.

Well, so much for that self-indulgent moment. She couldn't even masturbate without one of her kids interfering.

No, that wasn't completely true. Her kids were good kids, and they all usually slept through the night, even sharing a room, the three of them, but once in a while she had to deal with one of them waking up and needing her.

Even though she liked to say she was "off the clock" at

eight o'clock when they all went to bed, she was never officially "off the clock." She'd be a mom and there for her children whenever they needed her until her last breath.

She returned a clean and disappointed Jason Momoa to his purple satin bag in her nightstand, locked the drawer and leaned over to wipe the hair off Charlie's face.

He smiled in his sleep, appearing more baby-like than he did while awake.

Fucking Ashley.

He was missing watching his children grow up, missing this wondrous time in their lives because he'd been such a selfish prick.

She left her bedroom door open just a crack and headed downstairs, pouring herself a glass of cab sav in the kitchen before making her way onto the back patio.

She took up roost in a lounge chair and watched the clouds chase each other across the sky..

What had her husband been thinking?

Charlie was only six months old when Ashley started sleeping with his secretary, Opal.

Six months!

And it was the day BEFORE Charlie's first birthday party, to which all their friends were invited, that Ashley broke the news to her that he was leaving Bianca because he'd knocked up Opal.

He was leaving Bianca and the life and family they'd built because he couldn't *abandon* Opal.

But he had no problem ABANDONING his wife of ten years and his THREE children for the twenty-seven-year-old secretary carrying his twins.

When he told her about Opal and the pregnancy, Bianca didn't fight him. She barely even spoke. Was she angry? Of course she fucking was. But there was no sense showing her hand, no sense letting him see just how devastated, how broken, how utterly fucking shattered he made her. She cried when he told her but barely said a word.

She hosted Charlie's party, acted like nothing was wrong, smiled to all their friends, celebrated her child and laughed with Ashley's parents.

Until that night.

The kids were in bed. Ashley "went out," and she began to plan.

She planned and worried herself sick. She had no appetite. She dipped below one hundred pounds from the stress of it all. Because the only thing she could control was what she put in her mouth, so if she didn't put anything in there, it was one less thing to stress over.

She'd never been a big person to begin with, so it didn't take much for her to look skeletal and sickly. Her parents and brothers had all been very concerned.

But, as hard as it all was, she chose to look at the whole situation, at Ashley's betrayal as a way out. A reason she could finally go home.

She'd never liked Palm Springs. Having grown up in Seattle, she preferred cooler temperatures and proper seasons. She'd moved to Palm Springs for Ashley.

He was the major breadwinner with the fancy CFO job for a big golf resort and country club, so she went where he went.

But she didn't have to stay there when he decided to leave their bed. When he decided to leave their family. Putting his own selfish needs ahead of the needs of his children.

So she went to the two best divorce lawyers she knew. Her brother, Liam, and his wife, Richelle. Richelle was also licensed to practice law in California, and she went after Ashley's balls.

Neutered him in court.

He shouldn't have needed the neutering, shouldn't have

needed the divorce period if he'd just gone and gotten the vasectomy like he promised he would after Charlie was born.

But, no. He worried about the potential side effects. Like impotence.

So because *she* didn't want to ever be pregnant again, Bianca went under the knife and had her tubes removed.

She had over eight weeks of recovery due to complications. The only extra help she had with her three-month-old and four-year-old twins was when her parents and brothers took turns visiting her because Ashley refused to take any of his vacation time off work to help her.

She had a few friends in Palm Springs, but most of those friends were "couple" friends, and when shit hit the fan with her and Ashley, they either dropped off the face of the Earth or the husbands sided with Ashley and the wives went with them. She wasn't leaving anything or anyone behind in Palm Springs, but she was returning to a lot when she moved back home to Seattle. She was returning to family, friends and starting a new life for just her and her children.

Looking back, she realized a divorce between her and Ashley was inevitable. And perhaps if he hadn't cheated, it would have been her who filed for the separation. He just continuously proved time and time again how selfish he was, and after Charlie was born, she'd finally started to have enough of it—enough of him. But, had they separated amicably, without a mistress and love children on the way, she wouldn't have let Richelle go after Ashley the way she did. She would have agreed to shared custody, and she might have stuck around Palm Springs so the kids could see their father more.

But he fucked the dog, or Opal—both worked in this context—and for that, she let her sister-in-law rip Ashley to shreds.

She should have known after he refused the vasectomy

that he was a selfish prick who would only ever look out for his own best interests. But alas, she had more faith in people back then.

Ashley, Opal and now Rod were killing that faith though.

She was a much more guarded person now. Much more skeptical. Fewer and fewer people were innocent until proven guilty in Bianca's eyes. Now, they were guilty until they proved to her they were innocent.

Which reminded her ...

She grabbed her phone out of her back pocket and brought up Facebook. As sexy and charming as he was, she still didn't know this Jack Savage guy. Who was he besides a sexy, badass biker with a beard and blue eyes?

What was his angle?

It didn't take long until she found him on social media.

He didn't have a big presence. It appeared that the last photo he posted was from three years ago. But from the looks of things, he liked his motorcycle, gardening and fishing.

He was tagged in a few pictures by other people, all of them at some beach bar, tanned and smiling. That must be where he worked down in the Baja.

Sipping her wine, she continued to look through his posts and photos. Nothing nefarious jumped out at her, but that didn't mean he wasn't an expert at hiding who he truly was. He could be an ex-con, for all she knew. A drug addict looking to use her reno as a place to shoot up.

Had she messed up again hiring him?

She was beginning to second-guess herself. Something she'd done when she hired Rod but dismissed her unease about him and that constant itchy feeling she got at the back of her neck whenever she was in the same space as the man. She shouldn't have dismissed her gut.

But her gut wasn't being clear with her about Jack. Her gut was telling her to give him a chance. However, there was still something slightly *unsettling* about him, and not necessarily in a bad way, just a way she hadn't felt in a long time. A way that made parts of her body tingle and her heart rate pick up speed.

Letting the wine sit on her tongue for a moment, she zoomed in on his eyes. They were the most unusual shade of blue, almost like a teal. Deep, dark and dreamy.

And even from the photo, they bored into her in a way that had her feeling vulnerable, open and, for the first time since Ashley dropped the affair and baby bomb on her —seen.

Like Jack saw her for who she was, what she was and what she struggled to be each and every day for her kids. And he didn't judge her an ounce for it.

Maybe she hadn't messed up hiring him.

Or maybe she had, and he'd get the job done but steal her heart in the process.

She swallowed her wine and took a deep breath.

Monday was certainly going to be interesting.

5

SATURDAY NIGHT WAS Bianca's favorite night.

It was her night to put the kids to bed, pour some wine and then wait for her best friends in the entire world to bring over more wine, delicious food and, in Lauren's case, an equally delicious baby.

Bianca had certainly lucked out moving into the town-house complex she did when she first moved back to Seattle.

The townhouse itself belonged to her sister-in-law, Richelle, but now that Richelle was married to Liam, she didn't need the place. And although it was only a two-bedroom house, it worked perfectly for the four of them. For now.

The rooms were huge, so the girls had a bunk bed on one side of their bedroom with all their stuff, matching dressers and fluffy pink beanbag chairs where they could sit and read, and on the other side of the room was Charlie's domain.

He had his big-boy bed with the railing to keep him from falling out, a closet and a green dinosaur beanbag chair where he liked to pretend that he could read.

The kids bickered once in a while about all having to

share a room, but for the most part, they seemed to be picking up on the vibe that this was the new norm, Mom was doing her best, so stop your bitching.

Pulling the mini quiches out of the oven, she heard the gentle knock at the front door.

Mothers themselves, Celeste and Lauren knew better than to ring the bell after seven o'clock.

Ditching her oven mitts, she padded barefoot across the tile floor to the front door and swung it open.

"Well, that's a look I haven't seen on your face in a while," Lauren said, her cheeks flushed like she'd been overexerting herself as she thrust a six-month-old Ike into Bianca's arms. "You finally get laid?" She had to pause in her passing of her son, as Ike had his fist wrapped tight around his mother's blonde hair.

Celeste snorted, an amused smile curling on her lips as she stepped into Bianca's house after Lauren. "It's certainly a good look for you if you are."

Bianca rolled her eyes and kissed Ike on the head. "No. In fact, I tried to have a bit of alone time with Jason last night, but Charlie woke up and ended up sleeping in my bed."

They both groaned and said, "Been there."

They made their way into her home comfortably because they did so every Saturday night, and her home was their home. Nuzzling a wide-eyed Ike, she followed in their wake.

"I was too hot to cook," Celeste said, plopping a wicker basket down on Bianca's granite countertop and flicking her red ponytail over her shoulder. "So I made hummus, bought some pita bread and chopped up some veggies."

"I'm too hot and pregnant to cook," Lauren said, "so I went to Paige's bistro and bought mini cheesecakes and chocolate-covered strawberries."

"I accidentally bought a seven-dozen pack of eggs at Costco rather than a three-dozen pack, so I made mini quiches," Bianca said. "But I've had the AC cranked since the kids went to bed so the place shouldn't be too much like a sauna, even with the oven having just been on."

Celeste pulled her and Lauren's contributions out of the basket along with a bottle of wine and what looked like sparkling apple juice.

Lauren pouted. "I got two freaking months of wine-drinking before I had to stop again. I didn't even have a *chance* to get my IUD in or build up my alcohol tolerance. It's going to be zilch by the time I can drink again."

"Nobody told you to spread your legs for the sexy cop," Celeste teased, bringing down two wineglasses from Bianca's cupboard.

Lauren's blue eyes widened. "You both did!"

Bianca reached for the pinot grigio over ice she'd poured herself earlier and took a sip, smiling into her glass. She'd filled her friends in via text message yesterday on what had gone down with Rod, but she hadn't told them about Jack yet.

"So what's got you smiling like you've recently smelled colors?" Celeste asked, popping the cork of her Chablis and pouring herself a generous amount in the stemless wineglass.

Lauren dug around in Bianca's freezer, pulled out an ice cube tray and cracked a few cubes into her and Celeste's glasses. "Yeah, if Charlie interrupted you and Jason, does that mean you're getting your jollies somewhere else? From someone who has *more* than ten speeds?"

Rolling her eyes, Bianca reached for one of the chocolate-covered strawberries and brought it to her lips before crushing it between her teeth. "I've found a new handyman, and he comes highly recommended, so I think I might actually get to finish this fourplex on time for the college students in September."

Her friends' brows pinched.

"*That's* what's got you smiling like you heard angels, harps and danced on clouds?" Lauren asked, walking her sparkling apple juice and tray of food into the living room. Bianca picked up her wine but didn't take anything else because she had Ike in her arms. She followed Lauren.

"He's hot, isn't he?" Celeste asked, joining them in the living room with her wine and the rest of the food on a big platter from Bianca's cupboard. "You're hot for the handyman."

Heat flooded Bianca's cheeks. She could neither confirm nor deny that she might have slipped two fingers inside herself that morning during her shower, before any of the kids woke up, and all she thought about was Jack and whether she'd get to see if he had any more tattoos under his shirt.

"Those are the cheeks of a randy woman." Lauren laughed, sitting on the couch and awkwardly curling her legs under her, her hand resting on her growing belly. "I know that look *well*. That look stared back at me every day in the mirror during my first pregnancy and greets Isaac every morning now with this pregnancy."

Rolling her eyes again, Bianca let Ike grip her fingers and stand on her thighs so he could look out at the world. He was such a strong, alert little guy. It wouldn't be long before Lauren would have to leave him with a sitter or Isaac to come over here because he would be wanting to crawl away. Then she'd have another baby in a few months that she'd be packing up to bring to wine night.

Bianca loved the baby stage, but she was glad she didn't have to go through any more herself. It was wonderful but exhausting.

"So we need to discuss planning Eva's bachelorette party," Celeste said. Bianca sighed internally, grateful for the change of subject. She wasn't quite ready to tell her friends about Jack. Not that there was anything to tell besides how dreamy he was, delicious he smelled and the fact that he oozed danger like a powdered donut oozed jelly.

"Has she said what she wants?" Lauren asked.

"Low-key but fun. No strippers, but she's not opposed to going out. She just doesn't want your *typical* obnoxious twentysomething bachelorette party where everyone wears sashes, gawdy jewelry and gets plastered."

"We did that at my bachelorette party, and it was a blast," Bianca said with a shrug.

"I was eight months pregnant when I got married, and I was also eighteen, as were all of my friends, so there was no drinking. My mom threw me a bridal shower slash baby shower," Celeste said with a snort. "But I get where my sister is coming from. We're not twentysomethings anymore, and this is her second time down the aisle. She wants sophisticated fun."

"With shots though, right?" Lauren asked. "Because I can't even drink, and I've never been married, but you can't have a bachelorette party without shots."

Celeste nodded. "There will be shots."

Eva was Celeste's older sister and Bianca's brother Scott's fiancée. Both Bianca and Celeste, as well as Richelle, were in the wedding and tasked with throwing Eva a bridal shower and bachelorette party.

The wedding was on August first, but Eva didn't want to party too close to the wedding, so they had just over a month to figure something out.

"What about a stretch Escalade, dinner somewhere fancy and then back to someone's house for drinks and a sex-toy party?" Lauren suggested. "That Curiously Kinky at Home romance party is supposed to be awesome. Lots of freebies, games and the consultants know their stuff."

"You think they can top Tracy's Dog?" Bianca asked.

Both of her friends shook their heads.

"Of course not," Lauren said. "Nothing—besides a very talented man, *cough cough,* Isaac—can top Tracy's Dog."

"*Cough cough,* Max," Celeste added.

Lauren grinned at Celeste, and both women touched their noses as they nodded.

Envy reared its ugly head inside Bianca for a fleeting moment.

Lauren continued, "But those parties still offer other fun things. Other toys. And lube and lingerie. I know a friend of mine got this really neat lube gel that feels like Pop Rocks when you put it on your skin."

"That's not a bad idea," Celeste said. "Liam and Richelle's place is big enough to host everyone. Richelle would probably be fine hosting if we all help."

"I can book the sex-toy party," Lauren offered. "I think I have a coupon for like ten percent off your next party."

"I'll talk to Richelle," Bianca offered. "Figure out what weekend we can kick the guys out, make them have poker night elsewhere."

They all groaned.

"Right, poker night," Lauren said, sipping her sparkling apple juice.

Bianca's oldest brother, Liam, hosted The Single Dads of Seattle every Saturday night. It was a group of ten single dads —well, *formerly* single dads—who got together, played poker, griped about their kids and their lives. Liam started the group several years ago because as a single dad himself, as well as a divorce attorney, he saw the lack of support out there for single fathers, and he wanted to change that.

Now, all the men were in happy relationships so they just called themselves the Poker Dads, but they still felt the need to get together most Saturday nights.

That gave all their women an excuse to get together for wine night. Bianca, Celeste and Lauren were invited to join the women who were all their friends, but they preferred to do their own thing. They were The Single Moms of Seattle—even though Bianca was technically the only single one left.

"You're his baby sister," Celeste went on. "Just bat your eyes at him and say pretty please. I've never known Liam or Scott to tell you no."

Bianca kissed the back of Ike's head and scoffed. "It'd be better if Richelle asked him to move poker night to someone else's house. She can pull out those feminine wiles of hers that bring my brother to his knees. I don't think he's ever said no to her."

Celeste nodded. "Fair enough. I don't think Scott's ever said no to my sister either."

Ike must have spotted his mother sitting on the couch because his little jellybean toes dug into the top of Bianca's thighs and he started to lunge for Lauren, grunting.

"Hungry?" Lauren asked, taking her son from Bianca.

Ike smacked her chest.

"I guess so." She started to nurse him, but Ike was no longer a newborn content on nursing while gently gazing into his mother's eyes. No. He was a wild little six-month-old with busy limbs and curious fingers. He alternated between smacking his mother's chest and trying to kick her other arm. Lauren was completely unfazed by it all and would calm his limbs without missing a beat of the conversation.

Bianca was proud of her friend. She'd come a long way in motherhood since December, when she delivered Ike into the world in the back of her Pathfinder on a gridlocked interstate. She had come into her own.

"Okay, so it's settled then," Celeste went on. "Stretch Escalade. We'll get everyone to convene at either Eva or Richelle's house, then we'll drive down to dinner and then return back to Richelle's for the sex-toy party."

"Unless we should do the party first and pre-drink," Bianca suggested.

"But then we're going downtown to dinner pissed drunk, and that's not what Eva wants," Lauren added. "Better to be in public only tipsy and save the sloshed behavior for when we're with friends and behind closed doors."

"We're women in our thirties and forties," Bianca replied. "You really think we need to worry about inappropriate behavior from anyone?"

Lauren shrugged. "You know them all better than I do, so maybe not."

"Anyway," Celeste went on, "we first have to see what weekend works and if Richelle can host, then we'll go from there. But in the meantime, I'd like to hear more about this handyman that had Bianca's cheeks flushed and a big smile on her face when we first showed up. Do we have a name we can search for?"

"You mean *stalk?*" Bianca chided.

"You stalked Max," her friend replied. "Fair is fair."

Rolling her eyes, Bianca sipped her wine. "His name is Jack Savage, and he is on social media, though not much. He rescued me from Rod after the bastard shoved me to the ground and was winding up to hit me."

Celeste was already busy on her phone, but her bottom lip dropped open, and she lifted her green eyes to Bianca. Lauren paused mid-chew, having bit into a quiche, her expression equally shocked as Celeste's.

"Fuck," Lauren finally said, tugging her blonde hair out of her son's fist without missing a beat or even glancing down at him. "Were you okay?"

Bianca nodded. "Yeah. I shot my mouth off at Rod out of anger—"

"As the Dixons are known to do," Celeste added, her freckled nose wrinkling.

"As the Dixons are known to do," Bianca repeated with a head bob. "And he shoved me to the ground, said a lot of stuff and was poised over me ready to swing when Jack rode in on his Harley, hollered at Rod, climbed off his bike and got right up into his face."

"Whoa," Lauren said slowly. "Like a *true* hero."

"And you hired him because of that?" Celeste asked.

"I hired him because apparently he's a handyman. Has worked in concrete and drywall, framing, painting, construction and carpentry for like twenty years or something. He gave me references. I called every single one, and they all sang his praises like he's some lord and savior and not just a guy who fixed their deck."

"But he's hot," Celeste added. It wasn't a question.

Bianca slowly nodded. "He's very good-looking."

"Single?" Lauren asked.

"I don't know." But judging by the way he'd been shamelessly flirting with Bianca, she certainly hoped he was. That was no way for a man in a relationship to act.

"So when does he start?" Lauren asked. "I mean, that was quick work on your part, firing and rehiring on the same day. Look at you go."

"Sheer luck, I swear it. You know the grief that house has been giving me. I just want it done. And if this Jack guy can get the job done, then great."

"I bet he can *get the job done*," Celeste said, handing her phone to Lauren. "That right there is a bona fide bad boy, Bianca Dixon, and you have got it bad for the bad boy."

Lauren whistled. "Look at those arms. All that ink. God, I wish Isaac had ink. I could run my tongue over it." Her cornflower-blue eyes glazed over and a small, closed-mouth smile curled her lips.

Rolling her eyes, Celeste took her phone back from

Lauren. "I don't see any women he could be romantically involved with in his photos, so he's probably single."

"Was he flirty with you?" Lauren asked.

Nibbling on her lip, Bianca nodded as she sipped her wine, her face feeling warm again. "He was, yes. He also told me the only way he'd take the job was if I promised not to fall in love with him." The snort that came at the end of that sentence was unavoidable. "Who says those kinds of things?"

"Bad boys," Lauren and Celeste said at the same time with matching big smiles.

"Nobody says you need to fall in love with him," Lauren added. "Just take a swim in the sexiness for the summer. Get out of this dry spell and funk. Get wet."

"Subtle," Celeste snickered, elbowing Lauren. "Get wet." She rolled her eyes. "I'm not disagreeing with our thin-filtered friend though. If he's game and it doesn't interfere with the job, you could both have a little innocuous fun. Makes me wonder why he said that though. Does he turn into a pumpkin at the end of the summer or something? So you can't get attached because Jack will become a gourd at the equinox?"

"Lame pun," Lauren teased.

"I happen to think I *squashed* it," Celeste said with a giggle.

"He says he takes off down to Mexico at the end of August every year. Spends his winters down in the Baja."

Celeste dipped a pita triangle into the hummus. "That makes sense then. Doesn't want to get attached if he's a nomad."

"I say you jump those bones and let the handyman nail, screw and drill you," Lauren said, tucking her breast back into her bra as Ike sat up. He nearly fell off her lap when he lunged at the table so vigorously for the food. She handed him a pita triangle, and he instantly started to mow down on it, drool cascading down his wrist like a waterfall.

"Max is still able to help out on the house when school is over," Celeste added. "This Jack guy may need help if it's just him and not a team."

"Isaac has mentioned helping on his days off, too," Lauren said. "He's pretty handy." She bobbed her eyebrows. "If you know what I mean."

Celeste and Bianca snorted and rolled their eyes.

"I'll mention it to Jack." Bianca grabbed her phone from her pocket and hit Facebook. She was still on Jack's profile. Not that she'd been staring at it relentlessly for the last day and a half, but he was a very nice man to look at, and she'd certainly taken a peek at him before her shower that morning.

"Oh, she's got it bad," Lauren sang. "Look at that lip between the teeth and those *hot for you* eyes. She's imagining him drilling, nailing and screwing her right now."

She was.

But she wasn't going to admit that to her friends, even though they could probably see it on her face.

"You do know we're going to have to come meet this jack-of-all-trades hot handyman," Lauren said with a big grin.

"Did you just say *Jack-off-all-Trades*?" Celeste asked.

Lauren's smile grew. "No, but that's a good nickname for him. We'll have Professor Washboard, Sergeant Foxy McBig-Hands and Jack-Off-all-Trades."

"No, and no," Bianca protested.

Her friends burst out laughing.

"Hung and Handy?" Lauren offered.

"Oh, I like that one," Celeste said, biting into a mini cheesecake. "I *really* like that one. He looks like he'd be hung. Sometimes you just know, you know? The guy gives off a vibe, even from his photo." She glanced back down at the picture of Jack on her phone. "And he looks like he'd be hung."

Bianca buried her face in her wineglass.

Jack's hands were big. His boots too.

She glanced up at her friends, and both of them were giving her knowing, annoying and teasing smiles.

She rolled her eyes. "I just need my fourplex done."

"And all your holes filled ... with caulk. Or is it *cock?*" Lauren added with a laugh. "I bet he's got the right tool to fill *all* Bianca's holes. Fill 'em up good."

Bianca leaned over and grabbed a mini quiche off the table and crammed it into her mouth. Yeah, all her holes filled would be nice.

Maybe just for the summer?

6

MONDAY COULD NOT COME SOON ENOUGH for Jack. He'd never looked so forward to a Monday in his entire life. Not that he worked Monday to Friday, nine to five, like a regular working stiff, but he still enjoyed the weekends like everyone else.

Only this particular Monday was bringing a new something, or *someone* more specifically, he was really champing at the bit to see again. He had a feeling he was going to enjoy the midweek grind just as much as he enjoyed the weekends if it meant he got to spend time with Bianca. Their limited interactions with each other had been full of revelations, and even though he barely knew the woman, he could already tell she was stretched thin, struggling to keep her head above water, and her happiness and well-being came dead last on the priority list.

He liked that she treated herself to a little *green* to take off the edge—it humanized her. But it revved his engine even more that when she did enjoy a joint, she made sure safety measures and contacts were aware in case there was an emergency with her kids. That was a woman who put her children first, above all else, but was also grappling with her need to take care of herself. She knew she needed to do better by herself; she just didn't have much time for it.

If he could help her even just a little by easing the stress of the renovation, then he would. His parents had always taught him that if he saw someone who could use his help, to give it. Karma was real, but you needed to live with your choices and feel good about them in *this* lifetime too, not just future lifetimes.

He pulled up to the Arbutus Drive house in his black Ford F150. He preferred to ride his bike during the summer if he could, but he had a shitload of tools he needed to bring with him and couldn't exactly pack them over on his bike. He'd leave them here, as he had no other projects booked for the summer.

Bianca texted that morning to say she'd meet him at the house at ten, as she had to drop off the kids at school and day care first and preferred not to be rushed when they went over the plans.

It was nine fifty. He liked to be early. When her white minivan pulled into the driveway and she spied him sitting on the curb in his truck, the smile that graced her face fucking winded him.

He cleared his throat and opened the door to his truck, meeting her on the walkway to one of the units. "Mornin'."

She smiled again, a sexy blush blooming in her cheeks. Her hair was different today, looser, wavier. It suited her. He watched as she tucked it behind her ear, hooked her purse strap over her shoulder and approached him. "Good morning. How was your weekend?"

"Good. You?"

"Good, thank you."

She wore a flowy blue skirt that hit her at the knee and a white T-shirt with a V-neck. It showed off her tits like the creamy mounds of perfection he knew they would be and hugged her curves just right. Even her feet were cute in strappy tan sandals with little amber jewels on them. But he had a tough time ungluing his eyes from her ass when she climbed the three concrete steps up to the front door and unlocked the unit.

He shoved down the groan that burbled in the back of his throat at the thought of that ass jiggling as he pounded her hard from behind.

He needed to get his mind out of the fucking gutter and focus on the job he'd been hired to do. He could fantasize about banging his boss all he wanted, pretend his fist was her tight pink slit in the shower until his balls were drained, but he needed to keep things with Bianca professional. She'd already been through the wringer with carpenters. The last thing he needed to do was complicate her world even more or blur the lines.

"So you've already been in here. I'm assuming you assessed what still needs to be done with each unit?" She stepped into the living room, and he joined her, leaving the front door open.

"I did, yes. Seems doable, but it'll be tight."

She spun around to face him, her eyebrows lifted, expression shocked.

He hadn't even meant for that to be a sexual innuendo. *Doable but tight.* But she certainly heard it as one.

It made him laugh that that was exactly where her brain went first.

Her expression softened, and she coughed, though she was unable to hide the flush that rose up her chest and into her neck. "I mentioned to you earlier that my friend Celeste's boyfriend, Max, has offered to help for June, July and August, and another one of my friend's boyfriends is a cop and has offered to help on his days off."

Oh great, a pig in his breathing space. That was the last fucking thing that he needed.

Not that he'd seriously broken the law in nearly two decades, he just didn't like cops.

But all he did was smile. He'd cross the pig bridge if he came to it. Maybe this guy wasn't such a tool as he knew some of them to be.

"I have to go and pick up the *new* over-the-range microwave today, so I'll do that shortly and bring it back. A part of me would like to get all the kitchens to a point where I can call the plumber in to hook up the stoves. He's already done the toilets and sinks in each unit, but we've gone with gas stoves for the kitchens, so he needs to come back for that."

Jack nodded. "Makes sense. Kitchen first, then bathroom. You want me to paint too?"

Her brows furrowed before she shook her head. "I can come and paint. That way you can spend time on the things I can't do, like flooring, tiling, installing the cabinets and building the laundry room."

So he was going to see even more of her? Bonus.

"We working one unit at a time? Get each one to completion before we move to the next?"

"Besides the plumbing, yes, I think that's best, that way if in the event we are unable to get all four done by the end date, at least we'll have two or three units to rent out." She drew a tape measure out of her purse and held it against the far wall in the living room. "I'm furnishing the places, so I need to get area rugs and furniture. I need to order everything by the end of next week. Hold that there for me, please."

Smiling at the command in her tone, he made his way over to the end of the tape measure and held it against the wall.

She walked to the other side of the living room and murmured the length to herself. "You still need to tell me what you charge," she said, nodding at him to let go of the tape and allowing it to furl back on itself.

"How does forty-five an hour sound?" he said, gauging her reaction. He normally charged closer to sixty given his experience and skill, but for her, he'd do it for less.

Relief filled her face, and she nodded, though he could tell it was taking a lot of control on her part to temper her enthusiasm. She stuck her hand out. "You're hired, Mr. Savage. I look forward to working with you."

"Jack," he said, taking her hand and giving it a good, strong shake. "You need to call me Jack, darl—"

She lifted a brow at him.

"Bianca," he finished. "You need to call me Jack, Bianca." His grin was big. She'd said on Friday that if she hired him, he couldn't call her *darlin'* anymore. It'd take some work on his part, but he'd do it. The last thing he wanted to do was upset Bianca or make her feel like he didn't respect her as his employer. She'd caught enough of that shit with Rod to last a lifetime.

"Where are you going to start today?" she asked, releasing his hand.

"Gonna haul all my tools in, then probably lay the subfloors in that one bedroom ol' Rod *did* paint. Give you a chance to paint the rest before we lay any more flooring. I see all the plywood is in the basement unit there."

"Yes, and all the flooring is in the other unit next door. Laminate and tile."

"Then I think I can get going."

She nodded. "Then I will leave you to it. I'm going to go order the stoves, fridges and some furniture, and I will be back with that first over-the-range microwave, seeing as Fuckface McGee probably pawned the other one."

His lip twitched, and he snorted. "You doing okay after Friday? No PTSD or anything?"

The fire in her eyes turned from flames of anger to something else, and her small smile held so much sweetness, he fought the urge to grab her by the back of the neck so he could get some of that sugar for himself.

"I am, thank you. Had a quiet night by myself Friday, then did wine night with my two girlfriends on Saturday. Unwound and processed. Hopefully, that's the last we've seen of Rod Penner."

"From your mouth to the ears of the universe," he said.

She tilted her head skyward. "Hey, universe, can this be the *last* I see of Rod Penner, please? I would *realllllly* love to catch a break right about now."

He chuckled, the urge to tuck a wayward strand of hair behind her ear making his fingers itchy. Instead he shoved his hands into the pockets of his jeans. "What about me? I'm a caught break, right? Finally found the handyman of your dreams. I won't leave you high and dry or bring in hookers."

She dropped her eyes from the ceiling and back to him, her expression one-hundred-percent serious. "You're right, you are a caught break. Thank you for reminding me."

Their gazes locked, blue to brown, and he was forced to shove his hands ever deeper into the pockets of his jeans to keep from reaching for her.

He'd never met a woman he'd had such a visceral reaction to. A woman he wanted to take and claim as fiercely and primitively as he did Bianca. Something about her just revved him up, turned him on and brought out the animal inside him.

With a grunt, he turned toward the front door, pulled his hand from his pocket and tugged on his beard. "All right then, I'm gonna go unload my shit and start working."

Nodding, she followed him. "And I best start my day as well."

He was already unloading things from the box of his truck when she came up behind him, keys dangling from her slender fingers. "I almost forgot. I had the whole house rekeyed on the weekend. New locks on every outside door, just in case Fuckface McGee had duplicates made and wanted to sneak back in for old times' sake. Here are your copies to every unit."

He took them from her, unnecessarily brushing his fingers against hers. Her eyes flared, and a gasp snagged in her throat. "Good idea. You can never be too careful with Fuckface McGees. They're always looking for the next come up."

Taking a step back, she tucked a strand of dark brown hair behind her ear, hair he wanted to take a fistful of just before he crushed his mouth against hers. "Yes, you can never be too careful. I'm going to go. Text or call if you have any issues. Otherwise I'll be back in a few hours. I have to go buy more paint."

He shoved the keys into his pocket and reached into the back of his truck box for his tool belt. "Sounds good, darl— Bianca. See you in a bit."

Her laugh was like music. "You're going to struggle not calling me *darlin'*, aren't you?"

"Maybe for a bit, but I've always enjoyed a challenge."

Her brow lifted before she swung her curves behind the steering wheel of her van. "Bye, Jack."

"Don't be too long ... Bianca."

IT WAS one thirty by the time Bianca pulled back into the driveway at the Arbutus Drive house. Jack's truck was still parked on the curb, and she could hear the faint sound of music coming from the open windows inside the unit he planned to work on.

She'd had a productive morning on her own. She picked up a new microwave, priced out area rugs for the two top units, ordered a bunch of furniture and some appliances, and bought more paint for the living room, kitchen, bathroom and bedroom. She'd also stopped and grabbed herself—and Jack—an iced coffee at See You Latte Café near the college before making her way back to the house.

With paint cans in one hand and the cardboard tray of iced coffees in the other, she fumbled to lock her van as she headed up the walkway to the front door. It was closed, but unlocked, so she only had to set down the paint cans for a moment to turn the latch.

Classic rock greeted her upon entry along with a shirtless, grunting and slightly sweaty Jack, down on his knees, laying the subfloor.

The paint cans left her fingers, and she nearly dropped the coffees but managed to catch herself. She failed to keep her mouth from falling open though, and her bottom lip damn near hit her sandals.

With another sexy grunt, he finished what he was doing and glanced up at her, shoving his hair off his face and smiling. "You're back."

Bianca swallowed and thrust the coffee holder toward him, her eyes lasering in on the tattoos across his chest and the way his pecs and arm muscles flexed and bunched as he finished what he was doing with a manly grunt. "Coffee," she said with a squeak.

Still smiling, he stood up to his full height and stepped toward her, shoving his hair off his face and pulling a plastic cup free from the cardboard. "Ah, thanks."

Pulling the straw and lid off, he sipped it like it was a mug of hot coffee and not a refreshing to-go cup of iced coffee.

"Hate straws," he murmured before taking a sip and stepping into the kitchen area, where the counters had been erected and a hole for the sink cut out. He'd been busy. That hadn't been there when she left. He managed to put in an entire kitchen nook while she was gone as well as start laying the subfloors. He'd be done the whole house in no time if he worked this fast all the time.

She sipped her own drink, her eyes continuing to enjoy their journey over the hard planes of his body. Each defined pec was inked up beautifully, but his nipples remained uncovered. He'd probably look incredible with nipple rings, or even better, barbells.

He set the coffee down on the counter. It was already half gone. "Can I ask you something ... as a parent?" he asked, running his fingers through his hair, which only made his biceps tighten. "Don't got a lot of friends who are parents."

"You have a kid?"

How many kids did he have? How old? What was his relationship with the mother? So many new questions cannoned around in her brain that she almost missed it when he grunted, tugged on his beard and said, "Yeah, a son."

She had to stop herself from swallowing her tongue and simply nodded for him to go on. The thought of Jack holding a baby against his bare chest or singing a child a lullaby before bed made her weak in the knees. A man who was good with children, who was a good father, was one of the biggest turn-ons. It was one of the things she'd loved most about Ashley. For all his faults, he was a good father.

At least he used to be.

Jack's deep voice and crystal-blue eyes pulled her from her meandering thoughts and brought her focus back to him. To his lips and the way they moved when he spoke.

"So my son is twenty-six and ..." He cleared his throat and averted his gaze before continuing. "I'm like ninety-nine-point-nine percent sure he's gay. But I'm just not sure I'm comfor—"

She held up her hand, and he went quiet. "I'm going to stop you right there."

Shit. She knew he was too good to be true.

She'd hired a fucking bigot.

He'd come to her rescue, slathered on the charm like it was SPF 90, and all the while he was hiding his inner bigot.

Fuck. Now she'd have to go and find a new handyman again, and chances are she wouldn't get any of the units ready for school in the fall.

"I support the LGBTQ-plus community. Who your child loves should not change whether you love them. I think you should go. This isn't going to work, Mr. Savage. I'm sorry, but I can't work with someone or have someone work for me who is so close-minded." She took a step back, shaking her head.

If any one of her children came to her and told her they were gay, she would hug them and march in the next pride parade right beside them. She loved her children no matter what, and the fact that Jack was having issues with his son being gay made her gut churn with how wrong she'd been about him. About hiring him.

But it was his turn to hold up his hands. He shook them, along with his head, his expression that of panic. "Whoa, whoa, whoa. You've got me all wrong, Bianca. That wasn't what I was going to say at all."

Her head snapped back, a brow lifting on her forehead.

His nostrils flared as his gaze washed over her. Something tender creased his face, and for a moment, her anger dissolved—slightly.

He exhaled, worry clouding his eyes along with the panic. "I was going to ask you for your help. My son is twenty-six. He's been in my life since he was eleven. He is the best thing in this whole fucking world. But he hasn't come out to me, and I want advice on how to let him know that I love and accept him for who he is." He shook his head again, his blue eyes fiercely defensive and like a battering ram to her quickly erected walls. "I was going to say, I'm not sure I'm comfortable just asking him, *Are you gay?* Because all the books I've read say not to out your kid. I don't care if he's gay, bi, asexual, nonbinary, fluid or whatever else. I love him no matter what, and although he hasn't said this guy is his boyfriend, I'm again ninety-nine-point-nine percent sure he is. How do I let my son know that him being gay changes nothing about how I feel about him without making him feel uncomfortable? Can you help me?"

Oh fuck.

There she went assuming.

Damn, she could be an ass. Since Ashley had wronged her so horribly, and then Rod, she was beginning to question her judge of character and instincts. She thought everyone had an ulterior motive or a dirty little secret.

Maybe Jack was the exception to that rule.

Was he really as handsome and wonderful as he appeared to be?

Exhaling, she dropped her gaze from him and stared at the floor. "I ..." The man had gone from someone she wanted to jump and grind his bones to dust, to a man she quickly, wrongly assumed was a repulsive bigot, to a supportive, sensitive, shirtless mountain of sweaty sexiness.

"Look at me, Bianca. Not the floor." The deep rumble of his demand had her pussy clenching and nipples beading.

Like a chastised child, she slowly brought her gaze back up to his. Then her body was acting before her brain even had a chance to weigh in. She plastered herself against him, cupped his face in her hands and took his mouth like she owned it.

He didn't resist for a moment. His arms circled her, and he pulled her tight against him. The taste of coffee on his tongue mingled with the coffee on hers. He smelled like sweat, man and fucking heaven.

His body was warm, his skin smooth but his muscles hard.

"Bianca," he breathed, breaking their kiss for a moment and dropping his lips to her neck, "what are we—"

She went for his zipper.

"We're doing this?"

Oh hell, yes, they were doing this. She'd wanted to do this to him since the moment he stepped up and defended her against Rod, since the moment he let her son hop on his motorcycle. Since the moment he showed up on her doorstep with the keys and oozing sexiness and danger, looking like the answer to all her problems—because he might just be.

And now that she'd seen him without a shirt, found out what kind of a man, of a father he was, add all that tanned skin, tattoos and lickable abs, and she wanted him even more. She wanted all of him.

"We're doing this," she panted.

"Okay." It was like a light switch went on inside him, and he gripped her by the ponytail, tilted her head back and claimed her mouth, backing her up until the center of her back hit the counter.

He pulled his tongue back and she chased it with hers into his mouth, taking control of the kiss, taking control of everything. He deepened their kiss, the vibration of her groan only adding to the mix of it all. His one hand splayed against her back, holding her in place against him, while the other hand remained wrapped firmly around her ponytail, keeping her head angled just the way he needed it. His kisses were deep, thorough and made her toes curl in her sandals. His tongue massaged hers, explored the contours of her mouth, and when he finally broke their lip lock, she was unable to stifle the whimper that fled her throat.

His lips worked their way down her heated skin to her neck and collarbone.

Gruffly, he released her hair and back, grabbed her by the hips and lifted her up onto the counter, wedging himself between her legs, his evident erection grazing her inner thighs.

Swallowing, she lifted her gaze from his lips to his eyes.

Blue fire flickered before her. Slowly, his hands, warm, strong and sure, slid up her thighs, pushing her skirt toward her hips.

Her lips parted, and her eyes fluttered closed. Fuck, she might be able to come just from that. It'd been so long since a man had touched her, and a man like Jack had never touched her. He was her ultimate fantasy. Tall, dark and so damn bad, he could only be good at all the things that would make her purr.

With a slight tremor to her hand, she lifted it up and touched his bottom lip.

He had nice lips. Full lips. Lips that could kiss.

His hands continued to push her skirt up. Torturously slow. His eyes remained glued on her. "Afraid I'm just gonna have to eat you, darlin'," he murmured. "No wrap on me, unless you got one in that purse of yours."

Bianca quivered, curled her fingers around his beard and tugged his mouth against hers again. "I'm clean," she said between kisses. "Got checked after he cheated."

"Cheating motherfucker," he said with a snarl. "I'm clean too. But that's not all we gotta worry about."

"Had my tubes removed too," she said, letting go of his beard and pushing her fingers into his hair. It was slightly damp from sweat but still soft and thick. "No more babies for me."

His groan had her pussy throbbing, and he took control again, pulled away from the kiss, pushed her down with his hand on her chest until her elbows hit the counter. He sank to his knees.

With his fingers around her ankles, he pulled her forward until her butt cheeks hung halfway off the counter. He pushed her skirt up to her waist, made a frustrated growl and pulled so hard on her panties, they snapped off.

"Holy shit," she breathed.

Her sandals fell off her feet in two loud *clunks,* and he planted her bare feet on his shoulders.

"Now that's a pretty pink," he murmured.

She barely had a moment to process what was happening before his tongue found her clit and she nearly blacked the fuck out.

Bianca wasn't sure if it was the fact that she hadn't had her pussy eaten in forever or if Jack was just that good, but his head was only between her legs for thirty seconds before her core tightened and stars burst behind her eyes as the mother of all orgasms swept through her.

He hadn't even put his fingers inside her. It was all tongue. All lips. All teeth.

He sucked and he licked and he bit. He ate her like she was the best ice cream sundae he'd ever had and he intended to clean that bowl until it sparkled.

"Jack," she said between pants, her clit pulsing, spots clouding her vision.

He pressed on, drawing her clit into his mouth and sucking hard, so hard she had no choice but to lift her hips and accept the second orgasm that came out of nowhere.

Her head thrashed back and forth on the counter, her

ponytail hanging over the side, butt cheeks pressing into the other edge.

When the second wave of euphoria began to ebb, she lifted up onto her elbows with the little energy she had left. "Jack ... you need to ..."

He just kept going.

"Oh my God, stop. It's too much."

He shook his head, his blue eyes opening and tipping up to look at her, dark and searing. He drew her clit back into his mouth. "I'm not stopping until it looks like I've eaten a dozen glazed donuts, Bianca. You have more in you. I can taste it, and you taste fucking delicious." He swept his tongue up her folds. "Haven't tasted anything so fucking good in a long time, darlin'. Can't stop now. Couldn't if I tried."

"Fuck ..." was all she could say.

Her head fell back against the counter but then shot right back off it again when he dipped his head and his tongue poked her crease. His forearm rested across her lower belly, and the thumb from that hand strummed her clit. His tongue pressed harder against her tight hole.

She shuddered when he circled her anus a few times before flicking it.

"Oh my God." She wasn't against ass play, but she needed to draw the line somewhere today, right? "No finger in the butt," she whispered.

"It's my finger and my butt and I'll stick it there if I damn well please," he murmured before rimming her hole with his tongue again.

She tossed her head back and laughed. She hadn't expected that comeback.

"No finger in *my* butt," she corrected.

"This time." His thumb wiggled over her clit until she thought she might pass out.

She was just getting used to his tongue where it was, teasing her forbidden hole, when he pulled it away, removed his thumb and latched back onto her clit, shoving his face deeper into her pussy. The flat of his tongue brushed over her clit. A couple more flicks with the tip and a harsh scrape of his teeth, and she was there. Another orgasm ransacked her body. Pulse after pulse, the climax spread outward from her clit into her body, to her extremities, until the tips of her fingers and toes tingled.

Her back bowed on the counter, and she pressed her pelvis into his face, panting and murmuring things she would never remember when the smoke cleared.

Her fingers found their way into his hair and flexed against his head, her nails digging in against his scalp. As her orgasm recoiled once more to her center, her back met the counter again, and she tapped his head. "You need to ..."

He held her hips, stabilizing her, holding her from slipping off the counter to the floor, and he pulled his mouth away. His eyes opened again and tipped up to her, a challenging glint in the blue along with a sexy lifted eyebrow.

As his lips curled, she could see that they held a thick sheen of her arousal. His beard and mustache were covered in droplets. It did look like he'd been eating glazed donuts.

He stood up.

"You need to fuck me, Jack," she said, her gaze slipping down his sexy torso and lasering in on the long, thick iron bar in his jeans.

Her mouth watered, and heat flooded her belly.

With a nod, he grabbed her hand, hauled her up to standing and turned her around, his hand on the back of her neck as he pushed her face against the counter, making her body bend ninety degrees.

"Wanted you since the moment I fucking met you, Bianca. Imagined giving it to you like this, watching that ass of yours jiggle with each pound. Next time I wanna see you. Watch you come as I'm inside you. This time though, I wanna watch that ass dance."

Next time?

She heard the telltale sound of a zipper and couldn't stop herself from craning her neck around to get a glimpse of him.

He held himself in his palm. A thick string of precum hung off the head of his cock.

She breathed out. Fuck, he really was Hung and Handy.

Swallowing, she pushed up to her full height from the counter only to be met with a frown of curiosity. Ignoring him, she swept her index finger over his cockhead, gathering the cum, and popped her finger into her mouth, closing her eyes and tasting every drop of him.

She would have loved to see his expression, but judging by the way he growled, grabbed her by the back of the neck and forced her back down against the counter, she guessed he liked what she did.

"Fuck, baby," he murmured, rubbing the thick crown between her folds, hitting her clit and making her entire body tremble. "You're a dirty girl, aren't you, Bianca?"

She swallowed as he pressed his cockhead against her swollen, pulsing entrance. Sure, she fucked Jason Momoa several times a week, but he had nothing on Jack.

Would it be a tight fit since she hadn't been with a man in over a year? Or had three children entering the world ruined her forever?

She held her breath and hoped it was the former but prepared for the latter.

Gripping her hips, he slowly wedged his way inside.

"Fuck me," he breathed. "Fucking tight, woman."

Yes!

Score one for a year of celibacy ... and routine Kegel exercises.

"Fuck, Bianca." His fingers curled tighter on her hips, and

he slowed down even more. "Not gonna last long in this hot, tight cunt, darlin'. Not long at all."

His dirty, crude words only turned her on even more.

She went to move her hand between her legs to touch her clit, but he swatted her away and replaced her fingers with his.

"No," was all he said as he pinched her clit.

Finally, he was fully seated inside her, letting her know he'd reached the hilt with a low, guttural grunt.

"Your orgasms are mine, Bianca. For the whole fucking summer, my face is the only face you're sitting on. My dick's the only dick you're gonna be riding. Ya got it?" He started to move.

She thought her eyes were going to roll clear back into her head.

"Ya got it?" he asked again, pinching her clit until she yelped.

"Uh-huh."

His cadence picked up. The steady in and out of his cock inside her pussy, his balls slapping her ass, and her thighs and ass cheeks jiggling were enough to make her come again. But add those clit pinches, and it was all she could do not to explode around him for a third time. Or was it a fourth time? She'd lost count.

"Gonna come," he said, tightening his grip on her one hip. "You with me?"

"Yes," she whispered. She wanted to come with him, wanted to wait for him to get there so they could reach that last climax together.

"Fuck, Bianca. Gonna suck those sweet tits of yours next time. Get you sitting on my dick so when you come, you cream all over my balls."

"Jack ..."

"That's right, darlin'. Say my name. Can't wait to have those lips around my cock."

She couldn't wait either.

He stilled behind her, let out a surly grunt, pinched her clit hard, and came.

She came too. Another wave of bliss crashed into her, blasting outward like a firework in the sky. She squeezed herself around him, milking his cock, feeling it throb against her channel walls with each spurt of hot cum as he filled her up.

By the time the tingles of ecstasy had dissipated, Bianca barely had enough energy to open her eyes. But she felt like a million bucks.

A million exhausted bucks. But a million bucks no less.

Jack's fingers released her clit, and his warm hands ran gently over her ass cheeks. "So, am I still fired?"

She chuckled, opening one eye and finding him smiling lazily behind her. "I rescind my declaration of termination and instead offer you a promotion and a raise. Do you accept?"

He shook his head before leaning forward and pressing a kiss to her shoulder. "Nope." His lips were next to her ear. "The only one who's going to be giving anyone a *raise*"—he twitched his dick inside of her—"is me to you. Ya got it?" His teeth tugged on her lobe.

Bianca smiled. "I got it."

7

"I DON'T KEEP spare panties in my purse, you know," Bianca said, drying her hands on a paper towel after using the bathroom. "And I'm not one to go commando. Particularly since it's windy today and I have school and day-care pickup."

Jack shrugged and smiled. "Whoops. Guess you need to start packing spares then." He pulled her into his arms, ruffled her skirt behind her until her bare ass was exposed, and he cupped it. "But if you wear underwear, I can't do this."

Her smile stole the air from his lungs. "That's true. I guess I just need to keep a bag of spares in my mom van if you're in the habit of ripping them."

"I am. Particularly when it's your hot, tight little cunt that's beneath them."

The pink to her cheeks had him grinning until his cheeks hurt and ripped a laugh deep from his chest. "Does my choice of words embarrass you?"

She shook her head, hitting him with those soft brown eyes he couldn't wait to have looking up at him as his cock filled her mouth. "No. I like them. They're just ... dirty, and I have never had a man speak to me like that before."

"Never been with someone like me, you mean?"

She blinked. "No. I haven't."

"Still need your advice about my son if you're willing," he said, changing the subject before things went too deep. He didn't want to know just *how* much of a guy he was that she'd never been with before. Was it just a guy with tattoos? A guy with a beard? A guy who rode a Harley? Or all of the above plus more?

He knew he wasn't the kind of guy parents welcomed with open arms to the dinner table. And Bianca had a very "good girl" vibe to her. He was probably her first fuck from the other side of the tracks.

Though not once since meeting her on Friday had she acted afraid of him. And he knew what an afraid woman looked like. He saw enough of them give him the *look* when he was grocery shopping or sitting in the waiting room at the dentist. And forget about going into a bank or an airport without all eyes landing on him and people clenching their jaws so hard, he could damn near hear them chipping teeth.

But not Bianca. She didn't look at him like he was a threat. And that was part of the reason why he wanted her so fucking bad. Because she saw him as a person first, as a man first. She didn't see his tanned skin, beard and long nose and jump to conclusions.

Or maybe she did, but it didn't show on her face, and he liked that.

Was he a bad guy? No.

A bad boy, perhaps. But he followed the letter of the law and kept his nose clean.

He was a good man now, even if his history sent him to hell when the universe bid him farewell. He slept soundly at night knowing he'd turned his life around, gave his son a good life, was clean and made his money the honest way.

The rest was up to fate. He'd have friends in the clouds or

friends dancing in the fire as Satan poked them all with his pitchfork. Either way, he wouldn't be alone in the afterlife, and he didn't much care if he was on Santa's naughty list. He didn't wait around for a fat man in a track suit to get him what he wanted. He went out and bought it himself.

Nodding, she bit her lip for a moment. "Right, your son," she said, drawing him out of his thoughts.

He blinked a couple of times and shook his head as she hummed.

Fuck, she was cute. Sexy as fuck but also cute as fuck. She was the whole damn package. He squeezed her ass cheeks one more time before letting her skirt drop and releasing her. They both took their iced coffees, which were now devoid of ice, and sipped them.

"Has he introduced you to this guy he's seeing?" she asked.

He shook his head. That hurt too. He thought he and his kid had an open enough relationship that when Simon had someone special in his life, he'd want to introduce that person to his dad. Had he been wrong about how close he thought he was with his kid? "No. But Simon lives in the camper next to my Airstream, and I hear the guy leave every morning around six."

"Then mention that. Just say, saw a guy leaving your camper the other morning. You going to introduce me to your boyfriend?"

He pursed his lips, the taste of Bianca still lingering on his tongue. Fuck, she tasted good. "Yeah, maybe. I just envision him freaking out."

"Is he the freak-out type?"

No. Simon was the most relaxed person ever. Hardly anything fazed his kid.

He shook his head again. "No."

"Or don't bring up the guy at all and just say, *You know I love you regardless of who you choose to love, right? Gay, straight, asexual, bi, you're my kid, and I'll love you no matter what."*

He nodded again. That wasn't so bad, but whenever he thought long and hard about it, nerves prickled along his arms and stirred his stomach to the point of painful knots. Simon meant too much to him. He just didn't want to jeopardize his relationship with his son for anything. He'd even read up on how to support your gay child, and he knew that outing his son before Simon outed himself was wrong. Maybe Simon was just experimenting and wasn't ready to admit his sexuality to anybody—including his dad.

"What about casually mentioning a double date?"

He cocked his head. "With you?"

She shrugged. "I mean, we don't have to go out. But just say, *Hey, how about a double date with me, you, the chick I'm boning and the guy who leaves your camper at 6 a.m. every morning."* She'd dropped her voice to a bleak attempt at a manly voice, but it cracked at the end.

He smiled. "The chick I'm bonin'?"

"Fucking. Drilling. Screwing. Nailing. Pick a verb that works for you and the kind of relationship you have with your son. Casually having adult relations with?"

He set his coffee down and pulled her back against him. "We've fucked once, and now I'm *boning* you."

She lifted a brow. "I came like four times, plus you said your face is the only face I'm allowed to sit on all summer, *and* you said next time we have sex I'm going to ride your dick so you can suck my tits and I can, and I quote, *cream all over your balls.* So yeah, apparently this wasn't a one-time thing."

Grinning, he dipped his head until his lips hovered just over hers. "Every morning, darlin'. You come here, we fuck and then we work. That's how it's gonna be. Start the work day off with a—"

"Bang?"

His tongue ran along the seam of her mouth. "Mhmm."

"I can get on board with that."

"I'm fucking my boss."

She hummed. "You are."

"Wanted to the moment I saw you. Hadn't planned on it. Tried hard not to. But I like it."

One brow lifted. "You tried hard not to?"

"Believe me, darlin', if I hadn't tried not to, you would have been riding my dick Friday night when I dropped off your keys. I've got serious willpower. Would have had a celibate summer if you hadn't attacked me. But I like that you did."

She hummed again. "I do too. You're back to calling me *darling*."

"Only when I'm fucking you. When we're working, I'll call you *boss*."

"I like the sounds of that."

"Don't forget what I said when I agreed to take the job, though. Just 'cause it made you laugh doesn't mean it wasn't the truth."

She paused for a moment, her eyes turning serious. Damn it, was he wrong to remind her that this was only temporary? She needed to know he was only here for the summer. This was a summer fling, a summer job and nothing more. But she didn't pull away from him. Her gaze softened, and she flicked her tongue out to meet his. "Don't fall in love with you, right. Got it. I think I can manage to keep my heart out of the game as long as you keep your cock in it."

His cock was already growing hard again in his jeans, and he pressed it against her hip. "I think I can manage that."

IT WAS Friday before she knew it, and Bianca had had sex every day that week. She was in the best mood of her entire life. Her children, even when they whined, bickered and complained about dinner, never upset her. Nothing upset her. Nothing got her down.

Life was glorious.

She was orgasming left, right, center and all over Jack's face. He was literally fucking the bad vibes, bad mood and negative thoughts right out of her.

She'd even answered the phone pleasantly and genuinely wished him a good day at work when Ashley called Wednesday morning, saying he didn't think he and Opal would be able to take the kids at all that summer. He probably thought she was on some kind of new drug.

And she kind of was.

She was getting Jacked.

Dopamine and oxytocin pumped through her, and Jack's cum coated her thighs. She was on cloud nine all day, every day.

Friday morning, she showed up in her painting clothes, ready for more orgasms, but he stopped her at the front door, a stern look on his face.

"No sex this morning, woman."

Her smile dropped like a stone in a pond.

"You said yesterday your parents are taking the kids overnight tonight?"

She nodded.

"Then you're coming over for dinner tonight. I'll cook for you. We'll fuck tonight."

"Can't we fuck this morning *and* tonight?"

His grin made her practically have a mini orgasm right then and there. "Addicted to the *D,* are you, darlin'?"

She nodded unapologetically. "It's your fault. First dose is always free to get you hooked."

His face scrunched. "Every dose has been free."

"Just one quickie and then we can save up the rest for tonight?" she said, stepping into his space and trailing her finger over his chest, which was covered by a black tank top. "I promise not to take long." She bit her lip.

She could see his resolve crumbling. But he shook his head and stepped away from her. "No, you wanton beast. No sex. That way tonight will be all the wilder because we'll have denied ourselves today." His brows knit together. "Get to work. Stop tempting me with your tits and ass and such." He turned to go, still appearing disgruntled.

She smiled wide at his back. "What are we having for dinner? I hope it's a big piece of meat. I'd really like a *big, juicy* piece of meat in my mouth."

He glanced back at her, his smile playful as he shook his head. "Work, woman, or I'll report you to the foreman."

"I am the foreman," she said, heading over to the sink, where her brushes and paint rollers were laid out to dry from the day before.

"No lip," he called from one of the bedrooms where he was laying down flooring.

"Unless it's wrapped around your—"

His head poked back around the corner, his eyes blazing. "Bianca!"

She rolled her eyes and smiled at him innocently. "I was going to say Popsicle."

He grunted, then ducked back into the bedroom.

She went about setting up her painting station when he called from the room. "You allergic to anything?"

She ran her paint roller through the pan. "No."

"Okay."

Silence followed, then the sound of a man working with tools.

She shrugged and started painting the walls of the living room.

She could hire a painting team to come in and paint the units, and once the kids were out of school, she might have to. But for now, she wanted the money in her pocket rather than someone else's. She was paid by the hour, but also, painting soothed her.

She'd always loved getting into paint-covered clothes and tackling a new room. Turning drab to fab with a fresh coat of a bright color.

She'd never done anything impulsive like this in her life. Never had a one-night stand or kept a *lover*. She was a mom, for Christ's sakes. A single mother at that. And yet, the way Jack looked at her, the way his gaze roamed her body even when he didn't think she saw, spoke of nothing but appreciation and lust. Passion and desire.

A man hadn't looked at her the way Jack looked at her in a long, long time. He reminded her that she was more than *just* a mother. She was rediscovering herself as a woman. A woman with needs. Wants. Desires. This might just be for the summer, but for the summer, Jack was going to help her get to know herself again. Feel like a woman. Feel wanted. Feel beautiful. Even sexy.

"You like quinoa?" he called out to her. "Been eating a lot of quinoa lately. They say it's good for you."

She had to smother her snort with her elbow. "Yes, I like quinoa."

He replied to that with a grunt.

Silence followed.

Smiling, she returned to her painting.

"What about potatoes? You one of those no-carb freaks? Or can I put potatoes on the barbecue in foil with butter and shit?"

"Love me some carbs. I'm way too Irish to turn my nose up at a potato."

Another grunt.

"You drink wine or beer?"

She was smiling so hard, her face hurt. He was thinking awfully hard about cooking her dinner, and it warmed her heart that he cared so much.

"Wine," she finally said. "Though I'll drink beer too."

Another one of those sexy grunts was followed by the sound of a hammer hitting something three times. "Red or white?"

"Depends what you're cooking."

He murmured something she couldn't hear.

"I can bring the wine."

"Cooking steak. That goes with red, right?"

"Yes."

Another grunt.

"Can I bring dessert?"

He didn't respond.

Setting her paint roller down in the pan, she went to the bedroom and hung her head around the corner of the door. "Can I bring dessert?"

Jack was on his knees on the floor, his phone beside him and what appeared to be recipes on the screen.

Bianca rolled her lips inward to hide her smile. "Jack?"

As if he hadn't heard the first two times, he jumped in surprise and craned his neck around. "Huh?"

"Can I bring dessert?"

Frowning, glancing at his phone once more and then making the screen go black, he nodded. "Sure. Dessert."

She smiled. "Okay, then. I'll bring dessert."

His frown deepened. "Get back to work, woman, before I lose my job for nailing my boss on company time."

Bianca's grin grew to idiot-size, and she retreated back to the living room. "You know, I wouldn't tell the foreman you nailed your boss. It would just be our little secret," she said, picking up her paint roller again and getting to work on the wall.

He didn't respond.

She was nearly finished the one wall when heat behind her and a hand on her ass made her yelp and jump, sending paint flying over the plywood subfloors.

Spinning around with the roller still in her hand, she smiled brightly up at him, blinking. Doing her best to be the picture of innocence. "Can I help you?"

His sizzling smolder made her panties damp. Good thing she had extra pairs in the glove compartment of her van now.

Not saying anything, he took the paint roller from her hand, set it down in the tray and scooped her up, his hands on her ass. He carried her over to the kitchen counter and plopped her ass there, immediately going for his belt buckle. "If you tell the boss, I'm in big shit," he said, tipping his fiery blue gaze up to her.

She made a zip, lock and throw away the key motion with her hand and mouth before giggling and going to untie the drawstring of her painting pants. "It'll be our little secret, I swear." She shed her pants and panties, and with a growl, he grabbed her by the back of the neck with one hand, the ass with the other and impaled her in one deep, fulfilling thrust.

"Best way to start the morning," she sighed as he started to fuck her.

"You like roasted carrots?" he asked.

Bianca tossed her head back and laughed as Jack moved inside her. "Less food talk and more fucking. And that's an order."

He began to move double-time. "Boss, yes, boss."

BIANCA FINISHED PAINTING the living room, changed out of her painting clothes and left the reno house to go run some errands. She was also starving after her and Jack's morning fuck-fest and needed some calories to get her through the day.

What she really wanted was a Mediterranean chicken sandwich from the Lilac and Lavender Bistro, but she worried that the line would be around the block, seeing as it was only one o'clock.

Did she have time to wait in line before she needed to head for school and day-care pickup?

A quick drive by told her the line wasn't as long as she feared, and by the time she parked, she was only the third person to the cashier.

Paige, the owner and head chef at the bistro and also the wife of one of the Single Dads of Seattle, spotted her in the line and waved. Bianca waved back, but she was distracted by the blonde- and pink-haired girl walking down the sidewalk outside the bistro.

"Hey!" she called out, stepping out of the line and restaurant to stand in front of the girl. When the girl had been riding Rod's cock last week and dressed like a lady of the evening, Bianca figured she was around twenty-five. But now, without the makeup or the getup, the girl looked even younger. Nineteen or twenty at the most.

The girl's pale cheeks turned dark pink, and she cast her gray eyes downward, attempting to step around and away from Bianca.

"Hey," Bianca said again. "Do you recognize me?"

The girl's head barely bobbed.

"Can we talk a minute?"

Lifting her head slightly, the girl bounced her gaze around the sidewalk. "Am I in trouble?"

Bianca shook her head. The poor thing looked hungry and tired.

Glancing back inside the bistro, she noticed the line had dissipated completely and Paige stood behind the counter, waiting for Bianca.

"You hungry?" Bianca asked.

The girl's eyes widened.

Nodding, Bianca gently rested her hand on the girl's arm. "Come with me."

"Hey, Bianca," Paige greeted her as she stepped up to the counter.

"Hey, Paige. Busy day?"

"Every day is busy, but you won't hear me complaining about it." Paige grinned, the gold in her brown eyes sparkling. "What can I get you?"

"Mediterranean chicken sandwich, please. And I'll get a watermelon lemonade to go and one of those lavender churros."

Paige nodded and began punching the order into the computer. She glanced at the girl beside Bianca, her gaze curious. "And for you?"

"I ..."

"You a vegetarian? Allergic to anything?" Bianca asked.

The girl shook her head.

"Just double the order then," she said to Paige.

With a confirming nod, Paige punched a second order into the computer, and Bianca handed over her credit card.

Once she paid, she ushered the girl over to a two-top table in the corner where they'd wait for their meal. "I'm Bianca."

"Casey," the girl said timidly.

"Nice to meet you, Casey ... *again*, I guess I should say."

Casey's eyes were focused on the hem of her oversize gray T-shirt. She was twisting a loose thread around her index finger until the tip turned purple. "I'm really sorry about the other day," she finally said, lifting her head. "I didn't know that was your house. I—"

Bianca held up her hand. "It wasn't your fault. I don't blame you. But I would like to know your story, if you're willing to tell me. How you ended up with"—she shuddered —"that vile creature. You need to be very desperate to let that man touch you."

Casey's complexion was so fair, Bianca could see the veins around her collarbone like a blue roadmap beneath her skin. But red mottled the pale white, and her nostrils flared. "He offered me a hundred dollars ..."

"For drugs?"

Casey's eyes turned fierce. "I don't do drugs. I never have."

"Then what made you so desperate to sell your body to that man? Do you have a pimp?"

Casey shook her head. "No. I do what I need to do to survive. To get by, okay?"

"No, it's not okay. How old are you?"

"Turned twenty-one last month."

Jeez, she was just a baby.

"Where are your parents?"

"Back in Utah."

So she was a runaway?

"What brought you to Seattle?"

Casey's face went stony.

"Look, I'm not judging you. If you're running from a bad situation, I'm not going to turn you over to the cops or anything like that. You're an adult now, I have no obligation to report you to the police or anything. All I'd like do to is help you if I can. I have three children, and as a mother, as a woman, as a *person,* it hurts my heart to see you *doing what you need to survive.*" She held up her hands. "Not that I have anything against sex workers. If that's what you *want* to do, then have at 'er, but something tells me you'd rather not be selling yourself to eat."

Casey's lips were pinned together to form a flat line, and she was back to playing with the loose thread of her shirt. "You ever heard of polygamy?"

"Yes."

"Where a man takes like five or six wives and has a ton of kids."

"Yes."

She lifted her gaze. "You're looking at kid number fourteen from wife number three."

Holy crap.

"And when I turned sixteen, I was being handed over to a fifty-two-year-old man to become wife number four."

"So you ran?"

"So I ran."

"And you've been on your own for five years?" She thanked the server who brought their watermelon lemonades over and immediately took a sip. It was freaking fantastic and exactly what she needed after a morning of painting and sex.

Casey sipped her lemonade. "I wasn't on my own at first. A friend and I ran away together. She was sixteen too, and her dad was setting up a marriage between her and a man who was sixty-three, had five other wives and lived three towns over. So the night before her wedding, we both ran."

"Where is she now?"

Casey's chin wobbled, and she clenched her teeth to control herself. "She went back after three years. We worked odd jobs, shared a tiny studio apartment. Lied about our ages. We were making it, just barely, but we were making it— together. But she missed her family, and she went back. We were living in California then, and I worried she'd tell them where I was, so I hitchhiked up to Seattle and have been here ever since."

She'd been on her own for the last two years. No family. No friends. Surviving on her wits and selling her body to people like Rod.

"I heard one night while I was busing tables at a diner about this *club*. It's an auction where women—virgins—are auctioned off to men for the night. At that point, I was already living in my car after Becky returned to Utah. I was desperate."

"So you auctioned off your virginity." Bianca brought her voice down to a hush as the waitress returned with their sandwiches and placed two big plates in front of them.

Casey's eyes went wider than the plate her sandwich sat on.

"I ate only oatmeal for an entire week in order to be able to buy a dress for that night. I found some shoes at a thrift shop, went to one of those beauty schools where the students do your hair and makeup, and then I put myself up on the auction block." Casey hadn't touched her sandwich, but she was staring at it like it was the first meal she'd had in a week.

Was she living on just oatmeal again?

Bianca could have sworn she heard the poor girl's stomach grumble.

"Dig in," Bianca encouraged, picking up her own sandwich and taking a big bite. She was afraid to ask what a sicko with too much money would be willing to pay to take the virginity of a runaway so desperate to survive she'd sell her innocence to the highest bidder.

"I was *bought* for five thousand dollars."

Holy shit.

Her next question was: How much of that went to her?

"I got all of it, if you're wondering. The buyers have to pay to go to the party, then they pay to participate in the auction, plus drinks, and that's how the party-throwers make their money. But what they bid all goes to me." As she took another sip of her lemonade, she tilted her head and her eyes adopted an almost defensive gleam. "I wasn't taken advantage of if that's what you're thinking."

That was precisely what Bianca was thinking.

"The people who run the auction were fair. If girls who were up for auction decided no at the last minute that was okay. I know it sounds dirty and something you would expect to take place in an underground night club where everyone is in a mask and orgies are going on in private rooms, but it was nothing like that."

Her mention of masks and orgies had Bianca choking on her lemonade. That was immediately where her brain had gone and she was surprised someone as seemingly innocent and naïve as Casey knew about that kind of thing.

However, after living on her own since she was sixteen and selling her body to eat, maybe she wasn't as naïve as Bianca thought.

"And the man who bought you ..." Bianca probed.

She finally picked up her sandwich. "An older guy, maybe forty-five or fifty. Decent-looking. Fit. He was some millionaire investor from New York."

Was he kind to her, though?

Gentle?

"He didn't smell bad either," Casey went on between chews. "Unlike ..."

Rod.

"Was he ..."

"Gentle?" She took a sip of her lemonade to wash down the sandwich. "He had some *preferences*, but he didn't hurt me. No more than I've been told a first time can hurt."

What were his preferences?

She was afraid to ask.

It seemed that now that she had some food in her belly, Casey was open to chatting about her life. "He liked to role-play. I was the nanny, and he was the naughty daddy cheating on his wife. I was a virgin, so I'd never role-played in my life, but I apparently did the trick because he tipped me two hundred bucks when his limo dropped me off the next day."

"And that's when you started ..."

She shook her head. "No, I continued to waitress, but I wasn't making enough. I kept getting crappy shifts where the tips were bad. The hourly wage was awful, so I started supplementing my income by turning a few tricks. I lived in my car, showered at the YMCA and waited tables."

"How did you find Rod?"

"He found me."

Bianca didn't understand. Was Casey advertising in the newspaper?

"I was leaving the diner one night real late. He saw me, approached me and asked if I did anything *extra* for money."

"So you followed him back to the house I found you at?"

"Yeah. That was the first and only time I went with him though. But he said he'd been bringing girls to the house the whole time."

Of course he was, the motherfucker.

Casey finished the sandwich, and her eyes fell to the other half of Bianca's sandwich that was just sitting on her plate. Bianca pushed the plate toward her. "Eat."

It seemed the young woman was beyond shame now and snatched it off Bianca's plate.

"What kind of *skills* do you have, Casey?" She needed to get this girl off the streets, away from turning tricks and no longer living in her car. But a runaway at sixteen didn't have much to offer the working world. Most jobs—unless under the table—would require references and a Social Security number, an address and an emergency contact. None of which she figured Casey had.

Casey licked sauce off her thumb. "Skills like in the bedroom?"

"No!" Bianca practically shouted. "Dear God, no. I mean like what can you do for work besides waitress? Did you have any hobbies or skills back home that you could make money at?"

She shrugged, and her lips latched onto the straw in her lemonade. "I like plants and gardening and stuff. My family owned the local nursery. We grew almost everything we sold at our farm and in our greenhouses. Flowers, trees, shrubs and stuff. I worked in the garden, liked it."

Now that, they could certainly work with.

"I tried getting a job as a nanny too, seeing as I watched all my younger siblings and stuff, but most people want references if you're watching their kids."

Yeah, Bianca would require that too. Along with a criminal record check, clean driving record and more experience than *I babysat my brothers and sisters.*

"Let's focus on this green thumb of yours. I think I might be able to help you."

Casey grabbed the paper bag that held her churro in it and dove into the sweet treat, her eyes flashing open as the sugar hit her taste buds.

"Best in the city," Bianca confirmed, sipping her own lemonade. "Now, I have a yard that is in serious need of landscaper. I'm talking full facelift. New lawn, new shrubs, overhaul the beds. Transplant and prune. The works. Can you do that?"

Granules of sugar clung to Casey's lips. Her gray eyes turned unsure. "I don't have any tools or—"

"Leave that to me. I can supply you with what you need. I just need somebody to do it. Can that somebody be you?"

Casey's head bobbed enthusiastically. "Yeah, totally."

Bianca lifted her hand over the table and held it out for Casey to shake. "All right then, you're hired. I'll pay you twenty dollars an hour to start, thirty an hour for any overtime."

She thought the poor woman was going to have an apoplexy based on her facial expression.

"T-twent ... thir-thirty?" Casey sputtered.

Bianca lifted one shoulder and wiggled her fingers, prompting Casey to shake her hand. She did. "That's the starting rate for landscapers around here."

"Oh my God."

Bianca released her hand and pulled her own churro from the bag, taking a big bite. "Okay, now that we got you a job, and me a landscaper, let's go see the new place I have for you to live, because no fucking way are you sleeping another night in your car."

8

At six o'clock, Jack pulled his Harley into the lean-to beside his Airstream and parked it. Simon's car wasn't parked on the road yet, so he knew his son wasn't home.

After work, Jack ran to the grocery store, picked up four nice sirloin cuts, some potatoes, carrots and a dry petit syrah the dude at the liquor store suggested before heading home to go shower.

He was just drying off in the bathroom when he heard the crunch of shoes on the gravel outside.

Throwing jeans on with no boxers, he flung the door open to find Simon halfway up the stairs leading to the camper. "Hey, son."

Simon glanced back. "Hey, Dad. How was your day?"

"Good. Yours?" After Bianca left to run errands, he'd gone over and over in his head what he would say to Simon, how he would broach the subject. Each and every scenario made him nervous and had him feeling like he'd just taken a sucker-punch to the gut.

Simon nodded. "Pretty good." His dark brows pinched, and his gaze turned curious. "You okay?"

Shit.

This was not at all how Jack had thought this was going to go.

He was tired of Simon hiding his love life from him. If Simon was in love, or even if he wasn't but he was dating, Jack wanted to meet the person. Him. Her. They. He didn't care. He just cared that his son was happy.

Stepping down out of his Airstream in bare feet, he stalked across the gravel to the steps of the camper. Simon looked even more perplexed than ever.

Unsure if the metal stairs to the camper would hold them both, Jack reached up and tugged his son on the arm until Simon stepped down. Jack drew Simon into his arms and hugged him. "You know I love you no matter what, right?"

"Dad?" Simon murmured against Jack's shoulder. "Are you dying?"

Jack rolled his eyes. Fuck. Now his kid thought he was about to reveal he had the big *C* or something.

Pulling away, he ran his fingers through his damp hair and took a deep breath. Do it like a Band-Aid. "No, I ain't dying. I'm having Bianca over for dinner tonight, if you and ... the *guy* who leaves your camper every morning at six o'clock would like to join us?"

Simon's bottom lip dropped open, a look that reminded Jack so much of his own father. Simon looked a lot like Jack's dad. Same coloring, same expressions. He was tall like Jack and his father had been. Naturally slim but with muscles. Jack's dad would have been an amazing grandfather and loved the hell out of Simon. His mother would have too.

Clearing his throat, he pressed on. "I don't know if you're just experimenting or not ready to ... *whatever*, but I hope none of that is because of me. You should never be afraid to tell me anything. Gay, straight, bi, or whatever, I love you no matter what, son."

Simon blinked, his blue eyes growing damp. "You knew I was having a guy over?"

Jack shrugged. "We live like five feet from each other. I hear him leave every morning."

"But you haven't said anything."

"I figured *you'd* say something. But then I started to worry you thought your old man wouldn't approve or something. That's not what you thought, is it?" He scratched the back of his neck, terrified of the answer. If his son didn't feel like he could come to Jack with his truth, then Jack had seriously fucked up as a parent.

He'd already fucked up the first twelve years of Simon's life. He thought he was doing better now.

Maybe not.

"I read somewhere that you're not supposed to *out* your kids. That they'll reveal their truth when they're ready, so if I'm overstepping here, Simon, I'm real sorry."

Simon's lips curled at the sides into a small smile. "His name is Jared. And ... you're not overstepping at all, Dad. I just didn't want to make you uncomfortable. Jared's parents disowned him when he came out, so we just wanted to play it safe." Simon exhaled and raked his fingers through his hair. "Not that you're like them ... ah, fuck. It's not that I didn't think I could come to you or that you wouldn't approve. I just thought that maybe once Jared and I got our own place, it'd be easier—you know? Us being *here* so close to you, I thought it might be awkward for you."

"Your own place?" Jack whispered. "You guys are moving in together?"

Fuck, it was serious then.

Simon nodded. "Yeah. We're gonna buy a house together. I love him, and he loves me. We want to start a life together."

Emotion clogged the back of Jack's throat. He was happy for his son, but it still gutted him Simon thought it would be awkward for Jack. He'd known deep down that his son was gay or at the very least bi way back when Simon was still a teenager. It was then that he started doing some reading and learned that if Simon was gay, Jack needed to wait for his son to come to him.

Dread swirled inside him that he'd overstepped anyway and pushed his son too far.

"I talk about you all the time to Jared, Dad. He knows how wonderful a man you are. You're nothing like his parents. I know you wouldn't disown me. We're each other's first serious relationship, so we just wanted to take it slow."

Jack made a noise in his throat and nodded. "I'm happy for you, kiddo. Real happy. I wanna meet this guy that's swept my son off his feet." Every syllable of his chuckle was forced. "How long you two been together?" He sniffed and cleared his throat again.

"We met in California. He got a job here. He's an architect. It's part of the reason why I'm moving here permanently. Jared's from Eugene, and we've been serious for about a year."

A year. Fuck. And Jack was just hearing about him.

He shook himself mentally. It wasn't about him. It was about Simon. He needed to get the fuck over himself and end the pity party before it even started. He also needed to do better by his kid, obviously, because Simon still looked at his dad as someone he couldn't trust with his truth. And also, fuck Jared's parents.

"So ... you're okay with Jared sleeping over?" Simon asked warily. "I mean, we'd stay at his place, but he's in a small, noisy basement suite with two other roommates, and the walls are so thin. We're not worried about people hearing us. It's that his roommates are giant man-whores and have a new girl in their bed every night. I was worried I'd catch an STD from the toilet seat the first time I stayed there."

"I have no problem with you and Jared staying in the camper, Simon. That's your home, and you're welcome to have guests. Jared can move in there if you like. Like I said, I love you no matter what. I'm happy you have love in your life, and I can't wait to meet him." He only wished he'd met him sooner.

Simon's smile made the whole day seem brighter. "Did you mean what you said when you invited us to join you and Bianca for dinner? 'Cause Jared and I were just going to go grab dinner, but if the offer still stands ..."

"Abso-fucking-lutely," Jack nearly hollered. "Invite him. I bought four steaks, so totally. Call him up. Bianca is bringing dessert. I grabbed wine. Making spuds and roasted carrots, a quinoa salad." That reminded him, Bianca was going to show up and he wouldn't have anything started. He needed to get going on dinner. He stepped back over the gravel and into his trailer.

"You need any help?" Simon asked, following Jack.

Jack nodded, pulled a clean olive-green T-shirt out of his dresser and tugged it over his head. "Yeah, you wanna wash those spuds in the shopping bag? Oil 'em up and wrap 'em in some foil. Same with the carrots."

Jared nodded and saluted his father before washing his hands in the sink.

Jack grabbed the steaks from the fridge, tore the plastic wrap off them and sprinkled them liberally with salt and pepper.

Simon glanced over at his dad as he began washing the potatoes in the small sink. "I'm sorry I didn't tell you about Jared ... about *me* sooner. It's not that I didn't think you'd approve, it's just ... I don't know. He's my first serious, openly gay relationship, and I wanted to take it slow."

"Not sure how *open* it was if you can't share your happiness with those who love you the most," Jack said, grabbing a box of quinoa out of the cupboard but hitting his kid with a side-eye.

Simon nodded. "You're right. For a bad-boy biker, you're very open-minded and have always supported me. I should have told you sooner, and I'm sorry."

Jack nodded but kept his gaze laser-focused on filling the sauce pot with water from the sink. He was only inches from his son, but at the moment he felt a million miles away.

"How long have you known?" Simon asked softly.

Jack set the pot down on his stove and flipped the burner on high before turning to his son. "Since you were about fourteen, I kinda figured you might be. Started doing some reading just to be more prepared for whatever you needed."

Simon dropped the potato in his hand into the sink, and his mouth fell open. "I meant about Jared." He turned to face Jack. "You've known I was gay since I was fourteen? I didn't even know I was gay at fourteen."

Jack shrugged, turned to the fridge, opened it and pulled out a couple of bell peppers for the salad. "Had my suspicions. Wanted to be prepared in case you came out. If you didn't, well then, I just educated myself anyway and became a more accepting person of others. No harm, no foul. Was interesting reading either way."

"Dad." Simon's hand landed on Jack's arm. Tears brimmed his blue eyes. "You're the most incredible father. I ... I should have known you'd be cool with all of this. With me. And I'm sorry I didn't give you the benefit of the doubt."

A meow at the screen door had them both turning their heads.

"In a minute, Bob," Simon said before facing his father again. "I love you, Dad." He reached for Jack and pulled him into a hug.

Of course, Jack went willingly. He wrapped his arms tight around his son, his nose against Simon's head.

He'd missed out on twelve years of his kid's life because he'd been selfish and stupid. A drug addict, a criminal and overall fuck-up. So even though he'd had Simon in his life for fourteen years, he still took every hug, every embrace his son offered because he was making up for lost time. He was making up for his failures as a father the first half of his kid's life.

Simon's floppy, dark brown hair tickled Jack's nose, and he sniffled, pulling away and wiping his hand roughly beneath his eye. He cleared his throat and turned to the screen door, where a gray cat with a bobtail sat impatiently. "How was your day, Bob?"

Simon chuckled. "I'll text Jared now before I forget."

Jack nodded and opened the screen door so Bob could enter. "Tell him to grab more wine. I think tonight should be treated like a celebration."

HE'D MENTIONED EARLIER that week that he lived in an Airstream behind the duplex he owned, but Bianca had no idea just how "set up" Jack's living quarters were. The duplex itself was immaculate on the outside. The landscaping was of professional quality, and even the gutters were shiny and white without a streak of dirt or grime to be seen.

Parking her van on the road where Jack instructed her to, she grabbed her purse and her small overnight bag, along with the chocolate orange cheesecake she'd bought on her way out of Paige's bistro, and took the butterflies in her stomach up to the closed screen door of Jack's trailer.

"Knock, knock," she said. Her hands were full so she couldn't actually knock.

"Hey," came his smooth voice from inside. The screen opened, and there he stood, looking just as sexy as when she'd left him at the house all sweaty and wielding a hammer like Thor. He took the cheesecake from her and welcomed her inside the Airstream.

The man just continued to surprise her.

She wasn't sure what she was expecting when he said he lived in a trailer, but she definitely wasn't expecting it to look like the decked-out, renovated, contemporary mecca of tranquility and function that it was. It was clean, it was new, and it was one hell of a cool place to call home.

After he put the cheesecake in the fridge, he rested his hands on her waist and took her mouth. "Thought you were gonna come back to the house after errands before you had to pick the kids up," he said with a low, manly growl before dropping his lips to her neck. "What happened?"

"I'll fill you in over dinner," she said, tilting her head to the side so he could get better access to her neck. The press of his erection against her hip had her insides quivering.

"I invited my son and his boyfriend to have dinner with us," he said, stepping out of her space and turning back to where he was tossing cubes of feta into a big bowl with veggies and quinoa.

She set her purse and bag down on the kitchen table. "Does that mean?"

He nodded, his smile so big she had to catch herself from swooning. "I took your advice, invited him and his boyfriend to dinner. We had a good talk."

She sidled up next to him and rested her head against his arm. "I'm so happy for you. I can't wait to meet your son ... and his boyfriend."

A meow at her feet drew Bianca's attention from Jack to a beautiful gray cat with a bobtail. It weaved around her legs, meowing and rubbing its cheek against her ankles.

"You have a cat?"

He snorted. "Kind of. I guess so. Bob showed up one day

last month and just never left. I put up posters around the neighborhood, asked around and stuff, but nobody came to claim her, so ..."

"Bob's a *her?*"

He nodded. "Yeah. We thought she was a him or a he or a ... we thought Bob was a boy. Hence why we called him *Bob*. Also on account of the bobtail and all. But then when Simon and I realized nobody was claiming Bob, we needed to get him checked out and stuff. Took Bob to the vet only to realize *he* was a *she*. But we'd already been calling her Bob for a month and figured it'd just be confusing for her if we changed her name on account she's been who she's always been. We just didn't know who she was."

Bianca pressed her lips together to keep herself from smiling too widely. Jack was a man who was certainly full of surprises. "I think that's the most I've ever heard you speak," she finally said, unable to hide her smile any longer.

He grunted and shrugged. "Bob's a good girl. Hasn't brought me any mice or birds or anything like that. Just the odd grasshopper, which I think is her way of saying *thanks for the grub.*"

Bianca snorted at the same time the screen door opened and a very handsome young man with the same floppy brown hair and blue eyes as Jack stepped into the trailer. "You must be Bianca," he said with a big smile.

"And you must be Simon," she said.

He stuck out his hand, and she took it.

"It's so nice to finally meet you," Simon went on. "Dad talks about you *all* the time." He glanced at his dad teasingly.

"Do not," Jack said gruffly, his knife hitting the wooden cutting board extra hard as he chopped cucumbers. His glance at Bianca was filled with unease. "I mean I've *mentioned* you, but I don't talk about you *all* the time."

Simon lifted a brow but then grinned even wider. "Jared is

just grabbing wine. He wants to know if you want him to get red or white?"

"Red," Jack said. "Having steak."

Simon rolled his eyes and focused on Bianca. "Sometimes he goes into caveman mode. Have you noticed that? It's like words suddenly become too hard for him. Grunts are easier."

Bianca giggled and pushed up onto her tiptoes to kiss Jack on the cheek. "I have noticed that. But I happen to like the caveman grunts, so I don't mind."

That earned her a grunt and some serious side-eye from Jack.

"When are we putting the steak on?" Simon asked, tap-tapping on his phone for a moment before stowing it in the back pocket of his shorts.

"Steak only takes minutes," Jack said. "We'll do that when Jared arrives. How are the veg?"

"Potatoes and carrots both need more time."

Jack nodded. "We'll eat outside."

Simon must have understood the hidden words there because he opened up a cupboard to the left of the sink and brought out four plates and bowls.

"I can help," Bianca said. "Put me to work."

"You wanna grab the cutlery?" Simon asked. "Steak knives are in a special wooden box just over there in that bottom cabinet. Meet me out behind the trailer."

Happy to be helping, Bianca did as she was told and met Simon out behind the trailer on a concrete slab where a rectangular glass patio table was set up. Chairs surrounded the table, each with a plush cushion on top, and a big umbrella in the center of the table flapped gently in the warm breeze.

Shrubs and a few potted flowers decorated the concrete, along with a hammock in a hammock bar and solar lights on stakes hammered into the ground. It was a little garden oasis that Jack had built for himself, and she loved it.

Just another layer peeled back of the enigmatic man named Jack.

It was like a door she'd been wrestling with for ages finally swung open freely when Jack entered her life. Things were going her way. She was in a better mood. She was a better mother to her children, a better friend, sister and daughter, and the only reason she could think of was Jack.

He made her happy.

It struck her as outrageous that she'd only known the man for a full seven days, and yet, she was already crazy about him. Crazy and wary, of course, because she kept having to warn her heart not to interfere and mistake orgasms and attention for love. This *thing*, whatever it was, was temporary. Jack was just a man to finish the renovation and scratch her insatiable itches. Nothing more.

Then why was she having dinner with him, his son and his son's boyfriend?

Wasn't that what *girlfriends* did? Not booty calls.

"So, Bianca," Simon started, beginning to set the table, his voice startling her out of her own thoughts, "what's your story? Dad mentioned you have three kids. How old?"

Bianca's belly grumbled at the smell of the veggies on the barbecue from the smoking stainless-steel beast on the corner of the concrete, but she smiled through the hunger and folded napkins. "I do have three kids, yes. Hannah and Hayley are six; they're identical twins, and little Charlie is two."

His eyes flared. "Wow, life must be busy."

"That's an understatement, but that also means life isn't dull."

"You have family here in Seattle that can help?"

"Yeah. I was born here, so my parents and brothers and

their families are still here. Lots of support. The kids are with my parents tonight, actually." Was Simon simply curious, or was he digging deep to protect his father? Should she tell him that it was his dad who told her straight up not to fall in love with him because he was a nomad snowbird who would dick off to Mexico in a few months?

"And you work as a property manager?"

"Property manager, project manager. I do a lot. There are a couple of guys with money up in Canada. Their pet project is to buy up old, run-down houses in college districts, renovate them into multi-unit housing and then rent them out as furnished, affordable student housing. So I manage the project—the renovations—and then I manage the properties once they're rentable. If they can't rent to students over the summer, I put them up on Airbnb."

Which reminded her, she needed to tell Jack about Casey.

She'd cleared her plan with Justin and James, who gave the green light immediately, but she did want to give Jack a heads-up too.

Two sets of heavy footsteps on gravel interrupted them, and seconds later, Jack and another handsome young man with blond hair, green eyes, a white T-shirt, chinos and a megawatt smile came around the corner.

The blond man, who she assumed was Jared, stepped forward and offered her his hand. "Jared Jacobs. Nice to meet you."

"Bianca Dixon. Nice to meet you, too."

Simon stepped up next to Bianca. "Dad, this is Ja—"

Jack held up his hand. "We've already met. He popped into the trailer first. I asked him what his intentions are with my son. He said honorable, we had a shot of tequila, and now we're best buddies."

Jared winked at Simon before stepping into the man's space and looping his arm around his boyfriend's waist.

"You can be such a worrywart sometimes. Your dad is great."

"I never said he wasn't great. I just didn't want to make him uncomfortable."

"Babe, you need to have more faith in people," Jared said before lifting up a bottle of red wine and waggling perfectly threaded blond eyebrows, his sage-colored eyes twinkling. "Now, who wants to have some of this very expensive pinot with me? I splurged because I'm finally getting to meet Simon's dad, *and* bonus, I get to meet the beautiful Bianca."

"I'll have a glass," Bianca said with a laugh. "I'll run back into the trailer and grab some."

Jack grunted behind her and squeezed her ass after he put the salad into the middle of the table. "You stay here. I'll grab the wineglasses."

"Want me to put the meat on the grill?" Simon asked.

"Don't fucking touch the meat," Jack hollered over the trailer, having already disappeared around to the front of it again.

All three of them laughed.

"I like him," Jared said with a cheesy wink. "He's got the bad-boy biker look down pat, and it *works*." His lip rolled inward, and he turned to Simon. "If you grew a beard, got some tattoos and a Harley, you wouldn't hear me complaining."

Simon rolled his eyes. "You pay for it all, and I'll do whatever your little heart desires."

Giggling, Bianca finished folding napkins and setting out cutlery just as Jack returned from inside with four wine-glasses in his hands. He set the glasses down on the table in front of her, and his mouth next to her ear sent a shiver sprinting through her, landing with a heavy throb on her clit. "Is that an overnight bag I spied on the table inside?"

His hand on her ass squeezed, and she pushed back into

his palm. "I don't have the kids tonight, but if I'm being presumptuous ..." She craned her neck around and grinned at him. "You want me to leave after dessert?"

"Fuck, darlin', you *are* my dessert, and you're not going anywhere until the sun is up, high and hot in the sky tomorrow." His lips grazed her temple. "I hope you went home and had a nap because you won't be getting much sleep tonight."

"I heard that," Simon said, coming up beside Bianca and pouring wine into the glasses. "Should I be putting in earplugs tonight?"

"No," Bianca said quickly at the same time Jack said, "Not a bad idea."

Jared let out a loud, boisterous laugh. "You guys are awesome."

They each had a full wineglass in their hand and faced each other.

Jack was the first to speak. "To meeting new people. I'm glad to finally meet you, Jared, and I hope to see a lot more of you."

"Likewise," Jared said with reined-in emotion in his throat, causing his words to come out as a squeak.

"And it's really great to meet you, too, Bianca," Simon said. "I hope to be seeing a lot more of you, too." His gaze met his father's, and a brow lifted in challenge.

Jack did no more than reply with a grunt.

They all clinked glasses, sipped and enjoyed the very lovely pinot Jared brought.

"Let's get that meat on the grill, shall we?" Simon asked, the first to pull away and head toward the barbecue.

"Don't touch the meat," Jack warned. "I'll do it."

"I love a man who knows how to handle meat," Jared teased, which only earned him a groan and eye roll from all of them.

9

SHE TRACED the nail of her index finger around his nipple. "Your skin is such a beautiful color. May I ask what your ancestry is?"

He glanced down at her, naked in his arms in his bed, freshly fucked and the most beautiful thing he'd ever seen. She could ask anything of him right now and he'd do his damnedest to give it to her.

"Unless that's an inappropriate thing to ask." Her words tumbled out of her, and a new darker flush added to her already rosy skin from his earlier attention. "I don't want to offend you." She squeezed her eyes shut. "I'm sorry."

Chuckling, he squeezed her tighter against him. "Bianca, it's fine. Not ashamed of where or who I came from."

"You shouldn't be," she whispered.

Pressing his lips to her crown, he went on. "My father was Croatian and Irish. Hence the last name Savage."

She traced the tattoo over his collarbone with her finger. "Is this Croatian?"

He nodded. "*Nebu.* It means *heaven.* It was my father's nickname for my mother, and it just felt right to get it as a tattoo after she passed. Because its where they are together once again."

"What was your mother's name?"

"Sabine. She was Lebanese and Turkish—a true beauty inside and out. She had darker skin, which I inherited."

"I think it's beautiful." She gently tugged on one nipple before beginning her exploration of all his ink again.

"I get a lot of concerned looks when I go places. Brown skin, longer nose. I look like a lot of people's worst nightmare." He tugged at the hair on his chin. "Though the beard doesn't help. I've thought about shaving it off. The blue eyes are the only thing that I got from my dad—besides my height. My mom was a tiny thing."

"I think you're one of the sexiest, most handsome men I've ever met. And I happen to like the beard." Her fingers left his nipple, and she began to run her hands up and down his torso. "Keep the beard."

"Well, thank you, darlin', but not everybody thinks like you do. I've been called a lot of things. Not all of them nice. Been told to go back to my own country, to learn English— English is the only damn language I know. Dad's parents immigrated from Croatia when he was in his mama's belly. My mom was born a year after her parents arrived in the states. Her dad was a Turkish diplomat. But they only spoke English with me."

"People can be so ignorant."

"People can be a lot of things, and ignorant is just the tip of the damn iceberg."

"You said your mom died. What about your dad?"

He kissed the top of her head again before closing his eyes and pressing the back of his head deeper into his pillow. "Mom died of cancer when I was fourteen. And Dad drank himself to death two years later. He wasn't an alcoholic before she died, but without her, he just couldn't function, so he took to the bottle."

"Dear God, I'm so sorry."

"Up until my mom passed, I had the perfect life, the perfect family."

"Any brothers or sisters?"

He shook his head. "No. Mom miscarried a few times before and after me. So they took me as their one blessing, and she got her tubes tied."

"I got mine removed after Charlie was born. Ashley said he was going to get a vasectomy but then chickened out at the last minute. So I went and got a ligation, and he knocked up his secretary." Her laugh was brittle and, he knew, riddled with bitterness.

Jack wasn't sure what he'd do if he ever came face-to-face with this Ashley fucker. A swift kick in the nads so he couldn't father any more children was a good start.

"So if your dad died when you were sixteen, what happened to you? You were still a minor so ..."

"I went to live with my mom's sister. But she worked a lot, and I fell in with the wrong crowd. I got kicked out of school, started doing drugs, started dealing. I was a father by the time I was seventeen. Was a heroin addict until I was sent to prison at nineteen for dealing. When I got out, I decided to clean up my act and started working in concrete. But then I broke my back, and that gave way to an addiction to painkillers."

"Oh my gosh."

"By that time, Simon was eleven. He came to me one day and told me that things with his mom were not good. Both she and her new boyfriend were addicts. Her boyfriend was abusive, she was abusive, and he didn't want to live with her anymore."

"So you got clean again?"

"Had to."

When Simon showed up on his doorstep with a black eye, cut lip, bloody nose and tearstained cheeks, Jack wasn't sure his heart would ever fully recover. He'd done that to his son.

Not literally. He hadn't taken a swing at his kid, but he might as well have, not being there for him the first eleven years of his life. Protecting him from his mother and her junkie boyfriend. He hated himself for a long time, but it was that hate, that desperation to do better, that fueled him to get clean. Simon deserved better.

"That must have been hard." Her voice held a small quaver, but he didn't think it was fear or judgment, just uncharted territory, so she was slowing her roll and proceeding with caution.

He wasn't ashamed though. He'd done good. Not only for himself but for his kid too. His and Simon's story may have started off wrong, but it was going to end right if he had anything to say about it.

"Cold turkey, darlin'. I detoxed on my own. Hardest thing I've ever fucking done, but I did it. Didn't touch another pill, not even aspirin. I got clean for my kid. I got full custody of him, started a job in construction."

"You still drink though?" There was no judgment in her tone, just curiosity. Which was valid because he'd had a glass of wine with dinner, and often those with a narcotic addiction stayed away from alcohol as well because it meant they had an addictive personality and one was just as bad as the other.

He nodded. "I allow myself only one drink and one only. One beer. One glass of wine. I never have more. I buy a six-pack on Monday nights, and that lasts me until Sunday night. It's how I prove to myself I have the willpower. I don't get drunk, but I allow myself to celebrate my life and all that I've overcome with *a* beer if I so choose."

"That's willpower. I can't remember the last time I only

had *one* drink." She hummed. "Maybe the last time I had dinner at my parents' and needed to be sober to drive my children home."

Chuckling, he traced his index finger softly up her arm.

"How did you manage to afford all the properties you have if you don't mind me asking? I mean, I know construction workers make decent money, but you own a few houses, a place in Mexico ..."

"Yeah, my late-in-life success is a bit unusual, that's for sure. I have my aunt to thank for a lot of it. When she died, she left her house to me. She didn't have any children of her own, so Simon and I were her only beneficiaries. But the property taxes and home insurance were too much to keep up with, so I sold it, took that money and just saved. I got us a one-bedroom apartment, gave Simon the bedroom. I slept on the couch and saved every penny I could. I worked construction during the day and delivered pizzas at night so that by the time Simon was sixteen, I had enough money to buy and renovate my first duplex."

"Wow."

"It was a condemned, rat-infested piece of shit, but I did all the labor myself where I could. We moved into the first finished unit, then I started working on the next. Rented it to get the scratch for another piece of shit to do it all over again. It took me almost five years to get all four finished and three units rented."

"Did you hire a contractor?"

He shook his head. "Not if I didn't have to. Did most of it on my own if I could. Only contracted out for plumbing and electricity—don't need shit exploding out of the shitter because I cheaped out and installed it myself. Also don't need to electrocute my nuts because I cut the wrong wire."

She giggled, which started to make his dick hard. "You laugh, woman, but if I'd have cheaped out and gone the

YouTube route with the electrical, you wouldn't be in this bed as satisfied as you are."

Her hum and the way her nail flicked his nipples made him even harder. "Oh, I don't know about that. You have a pretty wicked tongue. I'm sure I'd still be in your bed. I'm just not sure we'd *both* be as satisfied."

He grunted. "True as fuck."

"Tell me more about when you remodeled two houses all on your own." Her croon had him glancing down at her in surprise.

"You turned on by that?"

Nibbling her lip, she nodded. "The idea of you all sweaty and hot, shirtless and wielding a hammer ... I know I get to see it in the flesh, but even just hearing about it gets me going."

"Wanton wench," he murmured. "Well, whatever revs your engine." He cleared his throat. "I worked on the duplexes whenever I had spare time. Weekends, evenings and shit. Eventually, I was making decent enough scratch from the rented units—and got a promotion on the construction site—that I only needed to deliver pizzas on weekend evenings or when it was too fucking cold to move my fingers and pick up a hammer. Simon helped when he could too."

Her warm body snuggled in tighter against his, her breasts pressed against his side. "But you did it."

He grunted again. "I did it. I did it for my son."

"And yourself."

"Yeah." She was right about that. He did it to prove to himself that he wasn't the piece-of-shit nobody he'd been called more times than he'd like to count.

"So then Simon went off to college, and I bought the Airstream so that I could rent all the units out. Make more scratch."

"That's incredible. You turned your life right around."

Pride prickled inside his chest. He wasn't a conceited man, but he was proud of all that he'd overcome and accomplished in his life. Despite not finishing high school, having a criminal record and being a drug addict, he managed to pull himself up by his bootstraps and put his past behind him in order to give his son—and himself—a better life, a better future. And he'd done it.

His arm beneath her was beginning to fall asleep, so he shifted slightly, and his hand grazed her lower back, his middle finger pressed against the top of her crease. "So you took in a runaway, huh?"

At that same moment, Bob meowed from the door to the Airstream. He pried himself out from Bianca's embrace, swung his legs over the side of the bed and went to let in Bob.

"Looks like we're both in the habit of rescuing strays," she said with a giggle, levering up onto her elbows as Bob sauntered her butt into the trailer, took one look at both of them and then went and leapt up onto the booth seat for the kitchen table. She curled up into a ball and closed her eyes.

Jack slid back into bed beside Bianca, and she curled herself around him again. "You don't think what I did for Casey was wrong, do you?"

"Not at all, darlin'. You've got a big heart. That girl had hit rock bottom. Particularly if she was riding that motherfucker Rod to feed herself. You sure your bosses are okay with you putting her up at their Airbnb though?"

She glanced up at him with those big brown eyes. "I'm not putting her up at it though. I'm paying her twenty dollars an hour to landscape, and I'm charging her twenty dollars a day to live there. It's only a ten-dollar discount from what I'd normally charge, but it's also the smallest unit. Just a tiny studio with a single bed and a shower, no bathtub. Just a beer fridge and a two-burner stove and a toaster oven. It's nothing fancy, but it's better than her car."

"What about when school starts? Don't you guys rent those places to students?"

She shrugged. "We'll see what September brings. I think they'll be fine letting her stay there if I ask them. We've all had our own misfortunes, so to be able to help someone else who has hit rock bottom—if we can, then we should. But this means no more morning sex at the house because Casey will be right outside. Can you live with that?"

"So long as you ride my dick or face as often as you're able to, I think we'll be okay. I'm not against riding over to your place and eating my dessert at midnight on your couch while your kids sleep upstairs."

Her nose wrinkled, and she plucked at his nipple. "So long as I get to eat *my* dessert too. Cream-filled is my favorite."

He growled, his dick now standing at attention and ready to party. "Darlin', you are something else." Rolling her over to her back, he caged her beneath him, his arms on either side of her head, her pussy juices leaking all over his hard cock as he settled between her thighs and rocked his dick up against her slit.

Bianca wrapped her arms around his neck. "Am I?"

"Mhmm?"

She smiled against his lips. "Here I thought I was just some frumpy, sad divorcee with three kids and a job I can barely keep up with. But if you say I'm *something else,* then it must be true." Her lips twisted against his, and she scratched her head. "Afraid I can't think of what that *something else* is though."

Growling, he spread her legs farther apart with his knees, notched himself at her core and drove in. "Not frumpy. Not sad. Fucking rocking your job. Don't say that shit again, ya got it?"

She nodded, her gaze glazing over.

"Fucking beautiful is one thing," he said with the second thrust. Her eyes flashed open. "Smart is another." She crushed her bottom lip between her teeth and arched her back. "Kind. Funny. Tough as fucking nails."

She shoved her fingers into his hair and tugged hard until his scalp burned.

"Great fucking lay too, can't forget that."

"No, you can't," she said, raking her nails down his back until they reached his ass as it flexed and bunched with each pump into her heat. She dug those talons into his skin, and he grunted, picking up fervor.

"Wanton," he panted, dipping his head and drawing one of her nipples into his mouth. "A smartass."

"Smartass?" She slapped his ass cheek. "Did you just call me a—ooh."

He tipped his eyes up to find her mouth in a sexy little *O* when he scissored his teeth over the nipple in his mouth. Yeah, his little smartass liked it rough.

"Do that again. Other side," she pleaded, shifting beneath him so her other breast was shoved into his face.

"Forgot to mention bossy," he grumbled, planting kisses across her chest and over the mound of her other breast until he found the tight, dusky nipple just calling to him to be sucked.

"I prefer *born leader*." She tightened her internal muscles around him, bowed her back and swirled her hips beneath him. Yeah, if she kept that up, he wasn't going to last very long.

Not that he needed to. They'd already had sex twice that night, and he had every intention of taking her whenever his dick said it was good to go. He'd sleep when he was dead, and she could sleep tomorrow night. Tonight was about him making Bianca feel fucking good and her draining his balls until they were empty

His fingers found the slick nipple he'd abandoned, and he tweaked it, earning a sharp inhale from the wanton beauty beneath him.

"Fuck, Bianca," he said, releasing her nipple from his mouth with a wet *pop* and propping himself up on his elbows to look down at her. "You're not just *something else*, darlin', you're fucking everything else. I don't know where the fuck you came from, but I'm sure fucking glad I found you." He powered up into her one more time, but his cadence faltered when he looked down into her eyes and found them watery.

Shit.

"Damn, baby, I'm—"

She released his ass cheeks, grabbed his face and pulled his lips down to hers, crushing his mouth and shoving her tongue inside. The kiss was hard. It was wild. It was fueled by a passion that scared the shit out of him.

She lifted her hips up to his, not breaking the kiss but encouraging him to keep moving. To get them both there. Her lips eased up on his, and their kiss became more relaxed. He took over. Brushing the hair off her forehead, he cupped her face and tore his lips from hers.

"Look at me, darlin'. Come with me, okay?"

She blinked back the tears and nodded.

He drove deep. He drove hard. He gave Bianca everything he had. She moved with him, their bodies already in tune with each other. He knew what made her tick. She knew what got him there. There was no guessing with Bianca. He knew her. She wasn't a head game or a puzzle. She was the real fucking deal, and he was one lucky bastard to even get to know a piece of her.

"Jack," she whispered, her eyes remaining glued on his. "I'm going to—" Her lips parted, and a strangled cry broke free from her throat. She arched against him.

"Look at me, Bianca. Look at me. Feel me inside you,

darlin'. Filling you up.

Her hair thrashed about the pillow as she tossed her head, the orgasm consuming her.

"Never had such good pussy as yours. Never. That's the fucking truth." He surged forward one more time. A tingle in his balls and at the base of his spine made him stiffen, and like a geyser, he finally fucking blew.

She watched him come just as he'd watched her. Their eyes on each other, feeling the other not just where they were connected but deeper.

He hadn't anticipated the feelings he was having for Bianca. Hadn't thought beyond a summer fuck buddy and helping a person who needed help. But Bianca was more than he'd bargained for. He'd known her for a fucking week, and already there wasn't much he wouldn't do for her. Wasn't much he wouldn't give her if he could.

She'd been done wrong by her ex, but she was coming out on the other side better than fucking ever. Had a good job, had good kids and now she had—he shook his head, rolled off her and tore out of bed.

He didn't even look back before he closed the bathroom door, hopped into the shower and let the cold water run.

He needed it cold.

He needed a fucking wake-up call.

He was thinking like this was going to stick. Like he and Bianca were a thing beyond the summer. She had a good job, good kids, and now she had him? What the fuck? Where the hell did that come from?

She might have him for the summer. Have him eating her pie, be fucking her good and finishing up her renovation, but by the end of August, he was on the road again. He had plans. He had a life. A life he liked. He summered in Seattle, wintered in Mexico. He couldn't just give that up for good pussy. Pussy that came with a shit ton of baggage in the shape of three kids, an ex and way more extended family than he cared to meet.

A gentle knock on the door had him lifting his head, the spray hitting his face.

"Jack? You okay?"

"Yeah, sweetheart, sorry."

She opened the door wearing one of his T-shirts, and she looked damn fucking good in it. The shower was all glass so she could see him too. "You sure? You just got this look in your eye, then you ran." Bianca wasn't a tiny woman. She wasn't overweight or even plus-size, but she looked tinier than ever in his T-shirt that nearly hit her knees.

"Got hot. When I get hot, I start feeling sick. Need to cool off right away," he lied. "Didn't meant to worry you."

She didn't look convinced.

He adjusted the water to not sub-zero, opened the door and reached for her. Seeing her standing there in his shirt already had his cock standing again. He might be in his forties, but he could still get it up like an eighteen-year-old.

He didn't even give her a chance to tear off the shirt before he had her hauled under the spray with him. "You're sure I didn't do anything?" she asked, blinking up at him through the spray. Her lashes began to cling together and form spikes, and the brown in her eyes seemed to grow darker the longer he looked at them. She really was the most beautiful fucking woman he'd ever laid eyes on. Fucking perfect.

He shook his head. "No, darlin'. You didn't do a damn thing wrong. Couldn't if you tried."

She snorted a laugh and rolled her eyes. "Get to know me a bit better. I do *plenty* wrong."

He fisted her hair into a clump behind her and yanked her head back. "Don't roll your eyes."

Need and excitement glimmered back at him. She stared

hard at him for a moment, then rolled those baby browns again.

With a growl, he tightened his hold on her hair. "Bad girls have to ask for forgiveness. And I think you're a bad girl, Bianca."

She rolled her eyes again, unable to hold in the smile that had her lips twitching.

He pushed her to her knees, her eyes directly in front of his cock, which bobbed heavy and veiny, the water pummeling them unable to keep up with the precum leaking from the tip.

He guided her head forward, and she opened her mouth, taking him to the back of her throat immediately. "That's right, baby. That's a good girl."

Her lips wrapped around him, and he started to work her over his length. Fucking her face, hitting her deep and making her cheeks puff out. She didn't gag or balk once. She took him, as much of him as she could.

Fuck, her hot little mouth was almost as good as her hot little slit. She'd hadn't let him in her ass yet, but he knew she wasn't against it either. They had time. They had the summer.

She tipped her eyes up to his and rolled them again, smiling around his cock as she did so.

Fuck him.

With a tight grip around her hair, he yanked her back up to her feet, hoisted her up onto his hips and drove into her hard, shoving her back against the wall.

She clung to him, her nipples beading beneath his shirt, hard and making tight points. He sucked on one over the shirt, tugged on it with his teeth until her back bowed and she gasped. He lifted his head and swallowed the tail ends of that gasp, shoving his tongue into her mouth and tasting her.

Her thighs squeezed him, and her pussy tightened. He'd

been inside her three times already, and yet he still couldn't get enough. Couldn't get his fill. Every time he slid inside Bianca, it was like fucking heaven.

"Darlin'?"

"Yeah?"

"Gonna come."

"Okay. You want me back on my knees?"

Fuck. Him.

Yes, he certainly fucking did. Those brown eyes watching him as he shot his load on her face would fuel his fantasies on those lonely winter nights down in the Baja.

She slid off his hips, back down to her knees, opening her mouth, ready for him.

A position like that. A look like that, how could he not blow?

Two hard strokes and he was letting go on her face, across her tongue, coating her mouth. That image would be burned into his brain for fucking ever.

For. Fucking. Ever.

Bianca, on her knees, a smile on her face, eyes wide and welcoming as he glazed her face.

With one final tug, he finished. She stood up and put her face into the spray, washing away his cum. Once she was clean, she glanced back at him, her smile so fucking bright, he should have had sunglasses on.

"Fuck, darlin', now it's my turn." He sank to his knees, lifted up one of her legs, put her foot on his shoulder and dove in ears-deep.

Now this was how he planned to spend his summer.

BIANCA FINISHED up in the bathroom, washed herself and her hands and then turned off the light before opening the door.

She was as quiet as she could be, tiptoeing around the trailer so as to not wake the sexy biker sprawled out naked in the bed.

The clock on Jack's stove said it was eight thirty in the morning.

They'd fucked most of the night, so she had no idea what time they finally fell asleep.

Either way, she'd be running on fumes for the day and needed a big cup of coffee to not fall asleep behind the wheel when she went to pick up her kids.

Her clothes were scattered throughout the trailer.

Jared and Simon had retired to Simon's camper first, leaving Jack and Bianca lying outside in the hammock together watching the sky change. He'd slid his hand down her pants while they lay there and he got her off.

But that just made her a randy beast who only wanted more, and she'd tackled him in the hammock, which subsequently sent them falling to the ground in a thud and a heap.

He'd then chased her into the trailer and stripped her as he backed her up to his bed, where he spent a considerable amount of time with his face between her legs before he finally gave her the cock she craved.

Speaking of the cock she craved, it was pitching a very impressive tent while he slept.

Should she hop on for one more ride before she left? Wake him up by riding him like the stallion he was?

His white sheet barely covered him. It was like he was posing for some sexy photo shoot with his hands behind his head, the sheet draped across his nether region with only a sprinkling of dark, trimmed, wiry hair peeking out.

He had to know how beautiful he was. Women probably drooled when he walked past, threw their bras at him when he rode his Harley down their street.

In just a week, the bearded, tattooed biker with a twenty-six-year-old son had managed to burrow beneath her skin, and even more surprising, she was finding that him being in her life was a balm to soothe her aching heart. A salve for her soul. Which was desperately needed after what Ashley and Rod had put her through.

She allowed herself one more moment to just watch him sleep, to take in his beauty, in the peace she felt just being near him before she continued to gather her clothes. He'd literally just flung them wherever when he stripped her. She found her underwear on top of his dresser, her skirt was draped over his headboard, and her tank top and bra were like a trail of naughty breadcrumbs through his small kitchen.

Her purse was next to her side of the bed. With her clothes still in her hand, she went to grab it but yelped like a stepped-on dog when a long-fingered hand attached to a tanned wrist with dark hair and tattoos reached out and grabbed her arm.

She tossed the clothes in the air, her entire body feeling like she'd just stuck a fork in a toaster.

"Where you going?" he asked with a lazy, sleepy chuckle, his blue eyes groggy but no less beautiful.

"I have to go pick up the kids," she said, her heart rate returning to rest as she went about collecting her clothes again with one hand. He still held the other arm. "You scared the hell out of me."

"When you gotta pick 'em up by?" The rough bass of his voice scraped through her.

"Noon."

"How long of a drive is it to your folks?"

"Twenty minutes."

"What time is it now?"

"Eight thirty."

He tugged hard enough on her arm she was forced to

drop her clothes and fall back into bed. "Good, then you can glaze my face until eleven thirty. Ten minutes to clean up, get dressed and then you'll be there on time." He yanked her over his body, maneuvering her with his strength until she was forced to sit on his face. Not that she struggled or protested or anything.

"Jack …"

But her argument dissolved the moment his lips found her clit. She melted on top of him, gripped his headboard and rode his face like it was a bareback stallion.

Because for the summer, he was her stallion. Hers to ride as often and hard as she wanted.

She was close, really freaking close, and he must have known it because with more gruff, harsh movements, he pushed her off him, flipped her over to her belly, sat up, shoved her to her knees and dove back in with his face between her legs .

"Better access to *here*," he said, moving his tongue higher up until he circled her crease. "When you gonna let me take you there, baby?"

Her pussy clenched and her belly tightened at the thought of being taken in the ass again. It had been years.

Ashley had no desire to explore that erogenous zone in the bedroom.

"I'm not gay," he would say when she'd bring it up. *"That's what gays do. Or guys in prison. I'm perfectly happy with the two holes I've explored. I have no need to venture further."* Then he'd shudder like a weirdo and change the subject.

Yeah, she'd stopped letting him explore the hole in her face long ago, too. When he decided he didn't want to explore her hole with his face, she stopped letting him explore her face with his under-average-size cock.

"Where'd you go?" Jack asked, pushing two fingers into

her pussy and sucking on one of her folds. "You in your head?"

She blinked a few times, tossed the thoughts of Ashley from her brain with a good head shake and craned her neck around to smile at him. "Little bit. Sorry."

"Get out of that head and into this body. Feel. Don't think."

Feel. Don't think.

She could do that.

With Jack, she could do that easily.

Too easily.

How much she'd come to feel for this man—whether it be lust and blinded by orgasms or not—she had feelings for him. She needed to remind herself that those feelings needed to stay buried, lest she ruin the good thing they had going.

"Get out of your head, Bianca." His tongue left her folds, along with his fingers. A hard slap on the left butt cheek had her crying out. "Feel, baby."

"Feel," she said quietly.

"Just feel."

His fingers slipped back inside her. His tongue made contact with her clit.

A thumb pressed against her anus. "When?" he asked, his warm breath against her damp folds sending a shiver racing through her.

"Now?"

He paused his movements.

She held her breath.

"No." He went back to business as usual.

"No?"

"Happy doing what I'm doing. But soon, I'm gonna take you here real." He wiggled his thumb over her hole. "Gonna fuck you on my bike, too."

"Yes," was all she should get out.

He was doing something with his tongue on her clit, and it was driving her wild. Not to mention those fingers still pumping inside her, hitting her G-spot over and over again.

Her face made contact with the pillow, and she opened her mouth just as the orgasm washed over her. A cry so loud, she was sure it would have woken Jared and Simon in the camper if she hadn't done it into the pillow, ripped up from the depths of her throat.

His tongue worked double-time. His fingers pumped faster. She convulsed on the bed, her thighs shaking, body trembling with each glorious wave that swept through her.

Her eyes hurt, she was squeezing them closed so tight. Her fingers bunched in the sheets until her knuckles ached, but damn did she ever feel good.

With a heavy sigh, she collapsed to the bed as the last of her climax receded. Jack pulled his fingers from her, rolled her to her back, spread her legs again and sank down to his belly.

With the little strength she had left, she tapped him on the head. "No. You don't ... you don't have to. I'm too sensitive."

"Told you what I'm gonna do. Gonna do it. Glaze my face until eleven thirty, woman. No back talk, or I'll spank that ass again." He reached up her body and tugged on a nipple at the same time the flat of his tongue swept up her cleft.

She shuddered but sank back down into the mattress, her muscles relaxing, fingers threading into his hair. "Well, if I must ..."

"You must. Just feel, remember."

"Just feel ..."

He pushed two fingers back inside her.

Oh, she was feeling all right.

Feeling pretty fucking amazing.

10

HOW QUICKLY TIME flies when thing in your life are finally going right—for once. It was hard to believe she and Jack had already been together for three weeks. Not only was she happy and more sexually satisfied than she'd ever been, but the progress fourplex was coming along nicely.

It was the last week of school, and Bianca was excited to have her children out of Miss Beatrice's class but also dreading the summer and having to come up with endless entertainment for her crotch fruit.

Since hiring Jack, she'd been early if not right on time for school drop-off. Something about having a handyman with the *right* tool just made her want to get to work on time.

With a smile on her face, a spring in her step and Charlie on her hip, she ushered the girls into the school, smiling at other moms and teachers in the hallway.

A few of them gave her bewildered looks, but most of them just smiled and said *hello* in return.

Were they used to seeing her as a bumbling hot mess running down the hallway five minutes late?

Probably.

Did she care?

Not one fucking bit.

She was early enough with drop-off today that Miss Beatrice hadn't even pried her butt off her chair at her desk where she was eating her granola and yogurt to let the kids in. Parents and children waited in the hallway outside the classroom, lining the walls.

Hannah and Hayley spotted a friend and were discussing all things unicorns when Gwynyth with Duchess and Duke in tow came prancing down the hallway. She zeroed in on Bianca, and her pace quickened.

Duke took off toward his classroom, but Duchess joined Hannah, Hayley and the other little girl in their circle.

Gwynyth's cool hand landed on Bianca's arm. "I'm so glad I found you. I'm getting a touch worried that we haven't received your email yet about the joint class gift for Miss Beatrice. I mean, the last day of school is this Friday. That's not a lot of time to take a poll."

Bianca smiled, pictured Jack's head between her legs and smiled even more. "I've got it covered, Gwynyth. No need to take a poll. I'll just put something together. In fact, I was going to do that this morning after I dropped Charlie off at day care."

Gwynyth's complexion darkened beneath her heavily contoured makeup. "B-but that's not how we do it."

"Then you should have taken care of it yourself rather than pawned it off on me. You gave me the job, and I'm going to do it my way. There are twenty-seven children in the class. At twenty dollars a child, that's a pretty nice gift—heck, at *ten* bucks a kid, that's a pretty nice gift." She hoisted Charlie higher up onto her hip better just as the classroom door opened and a still-chewing Miss Beatrice smiled with a closed mouth at all the kids.

Gwynyth still hadn't removed her hand from Bianca's

arm. She squeezed, stopping Bianca from moving into the class. "But that's not how we do it," she said with a hiss.

"It's how *I* do it," Bianca said, jerking out of Gwynyth's grasp and moving her daughters forward into the classroom.

Anger flashed in Gwynyth's eyes, and she glanced at a few other moms at the back of the pack for support.

Bianca ignored them all.

If they were going to force a job on her, she was going to do it her way. She had connections at some of the hottest spots and with some of the best distributors in town. She'd put together a gift basket for Miss Beatrice that would knock that woman's socks off. She didn't need an endless stream of emails clogging up her inbox with every parent giving their two cents on a gift idea.

If they wanted a democracy, they shouldn't have put a competent, efficient dictator in charge.

She set Charlie down on the floor and helped Hannah and Hayley out of their backpacks.

"Why are all the other mommies staring at you?" Hannah asked, still incapable of mastering a whisper, even at six.

Bianca tipped her gaze up only to find Gwynyth and two other moms standing in a little huddle, staring at Bianca and whispering.

"They look mad," Hayley added, her volume just slightly lower than her sister's but still way above whisper level.

"It's nothing, girls. Nobody's mad at anybody. We have one week left of school, okay, and then it's summer. Let's make the most of this last week." Cupping each girl's face in her palms, she kissed them on their foreheads one at a time, told them she loved them, plopped Charlie back on her hip and left the classroom.

Now, if only she could make it to her van without being accosted by—

"Bianca!"

Damn it!

The shrill sound of Gwynyth's voice had her cringing. She remained with her back to the other woman in the middle of the hallway. Other parents leaving the school had to skirt around her. She looked longingly at the exit only twenty feet away. Mentally pleaded with the other parents to help her escape.

Footsteps, and not just one set, grew closer behind her.

Finally, taking a deep breath, she turned around to find Gwynyth and the other two women she was conspiring with standing in front of her.

The movie *Bad Moms* popped into her head, and she started to channel her inner Mila Kunis.

"How can I help you, Gwynyth?" she asked sweetly, flashing all of them a big smile.

"We're going to have to ask you to follow protocol," Gwynyth said haughtily. "You need to ask all the parents for their opinions. You can't just make the decisions yourself."

"This is a democracy," one of the other mothers added, cocking a hip and crossing her arms over her chest.

"Wasn't much of a *democracy* when you appointed me as the gift organizer. Seems to me a democracy would have involved nominations, voting and the elected accepting the position. None of that took place. I was *given* the task of acquiring a gift for Miss Beatrice, and I plan to do just that." Her moment was stifled when Charlie tried to cram a Goldfish cracker into her closed mouth.

"Eat, Mama."

Resistance was futile, so she eventually accepted the cracker and chewed it.

"If one of you would like to take over the job, then go for it. I haven't bought anything, so the position is still available."

Not one of them looked eager to take on the task.

Bianca snorted. "Didn't think so."

"You can't just *tell* us what to do," the so-far-silent mom said.

"You sound as old as your child right now, Leni. I'm not telling any of you to do anything. I'm telling you what *I'm* going to do. Now—" She reluctantly accepted another cracker from Charlie. "If you'll excuse me, I'm going to go get this guy to day care and go and pick up Miss Beatrice's gift. Expect my *one* email tonight with a total cost divided by twenty-seven and directions for reimbursement." She remembered Jack's eyes and how heated they'd been when she took him in her mouth Friday night and smiled at the women in front of her. "Have a *wonderful* day, ladies."

Ignoring their grunts and huffs of protest, she turned around and headed to the exit, stepping up her pace to get out of there before one of them decided to tackle her to the ground and demand democracy.

Fuck democracy.

If they truly wanted the PTA to be ruled as a democratic organization, they wouldn't have *shoved* the job of teacher gift organizer on her.

But she was in too good of a mood to give Gwynyth or her lackeys any more thought. They were making amazing progress on the fourplex, she had more orgasms in one week than she'd had in her entire ten-year marriage, and Eva's bachelorette party was on Saturday.

So after over a year of feeling like she was drowning while simultaneously trying to keep three children's heads above water, the seas had finally calmed, she found a raft, and shore —a new life—was on the horizon.

She dropped Charlie off at day care, then headed downtown to Lowenna's chocolate shop.

Mason, a single dad who was no longer single, owned a favorite Seattle watering hole known as Prime Sports Bar and Grill. Mason had gotten together with Lowenna—one of

Seattle's best chocolatiers—and together they had Mason's daughter, Willow, and their six-month-old twin boys. Lowenna would certainly hook her up with something decadent that even a sourpuss like Miss Beatrice wouldn't be able to turn her nose up at.

Most days—particularly when a new bonbon flavor dropped—there were lines around the block for Lowenna's chocolate shop, but thankfully the crowds had either gotten their chocolate fix or Lowenna had run out of the fan favorites. Bianca was able to walk right in without having to queue up.

Lowenna spotted her and smiled wide, her gray eyes twinkling. "Come here for a fix?"

Bobbing her brows, Bianca rolled up to the front counter and patted her hands on the smooth granite rhythmically. "Always. But I've also come in search of a gift that will turn my kids' teacher's permafrown upside down."

"Say no more," Lowenna said, ducking out from behind the counter and wandering over to a display table where prepackaged chocolates were set in beautiful gold boxes. "I've been getting a lot of parents coming in here for teachers' gifts. This one is popular." She picked up a long box with beautiful gold paisley embellishments on it. "Twenty-four of my most popular bonbons. But for you, I'll also toss in this." She handed Bianca a round ball that looked similar to a Terry's Chocolate Orange, only this one was covered in red foil and had a little brown stem and a silky green leaf sticking out the top. It looked like an apple.

"Candy apple?" Bianca asked, turning it over in her palm.

"Not quite. It's my take on a Terry's Chocolate Orange, which in my opinion is absolutely brilliant, delicious and I wish I'd come up with the concept myself. But alas, I have made a modified version. It's a chocolate apple. Kind of like a blooming onion. When you open the foil, the wedges will bloom to reveal a caramel dipping sauce in the center. The chocolate wedges themselves have like an apple pie filling inside."

"Holy shit." Bianca grabbed two more of the apples from the basket. "That sounds amazing."

All grins, Lowenna shrugged and tucked a strand of her dark brown bob behind her ear. "One of my more brilliant creations, I will admit. We're having to ration how many we put out. I haven't even advertised them, and they're already going like hotcakes. I'm not sure I'll do a social media blast about them. I'm worried there might be a stampede."

"For your chocolates, I wouldn't doubt it." Bianca gathered up her treats and took them to the counter. "All set for the party Saturday?"

Lowenna's eyes gleamed as she slid back behind the counter and began to ring up Bianca's order. "*So* ready. I can't wait to cut loose and get some real girl time. I love our wine nights, but we're usually so laid back with them, it'll be nice to get out and do something extra fun. Get gussied up. I might see if Eva will do my makeup for me."

"That's not a bad idea. Like back in high school or going out clubbing when life was childless and simple. Get together, pre-drink, listen to '90s pop and try on clothes."

Lowenna beamed. "Exactly. Plus, we get to ride in a limo, which is always a blast." She bagged up all of Bianca's items, tossed in a few more goodies with a wink and handed Bianca the bag. "I hear you're seeing somebody. Is that why your smile is nearly touching your ears?"

Her cheeks were sore, now that she thought about it. She rarely went a full five minutes without thinking about Jack.

"You don't even have to answer that question," Lowenna said, chuckling. "It's written all over your face."

"It's just a summer thing," Bianca said dismissively. "He's the handyman working on the fourplex, and he's—"

"Got the right tool for the job?" Lowenna finished, her grin sly.

He had more than the right tool for the job.

"Something like that." Bianca pulled the bag off the counter and nodded at Lowenna. "I'm off to Paige's. Going to get a gift certificate to go in the teacher's gift bag. Do you have any other suggestions?"

"Go see Luna at The Rage Room. Get a gift certificate for that. I'm not sure how rage-filled first-grade teachers are, but even the chillest people like to smash stuff."

"She's not chill. Has a stick firmly embedded in her ass."

"Then she can pull that stick out and hit stuff with it," Lowenna added, popping a chocolate into her mouth.

Bianca laughed. "Yeah, maybe."

"Go see Mitch for a cool print or a photo shoot gift certificate. Definitely get Zara to do up a nice bouquet. Eva could do a gift certificate for nails."

"Get a therapy session with Tessa to work through all her bitchiness?" Bianca added.

"She really that bad?"

Shrugging, Bianca turned toward the door when the bell chimed to indicate another customer. "She just doesn't like me. Probably because I don't kiss her ass like the other parents, and I'm a single mom with three kids, a full-time job and I'm often a little late dropping off the girls."

"That's no excuse for her to be rude, though. You're a warrior, doing it all on your own, and your children are still respectable little humans who I have no problem spending time with." Lowenna stepped out from behind the counter in preparation to greet and help the customer. "Don't let her glares get you down. Kill her with kindness."

Bianca lifted up the bag of chocolates. "That's the plan. Put her in a sugar coma."

"I'm sure Mase will hook you up with a gift certificate to

Prime too if you go talk to him. He might even have some booze swag. Like a Budweiser T-shirt."

Bianca opened the door and rolled her eyes with a smile. "Exactly what Miss Beatrice wants, a Budweiser T-shirt, chocolate and a gift certificate to a place where she can pull the stick from her ass and demolish a toaster."

"I wouldn't say no to a gift basket like that." Lowenna waved goodbye.

"Thanks, Lo. See you Saturday." She headed down the sidewalk toward Flowers on 5th. Zara, another wife of a not-so-single single dad, Emmett, owned another one of Seattle's best-kept secrets. She was known all over the city for making some of the most beautiful bouquets as well as having a unique style of wrapping her flowers in eco-conscious gold paper rather than plastic like everyone else.

Bianca would order a bouquet with Zara to be delivered to Miss Beatrice the morning of the last day of school. Combined with chocolate from Lowenna at Wicked Sister Chocolates and a basket of primo gift certificates, the woman couldn't not love her gift.

Flowers on 5th was three doors away when a familiar face coming out of the flower shop had her stopping in her tracks and then darting behind a telephone pole like a gumshoe

Jack was coming out of Zara's holding a beautiful bouquet. He wore his construction man jeans, white T-shirt and raw animal magnetism. He didn't have his helmet with him, and she found herself surprised that he drove his truck and didn't ride his bike.

She wasn't quite sure why she was hiding, but she waited until he jumped into his truck, revved the V8 and pulled back out into traffic before she went in to see Zara.

"Hey, girl," Zara greeted her. "How's it going?"

Keeping her eyes peeled for Jack randomly returning to the florist for some reason, Bianca's head swiveled, and her eyes darted to the windows. "That guy, the one with the beard—"

"You mean the blue-eyed hunk?" Zara finished with a wily smile.

"Yeah." Bianca nodded. "What did he buy? Did he say who it was for?"

Zara's blue eyes narrowed. "You know him?"

"I—"

Understanding flashed across Zara's fine features. "Oh my God, is that *Double H?*" she whispered.

"Double H?"

"Yeah, that's what Celeste and Lauren have been calling him."

Double H?

"Hung and Handy?" Zara finished. "At least that's what I'm told it stands for. Is that the man you're—"

Bianca's hand flew across the counter and covered Zara's mouth.

Rolling her eyes, Zara stepped away. "Afraid if I say it out loud, it'll jinx things and you'll suddenly stop having multiple orgasms?"

The horror.

"No, I just … I really like him, but it's supposed to remain casual. Just a summer thing." Bianca glanced around, her eyes landing on each meticulous floral arrangement. "What did he buy?"

"Gerbera daisies."

"Did he say who they were for?"

Zara shook her head. "No sorry." She dropped her voice low and quit. "His voice was deep, like rolling thunder. Smooth, dark, deep." She bit her lip. "I mean, I love my Emmett, but that man who just bought flowers is very, very nice to look at—and listen to."

Yeah, he was certainly all of those things.

"He didn't say who he was buying the flowers for? Did he grab one of those little cards?" Curiosity burned inside her like a hot coal bouncing around her body.

Zara's head shook. "He didn't, sorry. Came in, must have had an idea what he wanted because he was in and out in under five minutes."

That just made her all the more curious. He was supposed to be at work right now. Not that she gave him *set hours*. He could work when it worked for him as long as he got all the work done.

Zara was the oldest of all the single dads' wives, and she had a very calming presence about her. She was close with Richelle, Bianca's sister-in-law. The two went to kickboxing together.

Zara and her gay best friend had a child together, and they co-raised him while she also ran her family's floral shop. Now, she was with Emmett, an ER doctor, and the two of them were raising Emmett's daughter, Josie, and Zara's son. Zara just seemed to have her life together. She knew her worth and what she wanted out of life. Head games were beneath her. She was who Bianca wanted to be when she grew up.

"You here for intel or something else?" Zara asked.

"Both," Bianca said with a huff. "I'm here to order a bouquet for my kids' teacher, and then I saw Jack leaving your store and ran in here for details."

"Jack." Zara's lips twisted, and she focused on the door as if Jack was suddenly going to walk back through like she'd summoned him. "It suits him."

"I have to go see Luna at The Rage Room, then I'm going to head to the house to check up on things. I'll see Jack there."

"And you can ask him who the flowers were for yourself," Zara said, setting a big, floppy calendar down on the counter.

"Now, what can I get this teacher?"

Bianca stepped away from the counter and wandered through the black buckets loaded with individual stems and premade bouquets. "I need it for Friday. I need a bouquet that says, '*Thanks for teaching our kids, but maybe over the summer, take a chill pill or two.*' You got anything like that?"

The laser-focused look Zara was giving her set her nerves on edge, and she squirmed. It was like when Isobel, Single Dad Aaron's wife, touched your arm. She was this freaky empath who could suck your feelings to the surface and then feel them all herself. Everyone claimed it was voodoo, and Bianca was inclined to believe it.

"You gonna tell me why you're looking at me like you want to peel my face off and wear it as a mask?" Bianca asked, her laugh coming out shaky. She knew Zara wouldn't hurt her, but the look on the woman's face was no less alarming.

Closing her eyes and shaking her head, Zara smiled. "Sorry, I get a little serious when I'm thinking. Who'd you say your kids' teacher is?"

"Miss Beatrice. Young thing. Maybe thirty. Stick up her butt."

"Yeah, I remember her. She bounced around schools for a bit when she first started teaching. Mostly substitute work. Nolan had her as a substitute a couple of times. I definitely got a smug vibe from her." She tapped her finger to her lips in thought and hummed. "Place an order, and let me see what I can come up with. I've been looking at a few new arrangement styles online that I want to try. New color combos. I might whip up something new as a trial for her."

Bianca shrugged. She didn't have much of a green thumb, not like Zara, so she knew Zara would come up with something far more spectacular than if Bianca had picked out the bouquet from the catalog. "I trust your judgment."

Zara nodded. "One stick-from-ass-removing bouquet

coming right up." She made a note on the calendar for that coming Friday.

"Thanks. You excited for Saturday?" Bianca opened her purse on the counter, drew out her credit card and handed it to Zara.

Zara rang her up. "Absolutely. I hear you and Celeste have lots of surprises in store for us."

Bianca bobbed her brows wickedly and smiled. Everyone knew about the limo, so that wasn't a surprise, but the sex toy party and the booze cruise on a big party yacht with like fifty other people was a big surprise. Celeste had found the booze cruise online and booked it. Four hours of cruising around the bay, partying on a beautiful boat while drinking fancy cocktails—yes, please.

"I'm just happy that my parents are taking the kids Friday night and my brothers are taking the kids Saturday night. Two whole nights with no children. What's a mama to do?"

Zara handed her the receipt. "He just left. That's what, or should I say *who,* a mama should do. Now, go find out if those flowers were for you, and if they weren't, send him back here, and I'll hook him up with a bouquet guaranteed to get him into your pants."

Heat flooded Bianca's cheeks.

Zara smacked her palm to her forehead playfully, her blue eyes twinkling. "Right. Silly me. He doesn't need a bouquet to get into your pants. I'm sure you throw them at him as soon as you see him, right?"

Bianca was nearly at the door but grinned back at Zara. "Why do you think I'm wearing a skirt?"

"I like your style, woman. Go get yours. You deserve it."

"Bye, Zara. See you Saturday."

Zara waved, her phone ringing just as Bianca headed back out into the heat of the day.

One more stop, then she would go and see Jack and find

out if those beautiful Gerbera daisies—her favorite flower—
were for her or not. She wasn't sure how she'd feel about it if
they were or how she'd feel if they weren't.

AFTER VISITING Luna at The Rage Room and getting Miss
Beatrice a thirty-minute smash session, Bianca headed to the
fourplex to go and check on Jack. For now, she was done
painting. She'd finished the entire top two units and would
get to work on painting the bottom units in the next week or
so. Or if Casey wanted to make more money, she could always
pitch in and paint a bit too.

With her gut in her throat, Bianca peeled herself out from
behind the steering wheel of her van, hiked her purse up on
her shoulder and headed into the house, but the slam of a
truck door behind her had her jumping.

She hadn't even noticed that his truck wasn't there. Yet,
now that she saw him coming up the pathway toward her, she
realized he wasn't working yet.

Where had he been?

Did he have another woman in his bed who he was
bringing flowers to?

She steeled herself for the possibility of this being
the end.

Last time, when Ashley ended things, she'd been blind-
sided. Now she needed to be prepared.

"Good morning," she said, forcing a smile onto her face,
though the corners of her lips felt extra heavy at the moment.

His smile was grim, but he pulled her into his side and
planted a kiss on the top of her head. "Mornin'."

She unlocked the house, and they stepped inside.

He was quieter than usual. Withdrawn.

A car door slamming behind them drew Bianca's attention. Casey was making her way around her car, which by the looks of things seemed to be jammed full of various bushes and shrubs in the back and front seat of the little sedan.

"Don't mind me," Casey said with a wave, opening up the passenger doors. "Just popped by the nursery, picked up all the shrubs I could fit in here. Might have to make a second trip."

"Let me know if you need to borrow my truck," Jack called to her. "Might be easier."

Casey nodded and waved again, her smile big and bright. She'd shown up midweek last week with a new hairdo. She'd ditched the pink and was sporting a super cute dirty-blonde bob. It suited her much better.

Bianca smiled at Casey once more before closing the door to the house and turning on Jack. "I saw you this morning."

He lifted his head, curiosity swirling in the blue.

"I saw you leaving Zara's flower shop. Flowers on 5th."

The corners of his mouth dropped, along with his head.

"Are you seeing somebody else? Because I'm fine with this being just a summer fling. But I need to know that I'm the only one you're *flinging* with. We're not using protection, remember? Just because I can't have babies anymore doesn't mean I can't catch syphilis or any of the other super fun and itchy STDs."

When he lifted his head to look at her, she had to take a step back from how dark and stormy his smolder was. If she didn't know any better, she could have sworn real flames flickered in his eyes. "Today is my parents' anniversary. Every year on this day, I take a bouquet of Gerbera daisies to their side-by-side headstones. They were my mother's favorite flower. I sit and I talk to them for a bit. Tell them about my life."

She swallowed. Shit. Now she'd stuck her foot in it. She

opened her mouth to say something, but he cut her off with just a look.

"I told them about how Simon finally came out to me and how wonderful Jared is. I told them about you."

"Me?"

"You're the only woman I'm *flinging* with, Bianca. You're all I need." He stepped into her space, but he kept moving, forcing her to back up and look up at him. He backed her up until they were on the threshold of the bathroom.

"Jack—"

"I get sad when I go see my parents. When I tell them about all the things that they're missing. Not knowing my son. Not knowing me, now that I have my shit together. Never getting to meet you. It hurts." He fingered a strand of hair that fell against her cheek. "They'd like you."

She rested her hand on his heart. "I'm sorry. I didn't mean to jump to conclusions. I'm just ..." She hung her head, her hand dropping from his chest. "Ashley has turned me into such a suspicious person. I wasn't like this before. But his cheating has made me second-guess everyone. I think everyone is leading a double life and knocking up their secretary with twins."

His finger below her chin and the slight bit of pressure had her lifting her gaze back up to his. "I need to be inside you. Now."

Oxygen left her lungs. Her lips parted.

"You. Me. It's how I feel whole. This is more than just a fling—even if it's temporary. We're connected. And when we're *connected*, I feel more ... *balanced* than I've felt in a long fucking time." His words were slow, careful and precise, but the heat they packed, combined with that stormy smolder he had going on made her panties instantly damp. Her heart thumped in her chest. He told her not to fall in love with him, so why was he saying all the right things to make that happen?

"Jack, we're ... Casey's right outside."

He pushed her into the bathroom, closed the door, lifted her up and plunked her butt on the counter, pushing her skirt up her thighs and pulling her panties down her legs.

He dropped to his knees, cupped her butt and pulled her pussy against his face.

Her head fell backward against the vanity, and her eyes shut as he latched onto her clit and sucked hard. "Ooooh," was all she could get out.

Her fingers splayed in his hair, and she pulled him tighter against her, riding his face. He was supposed to be working. She was supposed to be working. Casey was right outside. But something that felt so right couldn't be wrong, could it?

His thumb replaced his lips on her clit, fiddling back and forth, while his tongue fucked her like a cock. In and out of her pussy. The thrusts were shallow, but they still hit all the right spots, and she was biting her lip and convulsing on the counter in seconds, her fingers digging into his scalp as the orgasm tore through her.

You. Me. It's how I feel whole. This is more than just a fling. We're connected. And when we're connected, I feel more ... balanced than I've felt in a long fucking time.

His words came back to her.

How honest he'd seemed when he said them. The passion that burned deep in his blue eyes. He really was making it impossible for her not to fall for him. She was madly in lust, and if he kept up the pace, she'd be madly in *the other four-letter L word* soon enough.

When her clit became too sensitive and the climax ebbed, she pulled his head free of her pussy and glanced down her body at him.

"Inside you," he grunted at the same time he stood up, unzipped his jeans and pulled out his length.

She gasped when he gripped her butt cheeks, digging his fingers into flesh, and pulled himself hard into the apex of her thighs.

It wasn't an instant fit, though. She had to wedge her hand between them and guide him to her center. But once he found it ...

Their sighs mingled, their lips less than an inch apart as he fully seated himself inside her and began to move.

"Fuck ... never met a woman like you before."

She was barely perched on the counter now. His hands held her in place and moved her up and down his shaft. The pace was all him. She was just along for the glorious ride.

"Casey ... Rod ... your ex ... your kids. You're so fucking strong. So fucking good. Feel so fucking good." He dropped his head and latched onto a nipple over her shirt and bra. The heat and wetness from his mouth made her nipple throb and the other one demand attention too.

"Never met someone so fucking strong." His tongue swiped across her collarbone, and his teeth made contact with her shoulder.

He'd never met somebody so strong? How about if he looked in the mirror? Losing his parents so young. Drugs. Jail. A broken back. Another addiction. Finally cleaning up his act for his son and owning multiple properties in multiple countries. If that wasn't the definition of strength, she didn't know what was. She felt weak in comparison to all that Jack had overcome, all that he'd seen in his life. He'd probably forgotten more than some people would ever know in their entire lives.

The way his pelvis was raking across her clit, his mouth against her skin, his cock inside her hitting every button, and his words—oh, his words—she squeezed her muscles around him, held on to his shoulders for dear life and let go one more time.

Thank goodness the bathroom didn't have any windows, because the noises she was making would definitely have carried across the neighborhood.

Heat prickled along her arms and through her lower belly until every neuron fired, every cell woke up and even her scalp tingled.

Jack stilled, pulled his face away from the crook of her neck, took her mouth and came hard. She tasted her own release on his lips, and he breathed heavily through his nose, reveling in his release, his cock pulsing inside her. His tongue pushed her lips apart, and he deepened the kiss, the same time his body relaxing, his breathing evening out.

She loosened her grip on his shoulders, and he stopped digging his fingers into her ass. She'd certainly have bruises. But they'd be bruises she could hide from the world but see when she was alone. They would make her smile and think of Jack. Not that she needed a visual reminder. She thought of him nonstop.

He broke their kiss and pressed his forehead to hers, opening his eyes. A small smile curled on his plump lips. "Best fucking place on Earth, baby. Right here inside you."

She cupped his face, blinked and pressed her lips gently against his. "I couldn't agree more."

11

IT WAS the Saturday night of Eva's bachelorette party, and
thankfully, the single dads agreed to not head off to poker
night and instead to watch all the children.

Bianca's brothers were taking her children, so she didn't
have to worry about arriving home drunk and dealing with
yappy early risers come Sunday morning.

She and Jack were almost four weeks into their "relationship," and she'd already lost track of how many times they'd
had sex.

It was a lot. She was just going to leave it at that. Her
panties got wet and her cheeks got warm if she thought too
long and hard about it and tried to keep count.

For the last three and a half weeks, they'd been getting
together on Friday nights. She would stay at his place, they'd
spend most of the night in bed, then she'd go pick up her
children from her parents around noon. But this Friday, he
ended up working late at the house, finishing up on the bathroom tile and vanity. They planned to go pick out the kitchen
backsplash on Monday.

She thought she wasn't going to see him, so when he

knocked on her door at eleven o'clock that night, burst in like he was preparing to rob the place, threw her to her back on the wood floor and buried himself between her legs, she was, needless to say, surprised. If not completely thrilled.

"Need you to glaze my face, baby," he'd said, shredding her panties in his hands before tossing her legs over his shoulders and going to town on her.

She shivered at the memory of last night. He showed up, ate her out to within an inch of her life, fucked her until she saw spots in her vision, then took off home on his Harley.

She wished he'd spent the night, particularly since the kids were at her parents', but he said he had to be up early to start work. He needed his sleep, and her in the bed beside him would mean he wouldn't get any.

Her cheeks warmed at his words. He was unable to be in a bed with her without being inside her. The last time she'd been in a relationship like that with a man, she'd been nineteen. Was this just lust? Taking advantage of the temporary and letting it fuel the desire to go at this arrangement at full throttle? Or would he always be this insatiable, this attentive and passionate if they were an old married couple with matching track suits and weekly lawn bowling?

He was also so dedicated to his job. Working weekends and evenings. Keeping his promise to get the job done on time. Which only made keeping her promise and not falling in love with him all the more challenging.

With her children already off with her brothers for the night, she, Celeste and Lauren made their way over to Richelle's house early to help set up. Lauren was finally ready to leave Ike with a babysitter—actually two sitters. Celeste and Richelle's daughters were going to watch him until Isaac got home.

"You feeling okay?" Celeste asked Lauren as they all piled into Lauren's SUV. Since Lauren was pregnant, she was driving and would drive their drunk asses home as well. "Nervous about leaving Ike alone?"

Lauren turned over the ignition and backed out of her driveway. "I've left him with Isaac before and with the girls for like an hour. He'll be okay."

Bianca leaned forward from her spot in the back seat and squeezed Lauren's shoulder. "He'll be fine. Besides, Isaac will be home in a few hours."

Lauren and Celeste exchanged looks in the front seat and smiled.

What the hell was that about?

"Max was eager to start helping Jack today," Celeste said, rolling down her window.

"Isaac too," Lauren added, turning onto the road out of their townhouse complex.

"Haven't heard anything from Jack, so hopefully it's gone well today. I know he needs the extra hands. It's a huge job." Bianca sat back in her seat and rolled down her own window. They all had their makeup, party clothes and hair products in bags and were going to get ready at Richelle's house, like they were college kids again preparing to go out clubbing. It sounded stupid, but Bianca was actually really excited. She hadn't done anything like this with a big group of women in a long, long time. She needed this.

"Well, let's go see how they're doing," Lauren said, turning in the opposite direction of Richelle and Liam's house on Lake Washington and rather heading directly for the college district and the fourplex.

Shit.

"Yes, I'm eager to meet Jack," Celeste said, grinning back at Bianca. "I don't like that Max has met him before me. I mean, I'm one of your best friends. Surely I should get to vet this new man in your life before my man gets to."

Lauren nodded. "I agree."

Bianca nibbled on her lip. They knew what he looked like, but how would Jack react to being ambushed by two of her friends? He'd already had two men thrust on him today and forced to be his apprentices. How would he feel about having to meet two more people in Bianca's life?

Was that pushing it beyond the level of a hookup to something more?

He said it was more than just a fling, remember?

He also introduced you to his son and told his dead parents about you. If anybody is blurring the lines of hookup and "more," it's him.

She high-fived her conscience for talking some sense into her.

But that didn't stop the nerves from rattling around in her belly like marbles in a tin can.

Lauren pulled up to the fourplex, where three motorcycles were parked in the driveway.

Max's Bonneville, Isaac's Ducati and Jack's Harley.

"A biker gang," Celeste said with a chuckle, unbuckling her belt and climbing out of the SUV. She had a lollipop in her mouth, and it had made the whole vehicle smell like watermelon. Bianca's belly rumbled in hunger, upsetting those marbles even more.

"I think it's hot," Lauren added, meeting Bianca and Celeste in the driveway. "Though I doubt in *real life,* if they were in any kind of motorcycle clubs, they'd be allowed to associate with each other. Given their varying tastes in bikes."

Bianca ran her fingers gently over the chrome of Jack's bike. "That's probably true."

The sound of hammers and other power tools echoed from inside the house, along with rock music playing off someone's phone.

Lauren stepped inside first, followed by Celeste and then

finally Bianca. But they didn't even make it over the threshold before Lauren tossed on the brakes.

"What the—" Celeste said, crashing into Lauren's back, which caused Bianca to crash into Celeste.

"Holy. Shit," Lauren breathed, robotically stepping into the house.

Celeste moved. "Holy. Shit. Indeed."

Bianca followed, her eyes taking in what had caused Lauren to freeze.

Holy. Fucking. Shit. Indeed.

Three men, all hot as a firefighter calendar actually on fire, were shirtless, sweaty, with bunching muscles, working with power tools.

The lollipop in Celeste's mouth fell out and hit the floor. Lauren's eyes continued to get bigger. Bianca's nipples tightened beneath her tank top and bra, and her panties became instantly damper.

"Jesus," Lauren muttered. "Right into the spank bank."

Abso-freaking-lutely.

They stood there, mouths open, eyes not even blinking. The guys hadn't noticed them yet, and that just made it all the better. They worked with grunts and murmured curses but, for the most part, seemed to be enjoying working together. The kitchen and living room were an open floor plan, and Max and Isaac were finishing up the laminate flooring in the living room while Jack installed the fume hood and over-the-range microwave in the kitchen.

"Howdy, boys," Lauren finally said, which made each one of the men jump in surprise.

A startled "fuck" burst from each of their lips. But when they saw the women standing there, their frowns of surprise quickly faded into smiles.

Isaac and Max stood up and made their way over to their

women, bringing the tangy, intoxicating scent of sweat, male and hormones.

Bianca's body grew warm.

"You ladies off to your party?" Max asked, his gray eyes only on Celeste.

Her bottom lip was between her teeth, and she reached out and rested her hand on his glistening pecs. "Yeah."

"You guys wanna come? Make a bit more money. I know Eva said no strippers, but you're already half-naked, so ..." Lauren's lashes batted when Isaac cupped the back of her head in his big palm and ran his thumb over her bottom lip. His smile curled wickedly when she parted her lips and bit the pad of his thumb.

Envy enveloped Bianca as she watched her friends with their men. The wordless conversations between the couples, the hooded gazes, pheromones bouncing around the room.

"Hey." And there was her man. If only temporarily hers.

His body shone with sweat, only enhancing the beauty of his tanned skin and the ink down his arms and across his chest. He said the lion over his heart was for Simon—a Leo and the only constant love of his life. The griffin on his right pec symbolized all that he'd worked so hard to build and all that he'd continue to work so hard to protect. The griffin was a protector of treasure and priceless possessions, and Jack said he knew he was one of the lucky ones to turn his life around. Too many times to count, he should have wound up dead but didn't. The griffin was there to remind him of what he'd worked for, what he treasured. His freedom, his sobriety, his son and his life.

Swallowing, she allowed her gaze to roam across his body for another moment before lifting her head to look his eyes. Heat swirled in the dark blue, and a knowing smiled tilted the corner of his mouth on one side. "Like what you see?"

Damn, that deep, raspy voice. It made her insides quiver and her pussy gush.

She nodded, remembering last night and how animalistic he'd been. Taking her the way he had on her foyer floor. She'd woken up with a sore back, but it was worth it. So damn worth it.

"Thinking about last night?" He dipped his head, his beard tickling her cheeks.

"Yeah," she breathed, inhaling his scent, imprinting it on her memory for the winter when he was down in the Baja and she was in bed—alone—save for her vibrator, Jason Momoa.

He brushed his lips over hers before pulling away.

Max and Isaac stepped back too.

"You wenches need to get out of here. You're nothing but sexy distractions." Jack's tone was gruff, but his eyes sparkled playfully. "Coming in here with your feminine wiles, muddling the brains of my staff." Clucking his tongue, he furrowed his brow at Celeste and Lauren but pointed at Max and Isaac. "Look at these two. You've turned good workers into horny teenagers. Now they're going to just be thinking about you two in those dresses when they should be thinking about laying that flooring."

"I can think about two things at once, boss," Max said with a big grin. "Always thinking about sex."

"I should hope not, bro. You're a high school teacher," Isaac teased.

Max grabbed a water bottle from the counter and took a sip. "Not thinking about it at *work*. And if I am, it's only with Celeste's."

"I'm always thinking about sex with Lauren," Isaac said, his smile enormous as he stepped back toward his woman, one hand cupping her swelling belly, the other one on her lower back. "How you feeling?"

"Tired," she said, leaning into him. "But excited for tonight."

"I've got a couple more hours, then I'll go relieve Sabrina and Mallory. Ike and I are looking forward to our boys' night."

"Yeah? Watching sports and scratching balls?" Lauren's hand rested overtop Isaac's as they watched her belly move.

"Baby moving?" Celeste asked. Though they could all tell that it was. Lauren and Isaac opted not to find out the sex, though based on how this pregnancy was going compared with her last one, everyone's vote was that they were having a girl.

"Big-time," Lauren said, wincing. "I think it's doing somersaults." Both her and Isaac's eyes widened when the baby in her belly did another big roll. Even from where Bianca and Jack were standing, they could see the shape of Lauren's stomach changing.

"That's probably the only thing I miss about being pregnant," Celeste said. "That and the cute squishy baby you get at the end. But I'm good holding my friends' babies. I don't need any more of my own."

"Amen to that," Bianca said, her gaze pivoting back to Jack. Amusement glittered in his eyes, and he appeared to be fighting a smile.

Jack's rough and sudden movements had her losing her balance. Luckily, he'd pulled her tight against him so she didn't fall. "Give me your mouth, and then all of you get going."

He claimed her mouth before she could object or give it to him willingly—not that she wasn't willing. Unlike before, when his lips just brushed hers before pulling away, this time, he took her completely. Forced her lips apart, wedged his tongue inside and swept it through, tasting her need for him, sucking on her tongue like he did her clit.

She melted against him, wrapped her arms around his neck and let him lead. If he led her into the bathroom and shut the door, she would be helpless to resist. Jack had cast a spell upon her, and she was reluctant to find a fairy godmother or murmur any magic words in case the spell be broken.

"All right, all right," Lauren said with a chuckle, pulling on Bianca's arm. "We need Bianca in top bridesmaid form for this party. It won't do if she's a puddle of wanton goo because you've gone and made her melt with all your bad-boy bikerness."

"Bad-boy bikerness?" Isaac said, glancing down at his woman.

Bianca blinked a few times and turned so she was now facing her friends but with Jack's arm still wrapped around her. "I guess I should introduce you to my friends, huh?"

He stuck out his hand. "Jack Savage. Nice to meet you ladies."

One by one, Celeste and Lauren shook his hand, enormous grins on their faces.

"You got a nickname for him yet?" Max asked.

Oh shit.

Jack lifted a brow. "Nickname?"

"Yeah," Isaac interjected. "I'm Sergeant Foxy McBig-Hands, apparently."

"And I'm Professor Washboard. Even though I'm not a professor," Max added.

"Teacher Washboard just didn't have the same ring to it," Lauren said.

Bianca and her girlfriends all stared at the ground. She couldn't see herself, but her cheeks were warm. Glancing sideways, she saw that both of her friends were certainly blushing.

"You're Double H," Lauren finally said, looking at Jack.

"Double H?" Jack glanced at Bianca.

Now, her face was on fire. Damn it. Maybe these nicknames weren't such a good idea. Or they should have kept them just between the three of them.

Bianca dropped her eyes back to her feet. "Hung and Handy."

Isaac and Max snorted.

"That's a good one," Isaac said. "I like his better than mine."

"Big hands beget big ..." Lauren said to her man. "Yours is more tongue-in-cheek."

Isaac's cheeky smile matched the playful twinkle in his blue eyes. "And Jack's nickname is just *hanging* out, no innuendos and euphemisms required."

"Well, I *am* handy," Jack said, squeezing Bianca's hip before pressing his lips to the side of her head. "And I'll let the other word just *hang* without any confirmation. I've never received any complaints, right, darlin'?" He nuzzled the side of her head and pulled her tighter against him. "If you wanna introduce me as Double H or Hung and Handy from now on, I won't object."

Rolling her eyes, she shoved him. "Yes, because I'm sure if I introduce you to my parents or brothers, showing up with my booty call named Hung and Handy is sure to not raise any questions."

"He'll meet them at the wedding, won't he?" Lauren asked. "Are you coming to the wedding?"

Jack said *yes* at the same time Bianca said *no*.

Shit.

He glanced down at her.

Stumbling over her words, she resisted the urge to blot her forehead as beads of sweat tickled her brow. "I ... I didn't want to assume. You don't have to meet my family if you're not up for it. You don't have to come to a wedding and meet *all* my friends if you're not sticking around."

"Maybe let Double H decide what he's *up* for instead of deciding for him," Isaac said.

Jack shot Isaac a look. "For a pig, you're not half bad."

Indignation had Isaac rearing his red head back. "You got a beef with cops?"

Jack shook his head, a crooked smile curling his lips. "No beef with pork, just not a fan in general. I'm a law-abiding citizen. A home and business owner. But you, you're not so bad."

Isaac glanced at Lauren. "Am I supposed to take this as a compliment?"

"I would," Lauren replied blandly.

"You gonna bring me to the wedding?" Jack asked, turning his attention back to Bianca. She was having a hard time thinking clearly with all his hard, half-nakedness up against her.

"I'd love to bring you, if you'd like to come." Hope spun in her stomach, and her heart thumped heavy in her chest. Everyone who meant anything to Bianca was going to be at her brother's wedding. Jack was going to meet them all.

"Not embarrassed of me?" The curl to his lips dropped, and the shimmer in his eyes darkened.

She stepped out of his embrace, panic replacing all other feelings inside her. Her tongue felt larger than normal. Awkward. Cumbersome. Unable to remain in her mouth and desperately looking for an escape. "No. Not at all."

"Then why didn't you ask me?"

Giving her friends a quick glance, she realized they were all wondering the same question.

She sputtered. "Like I said, I wasn't sure if you would want to go. I've never done *this*"—she pointed back and forth between them—"before. Never done a casual, temporary thing. I've had a handful of monogamous relationships, where even though they ended, they had no expiration date. I'm taking your lead on this, Jack. I don't want to push to involve you too much in my life and then you get all *you're being too clingy* and back away. I'm fine doing what we're doing, having some summer fun, but you introducing me to your son blurred those lines. I'm just trying to figure out where the lines are and not step over them. But I'd like for you to come with me if you would like to come ... please?"

Was she begging him? She didn't feel like she was begging.

She was just making sure Jack knew she wasn't just with him because of what hung between his legs. She was with him because she enjoyed spending time with him. She enjoyed who he was and who she was when she was with him. It went deeper than just the physical with them. The talks they had while working, while they lay in bed in between marathon sex sessions. It might not be a forever romance, but it was definitely more than a temporary fuck-fest with her hot handyman.

At least to her.

His lips pursed, and he stroked his beard for a long, long moment—or at least it felt long—before finally speaking. "Taking you to the wedding. I'll meet your family, friends, everybody. Might be temporary, but it doesn't mean we can't do things besides fuck."

At least they agreed about that.

"Well, that was more romantic than a Shakespearean sonnet," Max said, chuckling. His laughter broke the tension that had settled thick around them. He turned to Celeste. "This *isn't* temporary, but it doesn't mean we can't do things besides fuck."

Celeste snorted. "Maybe that's *all* I want to do."

"That's all I want to do these days," Lauren chimed in.

"Second trimester libido is a demanding beast."

"And I am A-OK with that." Isaac kissed his woman's cheek, bent down and kissed her belly before standing up straight again and heading back to where he and Max had been laying down flooring. "Gotta get back to work. The boss is a pig-hating dictator. We get no breaks. Not even to piss."

Max kissed Celeste, then joined Isaac. Celeste and Lauren stepped outside.

Which left Bianca and Jack.

"I'd love for you to meet my family. I hate that I go to all of these group gatherings and *all* of my friends are coupled up but me. Taking you as my date to the wedding would mean a lot." She pressed her hand over his heart. "I'm not embarrassed of you, though. I'm not sure what the opposite of embarrassed is, but whatever it is, I'm *that*."

"Unashamed. Unabashed. Proud."

"Huh?" She wrinkled her nose and gazed up at him.

"Those are the opposite of embarrassed." He still hadn't cracked a smile, and his eyes remained dark and hooded. She was having a tough time reading him.

"Well, I am all of those things when it comes to you. I like being with you. I like who I am when I'm with you, and I want my friends and family to see that side of me."

He nodded. "All right then." His hand found her waist, and his head dropped until his mouth was once again just a hairsbreadth from hers. "Have fun at your party tonight, Bianca."

The shiver she felt earlier when she remembered how he'd taken her last night sprinted through her body, and she dissolved against him.

"Don't go too crazy," he whispered.

"Bianca, you ready to go?" Lauren called into the house.

"Just a minute," Jack hollered before taking Bianca's

mouth once again with his, dipping her low over his arm until she was forced to kick up one leg.

When he plopped her back onto two feet, she was breathless and starry-eyed but definitely smiling.

"Behave," he said again, smacking her on the butt and pushing her toward the door. "Only one you're allowed to *misbehave* with is me."

Grinning like an idiot, she stumbled out of the house but glanced back at him over her shoulder.

He was all smiles again. "Get going, Bianca."

Nodding, she skipped down the steps to where Lauren and Celeste were waiting for her. They all climbed into Lauren's SUV again and were about to drive off when Celeste slammed her hand into Lauren's chest and yelled at her to stop.

"What?" Lauren asked, frustrated.

"Look!" Celeste pointed out the windshield, where lo and behold, Max, Isaac and Jack were all standing on the lawn, each of them with a water bottle in their hand.

"What are they do—" Bianca didn't even have time to get the words out before all three men poured the water over their faces, the droplets and tributaries cascading down their tapered and muscular torsos, between their abs as they tossed their heads to and fro like models at a photo shoot.

"Holy. Fuck." Lauren killed the engine.

"I think I just had an orgasm," Celeste added.

"I know I did," Lauren said.

Bianca's eyes were glued to Jack. His eyes were fixed on her. When their water bottles were empty, the guys waved, smiled and headed back inside, Jack the last to go. He winked at Bianca before disappearing into the house.

A text message rattled her phone a moment later. *I'm not your booty call. I'm your boyfriend. —Double H.*

She smiled like an idiot when she texted him back as Lauren pulled out of the driveway.

Well, in that case, BOYFRIEND, get ready to meet my entire family. There are a lot of them.

He texted back. *Only one I care about is you. And your kids. Need to meet the girls too.*

"Are you two sexting?" Lauren asked, glancing back in the rearview mirror at Bianca.

They were doing something better than sexting. He was claiming her as his girlfriend.

Lauren continued to prattle on. "Isaac and I do that a lot. Gets us both really ramped up for when he gets home from work. I tell you, he can barely keep up with how much I need the *D* during this pregnancy. He *can* keep up, but barely. Says he's spent and barely recognizes his balls by the end of the week."

Celeste chuckled and spun around in her seat. "She's definitely texting with Double H. That smile says it all."

Bianca glanced up at her friend after reading Jack's last text about meeting her kids. "He's just continuing to prove to me how wonderful he is."

"Did he send you a dick pic?" Lauren asked.

Bianca and Celeste both rolled their eyes.

"No. He just said that he's not my booty call. He's my boyfriend, and he wants to meet the girls."

"Sounds like he also wants to be more than temporary," Celeste added, her smile cheeky. "Does he *have* to go down to Mexico at the end of August?"

Bianca texted Jack back. *Monday, as I'll have all three kids and we need to go pick out backsplash.* Then she stowed her phone in her purse. "He does it every year. Summers here, winters there. He owns a bar down there. I can't ask him to change his life, his plans for me. Not when he made this clear from the very beginning it was temporary."

Her heart hurt every time she said that word. *Temporary*.

Was she getting in too deep with Jack? Was temporary soon going to become impossible? He just kept showing her more lovable sides of him. Even less than a month into their "arrangement" and she already knew it was going to be nearly impossible not to fall in love with him by the end of the summer.

"We still have two months," Lauren added, turning into the Lake Washington neighborhood where Bianca's brother and sister-in-law lived. "Jack might feel differently come August when the job's done and he's set to leave. He may not want to."

"The heart wants what the heart wants," Celeste said. "And maybe by the end of the summer, his heart will want to stay here with you and the kids."

Bianca could hope for Jack to have such a feeling, but she wasn't going to bank on it.

Jack was just the kind of man who gave whatever job he was tasked with one hundred and fifty percent of himself. Whether that be renovations on a fourplex or renovations of a divorcee, single-mother's heart, he gave everything he had to it. But just like the renovations on the house, his time with Bianca would be temporary too.

He'd fix her, just like he'd fix the house, get her in working order and then move on to the next project. As much as she knew he was "in this," she was a project nonetheless.

It might be more than a fling, like he said, but it was still temporary. He hadn't failed to mention that, and her brain also wouldn't let her forget it, no matter how much her heart wanted her to.

12

"DO THE IMPRESSION AGAIN," Zara asked, her face a mottled red as she laughed on Richelle and Liam's couch. "I don't even know this Gwynyth woman, but the face you make of her seems spot-on."

All the women in their group were laughing as Bianca regaled them with her triumphant tale of vanquishing not only the stick-up-her-ass teacher, Miss Beatrice, but also thoroughly putting Gwynyth in her place.

Bianca curled her lips, bugged out her eyes and flared her nostrils.

"It's like she's smelling her own fart but also trying not to shit herself," Richelle said, wiping a tear from beneath an amber eye.

Bianca shrugged and sipped her wine. She was pretty damn proud of herself and of how she'd not only handled the democra-zy that was the PTA bitches, but also Miss Beatrice.

The laughter died down, and the women all chatted among themselves. Bianca sat back in her chair and remembered Friday afternoon at school as all the children sat in a circle on the carpet in the classroom, their parents lining the walls.

This was the traditional last day of school. The parents came early, and the students put on a little skit-type thing and showed their parents some of their art and what they were working on in class and had learned over the year. Then the students presented the teacher with a joint class gift before everyone said goodbye for the summer.

Bianca had put together the mother of all gift baskets, and of course, Zara's one-of-a-kind masterpiece bouquet had arrived right on time. It was unique and spectacular. Purple orchids, bright orange birds of paradise and butter yellow lilies not quite in bloom had all the parents and even the children oohing and aahing.

A pinch at Bianca's elbow had her turn to find Gwynyth and her lackeys sidling up beside her. She adjusted Charlie on her hip.

"You've got some explaining to do," Gwynyth said with a hiss, her eyes thin slits and serpent-like.

Bianca rolled her eyes. "We'll see."

Like two proud, rosy-faced little dolls, Hannah carted the basket and Hayley carried the bouquet up to Miss Beatrice at the front of the class.

"This is for you, Miss Beatrice," they said in perfect "Redrum" stereo.

"Thank you, girls," Miss Beatrice gushed.

"It's from the whole class and our parents," Hannah added. "My mommy picked everything out."

Miss Beatrice's eyes widened before her head lifted. She glanced at Bianca with worry in her expression.

Did she think Bianca was going to poison her?

Not that the thought hadn't crossed Bianca's mind, but it'd only hung around for maybe five minutes before she decided to go with chocolates and a bunch of gift certificates.

Murder wasn't in her wheelhouse. Neither was putting laxatives in someone's coffee just for super shits and giggles. Kill 'em with kindness, not arsenic.

Slowly, Miss Beatrice peeled back the plastic from the basket and started checking out the contents. In addition to all the gift certificates, Bianca bought a bottle of wine, some nice loose-leaf tea and an aromatherapy candle to hopefully help Miss Beatrice calm the fuck down.

With each new envelope opened, Miss Beatrice's cheeks grew even pinker until she reached the final envelope, the one for The Rage Room.

When she finally lifted her head again, her green eyes were glassy, and she swallowed hard. "Thank you, class. These gifts are ..." She sniffled. "These gifts are amazing. I—I'm speechless. So perfectly me." She held up the box of chocolates. "This is my favorite chocolate shop." Next, she held up the gift certificate to Prime. "And my favorite restaurant. And I've always wanted to try out The Rage Room." Finally, she lifted the bouquet and held it to her nose. "And this bouquet is incredible, the most beautiful arrangement I've ever seen. I feel so spoiled."

Setting Charlie down on his feet so he could run and sit with his sisters, Bianca leaned back against the wall, crossed her arms over her chest and smiled smugly—because she'd earned the opportunity to do so.

Miss Beatrice wiped away a tear. "Thank you, students. Thank you, parents." She settled her gaze on Bianca. "Thank you, Ms. Dixon."

A garbled noise next to her had Bianca turning to see if Gwynyth was choking on crow or just her own spit. The look on the woman's face certainly said she wasn't handling her own version of capitalist democracy very well.

She uncrossed her arms and patted Gwynyth hard on the

back, like she was trying to dislodge a chicken bone from the woman's throat. "You okay, Gwynyth?" she asked.

Gwynyth glared at her. "I'm fine."

Bianca removed her hand, crossed her arms over her chest again and glanced back out toward the students. "Good. Because I'd hate for you to need to go to the hospital and miss out on how happy the class gift has made Miss Beatrice. You know, I'd be more than happy to do this every year from now on if all the other parents are okay with it?" She glanced down the line of the classroom wall to see a series of nods and adults saying "totally" and "definitely."

"All right then. Then I will totally and definitely keep doing this." She rested her hand on Gwynyth's arm. "Don't worry. I'm sure Miss Beatrice knows it was you who pawned the job off on me. You'll get *all* the credit."

Eva, Celeste's sister and the bride-to-be, came up behind Bianca and hugged her, shaking Bianca from her thoughts of her mean-girl triumph. "Thank you so much for everything you've done so far. You, my sister and Richelle are amazing putting this on." She pecked Bianca on the cheek. "I'm so happy to be getting two more amazing sisters."

"I'm definitely glad my brothers smartened up and traded up," Bianca said, patting Eva's arms. They'd all spent the early part of the evening getting ready with Eva—the esthetician—helping her friends and sisters with their hair and makeup. Bianca couldn't remember the last time she'd worn that much makeup, but when she caught herself in a mirror or glass reflection, she paused and smiled. She looked good.

Taking a gamble at online ordering, she found a cute little black dress with a deep V-neck, ruffled cap sleeves and a wavy hemline that hit her several inches above the knee. Thankfully, it fit like it was made for her. She paired that dress with some strappy gold heels and some hoop earrings, and Eva did her hair into a wavy half-up, half down thing.

For a single, divorced mother of three, she didn't look too bad.

Thank goodness for Spanx!

The sex toy company representative had come and gone, leaving all of them in stitches as they played *Name that toy* and *Where does THAT go?* And everyone's favorite, *The Vibrator Olympics*. In teams of two, the women had to take a vibrator, put it on max speed, put it between their legs (on the outside of their pants) and then do a series of activities like jump rope, a three-legged race and, of course, *pin the penis on the man*.

The team comprised of Tori, Richelle and Violet won, with none of them dropping their vibrator or having an orgasm.

Bianca would neither confirm nor deny whether she climaxed during the Olympics or not.

"Celeste tells me you're bringing your new man to the wedding," Eva said, her chin resting on Bianca's shoulder as they watched all their friends and family laugh and enjoy time away from their men and kids.

"Is that okay?" Bianca craned her neck around to see her soon-to-be sister-in-law. She loved Eva so much. Nearly identical to her older sister, Celeste, Eva had two boys from a previous marriage and was now getting ready to marry Bianca's brother Scott, who had one boy from a previous marriage. Two people could not be better suited for each other than Scott and Eva, at least in Bianca's opinion. They were perfectly matched, madly in love, and after what Eva's ex put her through, she deserved a good man like Bianca's brother Scott.

"It's more than okay that you're bringing a date," Eva said, squeezing her tight. "I'm so happy you're moving on. I can't wait to meet him. Or I guess I should say I can't wait to meet *Double H*," she teased, bumping Bianca.

"Limo's here!" Richelle called out, after answering a knock at the door. "Everyone, grab your purses, your cash and your emergency foldable flats, in case you break a heel. We stop for no one. Even those with broken shoes."

Eva pried her arms out from around Bianca and rolled her eyes. Bianca returned the look.

"Gotta love our efficient, dictator of a sister-in-law," Bianca said with a laugh, snatching her purse from the dining-room table.

They all piled into the limo, and Richelle and Celeste started to pour the bubbly.

"To the bride, the groom and this wonderful sisterhood," Richelle said, lifting her glass in a toast. "I'm so happy you bitches wore me down and made me a part of you. I just needed a bit of prodding."

Bianca wrapped her arm around Richelle. "And now you're stuck with us."

Richelle smiled, sipped her champagne and leaned into Bianca. "Ain't no place I'd rather be."

JACK BLINKED, slammed his eyes shut again, groaned and buried his head under his pillow, convinced that the incessant knocking on his door was only in his dream.

"Jack!"

He tossed the pillow off his head to the floor.

"Jack! It's Bianca. Open up."

Naked as he was hard, he swung his legs over the side of the bed and padded across the cool floor of his Airstream to his door.

More knocking.

"Jack, open up!"

He glanced through the peephole to where, sure enough,

a sexy as fuck, drunk as ever loving fuck Bianca teetered on heels.

Opening the door and yawning, he lifted an eyebrow. "Awful late, darlin'."

She pushed her way inside, teetering on those gold heels that he wanted to see tipped up toward the ceiling as he pounded into her. "Yep. And I'm awful drunk. And high. And horny."

His lips twitched. Fuck, was she ever cute.

"I'd say take off your clothes but ..." She raked him with her drunk, wobbly gaze, her teeth snagging her bottom lip and a groan rumbling in her throat. "But you're already there."

"Saving money on PJs is how I make my millions."

Her small palm hit him dead center in the chest, and she pushed him toward his bedroom, closing the door behind her with a loud enough bang he was sure Jared and Simon probably heard it. They probably heard her knocking and carrying on outside too.

"You need us to call the cops, Dad?" Simon's voice called out from the camper, amusement coloring every syllable.

"Do you feel safe, Mr. Savage?" Jared said, his tone equally amused. "Need any help?"

"Got it covered, boys, thanks. Go back to sleep."

"Need to find the earplugs first," Jared called, chuckling.

Jack rolled his eyes before fixing them to the vexatious brunette eyeing him up like he was an ice cream cone she wanted to lick. "You're really drunk, aren't you, darlin'?"

She nodded. "Yepper deppers. Had Lauren drop me off here instead of at home. Looking for some good *D*. You know anybody around here with some?" The way she hadn't removed her gaze from his hard cock said she'd already found the "good *D*" she was looking for.

He cupped the back of her head and pulled her close. "I

wanna fuck Bianca, not the booze or pot. Does Bianca wanna fuck?"

Her hooded gaze turned heated and her nostrils flared. She shook free from his grasp and dropped to her knees. "Bianca wants to suck some cock, that's what Bianca wants. Drunk Bianca, high Bianca, horny Bianca and sober Bianca, they all wanna suck some cock."

Fuck, she was loud.

He hoped to God his kid and Jared had found those earplugs. Otherwise, he was sure going to get some snickers and eyebrow lifts in the morning.

His cock was heavy and hard, bobbing in front of her face. A thick string of precum connected the tip to his hip.

With her thumb, she swept the precum off the crown and popped it into her mouth, closing her eyes and moaning in delight.

"Fuck, baby," he whispered, his finger threading through her hair. It was crunchy with product and damp at the crown, probably from sweat from dancing.

Bianca's eyes flashed open. She gripped him at the root and tugged, pushing the head of his shaft into her mouth and twirling her tongue around the crown.

"Holy fuck, baby."

With her right hand, she pumped. With her left hand, she reached beneath him, found his balls and tugged gently. Her mouth kept up pace with her hand, her tongue a devious, slippery muscle that wiggled over his cockhead one minute, worming around the hole at the tip, only to twirl its way down his length, massaging every vein the next minute.

And then she brought out the teeth.

He inhaled sharply when she scraped them over his crown and again when she tightened her bite around his shaft. But nothing she did was ever too much. It hurt just enough to feel good but not so much the pain overtook the pleasure.

He resisted the urge to close his eyes. He wanted to watch her. The way her lips stretched around his length and her head bobbed against his lap. Even her delicate fist wrapped around him, squeezing the root and causing the veins to pop.

Fucking beautiful was what it was.

She deep-throated him. Bottomed out and inflated her cheeks. A slight strangled sound gurgled when he felt her tonsils, but she never gagged, never complained. She pulled him out again and stroked him, glancing up at him with eyes so full of happiness, he thought he might shed a fucking tear.

"Love you sucking me, baby," he said, tightening his grip on her hair. "But want to give you the *D* you came here for. The *D* we know you're craving."

She took him back into her mouth, smiling around his cock before shutting her eyes again and working him double-time. He was going to blow soon if she didn't let up.

He released her hair and tapped her head. "Bianca, gonna come soon. Wanna fuck you."

She tugged harder on his balls and sucked harder on his cockhead, her suction power going from a solid seven to an eleven in under a second. He shuddered as a wave of pleasure ricocheted through him. One more hard suck like that and he was going to fill her mouth with cum.

"I mean it. Gotta stop." Careful she didn't have her teeth around him, he backed away, forcing himself free of her mouth with a wet *pop*. She released his balls too.

"On the bed, darlin'," he ordered. "Everything off but those heels."

Blinking up at him, she complied, slowly, provocatively peeling the dress off her shoulders and unhooking the lacy black bra at the back. Her breasts tumbled out, the nipples dark, dusky, hard and calling for his mouth.

Her bra hadn't even hit the ground before he was on her, bending his knees and cupping both breasts, taking one nipple into his mouth and tugging on the other.

Her gasp and moan had him switching to the other breast, taking as much of it into his mouth as he could, twiddling his tongue over her nipple until it pebbled and the skin around it puckered. Releasing the other breast, he pushed his fingers down beneath the black thong she wore. It matched her bra.

Not that he gave a flying fuck if her underwear matched, but he noticed that this was the first time she'd worn matching panties and bra. And as much as he wanted to yank them off her until the G-string up her ass snapped, he bet she'd spent a bit of money on these and wouldn't be too happy if he wrecked them.

His middle finger brushed over her clit, and she trembled against him.

"I thought I told you to get on the bed," he said, swiping his tongue over her nipple once again before he dipped his finger lower to gather some of her juices. She was already soaked, dripping over his finger. Warm honey he would never be able to get enough of.

"I got distracted," she said, the sexy line of her throat bobbing on a swallow.

He pulled his finger free from her, popped it into his mouth and mimicked her closed-eyed groan from earlier when she'd sucked his precum off her thumb.

"My favorite flavor," he said, jerking his head toward his bed. "Leave on the heels."

Carefully, she slid her panties down her thighs and stepped out of them, doing as she was told and reclining onto his unmade bed, still in those gold heels.

His lips curled at the ends as he allowed his gaze to lazily roam over her body, her dark brown hair, brown eyes crinkled at the corners as she smiled drunkenly at him. Her perfect tits. Her beautiful curves. The slight swell of her lower stomach where she'd grown three children. The trimmed patch of dark hair between her legs. And finally, that shiny pink center.

Her eyelids dropped to half-mast and her teeth snagged her lip again. She palmed her breasts, pushing them together and tugging on the pebbled points.

"Fuck, you're a beautiful sight," he said with a growl, planting one knee into the bed, preparing to climb up her body and take her properly.

Her eyes widened, the lustful look she was giving him fading. Uh-oh.

"I'm not embarrassed of you, Jack. Please know that. I have nothing *to* be embarrassed about. You're a good man. A successful man with a kind heart." She reached up and rested her hand on his chest. "My family is going to like you. Truly."

Even though he'd said earlier that he didn't care if her family liked him or not, a part of him was lying. Bianca was rapidly becoming somebody very important to him, and it mattered whether those important to her accepted him or not.

"I'd be honored if you'd be my date to my brother's wedding." The honesty in her eyes, the hopefulness and sincerity in her face hit him hard, and he struggled to keep his arms from buckling, and from the two of them just lying in each other's arms for the rest of the night.

She wanted sex, and he'd give her that. But afterward, he was going to hold this woman.

Hold her. Smell her. Feel her. Watch her sleep and then fall asleep with her soft body wrapped around his.

He thought he had his whole life figured out. A man with a plan.

Make money on the rentals and then eventually retire

down on the Baja. Simon and Jared could come visit him for holidays and vacation.

But Bianca Dixon and those sexy brown eyes of hers were slowly unraveling his plans. What he *thought* he wanted.

"Don't got a suit," he said, hovering above her, their bodies aligned, eyes focused on the other person.

She cupped his cheeks and smiled. "Good. Suits are over-rated, and you'd cook in this heat. It's semi-casual. A nice button-down dress shirt and some clean chinos or dress pants. I don't even know if Scott is wearing a suit."

"You need me to shave my beard?"

Her slender fingers wrapped around the hair that dangled a good four or five inches from his chin, and she pulled him down so his lips hovered over hers. "Don't you dare."

"Don't got no fancy diplomas on my walls. Not like your brothers."

He wasn't sure why he kept coming up with excuses. He was going to this wedding with her. No way in hell was he going to let her go alone. But he just needed a little more of a push to actually *want* to go. A bit more convincing that he wouldn't be sitting at the "guests" table all alone while Bianca had a mini family reunion.

"My ex had a bunch of those fancy diplomas, and look what kind of a shithead he turned out to be. Diplomas do not *make* a man. Hard work and integrity do, and you have that in spades." She pulled harder on his beard and took his mouth, pushing her tongue between his lips and sucking on his tongue.

He'd let her control the kiss for a moment, take what she'd come here for, and then he'd step in, take over and *really* give her what she came here for.

She released his beard, and she wedged her hand between them, wrapping her fingers around his cock.

"Inside me," she murmured against his mouth, continuing to kiss him. "Now. Please."

She didn't have to ask him twice. Though the sense of urgency, of need in her voice made him all the harder.

She notched him at her center, and he pushed inside, both of them groaning when he hit the end of her, when her hot, slippery fist of a pussy squeezed him and she lifted her hips, taking him even deeper.

He broke their kiss, leveraged up onto his hands and stared down into her eyes. "You with me, baby?"

Her nails raked a trail down his back, and she nodded. "So with you."

He started to move. "Only place you need to be."

Her lashes fluttered, and she bowed her back. "Only place I want to be."

Yeah, with her, inside her was the only place he wanted to be too. What worried him was that when the time came to leave her, he wouldn't have the strength to go. She held a piece of him now, and the longer he stayed with Bianca, the more time he spent with her, the bigger that piece grew. By the end of the summer, she'd own him.

Her eyes opened, and they pinned on him.

Fuck.

She could own him. Mind, body and soul.

Maybe she already did. But he didn't care. Didn't give a flying fuck.

A fraction of a man who got to be with Bianca Dixon was better than a whole man deprived of her.

And he wasn't going to deprive himself one inch of Bianca.

Even if it destroyed him.

13

BIANCA'S PHONE buzzed on the nightstand, only when she reached over to grab it, she hit wiry hair and a nose instead.

Jack grunted. "Other side, darlin'. You're in my bed."

Right.

She'd spent the night at Jack's after banging on his door demanding he bang her.

And boy, did he ever.

Stretching, smiling, she rolled over and snatched her phone from the nightstand, putting it to her ear. "Hello?"

"Who are you and what have you done with my baby sister?" asked Liam, his tone full of amusement. "Because this is definitely not little Bianca Dixon. You sound like a woman with a very large Adam's apple and a penchant for Marlboro Lights."

She cleared her throat. "Har-har. What do you want?"

"Wanna know when you're going to come collect your mini mes."

"They tearing your house apart?"

"No, just trying to get a timeline."

"Your wife sound like me?"

"My wife isn't awake yet. Stumbled her ass in here around one thirty." He yawned. "Neither of us fell asleep until three or so though."

Bianca wrinkled her nose. "TMI, big bro."

Liam chuckled. "Thinking about doing a big family brunch. Mom and Pop can come over, all the kiddos. We can all touch base on wedding shit."

"Has the bride-to-be signed off on this?"

"Haven't talked to her or the groom. Scott took Eva home when Richelle got here, but they left all the kids with me."

The sound of little boys making noise that only little boys could make echoed in the background. She heard Charlie's very distinctive fire truck impression, followed by her nephew Freddie correcting him that that was the noise an ambulance made. Apparently, a fire truck sounded more like ... then he made some irritating siren noise Bianca swore sounded exactly like Charlie's original impression. She had to hold the phone away from her ear, it was so loud.

"Hey, guys, knock it off," Liam said. She could practically hear her brother's eyes roll in his head.

Jack grunted beside her, rolled over, grabbed her around the middle and pulled her into him, spooning her. A large, long object resembling a cucumber prodded her in the butt.

"Put the phone away, Bianca," he murmured in her ear, his teeth scraping her shoulder.

"Are you with someone?" Liam asked, his voice not quite a screech but as close to one as her brother could get. "Where are you?"

"None of your business," she said on a yawn. "What time do you need me to come collect my children?" Pulling the phone away from her ear, she checked the time. "Jeez, Liam, it's only eight thirty."

"And I've been up since seven with *all* the children."

"You poor, poor man. Your *Uncle/Brother/Father of the Year* awards are on back order. Expect them by Halloween."

"Who are you with, Bianca?"

Jack grabbed the phone from her. "You'll meet me at the wedding, bro. Bianca will come get the kids at eleven."

Bianca spun in his arms, her mouth open, eyes wide as she tried to wrestle back the phone. She was no match for him though. His long arms, his muscles. He held her at bay without even trying.

He put the phone back to his ear. "Thanks for watching Bianca's kids though, man, honestly. She really appreciates it ... and so do I. Nice having family you can rely on and who have your back."

Bianca smothered her laugh in Jack's chest when Liam yelled, "WHO ARE YOU?" into the phone.

"Name's Jack. I'm helping your sister finish the fourplex."

"Helping her do more than that," Liam said with a heavy dose of snark. "Put my sister back on the phone."

"No can do, man. Got things we need to do this morning. But she'll see you at eleven. Thanks again, and we'd be more than happy to watch your kids if you and your woman need a night alone."

"Who is this *we*? Bianca? Bianca?"

Jack hung up the phone, tossed it onto his nightstand and rolled on top of Bianca. "Big brother's got quite the first impression of me." He settled between her thighs.

She wiggled until he was notched at her center. "He'll get over it. He just told me he was up boning his wife for an hour and a half last night. Fair is fair."

"We can do better than an hour and a half," he said, dropping his mouth to her nipple.

She lifted her hips, and he pushed inside. "That we can."

AT TEN THIRTY, Bianca reluctantly peeled herself out Jack's bed. She had a shower in his trailer—with him, which left her all of ten minutes to get to her brother's. Looked like she was going to be late. Whoops!

Jack, ever the gallant gentleman, drove her home so she could change and grab her van, which meant she didn't pull into Liam's driveway until quarter to noon.

Her parents' car was parked next to Scott's truck. It even looked like Celeste and Max were there, probably with Sabrina, and Eva and Celeste's parents' SUV had managed to grab the only shady spot. It was going to be a full house.

Should she have invited Jack to come?

Maybe he needed to meet her kids first before he met *all* the Dixons. Particularly her brothers. They could be a little much.

With her purse over her shoulder, a Tylenol doing its thing in her bloodstream and a to-go coffee in her left hand, she strode up to her brother's front door but didn't bother to knock.

Family didn't knock.

At least family didn't knock when all the family was there.

She'd learned her lesson to knock at other times. Particularly when it was just her brother and his wife home on a child-free night. That image of Liam's white ass was forever burned into her brain.

The moment she stepped onto the concrete floor of her big brother's home, the sound of family, children and laughter hit her and made her heart swell.

Hannah and Hayley were sitting at the dining-room table with Mallory and Sabrina, all of them deeply engrossed in some hard-core beading. Every girl had a furrowed brow and was laser-focused on what her fingers were doing.

She ran her hands over the backs of her daughters' heads and kissed them. "I'm guessing I wasn't missed?"

"You were missed, Mom," Hannah said, not looking up from her beadwork. "We just have fun without you too."

Mallory, Richelle's fifteen-year-old, glanced up. "At least she's honest."

Bianca pressed her lips together and hummed. "Yes, I suppose honesty is the best policy."

"We're making friendship-cousin bracelets," Hayley said, turning around to look at Bianca, a huge smile on her face. "Mallory, Sabrina, Hannah and me will all have matching bracelets."

Mallory and Sabrina exchanged looks and smiles as they sat next to each other. Even though the girls were in their late teens, they still gave the little girls time and attention. And there were a lot of little girls in their big group of family and friends. Sometimes, they got tired of the kids and went off to do their own thing, but most of the time they maintained patience with the kids and were the best babysitters. Of course, the grown-ups compensated them generously as well, which probably amplified their patience.

"There's my girl." Bianca's father, Wayne, wrapped his arm around Bianca's shoulders and squeezed her against him. "Rough night, BeeBee?"

Bianca rolled her eyes and glanced down at the four beading girls. They were all staring at her, waiting for a response.

She groaned. "Just tired." *Among other things. Hungover. Sore from Jack's tireless attention.*

Mallory and Sabrina snorted and smirked before returning to their beading.

"Yeah, my mom's *real* tired, too," Mallory teased.

"My mom, too," Sabrina added. "No pounding in her head *at all*."

"Wiseacres," Bianca's dad said, turning his daughter away

from the table and leading her into the kitchen. "How you doing, BeeBee?"

Her father always called her BeeBee. It was a nickname only he was allowed to call her, and that was his rule, not hers. He'd always wanted a daughter and pushed her mom for one more kid after they had Liam and Scott. She was her father's little girl in every single way.

"Good, Dad. Just tired, like I said."

His lips turned up into a wry smile.

"Glad to see you're having fun again, sweetheart. Been too long with that long face. Hurts my heart when you're hurting." He reached into Liam's fridge, pulled out a can of sparkling water and handed it to her. "No hair of the dog for you, young lady. You need water to nurse that hangover. Plus, you're driving my grandbabies."

She rolled her eyes and popped the tab on the water, taking a big sip that instantly tickled her lips and tongue but was cool and refreshing going down.

Bianca was close with both of her parents, but she and her father had a special relationship. She could always tell when he had something he needed to get off his chest, and he often knew she was in a bad mood before she did. A rarity for fathers and daughters, apparently.

Jerking her head toward Liam's living room, she indicated her father should follow her. Under any normal circumstance, she'd feel bad not saying hello to everyone at the house, but these people were family, so she could get away with being a little rude.

Charlie ran past her, chasing Freddie, Lucas and Kellen. "Hi, Mama. Bye, Mama."

Bianca's dad chuckled behind her. "He's been doing his damnedest to keep up with the big boys all morning. He's gonna nap well."

"Fingers crossed," she said, taking a seat on Liam's couch

and patting the cushion next to her. "What's on your mind, Dad?"

His lips twisted, but he took a seat. "You know me too well, BeeBee."

"My whole life."

Her father took a deep breath. "Liam said you're seeing someone?"

Didn't Liam know snitches got stitches? She'd have to go and shiv her big brother later.

"By the expression on your face, I'm going to say he's not wrong."

"It's none of his business, Dad. It's not anybody's business but mine."

Her father took her hand. "I know, honey. You're a grown woman who has endured a lot this past year, and you deserve to be happy. I'm just doing my fatherly due diligence and checking up on you. Three minutes old, three months old or thirty-eight years, you'll always be my baby girl."

Bianca leaned her head against her father's shoulder. "I know, Dad. And I appreciate you looking out for me. You and my brothers—as much as Liam can be a tyrant sometimes, I know he means well."

"Broke us all to see you hurting so much last year. A shadow of your former self. Worried me sick you were going to have a heart attack, you'd gotten so damn thin." His voice cracked with emotion, and he squeezed her hand.

Chuckling through the ache in her heart, she patted her stomach. "Made up for it and then some."

"You're beautiful, honey."

"Thanks, Dad. But I'm okay. Truly."

"Does he treat you well, BeeBee?"

She smiled, more to herself than anything. "He does, Dad. Jack is a great guy. I'm just ..." She felt bad with what she was about to say, but she didn't want there to be any surprises for either party.

"Just what?" Her father released her hand and rubbed her back, tickling the nape of her neck like he did when she was a kid.

"He's nothing like Ashley," she said in one breath. "I mean, appearance- or personality-wise."

"Not necessarily a bad thing. What does he do?"

"He's a handyman. A carpenter. I hired him to help me finish the fourplex project after the whole Rod incident. He actually helped me with the Rod incident. Was there when I needed backup and muscle."

"Well, he sounds like a winner in my books already, sweetheart. If he helped you handle that wad waste squatter, then I don't think I'll have any issues with him."

She pressed her lips together. "He's got a lot of tattoos, too, Dad. Like *a lot*."

Her dad wrinkled his nose. "Like on his face? Is he one of those people who tattoos their face so they look like an animal? Is he a lizard man or a lion man or something? Did he file his teeth into sharp points? Get whisker implants in his cheeks?"

Pivoting to face him, she lifted a brow. "What kind of television shows are you watching?"

"It's your mother. She likes that weird shit. I guess it makes her look at me with more appreciation that even as I begin to depreciate, at least I don't have pointy tiger teeth."

Bianca shook her head with a laugh. "Okay then. Uh, no. He does not have any tattoos on his face or pointy tiger teeth. Just his arms, back, chest. He's my date to Scott and Eva's wedding."

A hum was the only response her father gave her for a long moment. It was probably no more than a minute, but the pregnant pause and sudden silence unnerved her. She hadn't introduced a man to her father since Ashley, and that had been over ten years ago. Even though she was a different person now, she felt reduced to a teenager with the feelings inside her at the idea of her dad meeting her new boyfriend.

"Well," her father finally said, "he sounds A-OK to me. What's his name again?"

"Jack. Jack Savage."

Her dad let out a sigh of relief. "Phew, that's better than *Ashley*. When you told me you were bringing home a new boyfriend and his name was Ashley, I thought you were shitting me. And then I found out you weren't and I had to look that preppy fucker in the face, shake his too-soft hand and call him *Ashley*. Not *Ash*, but fucking *Ashley*." His eyes bugged out. "And then you went and married him. So I had to continue to call a *man* Ashley." He shook his head. "You know, with you kids, I'm trying to evolve. I know I have some backward tendencies, some ideologies passed down from my less than open-minded parents. But I'm trying to grow. I am."

She knew he was. She saw how open-mindedly and equally he treated her children. A far cry from how he'd been as a father. Even though she was always daddy's little girl, he certainly treated her differently than he did her brother.

She was a girl, and her brothers were boys.

She had a curfew; they did not.

If she was caught drinking in high school, that was the end of the world.

Scott, Liam and their father shared a beer fridge when her brothers were teenagers.

Not that she held any of that against her father —anymore.

As a parent now herself, she realized holding on to all that shit just bogged down your mind and inhibited your own growth. As long as he was trying to be better with her children, that was all she could hope for.

"Particularly because of the grandkids," he went on. "I want to be as progressive as I can. Women's rights and equal pay and all that. But some things just shouldn't be fucked with. I'd be okay if you named the girls Ryan and Parker or something like that, but if you or your brothers had named my grandsons something like Bethany or Rebecca or Emily, I'd have lost my damn mind."

"Nope. His name is Jack, and his son's name is Simon."

"Simon. That's a good name too. How old is his kid?"

"Twenty-six."

"Oh. How old is Jack?"

"Forty-three."

Her dad's head bobbed. "He doing a good job on the house?"

Beyond expectations.

"He is, Dad. He's very good at his job."

"Well, I'm looking forward to meeting this guy. Shaking his hand, feeling some fucking callouses and not having to call him a woman's name. I think we'll probably have more in common, too. I know you loved Ashley at one time, BeeBee, but—"

"I know you weren't Ashley's biggest fan, Dad."

Her father sighed. "It wasn't that. I mean, it *was*. Guy seemed slimy to me, but we had nothing to talk about. He was all golf, sailing, money and boardrooms. Guy's hands were smoother than the ass of a newborn, and that just doesn't seem right. Even your brothers who are white-collar office guys know how to change a tire, build a fence and pour concrete."

"Well, Dad, I think Jack knows how to do all those things too."

Her dad nodded once. "Then I think we'll have plenty to talk about, BeeBee." He tickled the nape of her neck again before standing up. "I smell the grill Seems your brother has finally put the damn burgers on. Need to go make sure he doesn't burn them."

Smiling and exhaling in relief, she followed her dad out onto Liam's deck, where the rest of the adults had gathered. Richelle, Eva and Celeste all looked as hungover as Bianca felt. Meanwhile, the men—Max, Scott and Liam—all wore smug smiles. It made her wish she'd brought Jack along. He'd definitely get along with the men standing there. He seemed to get along with Max. Earlier that morning after sex and before they had more sex in the shower, she'd asked him how things went with Max and Isaac.

She hoped his shrug and dismissive "fine" were honest and not just a man's way of brushing off the fact that he actually couldn't stand either man, but since they were her best friends' men, he had no choice but to suck up their presence.

Now she wished she'd probed more and asked more questions.

"How you feeling?" Richelle asked, a mimosa in her hand, her eyes hooded and tired.

"Probably the same as you," Bianca said, sipping her water.

"So, like thoroughly fucked death?"

Bianca snorted. "That's my brother, thanks."

Richelle just grinned and bumped Bianca in the shoulder. "You didn't want to bring Double H over?"

She gave her sister-in-law some heavy side-eye. "He's coming to the wedding. Maybe even the rehearsal dinner party, but I don't want to push it. Besides, he needs to meet my kids first."

"When's that happening?" Eva and Celeste joined them, and they all stood against the sundeck railing, elbows keeping them upright as they watched the children play down on the grass.

"Tomorrow, I think. I have the kids all day, as camp this

week is only Tuesday to Friday, and Charlie's day care is on vacation for the week. But we need to go pick out a back-splash and a few other things for the houses that need to be ordered, so ..."

"Are you going to tell the kids who he is?" Celeste asked.

"Charlie's already met him and loves him. Jack let him sit on his motorcycle, so he's the bees knees in the eyes of my two-year-old."

"But it's the other precocious, curious little Bianca look-alikes that you need to be concerned about," Eva added. "The ones who never stop asking questions. The ones who know *kind of* what a boyfriend is."

Bianca's eyes followed the children, who all seemed to be gathering behind a big shrub. There were a lot of whispers going on down below, and some of them kept glancing up nervously at the adults. "I'm just going to tell them that Jack is the man helping me finish the rental house. Which isn't a lie. If this wasn't a temporary thing, I'd tell them more of the truth, but since Jack isn't going to be sticking around, there is no sense in the kids getting attached."

It was hard enough keeping herself from getting attached. The last thing she needed to worry about was three little hearts who didn't see their father every day anymore getting all hung up on a man who would be riding off into the sunset in a matter of weeks.

"That's smart." Celeste's gaze turned equally curious as she watched Freddie, carrying a blue beach bucket, duck behind the shrub.

"What the hell are those kids doing?" Richelle asked.

"No idea, but it can't be good." Bianca needed to go and find out for herself. Hannah and Hayley were no longer inside beading, but she also hadn't seen them running around the backyard. Come to think of it, she hadn't seen Charlie either.

Finishing her sparkling water, she set the empty can down on a table and headed down the deck stairs into her brother's backyard.

She kicked her flip-flops off and enjoyed the feeling of soft grass between her toes as she headed across the yard toward the sound of giggling children.

Liam's son Jordan was the first to spot her, guilt painted all over his face. "It wasn't my idea, Aunt Bianca. It was Hannah and Hayley's."

"Yeah," Scott's son, Freddie, added. "Not my idea, either." Both boys had mud up to their elbows, and they were carrying buckets of water from the inflated kiddie pool behind the shrub.

She braced herself for what she was about to walk up on. Hannah and Hayley were master co-conspirators, and when it came to their little brother, they always managed to get him filthy. Not that it was hard to get Charlie filthy—the kid ate dirt and hated baths—but his sisters didn't help in the matter.

Holding her breath, she followed Jordie and Freddie and peered around the shrub into the flower garden where, sure enough, her six-year-olds and Eva's sons, Lucas and Kellen, had covered Charlie in mud like you would sand at a beach, leaving nothing but his head exposed, a giant smile on his face.

"Mommy, my mud monster, raaaawrrrr," Charlie said. Even his white teeth were speckled with mud as he grinned.

Bianca groaned, pulled out her phone from her back pocket and snapped a picture of her kid. "Yeah, you're a mud monster all right."

Charlie smiled again, happier than a pig in shit. "Raaaaawrrr."

THANKFULLY, Bianca usually packed more than one change of clothes for her children when they went on any kind of sleepover. Given Charlie's inability to stay clean and his sisters' penchant for mischief, she typically packed a week's worth of clothes for just one night. It was just easier.

She hosed her child off in the backyard after he was finished being a mud monster, then hauled his wet, naked butt into the house, where she put in him dry, clean clothes.

The culprits, who would have pleaded the fifth if they knew what it was, were forced to clean up the mess in the backyard, clean up themselves and then come inside for lunch.

In the end, nobody was really upset. It was harmless fun, if dirty. Even as Charlie sat on Bianca's lap eating his hamburger, she noticed dirt behind and in his ears. She'd have to bathe him again when they got home, much to her child's chagrin.

With her head pounding far less than it was earlier, Bianca chatted and smiled with her family, loving how close she lived to her parents and brothers again. Ashley's job had taken them to Palm Springs—his hometown—and she'd gone because at the time, she loved him and he was the primary breadwinner. But no way in hell was she sticking around the devil's armpit if she didn't have to.

She loved everything about Seattle, and the fact that all the people she loved the most were in Seattle as well made it a no-brainer to return. She also liked that her children were going to grow up surrounded by their cousins.

Ashley had a sister, but she wasn't married yet and had no children. They also weren't close, so even if she did have kids, and Bianca had stayed in Palm Springs, the chances of Bianca's children growing up playing with their cousins was slim.

Nibbling on a French fry, she ruffled Charlie's wild hair at the same time two big shadows in the shapes of her big brothers boxed her in on either side of the picnic table.

"Hear you're bringing the handyman to the wedding," Scott said, reaching into the center of the table, dipping a baby carrot into ranch dip and popping it into his mouth. "Are we going to get to meet this guy before the wedding?"

"If you're good," Bianca said. Her brothers hadn't intimidated her when they were kids, and they weren't going to intimidate her now.

Truth be told, Bianca loved having two big brothers. She loved it growing up, and she loved it now. They were her protectors. Her champions. And two of her best friends in the entire world. She trusted them implicitly, and even though they often had egos the size of Jupiter, she knew no matter what, they always held her best interests at heart.

It'd taken a lot for Liam and Scott to not go down to Palm Springs and give Ashley a piece of their mind with their fists. Particularly Scott, who was the mouthier hothead of the two. Liam had more of a lover not a fighter vibe to him, but that didn't mean he wouldn't retaliate if provoked or protect what he loved.

"What do we know about this guy anyway? Heard you literally just hired him off the streets, and now you're letting him into your *bed*." Thankfully, Scott dropped his voice down a few notches when he said that last word.

"I know he's one hell of a handyman. He gave me a list of references a mile long, and I called every single one. Nothing but glowing reports from each."

"Yeah, but like what do we *know* about him?" Liam added. "Did you do a background check? Criminal record check? Want me to get McGregor on him? Do a bit of digging?"

"No!" Fuck, she'd yelled that way too loud and way too quick.

Her brothers' brows lifted.

"You know something?" Scott asked, leaning in closer to Bianca.

"My all done, Mama," Charlie said, kicking his legs beneath the table to get down.

She wiped her son's face, turned toward Scott and plopped her kid down to the ground on his feet. Charlie took off like a runaway train to where Jordie, Freddie, Lucas and Kellen were all sitting on the floor in the living room, looking at Pokémon cards.

"What do you know about his past?" Liam asked, tapping Bianca on the shoulder. "We heard about what happened with that Rod fucker. What if this Jack guy is the same? What if they were working together?"

"You really need to cool it with the conspiracy theory shit," she said. "You're getting as bad as Atlas and his belief that everyone is a serial killer."

Liam dismissed her comment about his best friend with a blasé shoulder lift. "We're worried about you, B."

"Don't be. Jack is doing a great job on the house, and ..."

Scott's face scrunched up. "Don't say he's doing a great job on you. Please."

She rolled her eyes. "You said it, not me. It's temporary. For as long as the job lasts. He rides down to a bar he owns on the Baja at the end of the summer, so we're just having fun."

"I don't like the idea of my little sister having a *fun* time with the handyman," Liam said with a snort.

"Is it because he's the handyman you have an issue?"

"Fuck, no, and you know better than to even ask that," Liam replied defensively. "Don't give a fuck what he does as long as he's an honest, hardworking guy."

She believed Liam when he said that. Their father was blue-collar, and until a comment by an old Southern biddy with one foot in the grave, Liam was set to be a mechanic just like their dad.

"So then it's because I'm your sister and I'm doing exactly what you both have done? Hmm?" She turned to Scott. "You and Eva hooked up at a nightclub. Had a no-strings sex fest with the understanding you'd never see each other again."

Scott made a noise in his throat and glanced away guiltily.

She faced Liam. "And you and Richelle had a no-strings, once-a-week booty call arrangement for three years before you wore her down to be more. How come you can both have no-strings fun, but the thought of your sister doing the same thing makes you both go all caveman, alpha-chauvinist?"

Her brothers both sported red cheeks and irritated scowls. She'd called them on their bullshit, and they knew it. Even though they had women in their lives who didn't put up with their crap, they still needed to be educated from time to time on male and female equality. Particularly when it came to their little sister's sexuality.

Taking a deep, fortifying breath, she looped her arms around their shoulders and kissed them each on the cheek before saying, "I appreciate you two looking out for me. I do. And I love you both for it. But I'm a grown woman, and I've got needs."

"Oh God," Liam groaned.

"Needs Jack is *very, very* capable of fulfilling. He caulks my tub just right."

Scott winced. "Please stop."

"Knows how to drill, screw, nail and hammer."

Liam put his fingers in his ears and started going, "La, la, la, la, la."

Her lips jiggled and her facial muscles strained as she fought not to laugh. "Jack has the right *tool* for me, and he knows just how to use it."

"Bianca, seriously, please stop." Scott's pleas were coming out more like whimpers.

At this point, Celeste, Eva, Richelle and Max were all watching and laughing, enjoying the distress and discomfort of the Dixon boys.

"Has earned himself the nickname Double H. You know what that stands for?"

"No, and I don't want to," Liam said, his whimper matching Scott's, faced bunched up as if he were in pain.

Unable to keep from grinning, she leaned over and whispered into Liam's ear, "Hung."

Liam made another garbled noise in his throat.

She turned her head and put her mouth next to Scott's ear. "And Handy."

At the same time, both of her brothers stood up from the picnic table in such an abrupt way, chip bowls were knocked over and a few cups of juice spilled.

"All right, that's enough. Clearly, Bianca can take care of herself," Liam said, shaking his head like he had water lodged in his ears. He tossed a few napkins onto the spilled juice.

"Fuck, I need to wash my ears out. Give my brain an ablation after that," Scott said, sidling up next to Eva and shuddering. He glared at Bianca. "You play dirty."

Smiling, she popped another French fry into her mouth and shrugged. "So does Jack."

14

MONDAY MORNING, Jack rode his bike to the fourplex, where a nervous-looking Bianca sat behind the steering wheel while three wild, smiling children bounced in their car seats and boosters in the back of the van.

Her smile was far grimmer than her children's, and the eye roll that accompanied that smile said she was already at her wit's end and it wasn't even nine o'clock.

Jack was surprised to find his stomach in knots as he approached the front passenger door and opened it. Yes, he'd met Charlie, and the kid was cool and cute, but now he was meeting the twins.

They looked like their mother. Did they act like her too? Was he getting into a van with three hard-headed females with enough sass between them for a dozen women?

"Mornin'," he said, nodding his head at Bianca as he slid into the passenger seat. He craned his neck around to glance at the kids. "Howdy. I'm Jack."

"We know. Mom told us," one of the twins said, all proud of herself.

He snorted.

"That's Hannah," Bianca said, glancing in the rearview mirror. "Manners, please. That's not how you greet someone."

"Hi," Hannah said, the wind only leaving her sails slightly.

"And I'm Hayley," the other twin said with a wave.

Although identical, the girls had different styles and lengths of hair, unlike some identical twins. It wouldn't be impossible to tell the girls apart.

"How is everyone today?" he asked, fastening his seat belt.

"Mom's still tired from her wild night out with Aunt Eva, Aunt Celeste and Aunt Richelle. They all got into the goofy juice," Hannah said, giggling.

Bianca put the van into gear and pulled out of the driveway, giving Jack some serious side-eye. "I'm fine, Hannah. Just have some sleep I need to catch up on. That's all. I'll do that tonight. Early to bed for this mama."

"So why do they call you a *handyman?*" Hannah asked. "What makes you so handy?"

Depends who you ask.

"I can think of a few things," Bianca whispered, glancing at him again, this time with a cheeky smile he wanted to kiss.

Jack smothered his own smile with his hand and tugged on his beard, glad to not be facing the children at that moment. "A handyman is a man—or woman, because there are handy*women* out there—who knows their way around construction, carpentry and tools. They can fix things, build things and know a lot about a lot of different things about home maintenance." He resisted the urge to turn around and see the kids' expressions.

"But doesn't *handy* mean *useful?*" Hayley asked. "Like, I keep a water bottle beside my bed so it's *handy* for me if I'm thirsty at night."

"You're a *useful* man?" Hannah asked, this time with a

definite upward inflection at the end of that question. Like she had a hard time believing Jack was useful for anything.

He glanced at Bianca. She looked like she was having a hard time deciding whether to laugh, roll her eyes or cringe.

"Am I *useful?*" he asked her under his breath.

She side-eyed him hard. "Very."

That made him smile.

"I'd like to think that I'm a useful person. I'm helping your mom with that fourplex. Wouldn't you say that's useful?"

"I suppose," Hannah said, the skepticism still very clear in her tone. "I still don't get why you're called a *handyman*. Why not a *workerman*? Or a *toolman*?"

"Fixerguy," Hayley offered.

"You're welcome to call me those things if you prefer." The large home renovation store he preferred to use was just up ahead. He pointed at it so Bianca knew.

"Another term used for handymen is *jack-of-all-trades*," Bianca said, turning off the road and into the parking lot for the renovation store. "Kind of cool that his name is Jack already, huh?"

But it would appear the children had already lost interest in their vocabulary lesson and were pointing at the enormous blow-up gorilla wearing sunglasses and riding a surfboard on top of the car dealership's roof next door.

"Orilla," Charlie said as Bianca got him out of his car seat. "*Biiig* orilla."

The girls managed to get themselves out of their booster seats and belts and met Bianca beside the van, eyeing Jack suspiciously.

"Your beard is really long," Hayley said. "Why do you keep it that long?"

Smiling, he stroked his beard. "You don't like it?"

Hayley shrugged. "It's not that I don't like it. I'm just saying it's really long."

"It is," he confirmed.

"Longest beard I've ever seen," Hannah added. "Our daddy doesn't have a beard. He shaves every morning."

"Is that so?" Jack asked, determined not to say anything negative about their two-timing douche canoe of a father.

Hayley nodded. "But I don't mind your beard. Looks like it'd be fun to braid."

"Do you know how to braid?" he asked.

"Only pantyhose," Hayley said. "That's how we're learning. Mom ties pantyhose together to create three 'legs,' and we practice. I'm gonna get real good at it so I can make special friendship bracelets."

Hannah scowled at her sister. "We're *both* learning how to braid, and we're *both* gonna make friendship bracelets."

Hayley rolled her brown eyes. "He knew what I meant."

Hannah glanced up at Jack. "You wanna bracelet when we learn how to braid smaller things like thread?"

He loved how chatty and precocious they were. And even though it probably drove Bianca nuts, their bickering was entertaining. Though he bet that novelty wore off quick.

Bianca slung her purse over her shoulder and made a noise that sounded like a strung together "'K, letsgo," and everyone started to move.

Should he help her with the kids?

From the looks of things, she didn't need help.

She gathered them like a collie collects sheep and expertly herded them across the parking lot to the front door of the store.

She seemed to have it down to a science.

Charlie sat on her hip, the girls held hands and skipped, and they knew exactly when to stop and check for cars.

He was seeing the real Wonder Woman in action.

"We need a cart?" she asked, stopping in front of all the metal shopping carts.

He shook his head. "We're just ordering shi—*stuff* today. Not taking anything with us."

Her smirk at his almost-curse got his heart thumping. "Good catch."

"Gonna take some real effort not to swear like a sailor in front of this lot."

Her nod and eyebrow lift said she wasn't a clean-mouthed mama. But he already knew how dirty she could be. "I slip up more than I care to admit. They're not little innocents you're going to scar and traumatize with an accidental F-bomb."

"My down," Charlie said, pushing at Bianca's chest so he could get down and walk.

She quieted his hands with one of hers and looked him in the eye. "You going to stay with us? No running away. No touching. Hands to yourself, mister. Got it?"

"Okay!" His smile was big and genuine, but Jack could see the twinkle of mischief behind Charlie's honey-brown eyes, even at two.

Bianca must have recognized the twinkle too, because reluctance filled her face as she set her son down on his feet. "Hold your sister's hand, Charlie."

"*Nnnnno!*" Charlie jerked his hand away from Hayley's outstretched one.

"Crap." Bianca went to grab her son, but he pulled away from her as well.

"My hold Jack hand." He looked up at Jack, his hand out and waiting, eyes hopeful, smile enormous.

How on Earth anyone could resist holding that kid's hand after a request like that was beyond him. "Sure thing, little man. Let's hold hands."

Charlie's smile grew even wider as he took Jack's hand, and the five of them proceeded to walk into the enormous warehouse-style renovation store.

Jack didn't find out he was a father until Simon was

almost two years old. Jack and Elodie met at a party, hooked up, and never saw each other again. She never contacted him to let him know she was pregnant. Until Elodie tracked him down through mutual friends to introduce him to his kid. Problem was, the day she turned up to tell him he was a father was the same day he was being hauled off to prison for possession and intent to sell.

He missed out on the baby stage with Simon. Met his kid again when Simon was five, but then Elodie's new boyfriend threatened to hurt Simon and Elodie if Jack kept coming around, so because he was on parole and didn't want to wind up back in prison for starting shit, he stayed out of their lives.

Weeks turned into months, which turned into years before he saw Simon again. He always sent his son a birthday card with money in it. Told him he loved him and that he was there if Simon ever wanted him in his life, but he wasn't in a position—financial or otherwise—to fight Elodie for custody. He needed to get himself set up and secure before he could do that.

Then he broke his back, and the addiction to painkillers happened.

It wasn't until Elodie's boyfriend (a different one than before) started beating on Elodie and Simon that his son, only eleven, finally reached out to him. Lo and behold, Elodie had been keeping the cards in a drawer—unopened, thankfully—and when she was high and unaware of what day it was let alone what her son was up to, Simon found the cards and the money, packed a bag and traveled from Olympia to Seattle on the bus by himself.

It took Jack nearly a year to get full custody of his kid, but he was damn glad he did. Took every ounce of self-control inside of him not to go and murder the son of a bitch who'd laid a hand on his kid. Thankfully, an overdose took care of that motherfucker, and last he heard, Elodie was turning tricks to pay for her meth addiction.

But holding Charlie's little hand as they made their way through the store toward the tiling section just reminded him of all he'd missed. He'd missed holding such a little hand. He missed having someone so wide-eyed, innocent and full of joy and promise look up at him the way Charlie did. He'd missed out on the baby talk and the butchered words.

He'd missed out on so much of Simon growing up, but he rarely spent time wallowing in the grief of that. At least he had his son now. At least Simon found him and Jack got to raise his kid for the second part of his life.

"What are we doing here again, Mom?" Hannah asked, running her fingers along white PVC pipe.

"We're picking out a backsplash for the kitchens."

"What's a backsplash?" Hayley asked.

"Tiles that go on the wall of a kitchen above the counters and below the cabinets," Jack added.

Hannah couldn't keep her hands to herself. Now she was stroking one of those bright green microfiber carwash gloves. "We have that in our kitchen."

"Hannah, stop touching everything," Bianca said, steering her daughter toward the center of the aisle with a gentle hand on her shoulder.

Jack snorted. Even when Simon was twelve, he was often doing things he wasn't even aware of, like tapping his pen or chewing on something. Kids were so lost in their own thoughts, their brains and bodies often disconnected.

"Down here," he said, turning right. "Aisle forty-three."

Bianca nodded, and she and the girls followed him and Charlie.

"My hold your hand, Jack," Charlie said, giving Jack's hand a squeeze and smiling up at him. "My like it."

Jack's chest tightened, and he grinned down at Charlie. "My like it too, buddy."

"He replaces *I* with *me* and *my*," Bianca said, chuckling. "The girls spoke in the third person. *Hannah no like this. Haywee want cwackers.* But Charlie is his own person, and he speaks in his very own way."

"That's right, little man," Jack said, ruffling Charlie's hair with his free hand. "My think you talk great. My can understand you just fine."

"He is advanced for his age when it comes to language," Hannah pointed out. "It's because he has two older sisters."

Bianca glanced at Jack, and he smiled back at her. "I'm guessing she's heard you say that once or twice, huh?"

Bianca snorted. "Once or twice."

"Need to pick out what kind of knobs you want on the interior doors, and the lighting. Fan of recessed myself, not those ugly-ass sun lights from the seventies."

"What's ugly-ass?" Hayley asked. "Lighting? How can lights be ugly-ass?"

"He means not nice-looking," Hannah replied. "But he did it with a *swear.* Like he doesn't like the lights that look like a big sunshine in the center of the ceiling. But I don't know what *recessed* lighting is." She turned to Jack. "Is that anything like recess at school?"

Jack shook his head. "Not quite. It means the lights are up in the ceiling rather than attached to it." Understanding nodded back at him in the form of two cheeky six-year-olds.

They made it to the backsplash tiles. At the speed of two-year-old legs, it'd probably taken them a good ten minutes.

"All right, let's get picking." He reached for his notebook and pencil from the back pocket of his jeans, releasing Charlie's hand, much to the protestation of his new best friend. "Sorry, little man, I need to do some writing."

Charlie's pout gutted him.

Shit.

"Here." He scooped Charlie up into his arms and passed off the pencil and pad to Hannah. "You write down what I tell you to, okay?"

She nodded.

"What about me?" Hayley asked, a pout similar to her brother's forming on her face.

Oh, for Christ's sake.

He took the book back from Hannah, ripped it into two, found a pencil lying on the desk of the home-reno station and handed it to Hayley. "There, now you each get one. Both of you write down what I tell you. This way we won't have any mistakes."

Or they'd write down different things, and he'd be left guessing which one was the correct one.

The girls smiled, poised, their pencils at the ready.

"I like these tiles," Bianca said from down the aisle. He followed her, Charlie now on his shoulders, the girls right beside him, ready to take down notes. He hadn't even asked if they knew how to write or spell. He'd have to get the employee to email him a copy of everything they were going to order.

Bianca was standing in front of a sample section of small, transparent green glass tiles.

He couldn't hide the flare of his eyes.

"A lot of work?" she asked, obviously reading his mind.

He nodded. "The smaller the tile, the more finicky. Let's find a bigger tile. Even just these nice clear big ones would look nice. They have a bit of a blue hue to them."

Bianca glanced over and read the description. "Morning mist blue in glossy glass."

He shrugged. "I like my morning mist blue. What about you?"

She snorted. "I like these tiles. Can you do that?" she asked with a glance his way.

"I can do that."

A hand on Jack's arm had him turning around to find a woman, probably in her early seventies, smiling at him.

"Can I help you?" he asked, hoping she just needed directions to the checkouts and not his expertise on all things home renovation. He did have to get to work on the house today. Thankfully, Max was already there laying the rest of the flooring in the basement suites.

The woman shook her head, green eyes twinkling, brown hair with strands of silver swishing. "No, I'm okay, thank you. I just wanted to say what a beautiful family you have here. And you're such a good father, really hands-on with the kids. It's so nice to see."

Jack's mouth opened, his tongue struggling to form words. "I ... uh ... we're ... uh."

Bianca's hand on his other arm grounded him, and he shut his mouth. "Thank you. He is really great with the kids. I'm lucky."

As if she'd just said she was pregnant with *his* twins, he stared down at her, full of shock.

The woman smiled again, nodded at Bianca and then wandered away.

"Mom, who was that?" Hannah asked. "Why'd she say Jack's our dad?"

Jack released the breath that felt like fire in his lungs.

"Jack's not our dad," Hayley added, looking up at Bianca curiously before focusing her attention on a scuff on the floor and kicking at it with her sneakers. "Though at least he lives here. Our dad's back in Palm Springs with Opal, Garnet and Emerald. Doesn't care much about us anymore. He's got new twins to love."

Holy. Fuck.

"Jesus," Jack murmured.

Bianca's face was stony as she cupped her daughter by the back of the head and drew her against her mother's body. "Your father loves you guys. He's just really busy. You remember how crazy life was when Charlie was a baby? Well, times that by two."

"Yeah, but why'd that lady think Jack was our dad?" Hannah asked.

"Because we're all here together and we *look* like a family. And he *is* good with you kids. Defused your argument over the notebook and pencil, and look at how happy Charlie is up there. That's all. It was just a harmless mistake, but I think we should take it as a compliment instead, don't you?" She ran her hand over the back of Hayley's head. "I mean, she called us beautiful. No sense letting a compliment like that go waste, right?"

Hayley blinked up at her mother.

Jack stood there, paralyzed.

"We're almost done here, and then let's go do something fun, okay? I'll take the day off work, and maybe we can go to a splash pad or that funky food truck down on the water for lunch. What do you think?" Was she deliberately avoiding Jack's gaze? It sure felt like it. She was looking only at her daughters. Though they were her main concern right now, so maybe she wasn't avoiding his eyes but just being the awesome mother he already knew her to be and giving her children her undivided attention when they seemed to need it the most.

"Can we go get lunch at the food truck *and* go to the splash pad?" Hannah asked.

"Spash pad!" Charlie cheered, jostling on Jack's shoulders. He needed to be careful. He was usually okay with most movements and heavy lifting, but once in a while, his back injury would show itself and he'd have to take it easy for a few days and schedule an appointment with his chiropractor. And Charlie bopping and jerking around up there might be one of those instances.

Bianca nodded. "Sure. We can do both."

The kids cheered, though the girls' enthusiasm was far less genuine than Charlie's.

Bianca kissed Hayley's crown. "Let's finish here, and then we'll take Jack back to the house and go grab your bathing suits and stuff at home."

The twins' brows narrowed in scary synchronicity.

"Jack's not coming with us to lunch or the splash pad?" Hayley asked with sadness. "We want him to come."

"I've gotta go to work, honey," Jack said, feeling her sadness and wanting to play hooky from work like Bianca and spend time with these tremendous, hilarious kids. Even thirty minutes with them had his heart feeling fuller than it had in ages.

Hannah blinked at him. "You're coming home for dinner, though, right?"

Home?

Bianca went to speak, but he cut her off. "I'd be happy to come for dinner if your mom's okay with it?" He glanced Bianca's way, the startled look in her eyes reminding him of the first time they hooked up. It was a good look on her. Flushed cheeks, bright, sparkly eyes. Turned her from gorgeous to drop-dead fucking stunning.

"I ... sure," she finally said. "I mean, it's just broccoli quiche. I have broccoli I need to use up, eggs and milk in the fridge. Need to go grocery shopping tomorrow."

The girls groaned. "A fridge scramble?" Hannah asked, her nose wrinkling in displeasure.

Jack chuckled.

Bianca rolled her eyes. "Yes, a fridge scramble."

Hayley rolled her eyes Jack's way, her tone bored. "A

fridge scramble is when Mom takes all the veggies from the fridge that are going to go bad and cuts them up and puts them in a pie plate with eggs and cheese. She uses a fancy name like *quiche* or *fruity ta-ta*, but we know what it really is."

"It's *frittata*," Bianca corrected.

Still laughing, Jack tickled Charlie's knees, making the little boy giggle. "A fridge scramble sounds delicious. My mom used to make something very similar before grocery shopping days. Waste not, want not, right?"

"I'd rather just have hot dogs," Hannah murmured.

"I hope she at least puts sundried tomatoes in it," Hayley whispered to her sister. "That just makes the whole thing taste like tomatoes, which I kind of like."

"Come on, my picky eaters, let's pick some backsplash tiles and lighting fixtures so Jack can get to work and away from this circus." Bianca waved at an employee who was passing by, and the man with the blue apron and bald patch on his head was smiling as he headed their way.

"Jack, you'll come for fridge scramble?" Hayley asked again, tugging on his shirt.

He glanced down at her and smiled, pinning Charlie's leg beneath his arm so he could run his hand over Hayley's soft brown hair. "I wouldn't miss a fridge scramble with you guys for anything."

And that was the God's honest truth of it.

15

BIANCA CHECKED on the quiche in the oven, realized it needed about ten more minutes and closed the oven door.

From the moment Jack walked in the door after work, freshly showered, smelling delicious and looking even better, her three beasts had glommed onto him, lugging him upstairs.

All she'd heard over the last thirty minutes was giggling.

Should she go check on Jack? Make sure her children hadn't tied him up and gotten into her makeup? Or worse, that the girls hadn't tied both Jack *and* Charlie up and were giving them makeovers against their wills.

Quietly, she ascended the stairs, the echoes of childish giggling drawing her to her children's room. She saw Jack's big socked feet first.

He was splayed out on the kids' bedroom floor while one twin did something to his hand, the other twin was near his face with a Barbie comb, and Charlie was sitting on Jack's lower back, raking his nails up and down.

"What is going on here?" Bianca asked, entering the room cautiously.

"Spa day," Hannah said, a Crayola washable marker in her hand, the tip covering Jack's nails and fingertips in purple marker. "It's just pretend nail polish, Mom. Will wash right off."

"And I'm getting all the tangles out of his beard," Hayley said with a proud grin. Jack's beard was flat over the carpet, and Hayley alternated between petting it and brushing it.

"And what's Charlie up to?" she asked, worried about Jack's back injury and her unpredictable, bouncy child sitting atop him.

"The best thing ever," Jack murmured. "Haven't had my back scratched like this in ages. Makes the manicure and beard-petting worth it." His eyes were closed, and his lips curled up into a placid, dreamy smile.

"You're okay with him sitting on your back like that?" She knelt down next to Jack's head, unable to resist the urge to touch him as well. She stroked his head. Luckily, her children didn't gasp or look at her funny.

"I told him I hurt my back so he needed to be gentle. Seems to understand."

"Jack owie back, Mama," Charlie said, his brows narrowing in concern. "My be cowful. No hurt Jack." He went from scratching to petting. "Jack owie. My mooch it." Charlie hinged at the hips and kissed the center of Jack's back. "All bettah, Jack?"

"Like a million bucks, little man," Jack said, opening his eyes and pinning them on Bianca. "Just still be careful, okay?"

"Okay, Jack." Charlie went back to scratching Jack's back, and Bianca was pretty sure she heard the big bad biker moan.

"Can Jack come for dinner every night, Mom?" Hannah asked, switching from purple felt pen to pink. "This is fun."

"Jack's a busy man, kids. And he has his own place. I'm sure by the end of the day he's tired and doesn't always want to spend the evenings being climbed like a tree by you three little squirrels." She tipped her gaze down to his, only to be met with a brow lift.

"Doing a lot of assuming there, *Mom*. Maybe I'd love to come for dinner every night?"

She sat back on her heels. "You would?"

His blue eyes twinkled. "Depends how good tonight's dinner is."

She swatted him playfully on the shoulder.

"Even though we're picky eaters, our mom is a really great cook," Hayley said. "She makes *amazing* pancakes. Like the bestest pancakes in the entire world. They're purple because of all the blueberries." She craned her neck to look Jack in the eyes. "Have you ever had purple pancakes?"

"I have not," he said with amusement.

"You'll have to sleep over one night and we can have pancakes for breakfast, unless one night we can convince Mom to do breakfast for dinner," Hayley went on.

"I *love* breakfast for dinner," Hannah added. "Sausages, bacon, pancakes, scrambled eggs, hash browns. I don't understand why we can't just have breakfast food for every meal. Who says we *have* to eat that food only in the mornings? Who makes up these rules?"

"Good question," Jack said. "I often have breakfast for dinner, and it's because it's so darn delicious."

Hannah's eyes went wide. "See, Mom? Jack gets it. Did you make up these crazy rules?"

"I think Nana did," Hayley said. "Nana says too much bacon will hurt Papa's heart, so she only lets him have it once a week. That's probably where all these breakfast-food-only-for-breakfast rules came from."

Jack snorted and glanced back up at Bianca. "Was it you or your mother who created such ridiculous rules?"

"I plead the fifth," she said, sticking out her tongue.

"Can we have breakfast for dinner tomorrow night, Mom?

And Jack can come home for dinner again and we can show him how amazing your purple pancakes are." Hannah's hopeful gaze melted Bianca's heart. She knew her children would like Jack. What was there to not like about the man? But just how *much* they'd taken to him made her heart close to bursting. It also meant that when he left at the end of the summer, it'd be hard on all of them, not just her.

Should she shut this down now? Save her children more heartbreak and the loss of another man in their life? Or should she just let them know that Jack was only around for the summer and then he'd be leaving? Prepare their little hearts for his inevitable departure.

"Mom?" Hannah's hand on her shoulder jostled Bianca from her thoughts. "Can Jack come for dinner tomorrow night?"

"And can we have breakfast for dinner?" Hayley added.

"Breckfass for dinnah!" Charlie cheered, bouncing on Jack's back.

"*Oof*," Jack said. "Careful, little man."

"Shaw-wee, Jack." Charlie leaned forward again and kissed the center of Jack's back. "You okay now, Jack?"

"All better, thanks. Just no bouncing, okay?"

"Okay." Charlie was now kneading Jack's back like it was bread dough.

"Can he, Mom?" Hannah asked, not willing to let this Jack joining their dinners or breakfast for dinner thing go.

"We can have breakfast for dinner tomorrow night," Bianca said. "I'll add what we need to my shopping list."

The kids cheered.

"And what about Jack?" Hayley asked.

Glancing down at Jack, she was met with another thick lifted brow. Her children's gazes remained hopeful.

"Just so everyone is clear here, Jack is welcome to have dinner with us as often as he likes. But just so you kids know,

Jack is leaving at the end of the summer, okay?" She was telling their hearts just as much as she was telling her own: *Don't get too attached.*

The searing look she got from the man being tortured by her children made her insides do painful somersaults.

"Where you going, Jack?" Hannah asked.

"I have a place in Mexico I go to for the fall and winter," he said, not taking his eyes off Bianca.

"But then you're back here in Seattle for the spring and summer?" Hayley asked.

He nodded. "Yeah."

The twins smiled at each other almost wickedly.

"Cool. So you have dinner here when you're in Seattle. That solves that." Hayley's nod was so cut-and-dried, Bianca was almost ready to go along with the plan.

"But we also can't get upset with Jack if he decides he's had enough of you or is too tired from work and chooses not to come over for dinner one night." The timer for her oven and the quiche downstairs started to beep, and she stood up. "You three are a lot. Little energy-zappers. Sometimes I wish I could not turn up for dinner."

"That's when you do *plates of little things*, right, Mom?" Hannah asked.

Jack's look was all curiosity.

"When Mom doesn't want to cook, she makes us *plates of little things*," Hayley went on. "It's the best meal ever. Cheese cubes, pickles cut into circles, pepperoni sticks cut the size of our pinky fingers." She held up her pinky in case Jack wasn't sure what she meant. "Crackers, apple slices, cucumber slices, PB&J sandwiches cut into like a million little squares and then she puts toothpicks in them so we can pick them up and pop them into our mouths by the toothpick. It's awesome. I wish we could have *plates of little things* or *breakfast for dinner* every night."

It's amazing how differently children and parents see things. Bianca made *plates of little things* when she was too tired to cook or they were low on food in the fridge and she needed to get to the grocery store. She felt like a failure of a mom giving her kids that for dinner because it wasn't warm or homemade, but her kids loved it.

Her heart felt lighter knowing she wasn't scarring them for life, and the softness in Jack's eyes said he understood exactly what she was feeling at that moment.

The oven timer downstairs beeped again. "Crap! Gotta go."

"You won't get tired of us, will you, Jack?" Hannah asked as Bianca left the bedroom.

"Can't possibly see how that could ever happen," Jack said blandly, his sarcasm completely lost on the children as they cheered again.

"Do you have any pets, Jack?" Hayley asked.

"I kind of have a cat. Her name is Bob."

"That's a weird name for a girl cat," Hayley said. Bianca couldn't even see her child, but she could hear the nose wrinkle in her voice.

No weirder than a father named Ashley.

"Can we meet your cat? Mom says we're too busy and not old enough or responsible enough for a pet. I'd even just like a fish. I wouldn't take it out to pet it. I'd just pet it in its bowl."

Oh Hannah, and that's why you do not have a pet yet.

Bianca pulled the quiche out of the oven, went to the foot of the stairs and called up to the rest of them. "Five minutes until dinner. Don't forget to wash your hands. Girls, help your brother wash his hands, please."

"Okay, Mom!" all four of them yelled down at her.

Smiling, she rolled her eyes and returned to the kitchen. Even if it was only temporary, seeing her children embrace Jack and having him in her home made Bianca happy. She was fine with the no-strings fling they had, but she was also enjoying it turning into more.

BIANCA SNATCHED a pillow off the couch and slapped it against her face to smother the cry that rushed up her throat as she pushed her pelvis harder against Jack's face and the orgasm tore through her.

The children were in bed and asleep. She'd ducked outside, smoked a J while Jack did the dishes. When she returned, feeling relaxed she was tackled by a big bad biker with a sexy body and wicked tongue.

He'd thrown her to the couch, pulled off her capris and panties, sunk down to his knees on the floor and set up camp.

She'd been helpless to his strength and determination. Not that she would have fought him anyway.

He'd already made her come once, and now he was making her come again.

From her center outward, the climax had her body quivering, her fingers bunching in the pillow and her mouth open, noises she never even knew she was capable of making bubbling up from the back of her throat.

She spasmed when he pushed one finger into her anus, having gathered enough of her wetness to provide easy passage.

She groaned when he curled that finger deep inside her.

"Jack," she mumbled into the pillow. "Too sensitive."

Just like that, his finger was gone, and so was his mouth.

With her orgasm having subsided, she pulled the pillow away and looked up at him with worried curiosity.

But she need not worry. He was merely gathering her clothes before he scooped her up over his shoulder and carried her up the stairs.

She dug down deep to supress any kind of giggle worming its way up her throat, and she managed to do it until they reached her bedroom door and he bit her butt cheek.

Though her giggle was less of a giggle and more of a yelp, which he only made her repeat when he slapped her bare ass.

Into her room he powered on his long, strong legs. He tossed her to her bed hard enough to make her bounce. He closed and locked her door, his eyes flicking to the wall of mirrors that made up one side of her room when he turned around. "That's kinky," he said, the blue in his eyes practically gleaming.

"My closet," she said with a sigh. "I love how big it is, but I don't *always* want to see myself. It's a bit much with all the mirrors, I'll be honest."

He shook his head. "No fucking way, baby. We have to take advantage of these." Gripping her ankles, he contorted her on the bed until she was on all fours, her ass facing the mirrors. He palmed her ass cheeks and pulled them apart. "Gonna take you here tonight." Fingers slid between her slippery folds. "Look how fucking pink and beautiful."

She trembled from his touch. She was still sensitive from the last climax.

"Look, Bianca. Watch me touch you."

Craning her neck around, she took in what he was doing. Watching his fingers slip in and out of her. He pressed his thumb against her anus and pushed in. She groaned when he moved it deeper.

"You got that favorite toy around here somewhere?"

She'd told him about Jason Momoa, so she knew what he meant.

Nodding with eagerness, she pointed toward her nightstand drawer, which was locked.

"Key's under the lamp," she said. "I have a very *curious, boundary-challenged* two-year-old."

He went about retrieving Jason from her nightstand. "Preventative or a lesson learned?"

"Lesson learned," she said dryly.

Jack made an amused noise in his throat. "I bet there's a story there."

That was an understatement. Only a few months ago, while Lauren was over for coffee one afternoon, Charlie, being the devious little snoop that he was, got into her nightstand, found Jason and came downstairs chewing on it. Yes, she thoroughly washed her toy after every use, hot soapy water and whatever else the manual said to do, but it was still terrifying to see her child using her husband substitute as a chew-toy. She couldn't blame him though. He was teething, and it did have the same silicone texture and material as his chew ring.

But that didn't stop her from nearly having a heart attack seeing him gnawing on Jason like that, or from ordering a new nightstand with a lock and key five minutes later.

Jack held Jason out to her. "Special trick to this fella?"

She shook her head, pushed up to her knees and turned Jason on.

Jack stripped.

Watching him take off his clothes in the mirror was like having her own personal striptease or peep show. She grew wetter just watching him reveal another patch of tanned, tattooed skin. He was muscular without being bulky, with thick thighs, a soft, wiry beard and the bluest eyes she'd ever seen. He was a bad-boy biker, correction, *her* bad-boy biker, and he had a good heart and a wicked tongue.

"Show me what you do with that," he said, putting one knee into the bed and smacking her ass. "Better yet, let *me* put it in. You tell me when I'm hitting the right spot." He took

Jason from her, and she fell back down to her hands, swallowing and quivering in anticipation of what was to come.

She felt the vibration of it first against the outside lips of her pussy. He was teasing her. Running the head of the toy through her folds. Lubricating it, hitting her clit randomly and making her leg twitch. When he finally pushed it inside, she moaned, and her back bowed.

She'd already turned on the suction, and when it latched onto her clit, her entire body tightened.

"You ever watch yourself do this, baby?" he asked, drawing some of her wetness from between her thighs up her crease, his finger swirling it around her tight hole.

She shook her head. She was having a hard time keeping her eyes open. She wanted to squeeze her eyes shut, tighten her muscles and let the pleasure take hold of her.

"Watch me, baby."

"I'm trying," she mewled, feeling another orgasm brewing in her belly.

"You got a hand mirror around here?"

"Bathroom, second drawer." As wonderful as it felt, when he pulled his finger free from her anus, the reprieve from the overwhelming pleasure was welcomed.

He returned in seconds and handed it to her. "That way you can watch, but you don't have to turn around."

"Always thinking about my needs." She wiggled her butt.

His slap wasn't entirely unexpected, but it did have her yelping. "Of course, baby. You should know by now your needs are all I care about."

Oh, if only that were truly true.

Not that she didn't love the time she had with Jack, but he'd quickly burrowed his way beneath her skin, and she knew that when the time came for him to leave, it was going to hurt. She needed him more than she wanted to admit. He'd brought her back to life. Jack had given her a taste of what it was like to have a man in her life that cared for her. A man who showed her respect and reminded her that she wasn't just a mom struggling to keep her head above water for her kids. She was a woman. A woman with desires. With passions and a libido that didn't disappear when her marriage ended.

But, since day one, she agreed not to fall in love with him. And she was determined to keep that promise. Especially since he'd delivered on his promises, at least so far.

What he was doing with his fingers, though, was making that not falling in love thing more and more impossible.

"You got lube, baby?" he asked, his finger curling inside her ass while Jason went to town on her clit and pussy.

"Nightstand."

A true contortionist, she watched him in the hand mirror pivot to get the lube from the drawer while still pleasuring her. He didn't miss a beat.

The squirting noise and cool drip of gel down her crease had her shivering. He withdrew his finger and pushed in two, scissoring them back and forth to stretch her. The pleasure from that movement made her body buck.

"Easy, girl," he said, stroking her butt like a cowboy might pet a horse. "Easy, girl."

Glaring at him in the mirror, she attempted to swat him in the stomach, but he deflected her strike. "My wild filly, do I need to tame you the old-fashioned way? Ride you until I break you?"

Even with the weird animal-cowboy innuendos, the idea of him "riding her until he broke her" had her pulse racing. Was it wrong she wanted to say "yes, please"?

"I'm far from a filly," she retorted. "More like a brood-mare. You and my foals came down those stairs earlier like Captain Thunderhooves and his band of wild ponies."

He snorted and his lips twitched, his smile doing a crappy job of not breaking through. "Captain Thunderhooves?"

"You're such a stomper. Captain Thunderhooves. That's the only way to describe you."

Drawing his finger up her slippery crease, he leaned over and whispered in her ear, "I'm sure you can think of other ways to describe me besides ..."

"Captain Thunderhooves?"

His teeth snagged her ear. "Mhmm."

Even through the unyielding pleasure of Jack's finger sliding between her cheeks and Jason between her legs, she struggled to not laugh. "I'm afraid that's the most accurate way to describe you. Can't think of anything else."

Reaching between her thighs, he pressed the buttons for Jason, increasing his speed.

Her body stiffened and jerked beneath his.

"Diabolical," she whispered.

"I'll take that over Captain *What's-his-hooves*."

His lips touched her neck before he retreated behind her once again, gripped her hip with one hand and rested his cockhead against her tight ring with the other.

"Godlike," she said on a shiver.

"Better." He pressed gently.

She pushed out with her muscles, took deep breaths and focused on the Jason inside her and on her clit. It'd been years since she'd had anal sex. Years. Over ten for sure.

There was such a thing as muscle memory, but she knew there'd also be discomfort, which was why she squeezed Jason inside her, tilted her hips so he hit her clit better and breathed deep.

"You okay?" he asked, pausing.

Even with all the lube, there was a burn there. But she was tough. She could power through. She knew what lay on the other side was exquisite pleasure.

Squeezing her eyes shut, Bianca nodded. "Keep going."

"Watch, Bianca. Watch me take you. Use the mirror. I'll stop and pull out at any point, but watching me disappear inside you, fuck, baby, it turns me on like nothing else."

She opened her eyes and looked into the mirror. He'd angled them on the bed just right that she had a perfect view of his cock disappearing inside her ass. And it really fucking turned her on.

"See. How hot is that?" He pushed in a little further.

"Really hot," she breathed.

"You okay?"

"Yeah, keep going."

"Almost there. You're so fucking tight. Not gonna last long. Your ass, around my cock, sexiest fucking thing I've seen or felt in my whole fucking life."

She knew when he was completely seated inside her. He let out a sigh of his own, and his hands relaxed on her hips.

"You okay if I start to move?"

"You better," she said with a laugh, glancing back at him in the mirror smiling.

"Gimme that," he said, reaching for the mirror.

She handed it to him and turned her head to look over her shoulder. He held the mirror in front of his chest, tilted downward so she could see everything he saw.

"How fucking hot is that?" His eyes tipped up to hers. Blue fire burned hot back at her.

"Fuck me, Jack. Now. Hard."

His nostrils flared, the mirror landed on the bed beside her, his fingers found her hips again and he started to move.

The muscle memory and how good it felt to be so full came flooding back to her, and her nails dug into the duvet cover to keep herself from detonating too quickly. Jack knew how to move. He had sexy-flexy hips, a killer rhythm and endurance for days.

She wasn't sure which one of them had the higher sex drive, him or her. Or maybe they were just equally randy.

"Jesus fuck, baby." His words came out in a strained groan. "So fucking tight."

"Jack ..."

If she flopped to the bed and ground against Jason, she'd come instantly. The mattress would press the suction part right onto her clit, and she'd potentially pass out from the pleasure.

"Not gonna last, Bianca ... you close?" His grip on her hips tightened.

"Can be."

"Then be, baby. Do what you gotta do. Tell me what I can do."

"Just don't stop." She dropped down to her belly. He followed her, never ceasing, his rhythm constant.

Jason's suction power gripped her clit and refused to let go. The angle of Jack inside her changed, and she couldn't even wait for the countdown to launch. Her body exploded.

Starbursts and bright lights lit up behind her closed eyelids as the pleasure streaked through her, not only from her clit but from her pussy, her ass and even her nipples as they rubbed against the raised threading on her bedspread.

Her muscles tensed, fingers bunched in the duvet and toes curled until the crescendo was reached and everything started to relax. Warmth flowed into her limbs until they became pliant. Like stepping into a warm bath after a long run or a cold walk in the rain.

Jack grunted above her, stilled, and she felt him find his release inside her. His teeth scraped her shoulder, followed by his tongue and finally his lips. When he finished, his sigh ruffled the hair against her ear, and he collapsed on top of her. "I'll get off you in a sec, baby. Just need to gather my wits." He spread his hands along hers and laced their fingers together.

She squeezed his hand and giggled. "You're not that heavy."

"You okay?" He kissed her shoulder again, the heavy thumping of his heart against her back mimicking his ragged breathing.

"Better than okay," she whispered.

Her cheek was against the bed, and he lifted up slightly, hovering over her. "Give me that mouth." He didn't wait for her to give it to him though. He just took it. Which she preferred. He took her mouth with a fervor she felt right down to her toes. His tongue pushed between her lips and explored her mouth, tangoed with her tongue. When he finally broke the kiss, they were both breathless again. "Jesus, Bianca, you are something else. You know that?"

She smiled. "So are you."

Squeezing her fingers before pulling his hands away, he gently lifted off her and slid out. "Come on, baby. Let's have a shower." He slapped her ass. "I might have one more fuck in me before I need to sleep. Gotta wash first."

Smiling like a lovestruck buffoon, she lazily peeled herself off the bed and followed him, loving the view of the naked man in front of her, comfortable in her home and running a shower for the both of them.

How easily had he slid into their lives? Into her heart, her home, her bed.

Would he be able to slide back out just as easily, or would his departure leave a wake of broken hearts big and small, as she was beginning to fear?

16

It was the weekend of Bianca's brother's wedding. Friday night—tonight—was the rehearsal dinner, and tomorrow was the big to-do at some fancy rentable garden complete with an outdoor pavilion for the reception.

For the past three weeks, Jack had been having dinner at Bianca's nearly every night. Some nights he worked late on the house and missed dinnertime—which he hated. He loved those kids. Loved their energy, their quick wit and how wide-eyed and curiously they viewed the world. The girls' questions were endless.

Precocious and sassy Hannah and Hayley were double trouble and two people he never wanted to get into an argument with. Not because he figured he'd lose but because it would never end.

And Charlie was the life of the party. The kid growled almost as much as he talked, and his laugh was equal parts sinister as it was hilarious. He lived for laughs and smiles and offered up just as many as he sought.

Last Sunday night, Bianca invited Simon, Jared and Casey for dinner as well. It was Jack's first big family dinner where he sat at the head of the table, like many patriarchs do, while Bianca sat at the other end, smiling at him lovingly as their table of children young, old and "adopted" got along like they'd known each other for decades.

He'd never had a dinner like that before, with so much family and love around one table. The amount of pure joy he felt watching the people he cared about most laugh over barbecued chicken and potato salad still warmed him when he thought about it weeks later.

Simon and Jared came bearing big news that night too. News Jack already knew about, as he'd gone with them to check out the place, but he was no less excited to celebrate again. They'd closed an offer on a house and were set to move in September 1. They also seemed to have "adopted" Casey and were taking her in to live with them. They wanted to help her get her GED and give her a family. In exchange for free rent, she would clean for them and help out with meals, as both men worked a lot.

Casey was all over it and excited because they said she could decorate her room however she wanted—even paint it.

Hannah suggested purple with unicorn decals, and Hayley suggested aquamarine with mermaid decals. And of course, Charlie had to add his two cents with a growl and a scowl and say "geen dino-saw."

Jack worked only until four today, then headed straight to Bianca's, where he would shower and they would get ready together. He hadn't spent the night yet, even though the kids kept asking him to, but they did seem to know that Jack and Bianca were more than just friends.

Max and Isaac had helped out today too, but only Max was coming to the rehearsal dinner since he was dating the bride's sister. It'd be nice to have a friendly face at the table, seeing as everyone else would be a stranger. A stranger who undoubtedly knew more about him than he did about any of them.

If things got weird or awkward, he'd just go sit with the kids. He'd already decided that. He wouldn't abandon Bianca and the kids, but he wasn't going to pretend to be somebody he wasn't just to fit in with a crowd he wasn't sure he belonged with.

Exhausted from an early start and a tedious day spent doing drywall on the laundry room, he parked his bike in front of Bianca's house only to see the door fly open and all three children run out to greet him wearing big smiles. None of them had shoes on, and Charlie wasn't even wearing a shirt. His toddler tummy stuck out over his denim shorts, the waistband of his diaper peeking up over top.

"Hi, Jack!" Hannah said with a huge grin, a sneaky grin.

He swung his leg over his bike and peeled off his helmet. "Hi, Hannah." He lifted a brow, his gaze flicking between the two girls. "What's going on?"

Their matching brown eyes gleamed. "Nothing," the said in stereo.

"Mama buy you new shirt, Jack," Charlie said. "It bwoo. My like bwoo. It my fave-it color."

The girls rolled their eyes.

"You ruined the surprise, Charlie," Hayley said, shaking her head.

Picking Charlie up like a sack of potatoes, Jack swung the little guy up onto his shoulders and followed the girls into the townhouse. "She bought me a shirt, huh? What, does she think all my shirts are garbage?"

The air inside the house was cool, particularly because the air outside was trying to roast the Earth's inhabitants. He toed off his work boots without putting Charlie down, then continued on into the house after the twins.

Bianca was in the kitchen adding ice to the blender and a

bunch of different berries. "How was your day, dear?" she asked with a sexy smile.

"Long," he said blandly.

She hit the button on the blender, and it pulverized the ice and fruit in a nerve-grinding whirr until everything blended together to create a purple smoothie.

"This is just to tide us over until dinner," she said, pouring five glasses. "My parents are hosting the rehearsal dinner, and my mother always goes over the top for food. We'll probably get sent home with containers of leftovers."

"Don't spill any of that on my head," Jack said as he followed Bianca's hand and the cup she gave to Charlie, who was still on his shoulders.

"Me won't," Charlie said, patting Jack's head.

He took a sip of the smoothie, and his whole body cooled down. Fuck, that was good. "So I hear I have a new shirt?" If he'd been alone, he would have downed the smoothie in two gulps, but he was with children and needed to set a good example, so he took sips, his stomach grumbling as the flavors burst across his tongue.

Bianca's cheeks pinked. "You don't have to wear it. Either tonight or tomorrow or not at all. We were at the mall today because I had to find new dress shoes for the girls, as they've grown out of the ones they fit in May, and we saw this shirt on the mannequin at the men's store, and I thought it would go nice with your eyes. Like I said, you don't have to wear it. I can return it. I'm not trying to change you or tell you your wardrobe sucks."

She was rambling.

Why was she rambling?

He hadn't even been paying attention to the twins or the fact that they'd taken off upstairs, but when two thunder-hooving ponies came galloping back down, he realized they'd disappeared.

"Here's the shirt, Jack," Hannah said, holding it up. "Isn't it beautiful? I love this blue."

Hayley clasped her hands together and tucked them beneath her chin, batting her lashes. "It goes with your dreamy blue eyes."

Jack's brows shot up, and his gaze pivoted to Bianca. "Did you say I had *dreamy blue eyes*?

"I said you have *blue* eyes. I don't know where they got the dreamy part from."

He took the shirt from Hannah and held it up. It was a nice shirt. A deep, dark blue button-up with tiny white polka-dots. It was short-sleeved, which was a bonus, and seemed well made. The fabric was soft.

"What do you think, Jack?" Hayley asked, wide-eyed and eager for an answer.

"I'll try it on after my shower, and if it fits, I'll definitely wear it. It's a very nice shirt. Thank you."

The girls cheered.

"Yay! That's good, because we got you like four other shirts, too," Hannah said with a laugh.

Fast enough to give him whiplash, he faced Bianca again, but before he could say anything, a damp, icy feeling began to work its way down his scalp and into his ear.

"My uh-oh," Charlie said above him. "My mess. *Big* mess on Jack head. Mama clean it, pwease?"

Squeezing his eyes shut and breathing deep, Jack crouched down so Bianca could pull Charlie from his shoulders. The little guy's face and chest were purple. Jack didn't want to see what his head looked like.

"You needed to shower anyway, right?" Hannah asked with a shrug. "Now you just have to wash your hair a little extra long."

"And it'll smell like berries," Hayley added with a giggle.

"Extra shirts are on your bed with my bag, I take it?" He glanced Bianca's way as he started climbing the stairs.

Sheepishly, she nodded. "I can return them," she called up to him as he ascended the stairs.

Nobody since his own mother had ever bought him clothes before. He hated clothes shopping, but he did like to look nice. Not that he had very many excuses or opportunities to dress up, but when he had to, he liked to be able to wear something that fit and made him look like less of a handyman or biker.

He hadn't wanted to say anything downstairs in front of the children, but Bianca thinking of him and buying him something even as simple as a few shirts meant a great deal.

Now, he needed to figure out a way to show her that she meant a great deal to him too. As much as he didn't want to go to this party tonight, he would. For her. For those kids downstairs that he'd grown to love so damn much in a short amount of time.

Entering her room, he spied his duffle bag with his dress clothes in it. He'd brought it over last night so he could just come straight over after work today. The rest of the shirts were all laid out next to it. Each one was soft and he knew would fit. They were also shirts he never would have thought to pick himself but liked when he saw them waiting there for him.

But first he needed to wash out all the smoothie from his hair and the drywall dust from his skin. Glancing in the wall of mirrors, he saw that indeed he had a beanie cap of smoothie, and it was still dripping down his neck and ears.

Charlie needed a sippy cup with a lid.

ONE HOUR and seventeen minutes into the family gathering that was Scott and Eva's rehearsal dinner and so far, so good. Jack was introduced to all the Dixon men, and to Bianca's relief, her brothers had behaved themselves.

Not without a healthy dose of male chest-puffing and testosterone floating in the air, but nobody's hand was crushed from a handshake, and when Bianca glanced out the window into her parents' backyard, she could see Jack smiling and laughing with Scott.

Phew.

She wasn't worried about people not liking Jack—that was nearly impossible—but she had been worried about her pigheaded brothers deciding to go all he-man on Jack and reading him the riot act for defiling their little sister.

"Mama!" Charlie's voice behind her made her jump and spin around. "My done."

Over the last week, her baby had decided he was no longer going to go to the bathroom in a diaper and refused to go anywhere but on the big people toilet.

The girls had been easy to potty-train, with M&Ms as reward incentive, but Charlie was an even bigger breeze. He wanted to "pee like Jack," as he said, not that he'd ever seen Jack pee except for when they went for a few Sunday evening walks in the woods. But that had apparently been enough of a push, and Charlie wanted to embrace the potty.

So there she stood, in her parents' downstairs bathroom, while her son grunted, groaned and made faces that turned his cheeks red.

"You wipe me," he said, holding his arms up so she could take him down off the toilet insert for children.

She lifted him down and went to wipe his butt when Charlie gasped.

"What's wrong?"

"My made snake poo. Look!"

He pointed his finger down into the toilet so far, she had to swat it away before he touched his *snake poo*.

"My go tell Jack. Hurry, Mama. Wipe my butt. My go tell Jack about my snake poo."

As he stomped his feet repeatedly in excitement, Bianca cleaned up her kid. She washed both their hands and had barely opened the door before Charlie took off out of the bathroom and out into the yard.

"Jack!" she heard her kid yell as she exited her parents' basement into their enormous, perfectly manicured backyard. "My made snake poo."

Jack was standing, talking to Liam next to the refreshment table, the words *Dirt Fish Rally, heli-fishing* and *brewery tour* floating on the air. They were talking about Scott's bachelor party last weekend, which Liam organized.

"Next time you should come," Liam said, his eyes following Charlie as he continued to race toward them.

Each man had a bottle of beer in his hand. Jack set his beer on the table, crouched down and looked directly into Charlie's eyes. "You did what, buddy?" The confusion on his face was priceless. But boy, did it warm her heart to see Jack give her kids such undivided attention. He really had taken to them, and them to him. They hated when he left and raced out to meet him when he arrived. And when he wasn't around, he was often a topic of conversation. Just like their mother was, Bianca's children were smitten with Jack.

Charlie held up his arms, and his eyes widened. "My made snake poo. Was *this* big." He held his hands almost two feet apart.

Liam's mouth split into a big smile at the same time Bianca rolled her eyes.

"He just had a big poop on the potty, and apparently, it looked like a snake. He was desperate to come out and tell you about it." Shaking her head, she ruffled her son's hair. "Is this the beginning of all the potty talk in my house?" She glanced at her brother. "I remember you and Scott made everything a bathroom joke. Is this the beginning?"

"Still do," Liam said with a snort. "And yeah, pretty much from now until forever, Charlie will look for a way to make things about the bathroom hilarious, and he will tell you about them. And if not you, someone else. Welcome to the life of having sons."

Bianca groaned.

"You pooped on the potty, little man?" Jack asked, giving Charlie his full attention again.

Charlie beamed and nodded. "A *snake* poo. *Huge*, Jack. *Huge.*" He spread his arms wide again.

Struggling not to laugh, Jack stood back up to his full height. "Good on you, buddy. High five for pooping like a big kid." He held his hand out, and Charlie wound up his arm, leapt and smacked his hand against Jack's. "I still wish people high-fived me after a good crap."

The men snorted laughs and nodded.

Charlie hopped where he stood. "My go tell Jordie and Fweddie about my snake poo." Then before Bianca could tell him to stop talking about poop, the little guy took off into the yard in search of his older cousins, who would undoubtedly find the story hilarious and wish Bianca hadn't flushed the toilet.

Liam snickered and sipped his beer. "You lucked out with Hannah and Hayley being so *proper*. Girls have potty-humor brain too. I remember you busting out the odd poop joke, B."

Bianca snagged Jack's beer off the table and took a long sip, shaking her head and making a "nuh-uh" sound in her throat. "Me? Never. I have always been a lady. Just like my daughters are ladies. Toilet jokes are beneath us." She lifted her nose in the air haughtily.

Liam snorted. "Sure."

"Quite the spread of food," Jack said. "Your mom make it all?"

"The mains, yes, but she ordered the baking from Paige's bistro," Liam said. "Mom always overdoes it though. They'll be eating leftovers for weeks."

Bianca watched as Jack's long fingers reached for a glazed donut off the top of the pile near the back of the dessert table and he brought it to his mouth, sinking his teeth into the pastry, icing catching on his lips.

"Paige makes a mean glazed donut," Liam said, oblivious to what was going on in Bianca's head.

But Jack knew.

Jack knew exactly what she was thinking.

His eyes hit hers hard, and a knowing, dirty and panty-soaking closed-mouth smile spread across his lips.

Fire ignited in Bianca's belly, and her pussy began to throb. Warmth grew in her cheeks, and she could only imagine they were growing pinker by the second. She needed to avert her gaze, but he had her transfixed. Watching his mouth as it moved with each chew. His lips, perfect, talented and oh so delicious, covered in icing, moved as he devoured the donut.

"Dude." Liam's voice broke the trance Jack held over her. "What is going on with you and my sister right now?"

Jack finished his donut, licked his thumb and reached for another one off the pile. "Nothing's going on, bro, just enjoying some of these dee-licious donuts."

Liam shook his head, his brow furrowed. "While staring at my *baby* sister all weird like. I don't like it. Stop it."

Jack didn't take his eyes off Bianca as he answered Liam. "She ain't a baby, man. Nothing about Bianca is baby-like, and I'm appreciative for that." He bit into another donut, turned to face Bianca's brother and smiled cockily at Liam as he chewed. "She's a grown woman who just happens to *love* watching me eat donuts."

Bianca had to keep herself in check. Keep herself from snorting a laugh while hiding her face in embarrassment.

That wasn't all she liked watching him eat.

"Dude, something about the way you're eating that and looking at my sister feels impure. Cut it out. I happen to love Paige's donuts, and you're making them feel dirty." Liam's brown eyes shifted back and forth between Jack and Bianca, his gaze growing increasingly frantic.

Jack's tongue swept across his bottom lip, then his top dramatically. "You mean like when I do this?"

Bianca snorted and hid her smile behind the back of her hand.

Liam grunted. "Fuck, man. Knock it off. I know you're boning my sister, and I already don't like thinking about that, but you're tainting something pure and delicious like a donut. Have a heart."

Jack finished the donut, reached for his beer from Bianca and took a long pull, finishing it. "Haven't done anything wrong, just enjoying a couple of donuts. You got a wild imagination, man." He wrapped his arm around Bianca's waist. "Want a drink, baby?"

Bianca flicked her gaze up to a feather-ruffled Liam and smiled. "I'd love a drink. And I bet you're pretty parched after those donuts."

"Very parched indeed," Jack said, squeezing her hip and leading her over to where her parents had coolers set up with pop, beer and ciders nestled in ice.

"Not cool," Liam called after them.

"I happened to think it was *very* cool," Jack said, bending down but not releasing his grasp on Bianca to get her a cider and him a bottle of water from the cooler.

"Bianca Dixon?" a voice behind her asked. She knew everybody at the party and didn't recognize the voice.

With one hand wrapped around Jack and the other wrapped around the neck of her cider, she turned to face the man. "Yes. How can I help you?"

The short, skinny guy of about thirty, with dark hair and dark hipster glasses, smiled nervously and flicked an orange manila envelope in her direction. "You've been served. Have a good night."

"What the hell?" Jack released his hold around her and lunged for the man. "Hey, what the fuck, man?"

With a shaky breath, she pulled on Jack's shoulder. "Let him go. He's just doing his job."

Growling, Jack let go of the terrified-looking man's arm. The process server ran away as fast as his wrinkly khaki-panted legs could take him.

Unable to take a deep breath for the sudden weight of a lawsuit sitting on her chest, Bianca was guided by someone—she wasn't sure who—over to a plastic lawn chair.

Looking up, she found Liam; his wife, Richelle; Atlas, Liam's best friend; and Aurora, Zak's wife—all lawyers—staring at her.

Shaking her head, she held out the envelope for one of them to take it and open it.

"It's probably Ashley suing for more custody or something," she murmured, dropping her gaze to her feet.

"No, that would have come through the lawyers," Liam said, watching as Richelle opened the envelope and pulled out the contents.

Liam, Atlas and Aurora read over Richelle's shoulder.

"You're being sued for wrongful termination and withholding payment?" Aurora asked, lifting her light brown eyes to Bianca.

What?

Now that got her attention.

"Who is Rod Penner?" Atlas asked. "You fired him and didn't pay him?"

"Shit," Jack said, pushing his fingers into his hair and taking a seat next to her with an exasperated sigh she felt in every fiber of her body. "That's the guy she hired before me. The one who stole shit, wrecked shit and was squatting in the house and bringing in hookers. I stepped in before he hit Bianca."

Aurora gasped, which drew the attention of more people around them. "And he's claiming you promised him four thousand dollars, of which you only paid him five hundred," she went on.

A few people in their enormous circle of friends knew the whole story, but for the most part, Bianca had kept the whole Rod, the contractor from hell debacle on the down-low. She was embarrassed to have been duped by him and his idiot sister in the first place.

Oh yeah, Lorene—Hannah and Hayley's piano teacher and Rod's sister—turned out to be an almost bigger piece of work than her brother. When Bianca brought up Rod and what happened, Lorene said, "This does not concern me. This is an employee-employer issue. Rod is your problem, not mine. You hired him."

She hired him because Lorene vouched for him. Lorene asked Bianca to give her down-on-his-luck brother a job. If this were a real job, Bianca definitely would have been calling the references of the employee she hired and asking them if their glowing reference was fake or not.

Needless to say, after Lorene washed her hands of Rod and Bianca's problem, Bianca washed her hands of Lorene teaching her children piano, and she made sure any and every parent she spoke with or came across knew exactly what kind of a person Lorene really was.

Bad news and bad reviews didn't just travel fast in a small town; they traveled fast in a big city like Seattle too. Lorene messed with the wrong mama bear when she turned her back on Bianca.

"Asshole didn't do the work. That's why she didn't pay him all the money," Jack said. "Did a shit job of what he did do in the ten days he worked for her." Bianca was grateful he was speaking for her because at the moment, her head was spinning, and she couldn't form words to save her life. "We paid him five hundred bucks to get gone and never come back. I said if I saw him even look at Bianca, let alone step on the property, I'd staple his tongue to his taint so he could watch me kick his ass."

Atlas lifted his chin. "I like you."

"He has no leg to stand on, does he?" Bianca asked, hitting the four lawyers standing over her with a pleading look. "I can't go to James and Justin and tell them we're being sued for wrongful termination. I can't."

"If what you say is true—" Richelle held up a hand. "Sorry, I mean, obviously, what you're saying is true, but if this is all it is, the guy is grasping at straws. He had no case, and any *good* lawyer would know that, which is why he's filing through small claims court. The process server was pomp and circumstance hired to undoubtedly scare you. At the most, this would go to arbitration, but likely the civil resolution tribunal will be assigned."

Liam made a noise in this throat. "Ol' Roddy boy didn't expect you to have a bunch of lawyers in your family though. Gonna tear this guy a new asshole so when Jack staples his tongue to his taint, all he's smelling is shit." He rubbed his hands together maniacally and took the papers from his wife. "Guy tried to hit my baby sister, scared her, took advantage of her kindness. He's going to wish he took his five Benjamins and left fucking town when we're done with him."

Jack rubbed Bianca's shoulder with his long, strong fingers. "You okay?"

She tried to swallow, but her throat was thick and raw.

Just when life was starting to get good again, when she thought the hand she'd been dealt had promise and might even win some chips, the universe threw another wild card like Rod Penner back at her.

Anticipating her needs, Jack released her shoulder, found her unopened cider on the ground next to her chair, popped the cap and handed it to her.

She took a long sip, the alcohol immediately taking off the edge and calming her nerves—somewhat.

"This is honestly an open and shut case, B," Richelle said with sympathy in her amber eyes. "This douche has no case. We'll follow up with it on Monday and handle everything from here. Don't worry about a thing. Don't let it ruin the weekend or even the rest of your night. We may need a statement of what happened, an account of what he took, what the agreement looked like, and if you have anything in writing, we'll definitely need that."

Bianca nodded as she drained nearly half her cider. "There are a few text messages between us."

"Then we'll need those."

Jack was back to rubbing her shoulder, his nimble fingers turning her tense muscles into butter. "The guy is fucking scum. Probably doesn't have a pot to piss in and now he's coming after Bianca."

Liam, Richelle and Atlas nodded.

"We'll make it right," Aurora said, turning around when Zak, her husband, approached and handed her their eight-month-old son, Dawson, who immediately started pulling on his mother's shirt. "Excuse me, I need to go feed a starving child." She took Dawson and went to go sit down.

Zak didn't leave with her though. "What's going on over

here? Not a smile among you. Everything okay?" To look at him, you'd never expect Zak to be the teddy bear that he was. Six feet four or something, red hair and two full sleeves of tattoos. He also owned a gym franchise, so his muscles had muscles.

"Old contractor suing Bianca," Liam muttered, sipping his beer. "Fucker was bringing in hookers. Took a swing at Bianca, did a shit job, and now, weeks—fuck, a couple of *months* later, he's coming back saying he was wrongfully fired and not paid what he was owed."

Zak rolled his eyes, flared his nostrils, and his cheeks became ruddy. "Scum." Just as quick as his temper had flared in defense of Bianca, it vanished, and his gaze became concerned. "You okay, B? Need Mase, Aaron and I to go have a *conversation* with him?"

If only she could say *yes*. Mason and Aaron were nearly as big as Zak. All of them were tatted up and could bench-press a small vehicle. This wouldn't be the first time they'd used their size and appearance as a form of intimidation. She'd heard stories about the three of them showing up to a custody hearing for Atlas's wife, Tessa, and scaring the crap out of Tessa's ex.

"I'd be there too," Jack said, moving his hand along her upper back. "Fucker got off easy last time 'cause Charlie was there."

Closing her eyes, Bianca shook her head. "I'd rather do things the legal way *first*, then take it where it needs to go if he pursues this further."

She should have known Jack swooping in to save the day was too good to be true. Not because he wasn't a hero and hadn't helped her, but because they'd let Rod go free.

Not only was Jack just a flash-in-the-pan romance, a summer tryst that turned into a deep love she had to keep a secret from him, but he'd only saved her from Rod that day.

Rod was still out there, still a threat. Jack stepping in had probably only angered Rod even more, and with nothing else to do but stew and plot, Rod waited until Bianca was complacent and unarmed before he came after her again with a bullshit civil suit.

Would he keep coming after her, only in different and creative ways? This time it was with a lawsuit. What would it be next time? Vandalism on the house? Arson? And with Jack leaving, she was going to be alone again. Forced to face the demon contractor on her own.

"He's desperate if he's coming after you with such a weak case," Richelle said. "We'll shut him down. Make it *all* go away. Don't worry."

"Need to make *him* go away is what is sounds like," Zak said. "A desperate man can be a dangerous one. Means he has nothing to lose."

Oh God.

The pointed end of an icicle scraped down Bianca's back.

Rod might not have anything to lose, but Bianca sure as hell did.

17

IT WAS the day of Scott and Eva's wedding, and Bianca felt like garbage. She'd barely slept at all after returning home from the rehearsal dinner. She just couldn't shut off her brain.

Rod was a plague of her own making, and even though Jack had eradicated the plague from the fourplex, it still loomed in her life. Threatening to infect again. There was no immunity, no vaccination, no antibiotic ointment to rid her world of Rod and the rash he created. The man contaminated everything he touched. He was toxic. Pure poison.

Would Rod forever be a disease? Always around, always a threat? How could she protect her family, her livelihood and herself if he was always lurking, waiting to pounce, waiting to pollute her world when her defenses were down?

The kids were up at six thirty like they always were, despite the fact that they'd gone to bed nearly three hours past their regular bedtime, and all three of them were bouncing off the walls before Bianca even had the cream poured in her coffee.

"It's wedding day!" Hannah cheered, wearing a dress-up

veil on her head, still clad in pajamas and pretending to walk down the aisle down their hallway while holding a rolled-up hand towel in her fists like a bouquet. Charlie stood at the "altar" waiting for her, wearing nothing but Paw Patrol undies, and Hayley was waiting like a reverend with a Berenstain Bears book open to a random page.

"Dearly bee loved did, we are gathered for today to see this man and this woman join in owly matrimony," Hayley began when Hannah stopped in front of her. "Charles Wayne Loxton, do you take this woman to be your wife?"

"Yup," Charlie said with a nod before pulling his underwear out of his butt crack.

"Hannah Jillian Loxton, do you take this man to be your husband?"

Hannah hummed, stroked her chin and wrinkled her face. "Charlie, do you promise to do as I say for as long as we're married?"

Charlie nodded. "Yup."

"Do you promise to make me food, take care of me when I'm sick and not eat the last of the peach and vanilla yogurt?"

Charlie nodded again. "Yup."

Hannah's head bobbed. "Okay, then, yes, I do."

"You may now kiss the bride," Hayley said, dramatically closing the book.

Hannah bent down, puckered up and closed her eyes.

"Yogurt!" Charlie exclaimed, done with the wedding and tearing off into the kitchen, where Bianca was leaning against the counter, cradling her mug of coffee and trying not to let her head explode. "My want yogurt, Mama. Peach and 'nilla."

"Charlie, you didn't kiss the bride," Hannah said, coming up behind her brother. "And you promised you wouldn't finish the peach and vanilla yogurt."

Charlie was now yanking on the front of his underwear,

but he craned his head around only enough to fix his sister with a look and go, "Nope."

A *knock knock* on the door had Bianca sighing in relief as she set her coffee down on the counter and opened the fridge to start preparing the children's breakfast.

"I'll get it!" Hayley yelled, her pony hooves thundering into the living room, her sister and brother's hooves echoing behind her.

"Jack!" All three children hollered. Then there was unrelenting chatter from the children, most of them questions, and then some kind of whining noise from Charlie followed by a, "No, Hannah, my do it."

Bianca pulled another mug down from the cupboard, poured Jack a coffee and set it on the counter. Unlike Bianca, who preferred a splash of milk and sprinkle of cinnamon in her java, Jack took his black and the stronger the better, apparently.

He appeared around the corner with Charlie on his hip. Hannah, pouting, held the hand that was supporting Charlie's butt while Hayley held his other hand.

"Good morning," he said with an amused smile before setting Charlie down on his feet. "How was the rest of your night?" He picked up his coffee mug and took a sip.

"Can we watch *Frozen*, Mama?" Hayley asked.

"Into unknown," Charlie added, which meant he wanted to watch the second *Frozen* movie.

Bianca nodded. "You turn on the television, and I'll cast it from my phone."

The kids took off into the living room, and in less than two minutes, the movie had started and she took the first deep breath she'd taken since before the process server showed up with the lawsuit.

Jack put his coffee down on the counter and moved into her, concern in his blue eyes. "Did you sleep at all?"

She shook her head, the turmoil inside her only slightly less raging because he was close. "Not much."

His hands on her hips were not nearly as reassuring or calming as she wished they were. Her head fell forward against the hard plane of his chest. "Thank you for taking the kids this morning so I can go and do bridesmaid stuff." Since everyone she'd normally leave her children with was involved in the wedding somehow, Jack offered to take the kids and occupy them until the wedding. She still couldn't believe her luck in finding such a wonderful man. He hadn't dropped out of the sky like an angel, but he might as well have.

"Anything you need. Just let me know where I need to be and when, and I'll bring them dressed, fed and ready to throw flowers and bear rings." His hands moved from her hips to her back, and he pulled her against him. "I'm also not going to let Rod fuck with your head like this. We're almost done with the fourplex, and your brother and all those other lawyers are going to nail him to the wall by his foreskin."

She tried hard not to conjure such an image. "Thank you. The kids' clothes are all laid out on the leather ottoman at the foot of my bed. If you can tame Charlie's hair, I will be forever in your debt. The girls need to be dropped off with me at one o'clock so they can get their hair done with the rest of the wedding party. Ceremony is at three, and Charlie doesn't need to be there until shortly before, or you can drop him off with me at Scott and Eva's, where we're getting ready, and he can ride in the limo with us. The men are getting ready at my parents'."

His finger under her chin had her lifting her head. The fatigue in every muscle of her body made it difficult to keep her eyelids open. "When do you have to go to Eva's?"

She glanced at the clock on the stove. It was just past seven thirty. Jack had called her at six forty-five to see how she was doing after last night, and she immediately got choked up on the phone with him, which was why he was there so early now. The man was amazing. "I need to be at Eva's at ten, I think."

"So you have time to run upstairs and close your eyes for an hour or so."

The huff of laughter out of her nose ruffled his beard hair. "I have time, sure, but I'm not going to do that. I need to make the kids breakfast, there is a mountain of laundry that needs to be folded, and I think the dishwasher needs to be unloaded. I'll sleep tonight." *Maybe. Hopefully.*

Shaking his head, he reached for her hand and pulled her over to the bottom of the stairs. "No, get your ass up there, crawl back into bed and close your eyes for an hour or so. Then shower and come down when you're ready. I'll make sure the children don't starve." He smacked her butt but didn't remove his hand from her cheek until she took the first step up. "I'm not asking, Bianca. I'll carry you up there and tuck you in if I have to."

Well now, didn't that conjure all kinds of images in her brain, even through the fog of fatigue. Jack carrying her caveman-like and "tucking her into bed" was right up there with him sliding his fingers down her pants as she rode in front of him on his bike.

A sob caught in her throat at the idea of crawling back into bed and hugging her pillow with her eyes closed. She took another hesitant step up, paused and turned back to face him.

His brows pinched. "I'm not lying, Bianca. I will haul you—"

She tugged on his beard and pressed her lips to his. "You're amazing, Jack. I don't know what I'd do without you right now. I ... I lo—*like* that the kids have taken to you so well." *Phew.* She nearly let the lovesick cat out of the bag.

There was no denying it now though, at least not to

herself. She'd gone and fallen head-over-heels in love with Jack Savage, even though she'd promised him she wouldn't.

His eyes widened, and the blue in his irises grew darker, as if he knew what she was about to say and was scared shit-less of it.

Shuddering, she tamped down the bubbling emotions inside her, released his beard and kissed him once more. "Thank you."

Jack only nodded.

She ascended the stairs, peeled out of her housecoat, tossed it to the foot of her bed and climbed under the sheets.

It was the first week of August. They had three weeks left of their fairy-tale summer tryst. Three more weeks of orgasms, laughter, and falling deeper in love with a man she knew would never love her back and would be gone like a snowbird down to warmer weather before the leaves began to change.

She knew she never should have gotten involved with Jack, knew she should probably end things now before her heart and her children's hearts wound up broken beyond repair, but she just couldn't.

She loved him, and any time she could have with him was time she'd take gladly, willingly. Consequences and heartache be damned.

Those were for future Bianca to deal with.

Present Bianca was going to soak up as much of Jack as she could and enjoy the feeling of being respected and cared for. Relish the orgasms she didn't have to take care of herself, and being with a man who repaired the damage of her divorce.

She laughed at that thought. He really was a handyman. He'd not only fixed up her fourplex, but he'd mended her heart as well. A true-blue Jack of *all* trades.

Bianca planned to enjoy the moments where she was

more than just a mother, more than just a daughter, a sister and an employee. Jack made her feel more like a woman, like a sexual being than she had since before her children were born, possibly since before she got together with Ashley.

He made her feel alive, and even if when he left, it damn near killed her, she was going to live life to the fullest with him while she still could.

WITH BIANCA OFF at Eva's doing bridesmaid things and getting ready, Jack did his best to keep the children—mainly Charlie—from getting filthy.

Easier said than done.

While Bianca napped, he fed the kids his mother's special maple syrup and apple baked oatmeal, which they devoured, and he folded all the laundry and emptied the dishwasher. When Bianca woke up and came downstairs, he worried she was going to jump his bones in front of the kids. The look she was giving him was pure female in estrus.

"Jack made the *best* breakfast *ever*," Hannah had said, using her finger to wipe the remaining bits of food from her bowl. "It's sooooo good."

Bianca's lip twitched before she took the fork from Jack's hand and tried a bite. Her eyes lit up. "I'm not going to argue with that. This is pretty delicious."

"Can we have this every morning?" Hayley asked. "Can Jack make us breakfast every morning?"

Neither he nor Bianca answered.

These kids were making his leaving in three weeks damn near impossible. These kids *and* their sexy, smart, incredible mother.

Bianca damn near gave him a heart attack on the stairs earlier when she grabbed his beard and started to say a word that started with *L*. Had she caught herself? Was she about to say a word he'd made her promise not to say? Made her promise not to feel?

He'd fucked up royally getting involved with a single mother and meeting her kids. It didn't help that the kids were cool as fuck and he wanted to spend time with them. He'd never really done the single mom thing, and now he knew why. It was hard enough falling for one person, let alone four.

And three of those people were currently blowing bubbles and scribbling chalk on the sidewalk in front of Bianca's townhouse. So far, nobody had scraped a knee or decided to dump bubble soap on themselves.

So far.

Two men he was getting to know well ran up in front of Bianca's townhouse, one of them pushing a stroller, both of them sweaty from a run.

"You on babysitting duty?" Max asked, his chest heaving beneath a black sports tank top, which he used the hem of to wipe his face.

Jack nodded. "Bianca's part of the wedding party, had to go get ready."

Squinting, Max cleared his throat and bobbed his head. "Yeah, Celeste and Sabrina too."

"Lauren is helping with hair and makeup, so Ike and I are bro-ing out with Max until the wedding," Isaac said, craning his body around to check on baby Ike, Lauren's son.

With a groan, Jack pried himself up off the grass and stood to peek into Ike's stroller. The little guy was passed out in the shade with a big floppy sunhat on and a sky-blue T-shirt that said, "Feminist and proud of it."

"You're really getting in thick with the fam, huh?" Max said, dropping his voice to a whisper. "Babysitting, coming to the wedding. I hear you're pretty much here every night for dinner."

Jack lifted a brow Max's way. "Yeah, so?"

"So you still planning to leave in a few weeks?"

Jack glanced at the kids playing nicely on the concrete. The more time he spent with Bianca and her kids, the less resigned he was to taking off and leaving them until the spring. What if she found another guy in the meantime and neither she or the kids wanted anything to with Jack when he returned?

He couldn't blame them if that did happen. He was leaving, after all. Doing what he always did. Making the most of his freedom. It'd been a long while before he was able to cross the border, given his criminal past, but now that he could, he couldn't give that up. He had a bar to run in Mexico. A home down there that needed tending to. A life. A plan.

And just because he was enjoying his time playing family with Bianca and the kids didn't mean he could just abandon his plans, could it?

"That's not the look of a man who's convinced leaving is the best idea," Isaac said with a snort. He lifted a water bottle out of a compartment near the handlebar of the stroller and squirted water into his mouth. His dark red hair was damp and glinted in the sun when he moved. "These kids know your plans? Know your *expiration* date?"

Jack made a noise in his throat and focused on Charlie, who was now covering the palms of his hands in blue chalk and dipping them in the bubble mixture to make blue hand prints on the sidewalk. "They know," he finally said, lifting his gaze back to Isaac and Max. "Bianca made sure they knew before we started spending so much time together."

The other two men's heads bobbed.

"Heard about the civil suit," Max said, changing the subject, which Jack was grateful for. Not that he couldn't or wouldn't talk about the fact that he was leaving in three weeks, because it was no secret to anybody, but he just didn't like talking about it.

"Yeah, fucking prick coming after Bianca like that. He's determined to make her life hell. We're reaching out to the guys from Grant Cabinets, as they were witnesses to what happened, so it's not just our word against Rod's." It shouldn't be anybody's word against anybody's though. This shouldn't even be fucking happening.

"Definitely get that hooker's statement. The one who is now doing the landscaping," Isaac said, doing the same as Max had earlier and wiping his brow with the hem of his white tank top.

Jack dropped his voice deep and narrowed his gaze on Isaac. "Her name's Casey, and she's not a hooker. Never was."

Isaac's already ruddy complexion turned darker. "Sorry."

Max glanced at his watch on his wrist. "Closing in on noon. Need to shower and eat something. Then get dressed in the clothes Celeste laid out for me." His grin was cheeky, but the glimmer in his eye said he didn't mind.

Neither did Jack.

In fact, he liked that Bianca had picked out clothes for him. He'd never had a woman—not since his mother—pick out clothes she thought would look nice on him. It wasn't a mothering or controlling thing. It was a way she showed that she cared about him.

It's her love language. At least that's what his mother would have called it.

People showed they cared about others in different ways. Some used food, baking and cooking for others to show them they cared. Others used gifts, while some people went above and beyond in other ways.

Since Jack's father had been a quiet, more reserved man, he didn't say the *L*-word very often. But he showed it in different ways. He always made sure Jack's mother had a warm cup of tea beside her when she sat down to knit in the evening. He rubbed her feet after a long day of work, and he brought her flowers "just because" at least once a month.

Jack's parents' love was a love worth aspiring to. Honest, pure and eternal.

"You taking the kids with you to the ceremony?" Isaac asked.

Jack shook his head. "Maybe Charlie, but I've gotta run the girls to Eva's in an hour for hair. I can either take Charlie to Eva's just before three or keep him with me and meet the wedding party at the park for the ceremony." He ruffled Charlie's hair. "Probably just keep the little man with me. He can keep me company. Right, bud?"

Charlie tilted his head up and smiled at Jack. "My lub you, Jack."

Well, fuck, if that didn't hit him in the heart like an arrow in a bullseye.

Exhaling, Jack ruffled Charlie's hair again. "You got chalk all over your hands, buddy. Mama's not going to be too happy if you show up to your uncle's wedding looking like a Smurf."

With a confused expression, Charlie rubbed his cheeks with his fingers.

"Ah ... no ..." Jack hung his head as he watched Charlie wipe his blue hands down the front of his shirt and shorts. Now he really did look like a Smurf.

Max and Isaac snorted laughs.

"Good thing it's chalk and not Sharpie," Max said. "You should ask Atlas about when his little girl decided to give herself some *permanent* pajamas."

Jesus, Jack could just imagine what that meant.

"Need to bathe this beast before I take him to his mother," Jack said as Charlie dipped the chalk into the bubbled mixture and then proceeded to wipe the chalk stick on his bare arms and legs.

"Better get on that, then," Isaac said. He turned the stroller to head down into the complex toward his and Lauren's unit. "We'll see you at the wedding."

Jack nodded, distracted by the Smurf-child smiling up at him with messy hair, bright brown eyes and so much affection Jack thought his heart might damn near explode.

He'd missed all of this with Simon, but the fact that he was getting to experience it with Charlie was a dream come true.

"Need to get out for a ride, the three of us, before you leave, too," Max said, following behind Isaac. "Once we get the house done, we can go for a celebratory ride and a beer."

Now that, Jack liked the sound of.

He nodded again, this time catching both men's gaze, before he scooped up a giggling Charlie and asked the girls to start packing up the toys. "I have a child to de-Smurf," he said, blowing a raspberry on Charlie's stomach when his T-shirt rode up. The little guy squealed. Just before he, Charlie and the girls entered the house, he tossed one more glance outside, where he found Isaac and Max standing in front of Celeste's house, watching him and smiling.

"Looks good on you," Max called out. "The whole *step*-dad thing."

Jack lifted his hand in the air and flipped Max the bird, which only caused him and Isaac to start laughing.

As far as weddings go, Bianca would have to say that Eva and Scott's was one of the most beautiful she'd ever been to. Eva had taken care of every detail imaginable, right down to the punched-out heart-shaped dried leaf confetti and the allergy-sensitive menu.

Unlike most weddings, where the wedding party sat at a

head table, Scott and Eva chose to sit at a table with their sons, while everyone else was free to choose their own seats.

Bianca, Jack and the kids sat with Lauren, Isaac, Celeste and Max as well as Bianca's parents. Bianca hardly saw Charlie the entire night. He was either on Jack's lap or with one of her parents. Once the dinner was over, the twins took off with some of the older girls to go dancing in the grass in their bare feet.

"What time is it?" Celeste asked, leaning into Max and letting her eyes close. Bianca and Celeste were in similar butter-yellow long sleeveless dresses. Bianca had to hand it to Eva. She'd picked some unbelievably beautiful dresses for her wedding party. And with a color palette of dove gray, butter-yellow and mint green, the bridesmaids and groomsmen looked striking together. The whole venue was gorgeous.

"Almost eight," Max said, checking his phone. "What time are the kids set to leave?"

"Babysitters are arriving at eight thirty," Bianca said sleepily, sipping her wine.

"Smart fucking bride and groom," Jack said, tipping up his beer to his lips. "Let the kids come to the ceremony, then stick around the reception, but only past dinner, then boot them out so the adults can party properly. Freaking genius."

Bianca smiled. "It's nice that we have so many babysitters on call and willing."

"When they get paid as well as they do, they'd be stupid to turn us down," Lauren added, rubbing her belly. "Not that I think I'll be able to last much longer than the kids."

Isaac's hand landed on her stomach. "Need me to rub your feet?"

Lauren's cornflower-blue eyes gleamed. She kicked off her heeled sandals and lifted her legs into Isaac's lap with a grunt that could only come from a woman in her final trimester.

"Sabrina taking your kids home?" Isaac asked Bianca, his thumbs working the pads of Lauren's feet enough to make her moan and shut her eyes. His sexy grin made Bianca shiver.

"Yep."

"We're putting Ike's car seat in Bianca's van, hun," Lauren said. "Girls will take the kids back together."

Isaac nodded, seeming to relax a bit, his fingers still working at Lauren's arches. "That eases my mind about my kid driving around with a teenager. They're good girls. Got level heads. Took care of my kitten real well, too."

Lauren popped one eye open and snagged Bianca with it. Lauren didn't have to say anything for Bianca to know her friend's heart was close to bursting from Isaac calling Ike his son. Isaac wasn't Ike's father, but he was the closest thing Ike had to one, and since Lauren and Isaac were expecting a baby together, it was only a matter of time until they made things official and Isaac properly adopted Ike.

"Grandparents, parents and babysitters are going to take the rest," Celeste added. "Freddie and Jordie are going to their mothers."

Jack grunted beside Bianca, shifted and pulled his phone out of his back pocket. "I should show you these." Unlocking his phone, he brought up the photos and what appeared to be Charlie covered in something very blue.

"Was this today?" she asked, sitting up and taking his phone from him.

"Yeah, earlier. Kid figured out how to make a clay-like paste with chalk and bubble soap. Painted himself with it until he looked like a Smurf."

She held the phone out so the rest of the people at the table could see, then she started flipping through the rest of the photos on his phone. There were over twenty photos of the kids. And then there were even more of Jack and the kids doing goofy selfies.

He snorted. "Hannah got ahold of my phone and demanded we take a bunch of selfies. Then they started making silly faces." It was clear as day in the photos just how much fun her children had with Jack. It was also clear just how much fun he had with her children. The smiles were real. There was no faking with any of them.

Her chest ached with how much love she saw in each picture. The way her children were looking at Jack and Jack at them.

"Mama, my tired," Charlie said, coming up to her and putting his hand on her thigh.

She went to scoop him up, but he shook his head and climbed into Jack's lap, snuggling in against his chest and the soft, dark blue shirt she'd bought for him. She loved that he wore the shirts she'd bought him. He looked damn good in them too. But she knew firsthand the man looked good in anything—and also nothing.

As if second nature, Jack hugged Charlie right back and started running his hand down the little boy's head and back.

"You'll be heading home pretty quick," Bianca said, stroking Charlie's cheek with her knuckle.

Mallory and Sabrina appeared.

"We're cool to start packing everyone up now if you want," Sabrina offered, her fiery red hair done up in a side bun below her ear, with rebellious wisps escaping around her face. She looked just like her mother.

"You want to head home to bed, buddy?" Jack asked, pressing his lips to the top of Charlie's head.

Charlie simply nodded.

"We'll go gather the twins," Sabrina said.

"Anybody seen Ike?" Mallory asked, glancing around the

outdoor pavilion. "He's only eight months old. He couldn't have gotten that far."

Lauren opened her eyes again. "I think Bianca's mother stole him and went to go put him with other babies so they could talk about the depressing state of the world together."

Isaac made a noise in his throat. "Or plan to all shit their pants at the same time."

Max pressed his finger to his nose before pointing it at Isaac. "My money's on that."

"I'll go find him," Mallory said, taking off into the crowd.

"If he's shat himself, feel free to just take off his diaper and drag his ass around on the grass to clean him off," Isaac called after her with a goofy smile, earning chuckles from the other men at the table.

Mallory gave him a grossed-out look, which only made him laugh.

"Should get Casey babysitting," Jack said with a wince when Charlie pulled on his beard, the little boy's eyes closing.

"I'd like to," Bianca said. "I'll let her get sorted at Simon and Jared's first, then get her to take the babysitting course and first aid course. I'm sure she's great with kids, and I really like her, but I know for a fact Mallory and Sabrina have taken both courses, and that eases my conscience tremendously."

"Agreed," Lauren said. "I don't care if Casey was a lady of the evening before she started mowing lawns or that she had fifteen brothers and sisters who she looked after. I just want to know she can administer infant CPR if need be."

Within ten minutes, Bianca was escorting two tired-looking six-year-olds and Jack was carrying a sleeping Charlie to Bianca's minivan.

Lauren was driving all the adults back to the complex later, since she was sober and "obnoxiously pregnant," as she put it.

"You'll come back later, Mama?" Hayley asked, her eyes taking ages to blink.

Bianca fastened Hayley's seat belt and pecked her daughter on the forehead. "I will, angel. I'll be back tonight. But it's a grown-up party now. Kids are off to bed."

"You going to have goofy juice?" Hannah asked before yawning.

"Lots of it," Bianca said with a smile, kissing Hannah on the forehead as well.

"My stay with you, Jack," Charlie said sleepily as Jack plopped the little guy into his car seat. "My drink goofy juice with you, Jack."

Jack went about strapping Charlie in. "I'd love nothing more than to drink goofy juice with you, buddy, but I think you'd be a crazy drunk, and I'm not ready to see that."

Bianca snorted.

"My lub you, Jack," Charlie said, reaching out for Jack. "Hug, pwease, Jack. Night, night hug, pwease."

"Damn," Celeste whispered behind Bianca. "My ovaries are going to fucking explode seeing this."

Isaac made a noise in his throat as he finished getting Ike all buckled into his car seat in the very back of the van.

"I can't turn down a Charlie hug," Jack said, leaning his big frame in over Charlie and hugging him awkwardly. Charlie's little arms wrapped around Jack's neck and held on.

"Me too," Hayley said.

"Me too, too," Hannah added.

Jack finished hugging Bianca's children and stepped out of the van.

"You want hugs from your mom?" he asked at the same time Sabrina started up the engine of the van.

The kids shook their heads.

"We always hug her," Hannah said.

"But we only have a few weeks left to hug you," Hayley added.

Jack glanced at Bianca and shoved his fingers into his hair. "Jeez, guys, way to make me feel bad."

"Kids are the ultimate guilt-trippers," Celeste said. "They have an uncanny ability to make us feel loved but like garbage all at the same time."

"No shit," Jack muttered.

"See you amorrow, Jack," Charlie said just before the sliding doors of the van were closed.

They could see the kids waving through the tinted windows.

Sabrina rolled down the window. "I'll send you all a message when we get home."

"Thank you," Isaac said, wrapping an arm around Lauren's waist.

Mallory and Sabrina waved, then Sabrina pulled out of the parking lot and onto the street.

"All right, now that the kids are gone, it's time for the grown-ups to get wild!" Celeste cheered, grabbing Max by the hand. "Let's dance, Professor Washboard."

"I keep telling you I'm not a professor," he said with a laugh, following her back toward the tented and decorated area of the reception.

Lauren and Isaac were all wrapped up in each other and slowly following. Lauren craned her neck around to glance at Bianca. "You guys coming?"

They would. But not yet.

Bianca had other plans.

Seeing Jack with her children, the silly photos of them, how much they loved him and wanted him in their lives, it struck so many chords inside her, she was now a burning ball of need. Of passion.

"In a minute," she said, lifting her chin at Lauren.

"Have fun." Lauren's eyes gleamed, and her smile turned wicked. Even seven months pregnant, the woman was a radiant beauty in her dark red, floor-length maternity dress. The deep V that showed off her killer cleavage wasn't anything to scoff at either.

She waited until her friends were gone before taking Jack by the hand and leading him into a thick copse of trees, where an old potter's shed was buried beneath ivy and aggressive morning glory.

It was dark now, and in a moment, they would blend in with the shadows and become invisible.

"What was this place?" he asked, his hand warm in hers.

"Property used to belong to a wealthy couple who were big into gardening and the arts. They never had any children, so they donated their land to the city with the caveat that the gardens be rented out at a reasonable price for weddings and parties. They were big partiers, apparently. Their house now serves as the washrooms for the venue, the prep station for caterers and if a bridal party needs space to get ready."

"It's really cool. All the fruit trees, the gardens and the field, set right along the river. I'd get married here. And that gazebo. I was checking it out earlier, a true work of art."

"They lucked out getting it. Another couple canceled, and Eva and Scott jumped at it when it was offered to them. The wait list to get married here is like three years long."

Jack whistled.

She tugged him behind the potter's shed and shoved his back against the outer wall.

"What's going on, baby?" Jack asked with a throaty chuckle. "You plan to kill me? Bury my body?"

Stepping into his space, she let his heat and scent wash over her. Intoxicate her better than any joint or shot of tequila ever could. Her fingers fell to his belt, and she began to unfasten it. "I only have a few weeks left," she said, pushing up onto her tiptoes and taking his bottom lip between her teeth. "Need to get mine while I still can."

No light from the reception area reached where they were, so it was a struggle to see him smile, but the way his beard tickled her chin said his lips had curled up. "Is that what we're doing here?" His voice was now the purr of an alpha male, setting his sights on his mate and preparing to claim her.

"It is. You've been incredible today. Now it's time for me to show you how much I appreciate you." She made to sink to her knees, but he caught her before she could.

"Then let me do what *I* want to do, baby." Gruffly, he reversed their positions and pushed her back against the ivy leaves and rough wood of the shed. He dropped to his knees and pushed the hem of her dress up enough to duck underneath.

"Jack ..." Her hand fell to the top of his head.

"It's like you said, baby. You need to get yours while you can." Then he tugged her lace panties to the side and swept his tongue up between her folds.

BIANCA IN A GUNNYSACK would make him hard, but Bianca in that dress with her hair all done up and a little bit of makeup made Jack worry he was going to blow his load in his dress pants during the ceremony. Seeing her standing up behind Eva, with the sun on her face, her damp eyes and unbelievable smile, Jack was unable to look anywhere else. He was pretty sure two people got married, but he hadn't heard a damn word of it. His eyes, his attention, his sole focus was on Bianca.

He figured he'd have to wait until the wedding ended and

they got back to her place before he could bury his face between her thighs, making her leave the dress on.

But she had other plans.

In pitch black, with the scent of his woman surrounding him, he held her panties to the side and drew her clit into his mouth, reveling in her moans and heavy breathing.

She ground down against him, tilting her hips to give him better access and so he could push two fingers inside her.

"Oh fuck," she breathed, her hand pushing down just slightly harder on his head.

He loved it when she got a little bossy and took what she wanted. She needed to do that more often. Get hers. Put herself first. She was a selfless woman, a generous mother and gave so much of herself to others, Jack often wondered if there was anything left for Bianca at the end of the day.

Today he knew there would be.

Drawing her swelling clit into his lips, he lapped up her juices and was about to make her come with a hard suck when voices nearby made him pause.

"I'll fuck you like I did on the balcony that time," a male voice said with a deep purr. "Spin you around, put your hands on that tree trunk there and take you from behind, you filthy thing."

"Afraid to get your suit dirty there, stud?" Now it was a woman speaking.

"Not if you're going to ride me, Tink."

"Shit, that's Liam and Richelle," Bianca whispered, her hand relaxing on Jack's head.

The crunch of dry leaves and shoes drew nearer.

"Think anybody can see us here?" Liam asked.

"I can barely hear the music. I think were fine."

"Um ... guys?" Jack spoke, hoping to God he didn't pop out from beneath Bianca's dress to see her big brother standing there ready to kill.

"Who's there?" Richelle asked, her voice startled. "Did you know somebody was here?"

"Just me ... Jack."

"You're here by yourself?" Liam asked, the skepticism in his tone tangible.

"No," was all Jack said.

"Is Bianca there with you?" Richelle asked.

Their voices were loud enough now they were probably just on the other side of the shed. Jack needed to make sure they stayed there.

"I'm here," Bianca said sheepishly, unable to keep the groan of being caught in the act out of her tone.

"What are you guys—" Liam wasn't able to finish his sentence. Richelle must have elbowed him because he made a strangled sound, which was followed up by an "Ow."

Richelle chuckled. "We'll leave you two be."

"Appreciate it," Jack murmured.

"Are you and my sister— Ow! Stop pinching me!"

"Then stop being an idiot."

"I'm not being an idiot. I'm being a big brother. Hardly seems seemly for Bianca to be sneaking off and—"

"Doing what we were just about to do?" Richelle interrupted him.

"We're *married*."

"Which is completely irrelevant," Richelle pointed out. "We were fuck buddies for three years until you wore me down to be more. Give it a rest, you antiquated old coot. Join the rest of us in the twenty-first century, where women can get their orgasms without a ring on their finger first."

"Please don't talk about my sister and orgasms."

Bianca groaned again. "Can you two go argue about my orgasms somewhere else, please?"

"Sure thing," Richelle called out. Leaves crunching echoed through the trees again. "Come on."

Jack could just picture Liam's pout of frustration as his wife led him away, the high-powered attorney disgruntled that his little sister was also a woman who liked to partake in some outdoor extracurriculars.

"Much obliged," Jack called after them.

"Don't push it," Liam said. "Ow. Stop pinching me, woman."

Bianca's snort of mirth above him had Jack smiling. She started to shake with laughter, which in turn made him start laughing. He pressed a kiss to the inside of each of her thighs before ducking out from beneath her dress. "Moment gone?"

"My big brother murdered it," she said, still laughing. "Even with Richelle's best efforts, Liam interfered with my orgasms."

Jack stood up, licked his fingers clean and let his hand fall to the small of Bianca's back. "Well, let's hope he stays the fuck away from the bed later tonight." He steered her back toward the party. "By the way, you're leaving that dress on. Wanna fuck you in it."

She giggled and leaned her head against his shoulder. "I think that can be arranged."

"Heels too."

"I took them off ages ago, put on my emergency flats."

"Don't care. Find 'em, put 'em on and throw them legs in the air."

"Yes, sir." Her lips pressed against his shoulders. "Thank you for coming to the wedding, Jack. I'm glad you're here with me."

He turned his head and pressed his lips to her hair. "Anything for you, darlin'."

18

AND JUST LIKE THAT, the days turned into weeks, and before she knew it, it was Saturday night and Jack would leave that coming Monday. Bianca still couldn't believe that the month of August had gone by so quickly. One minute it was warm in the evenings and her brother was getting married, then the next minute, sharp bites of fall clung to the late-afternoon breeze and she was getting emails from the twins' school about the first week back.

Jack spent the better part of that day working at the house. It was nearly done. He figured between him, Max and Isaac, they could get everything done Sunday and they'd be good to go.

Literally and figuratively.

Finally, Bianca could see the light at the end of the tunnel with the fourplex. At the exact same time, the walls around her felt like they were closing in when it came to Jack's impending departure. The light was there, just within reach, but she couldn't enjoy its luster for the squeeze of the walls around her, the ache in her heart and the inevitable sadness that would surely fall over her own household.

It was particularly rough when she went to his place on Friday night and saw the saddlebags for his bike out on the kitchen table of the Airstream and he already had rolls of clothes tucked in them.

He'd almost caught her sad face when he turned around, but she quickly stowed it, flashed him a big fake smile and smothered the last signs of her disappointment with his lips against hers. The easiest way to ease her heartache about him leaving was spending as much time with him as possible. And if the children weren't around, that time was spent in Jack's arms, one way or another.

But alas, it was Saturday night, and not even for good dick was she going to bail on her chicks and cancel wine night at her house with Celeste and Lauren.

"And he's still hell-bent on leaving?" Lauren asked, sipping the basil-mint water Bianca had made earlier that day. "Even after getting to know the kids, falling for you, he's still going to leave?"

Bianca sipped her wine and nodded. "I don't know if he's *fallen* for me though."

Celeste shook her head and scoffed at the same time. "Guy's hot, nice and handy, but he's nuts to walk away from you and the kids."

"Don't forget hung," Lauren added. "But still nuts. I agree with that."

"He's not nuts," Bianca said with exasperation. "He was up front from the get-go about his plans and his intentions. I was the idiot who fell in love with him even when he made me promise not to. I'm the one who's nuts."

"False," Lauren said. "You're not nuts."

Bianca rolled her eyes. "Well, I'm not sane. I went and started sleeping with my handyman, knew from the very beginning it could never amount to anything, and then I went and introduced him to my children and fell in love with him anyway. No *sane* person does that."

"Most sane people would do that. You're human. You're ready to move on, and you found something in Jack." Celeste's face of sympathy ate at Bianca. She didn't feel sane when she was around Jack. She felt like a lovesick teenager. When she was seventeen, she'd fallen hard one summer for Darren, her neighbor's nephew. He was staying with his aunt and uncle for the summer until he started college at U of W. Darren had been her first love, her first *everything*, but he'd dumped her at the end of the summer, claiming he wasn't ready for a serious girlfriend and wanted to "play the field" because that was what college was all about.

But Jack wasn't Darren.

He'd leave her with a broken heart, but hopefully, unlike Darren, not a case of gonorrhea.

At this point, she'd take the gonorrhea over the heartache. At least there was a cure for the former.

"So if he's leaving in two days, why are you sitting here with us and not getting pounded into the mattress?" Lauren asked, adjusting her position on the couch with a grimace and a grunt.

"Because chicks before dicks," Bianca said plainly. "He'll be gone. You guys won't be."

Her friends beamed at her, and Celeste reached out and squeezed Bianca's foot. "You know we love you and wouldn't get upset if you canceled tonight to spend some extra time with your man. We've both been there."

"But you're also *still* there." She wanted to change the subject. Talking about Jack was just hurting her heart, and sooner or later, she'd start to cry. Unlike Bianca, who was only temporarily not single, her friends had found their forever men and were legitimately not single anymore. She was the only single mom left of their single mom group.

How depressing. Maybe she needed to find a new group of single moms to spend time with, women with kids her children's ages so they could commiserate and bitch about the same things.

"I think he's an idiot for leaving," Lauren said, her hands resting on her belly. "Plain and simple."

Bianca shook her head. "I think he's a man with a plan, and nothing gets in the way of that."

Lauren's brows knitted, and she tucked a blonde strand of hair behind her ear. "Not even love?"

"He made me promise not to fall in love with him."

"Which you failed to do." Celeste sipped her wine.

"Which I failed to do. But that doesn't mean he feels the same way. He probably does this every summer. Finds some woman to warm his bed for four or five months, takes off down to the Baja, finds a woman down there to do the same, then lather, rinse, repeat." She knew Jack well enough to know that probably wasn't quite the case, but it eased the pain in her chest somewhat to think of Jack as some playboy jerk just out for a good time.

Feed into her friends' bashing of him.

"The heart wants what the heart wants, right?" Celeste's gaze was sympathetic, and Bianca's hackles rose at the thought of her friends pitying her.

Lauren munched on a chip, a couple of crumbs escaping into the napkin she held beneath her chin. Since her last pregnancy, she'd learned how to eat tidier. The woman was rather klutzy even when not knocked up, but when pregnant, she was a bull in a China shop twenty-four seven. "So, what's so special about the Baja anyway?"

"He owns a bar down there and a house. He winters there, runs the bar and does odd handyman jobs during the high tourist season. Mostly works on houses for other expats or rentals. He's been doing it for years. I can't expect him to change his pattern, to change what has become the norm, for me."

Celeste pressed her lips together. "Max says the house is nearly done."

Good, a less volatile topic.

Bianca nodded. "Yeah, just have to paint the trim, install the fume hoods over the stoves, do some grout and caulking around the tubs, sinks and toilets and then move in the big pieces of furniture. Washer and dryer arrived on Thursday, and they got them all installed."

"Max has really enjoyed working on the house, and he likes Jack."

Lauren's head bobbed. "Isaac too. He wasn't sure at first because Jack seemed put out about Isaac being a cop, but they seemed to have smoothed out whatever rough start they had."

Hmmm. Jack hadn't mentioned anything about not wanting to work with Isaac. Did it have something to do with his criminal history?

"I'll cut the guys' checks at the end of the week. I know their help has meant a lot to Jack, and it's definitely meant a lot to me."

Her friends nodded.

"Come to think of it, I think they're all at my house now having a beer and comparing dick—I mean *bike* sizes." Lauren snorted. "What I'd pay to be a fly on the wall if they were actually comparing dick sizes."

"Dear God, woman, no more babies for you after this one. You turn into a very horny, borderline inappropriate monster." Celeste's disgruntled face and headshake of disgust was met with Lauren sticking her tongue out.

Soon they were all laughing.

Jack hadn't mentioned going to Isaac's for a drink, but the

thought of him getting to know Max and Isaac better outside of working on the fourplex did make her happy.

"Is he coming over after we leave?" Celeste asked, topping up her and Bianca's wine.

Bianca nodded. In all the weeks they'd been together and Jack came over for dinner and hung out with her and the kids, he'd never spent the night at her place. She'd spent a few nights at his trailer, but mostly they were at hers because she had the kids and he was gone by midnight.

What would her children think if they woke up, came into Bianca's room in the morning and found Jack in bed with her? She'd been very careful about not being too affectionate with him in front of the kids as well. No kissing, no hand-holding or hugs. As far as she could tell, the kids just thought Jack was Bianca's new friend.

Then again, kids were far more astute and perceptive than adults gave them credit for. Maybe they did know Jack was her boyfriend and wouldn't bat an eye to see him in the morning. The girls would probably ask him a million questions about the lion and griffin tattoos on his chest. Charlie would probably grab a Sharpie and try to give himself chest tattoos.

Her son's adoration for Jack was both sweet and unnerving. It meant Charlie was starving for a stable male role model in his life. Briefly that focus had shifted from Ashley to Bianca's father, but it would appear it'd shifted from her dad to Jack. And that rug was about to pulled out from beneath her little guy's feet in two days.

Another reason why she didn't want Jack spending the night. It would just promote hope in her children's hearts. Hope she couldn't bear to see demolished.

And now nearing the end of their relationship, she definitely wasn't going to take that chance. He'd come by when her friends left, they'd have fun for a couple of hours, and then he'd leave.

Lauren yawned and stretched. "I actually think I might head home now. Pregnancy makes me tired all the time."

"Another reason to not have any more babies for a while," Celeste said. "That and so you can actually participate in wine night."

Lauren's tired blue eyes widened for a moment as she nodded theatrically. "Amen, sister. I miss my wine."

"I should probably get going too," Celeste said, finishing her wine and standing up from the couch, taking her empty glass and an empty tray to the kitchen.

Bianca gathered dishes and joined her in the kitchen, followed by a grunting and waddling Lauren.

They were on the threshold of Bianca's front door, the cool, crisp late August air ruffling their hair, when Bianca's phone in the back pocket of her jeans started to warble.

She pulled it out to see Richelle's number on the screen.

"Isn't she supposed to be at her own wine night?" Lauren asked.

Bianca hit the green button and put the phone on speaker. "Hey Richelle, what's up?"

"I'm here, too," Liam said.

"Poker and wine night end early?" Bianca asked.

"Just got home," Richelle said. "Came home to find a bunch of emails regarding your civil suit with a one Rodrick Penner."

Dread slammed into the bottom of Bianca's gut like an anvil.

"We filed a countersuit with regards to damages and theft, and he's gone and withdrawn his claim," Richelle said, the relief in her tone wrapping around Bianca like a blanket fresh from the dryer.

"So it's over then?" Bianca asked. That seemed way too easy.

"It would seem so," Richelle said. "I'll look into things further on Monday, but from what we can tell, since our lawsuit exceeded the amount that he was asking for, we have evidence of damages and witnesses to corroborate your story—"

"Not to mention the fact that he's one hundred percent guilty and fucking knows it," Liam added.

Richelle clucked her tongue. "Yeah, but he's a vapid narcissist and borderline psychopath, dear. Even if he knows what he did was wrong, he'll justify in his head to convince himself he was in the right."

"Fair enough." Bianca's brother grunted.

"Like I said, we'll follow up on Monday and get the details and then be in touch. But we wanted to let you know now, to ease the weight on your shoulders, that he's withdrawn his claim." The unsaid words as Richelle spoke tightened the strings around Bianca's chest. Richelle knew this was Jack's last weekend, so she probably wanted to remove any additional stressors for Bianca if she could.

Bianca loved her sister-in-law.

"Well, thank you," Bianca said, finally feeling like she could breathe deep again.

"Yeah, thank you," Lauren said.

"We're just heading home, but glad we stuck around to hear the good news," Celeste chimed in.

"Hi, ladies." The smile in Richelle's voice was obvious.

"I'll tell Jack the good news," Bianca said.

"Say hi to ol' Jackie boy for me." Richelle's teasing tone could only mean she was thinking about the near miss they had back at Eva's wedding. Liam hadn't been able to look at Bianca for the remainder of the night, and he'd only glared at Jack like he wanted to gut him like a fish.

"Will do," Bianca sang. "Hi, big brother. I love you. I can't wait to see you again."

Lauren and Celeste snickered, as they knew the whole story.

"Not funny, Bianca," Liam gritted out. "If I'd seen what I'm pretty sure was happening behind that shed, I'd be scarred for life. I'd probably go blind. Do you want to blind me, little sister?"

Bianca chuckled. "Good thing you didn't see what was behind that shed then, huh?"

"Not. Funny."

"I happen to think it's hilarious," Richelle chimed in.

"Good night," Bianca said, still in a teasing singsong voice. "Miss you, Liam. Jack misses you too."

Laughing, Richelle said, "Good night," then hung up.

The girls were just waving goodbye and heading through the gate in Bianca's front yard when a sexy bearded biker with full tattoo sleeves walked up, oozing all things heart-stopping.

Bianca watched her friends give Jack the mental shakedown, cruising their eyes over him from top to toe like he was a bad boy from high school and set on ruining her reputation.

Bianca couldn't give two shits about her reputation. She just wanted the bad boy, heartbreak and a scarlet letter be damned.

"Ladies," Jack said, passing them at the gate. "How was wine night?"

"Lots to talk about," Lauren said with attitude. "You were a topic that came up a fair bit."

Jack's head reared back like he'd been smacked.

Bianca called out to her thin-filtered friend. "Knock it off, Lauren."

Lauren shrugged, leaned in toward Jack and whispered

something to him that had his eyebrows shooting up to damn near his hairline.

A tug on Lauren's arm from Celeste had both women moving down the sidewalk.

"Call us if you need us," Celeste said loudly, already nearly at her own front door. "Call me first though. This cranky pregnant beast needs some sleep."

"I won't argue with that," Lauren said, out of sight with only the *slap slap* of her flip-flops on the tarmac letting Bianca know she was still within earshot.

"I love you both," Bianca called out into the dark.

"And we love you," they both said.

Jack's hand landed on her waist, and he guided her inside the house, closing the door behind them. "Lauren needs to have that baby," he murmured, burying his face in her neck. "Isaac says she's much nicer when she's not pregnant."

"I won't argue with that," she said, rocking against him and his growing erection. "Richelle called."

He lifted his brow. "And?"

"And they threatened to countersue and Rod withdrew his claim. It looks like there is no longer a case. Bullet dodged."

A deep, satisfied laugh rumbled in his chest as he scooped her up around the waist and spun her around. "Thank fucking God, huh? Now all we need is that fucker to drop dead and all is right with the world."

Giggling, she wrapped her arms around his neck. "From your mouth to the ears of the universe."

He tilted his head skyward. "Hey, universe. Jack Savage here. How's it going? Good to hear. I'm not so bad. Thanks for asking."

She rolled her eyes.

"Just a small request, universe, but could you dispose of

the trash that is Rod Penner, please? Don't care how, just get 'er done when you have a moment, huh?"

Bianca snorted. "Think the universe will listen?"

He shrugged and glanced back down at her. "You don't get what you don't ask for."

Well, if that wasn't a read-between-the-lines thing to say if she'd ever heard one.

Was he saying that if she asked him to stay, he would?

"What did Lauren say to you?" she asked.

Growling, he dipped his mouth to the crook of her neck. "Need to be inside you."

Bianca's head snapped up. "Is that what she said?"

"Mhmm. Told me to pound you into the mattress. I like your friends, they're straight shooters."

An ache pulsed in her lower belly, and her pussy clenched. "Couch or bed?"

Jack lifted his head, the intensity of his blue gaze causing the air to catch in her throat like a hiccup. Subtle beer breath puffed against her lips, but it wasn't bad. It was Jack, and she loved it. "Bed. I plan to spread you out and take my time." The rumble of his voice had her shivering, not to mention the anticipation of what he just said he wanted to do to her.

"Then I guess we better get upstairs." She took his hand and turned around, leading him toward the stairs, but they didn't quite get there before he had her pinned against a wall in the kitchen.

He drew his nose along the side of her neck and up until his mouth hovered next to her ear. He wedged his knee between her legs and pressed against the apex of her thighs. Shamelessly, she ground against him. "You're incredible," he murmured. "Sexiest woman I've ever met. This summer ..."

She swallowed hard and shut her eyes, determined not to let her love for him show.

"Fuck, Bianca." He grew harder against her inner thigh,

and his forehead rested on hers. "Best fucking everything. Woman, mother, lay, you are the best. And this summer has been the best."

But you have to go because as much as it's all been the best, you don't love me and have a life and a plan.

Was he purposefully twisting the knife? Because every word that came out of his mouth was just making his inevitable departure more unbearable. Her heart was going to need time to heal from its upcoming shatter.

She swallowed again, opened her eyes and smiled through the pain in her chest. "Take me upstairs and show me what *you're* the best at. I can think of a few things, but I bet you're the best at so much more."

His smile turned wily, almost sinister, and he tightened his grip on her hand and tugged her toward the stairs. "Oh, darlin', you have *no* idea."

19

And so came Monday.

Heavy-hearted and struggling to smile as she prepared breakfast for her children, Bianca went through the motions and got their food ready, but her mind was on the past three months and Jack.

She'd come a long way since moving back to Seattle from Palm Springs. Not only were her children happy and healthy but so was she. She'd put on weight, was succeeding at her job and had a growing social circle. And even though she knew she'd come a long way since moving to Seattle, she felt like in the last three months being with Jack, she'd grown more than ever. He made her feel more beautiful and comfortable in her own skin than she had in ages.

Even though she'd promised him she wouldn't, she'd gone and fallen in love with him and all he brought to her life. All he added. Her children loved him too, which only made her love for him all the deeper. But that was her cross to bear. She wouldn't tell him how she felt because she'd made a promise. The least she could do was keep her true feelings to herself. Let him believe she'd upheld her end of their agreement. Even if it was a big fat lie.

At the children's request, she made breakfast for dinner last night, so for breakfast this morning, it was leftover pancakes and fresh fruit. Jack showed up last night with his mother's famous baked apple and maple oatmeal, but there wasn't any of that left. The kids devoured it—so did she. Which was why there were still purple pancakes in her fridge.

Setting three plates down on the kitchen table, she turned to beckon her offspring when a knock at the front door had her pausing.

"My get it!" Charlie hollered, leaping off the couch and running to the door.

"You can't turn the handle yet," Hannah said, her voice containing an eye roll. She helped her brother and opened the door. "Jack! Yay!"

Bianca had wandered into the living room, and her breath snagged hard and jagged in her lungs seeing him. Even though he'd been there last night and they were in bed together until past midnight, seeing him now at seven thirty pulled the strings of her heart taut.

"Figured we could all go grab breakfast," he said, focusing on Bianca, who was still in her pajamas and robe. "Unless I'm too late and you've already eaten?"

"We only had a cereal bar," Hayley pointed out. "Mom was in the kitchen preparing second breakfast."

Jack lifted a brow at Bianca. "Second breakfast?"

"They get a cereal bar when they wake up. Enough to curb the hunger pangs until I can get a coffee into my bloodstream and prepare them something more substantial." He looked just as yummy in jeans and a fitted black T-shirt as when she'd had him naked in her bed only a few hours ago.

His nod of understanding was all she got because the kids

were on him, drawing his attention away from her with millions of questions and Charlie somehow maneuvering his way into Jack's arms.

"So, breakfast?" he asked her, once the door was closed and the children had calmed down a bit.

"It was just going to be leftover pancakes and fresh fruit," she said with a shrug, just as eager as her children to spend any extra moment she could with Jack.

"How does ... the Lilac and Lavender Bistro sound?" he asked, tossing Charlie up into the air and causing her son's hair to fan around him like a halo.

He started to giggle and shouted, "Again. Again!"

"That's Aunt Paige's place," Hannah said. "We love it there." She glanced up at Bianca. "Can we, Mom?"

Bianca had already made up her mind before her children looked at her with their innocent and wide puppy-dog eyes.

"Give me twenty to get dressed," she said, spinning on her heel. "Hannah, Hayley, I brought down clothes for your stubborn little brother. Could one of you wrestle him into them, please?"

"My wear my jammas alllll day!" Charlie said.

"I'll get 'er done," Jack called from the living room while Bianca was already halfway up the stairs. "Come here, you little turkey!"

Charlie's squeals and giggles echoed through the house.

"What will I do without you?" she said loud enough he'd be able to hear her downstairs. The truth in those singsong teasing words hit her harder than she wanted to admit.

What *would* she do without him?

Go on living her life, that was what.

But she'd be a hell of a lot less happy and a lot less fulfilled with him gone, that was for sure.

Would his leaving kill her? Of course not. But it would

leave a scar that would take a while to heal. Particularly because she would be forced to bear her children's scars as well to save them from their own heartache of Jack leaving. And every time one of them would ask about him, unlike when they asked about their father, that scar would grow deeper, the scab would get picked, and fresh blood would pool.

A small price to pay for the happiness of her children. She'd already ripped one man from their life, and now she planned to do it again. The least she could do was make their pain hers.

JACK SAT NEXT to Charlie and Hayley in the booth at the Lilac and Lavender Bistro, each kid shoveling their jaffles—toasted bread pockets—into their mouth like they hadn't eaten in a week.

"What's in these things? Crack?" he asked, glancing at an unusually quiet Bianca across the table.

"Turkey, bacon and cheese," Hannah said. "We're picky eaters, but Aunt Paige's jaffles are amazing." She bit into a juicy-looking strawberry and fixed Jack with a curious look. "What's *crack?*"

Snorting, Jack sipped his coffee. "Nothing you need to worry about, sweetheart. Bad stuff. Never touch it, okay?"

Hannah nodded. "Why would Aunt Paige put crack in her jaffles if it's bad?"

"Let it go, honey," Bianca said gently, running her hand over the back of her daughter's head and picking at her own plate of food. Jack and Bianca had each ordered the Monday special, which consisted of two crab cakes with poached eggs on top, fresh fruit and sourdough toast.

"So who gets Bob while you're down in Mexico?" Hannah

asked, abandoning the crack conversation, much to Jack's relief.

He shook his head and sipped his coffee. "Funny you should ask, 'cause I haven't seen Bob in three days. She's supposed to be going to live with Simon, Jared and Casey once they move into the new house, but she's been MIA since Friday morning." He didn't want to say anything to the kids, but the fact that Bob hadn't shown her furry little face at his screen door was beginning to worry him. Sure, she was a *stray*, but she never strayed far from the house. Some days she rarely went outside and was content to just sleep on the booth seating of the kitchen table in the Airstream.

None of the fliers they put up the neighborhood yielded any results, so he figured after five months of feeding her and letting her sleep in his trailer, she was his and he was hers. Why would she take off now? She'd spent every night either in his trailer or in the camper with Simon since they found her.

Was she okay?

He'd always been reluctant to have an outdoor cat. His parents had a cat—Telemachus—and he'd been an indoor cat only. His mother adored that cat, and Telemachus adored her. He'd actually died (his father figured of a broken heart) only two months after Jack's mother passed away. Jack figured it was because the cat was nearly twenty, but he never said that.

"What does *MIA* mean?" Hayley asked, a long gooey string of cheese bridging the space between her lips and the jaffle.

"Missing in action," Bianca said. "It means she's missing."

Hayley and Hannah's eyes turned serious.

"We can help you look for her," Hannah said. "Put up fliers and go wander around your neighborhood calling her name."

If only he had the time for that. He planned to leave that afternoon.

"I'm sure she's just off exploring and will return to Simon's camper tonight," Bianca said gently, the care in her eyes as she gazed at her daughter also easing the emptiness and worry in Jack's own heart.

Hannah's eyes perked up and she sat up straighter in her seat, waving emphatically. "Miss Beatrice, hi!"

Bianca's brown eyes flared and she jumped where she sat before her posture grew stiff and her expression became a stony mask.

A woman in her late twenties or early thirties approached, wearing a big smile. "Hello, Hayley and Hannah. How was your summer?"

Hayley was the first to speak. "We were flower girls in our Uncle Scott's wedding."

Miss Beatrice's smile was warm. "That sounds lovely. You'll have to bring some pictures of yourselves all dressed up for show and tell."

The girls both nodded.

"Are you going to be our teacher again?" Hannah asked.

Jack watched Bianca's nostrils flare. The rest of her remained still and silent.

"I might be," Miss Beatrice said. "We don't know for sure yet, but it looks like I might be teaching the second grade this year. Would you like that?"

Hannah and Hayley cheered. Bianca grimaced, and her eyes closed for a moment.

She'd mentioned in passing a couple of times that the girls' teacher, Miss Beatrice, was judgy and bitchy and how she was glad to be done with the woman for a few years. He could only imagine the devastation Bianca felt knowing she might have to endure the woman's wrath for another ten months.

"Well, I best be on my way. I just came here to grab some baked goods for a baby shower I'm hosting for a friend." Miss Beatrice adjusted the white cardboard box of goodies in her arms and knelt down so she was right next to Bianca. She dropped her volume a few notches. "I have a feeling we got off on the wrong foot, Ms. Dixon, and I think that was mostly my fault. I'm sorry if you felt like I was hard on you. Like I was judging you. I know you were the one who spearheaded the class gift, and I just want to extend my gratitude and say how wonderful the gift was. So incredibly thoughtful. I'm hoping that if the girls are in my class again, we can start fresh. I'm truly in awe of you. A single mom to three really, really *good*, kind kids, and you have a full-time job." She shook her head and rested a hand on Bianca's arm. Bianca was glancing down at her, her body still stiff, expression still stony. "I'm sorry, and I hope we can move forward."

Jack's eyes flitted back and forth between the two women, but he maintained his focus mostly on Bianca. She'd been weird all morning. Did it have something to do with Miss Beatrice?

Finally, after a deep inhale and a painful moment of awkward silence, Bianca's shoulders slumped, her expression softened, and she placed her hand on Miss Beatrice's. "I would really like that. The girls love you, and you are a wonderful teacher. I might have over reacted in some cases to your emails and manifested your disapproval of me in my head. So I owe you an apology as well."

Miss Beatrice's smile softened and she closed her eyes for a moment. "Thank you." She opened her eyes again and squeezed Bianca's arm.

"Thank you for the apology, and I accept it." Bianca's smile was small but true, the gentle creases around her eyes deepening just a touch.

Miss Beatrice smiled again, nodded and stood up, pulling her hand away. "I'm glad we bumped into each other."

Bianca nodded as well. "Me too."

"See you in a couple of weeks, girls," Miss Beatrice said, glancing back at Hannah and Hayley.

The twins had their mouths full, so they simply waved and smiled.

Miss Beatrice took her leave of them, and Jack reached over and grabbed Bianca's hand. "You okay?"

Her nod was stiff, and she didn't look at him. "That was a surprise."

"But a pleasant one, right?"

Another stiff nod. "Yeah." She blew out a long, deep breath. "Very pleasant. I just hope Gwynyth had the stick removed from her ass this summer as well."

Jack snorted. "One stick at a time, darlin'."

"Do we *have* to go to camp today?" Hannah asked, breaking some of the tension at the table, tension Jack couldn't put his finger on. "I'd rather we just all spend the day together. Like a family."

"Yeah, like a family," Hayley chimed in.

"A fam-i-wee," Charlie added.

Well, fuck if these kids didn't know how to gut him until he was damn near unrevivable.

"Jack has to head out, kids," Bianca said quietly, still not looking at him. "I'm taking you to Nana and Papa's. Charlie's day care is closed this week, as the teachers are on vacation, and they canceled the last week of camp because of low enrollment."

"Good," Hannah said, her brows scrunched. "I was sick of camp anyway."

"Me too," Hayley added. "I still don't see why Jack can't leave later or tomorrow."

"Or never ..." Hannah said under her breath but loud enough for all of them to hear.

"That's enough, girls," Bianca said, setting her fork and knife down. She pushed her plate away unfinished.

"My sit with you, Jack," Charlie said, clambering into Jack's lap and facing him. He cupped Jack's face and rubbed his hand over his scruff, his little fingers a touch sticky but still pudgy, soft and adorable. "You going soon, Jack?"

Swallowing past the jagged lump of growing grief in his throat, Jack nodded. "Soon, buddy. Gotta go work my other job."

Charlie released Jack's face and flung his arms around his neck, squeezing so freaking tight, the kid started to shake. "My miss you, Jack. Too much."

Pain funneled into his heart, intensifying so rapidly he worried for a moment he might be having a heart attack. He wrapped his arms around Charlie and ran his hand down the boy's head and back. "I'm going to miss you, too, buddy. Too much, too." He hadn't realized his eyes were closed until he opened them and pinned his gaze on Bianca, and what he saw her doing made his chest hurt even more.

She was staring down at her lap and playing on her phone.

What. The. Fuck?

It was all Jack could do not to cry as he said goodbye to Hannah, Hayley and Charlie in Bianca's parents' driveway later that day. His throat was rigid, refusing to let him swallow, and his jaw was clenched so tight, he thought he was going to chip a tooth. But nothing compared to the pure agony that filled him. The heartache he felt saying goodbye to those children was like a hostile squatter inside of him, occupying every square inch of his chest and radiating outward until even his limbs ached.

Bianca had remained quiet and stoic, standing with her father to the side and chatting softly. Her mother had handled the children's tears and swept them inside with the promise of homemade ice pops and a movie in a blanket fort.

And then there were two of them.

She drove him home so he could grab his bike, then he met her at the fourplex, where the owners, Justin and James, were waiting for them.

They shook Bianca's hand first, giving her their attention and showering her with praise for pulling off what Justin called "the makeover of a lifetime."

"I have to admit, I think I've developed a bit of a *My Fair Lady* complex," Bianca said with a laugh as she and Jack gave their bosses a tour of each unit. "This place was in worse condition than any of the others you've handed me, but I was determined to turn it into something great."

"And you delivered and then some," Justin said with a whistle, his hands in the pockets of his jeans while he rocked back on his heels. "This beast needed more than a makeover."

"Facelift, lipo, Botox and some serious electrolysis," Jack added, causing them all to laugh. "Though we have Casey to thank for the *hair* removal. Kid's done a bang-up job on the yard. Nothing but a sexy landing strip now."

With a snort of amusement, James peered out into the backyard through the kitchen window. "I see she's marked off a small plot for a possible veg garden. Nice touch. And that tile job on the patio looks like a pro did it. She's got talent."

"Casey has been a godsend," Bianca said.

"You've really outdone yourself here, Bianca," Justin said. "We could not be happier with how the place turned out." He focused on Jack. "And we're sorry to be losing your talents for the next seven months. We're already looking at a couple more projects in the neighborhood, would love a man with your skills on the team." He bobbed his light brown brows over Caribbean Sea-blue eyes. "Can we convince you to stay on?"

Chuckling, Jack scratched the back of his neck and glanced away from Justin's waiting gaze. "Ah, got a plan of my own, I'm afraid. Like my warm winters and freedom."

"Next summer," James said, thrusting his hand out toward Jack, who took it. "We'll have something for you next summer, then, if you're interested. We need to keep this woman here happy and flush with cash, so we're just going to keep expanding. Keep her busy."

"Bianca," Justin said, his volume increasing a few decibels, "we cannot thank you enough. You've truly made our vision become a reality. Affordable student housing for the next generation." He glanced at the dark-haired James, who was all nods. "Even though we have money now, our heads aren't so far up our asses that we don't know that there is a serious housing crisis here in the Pacific Northwest—fewer and fewer rentals, and housing prices are out of control. Which can make it difficult for families and students to find decent accommodation, particularly rentals."

Jack and Bianca both nodded. The real estate market all up and down the Pacific Coast was indeed out of control. He knew the housing prices in Vancouver, Canada, were obnoxiously expensive as well, and Bianca had mentioned that the guys were doing the same kind of thing there too. Buying up old run-down houses and instead of demolishing them and putting in high-rises or million-dollar mansions, they were fixing up the houses and renting them to students and mature students with families.

Jack looped his arm around Bianca's shoulder and pulled her in, which had both James and Justin's eyes widening with curiosity. He kissed her crown. "She is a machine. Kick-ass mama, daughter, sister, friend, and she's the best boss I've ever had. Gets shit done but is fair and flexible."

The nostrils of the two men in front of her flared at the way Jack said *flexible*. He resisted the urge to check to see if she was blushing. He knew her well enough to know she probably was. Did they not know Bianca and Jack were seeing each other?

Justin made a noise in his throat, and both men regained their composure. "Well, that's great to hear. We've got no complaints. And we're definitely glad that Rod fucker is out of the picture."

James's hand rested on her shoulder. "Don't sweat it. We all have a Rod in our past. Consider him a badge of honor. You're one of us now." He squeezed his hand. "And it all worked out in the long run anyway, right?"

Jack could only imagine Bianca was having a hard time considering that waste of skin a *badge of honor*. Rod was more like a tumor the doctors just couldn't remove all traces of. Jack was still waiting for confirmation from the universe that it'd done as he asked and properly *disposed* of the fuckwad.

"We're grabbing dinner at the Windward Pacific tonight, which is where we're staying. We'd love it if you joined us to celebrate finishing this place," Justin offered. "Both of you." He pinned his gaze on Jack. "You were just as integral as Bianca was to getting this place finished. We'd love it if you could join us. Our wives will be there."

James nodded. "Kids too. Can't go anywhere without them these days."

"And bring your kiddos, too," Justin added. "We know the owners of the Windward, so we've booked the patio nook for dinner so we won't bug the other guests. Lots of room, tables, chairs, and they even have a small play structure for kids."

Shit. Well, that sounded like a good time, particularly

since Jack found himself really liking Justin and James. Despite the fact that he knew the men to be multimillionaires, they had a down-to-earth vibe about them that Jack was drawn to.

He needed to get on the road though.

"I'm afraid it'll just be Bianca and the kids," Jack said, squeezing Bianca once before removing his arm from around her shoulder. "I'm heading out in about an hour. Just gotta do the final run-through with the boss-lady here, go home and finish packing, find my cat, then I'm on the road."

Justin and James's eyes both landed on Bianca, so many questions being fired at her without a word being uttered.

Yeah, he heard those questions loud and clear. They were the same questions that had been filling his head for the past three months.

Do you really want to leave her? Leave them?

Is living in Mexico necessary to your happiness?

Does she love you? Would staying just cramp their style?

All those questions, plus nearly a million more, had rendered his nights rather sleepless, particularly for the last week, as the countdown to their final night and day together grew nearer.

"Okay, then, Bianca, we'll see you tonight at the Windward?" Justin's phone must have vibrated or pinged as he pulled it from his back pocket, glanced at it and lifted his chin at James. "Kendra and Em say the kids are done at the Space Needle and we need to meet them at the aquarium."

James nodded. "I guess we're on our way to the aquarium then."

"Be sure to check out the giant octopus," Jack added as he and Bianca followed Justin and James to their SUV parked along the curb. "Charlie loved it when we took the kids there a couple of weeks ago." He glanced at Bianca. She'd been distant all morning, and even though he knew she was probably sad about him leaving, she wasn't showing it. She was aloof and almost ... pissed. "Right, babe?"

Nibbling her lip and shoving her hands into the pockets of her white denim capris, she nodded but didn't look at him. "Yep. Loved it."

They all shook hands one more time, Justin and James giving Bianca hugs as well, thanking her repeatedly for her hard work before James slid behind the steering wheel and they pulled off into traffic.

Casey was busy at work inside, doing the post-construction clean.

Since Jack, Max and Isaac had worked until six o'clock last night finishing up the place, Bianca hadn't had a chance to do the final walk-through.

They were going to do that now.

Then they were going to say goodbye.

"The place looks great," she said, walking back into one of the upper units and swiping a finger on the wall, coming up with a layer of dust. "Need to wash these walls."

"Construction dust gets everywhere," he said, wandering behind her quietly as she drifted through each room in each unit. "Max said that if there is anything you need tweaked or done to just give him a call. Even though he's already started work, what with high school having started last week, he says he can help finish up on the weekend."

She nodded and hummed a response, showing him her back.

Without saying anything, she left the top unit, made her way around the outside of the house to the backyard and opened the door to the laundry room. "Looks great in here. Hoyt and Bill did a nice job with the cabinets, and you guys did an amazing job with the drywall and flooring." Like she hadn't picked out the appliances herself, she opened the top-loading dryer and peered inside.

Her silence, lack of eye contact and overall demeanor were killing him. Was she giving him the cold shoulder because she was upset he was leaving? They'd spent a hot as fuck night together last night, and she'd been affectionate, warm and soft as ever. But when he knocked on her door this morning, it was like a robot had replaced his woman. The vacancy in her eyes, in her expression was like a machete to his insides.

Nodding and humming, she opened up a few kitchen drawers inside the last basement suite, twisted her lips in thought as she ran her finger over the grout in the tub, then finally, at long last, turned to face him. "Thank you."

It wasn't the words he thought were going to come out of her mouth, but it was better than nothing.

Jack nodded, hating how the air between them had grown thick and awkward, like he hadn't had his face between her legs and his dick her inside her for hours last night. Or that he hadn't spent every dinner at her house with her children. She was looking at him, speaking to him like he was just another contractor, just another jack-of-all-trades with a tool belt and sawdust in his hair.

"You did a great job, Jack," she said, stepping past him and out into the sunlight. "I couldn't have pulled this off without you. Justin and James were right. You were integral to getting this project to completion." Her bottom lip wobbled. She shoved her closed fist in front of her mouth and coughed, but even an idiot could tell she was faking it. Quickly, she spun on her heels, showing him her back once again, and circled around to the front of the house and the curb where his bike was parked.

Her purse was against her hip, and she swung it to her front and fished a hand inside. "Justin, James and I want to say thank you for all your hard work." She handed him a check. He didn't even bother looking at it and stuffed it into his back pocket.

He didn't give a flying fuck about the money.

He gave a flying fuck about the woman in front of him.

"Bianca ..." Reaching for her, he took her hand. "You can be sad, darlin'. I'm sad too. Had the best fucking summer of my life with you and those kids."

Her throat bobbed hard, and she looked anywhere but his face as her teeth crushed her bottom lip and tears welled up in her eyes.

Fuck. His head was going to explode. And if not his head, then definitely his fucking heart.

Shaking her head, she released his hand and took a half step back, thrusting her hand out like she wanted him to shake it, only it trembled like she'd just taken a double espresso shot intravenously. "I ... it was a pleasure working with you, Jack."

Now he was going to have a straight-up aneurysm followed by a heart attack and, for good measure, maybe a stroke.

He batted her hand away, grabbed her roughly around the waist and drew her against him. "The fuck's going on with you, woman?"

She shook her head, pressed her hands into his chest for a moment to rear her head back, attempting to get away from him. He wasn't letting her go though.

"Nothing's going on," she said, her voice quavering just slightly. "I'm thanking you for your services, paying you and saying goodbye."

"For my *services*," he spat out, releasing her and shoving his fingers into his hair. "For my *services*. You talking about the drywall in there or when I had my tongue in your ass last night? Which *service* you *thanking* me for?"

Her gaze darted around the empty street, and color filled

her cheeks, her eyes becoming watery. "I'm *paying* you for the work you did here, and thanking you for *everything*," she made out through gritted teeth.

"Everything? You mean the last three months?"

Bianca nodded, swallowing again. "Yes."

All he managed was a snort. He was speechless. Did the last three months not mean anything to her?

"We've had fun, Jack. Lots of fun. You're great with my kids, a wonderful man, and I'm a better person for knowing you. But it was just a summer fling, right?" The haughty laugh that burst from her throat made his blood bubble. "We both knew that going in. Why are you getting upset?" A cord in her throat bulged as she swallowed. Her fingers had knitted together in front of her. "I wish you well and a safe trip down to Mexico." She held out her hand again.

"Fuck that," he said batting her hand away again, grabbing her by the ponytail and pulling her against him. He took her mouth like he owned it. Because he fucking did. She was his. Fling or no fling, Bianca Dixon was fucking his.

She remained stiff at first, but her demeanor softened, and she eventually melted against him, wrapping her arms around his neck and letting him lead the kiss like an erotic dance.

When they finally parted, they were both breathless. He pressed his forehead to hers and cupped her chin with his free hand. "Don't treat me like the fucking handyman. I'm more than that, and you know it. What we have is real."

Her lashes fluttered, and she glanced away as more tears brimmed her eyes.

"Look at me, Bianca."

He could feel her reluctance to obey, but she did.

"Say it. What we have is real."

She looked him square in the eye, defiance staring back at him. "You're right. What we *had* was real. But it's over, right?

You're leaving. That's the plan. That's always been the plan. A summer fling." A fat tear slid down her cheek.

Fuck.

His grip on her hair and chin tightened. "You fall in love with me?"

Her head shook, and another tear slipped down along the crease of her nose. "No. You told me not to, so I didn't."

The sledgehammer to his chest was unexpected.

He'd told her not to fall in love with him. Made her fucking promise not to—it'd mostly been a joke, something to add to their "deal"—but as they grew closer and their fling morphed into more, he realized it wasn't such a joke anymore. He was a man who liked his freedom, and hanging out with Bianca and her kids had been fun for the summer, but he knew if they said the *L*-word, hearts all around, big and small, would break. It was better if they kept it casual. Casual was safe.

And hanging out with her and her kids every fucking night for the last two months was casual?

The look on her face said she was lying. She'd gone and fallen in love with him but was too stubborn to admit it. He'd made her promise not to, and she was determined to keep that promise.

Did he want her to reveal that she'd broken her promise? Ask him to stay and be with her and the kids?

He didn't know what the fuck he wanted.

Maybe that was the problem. Bianca knew what she wanted—stability for her and her kids and a fresh start.

Jack wasn't sure he could offer her any of those things.

He let go of her ponytail, pulled her in by the chin for one more quick kiss and finally let her go. Clearing his throat, he stepped away. "Good. You kept your promise, and I kept mine."

Agony filled the soft brown of her eyes, and her words came out as a croak. "I did."

Fuck, why couldn't she just say what she felt? That she'd fallen in love with him. Ask him to stay. "You think I fell in love with you?"

Why was he torturing himself? He needed to get the fuck out of there. Bianca was strong, she was fierce and had proven to him time and again that if she wanted something, she went for it. She wasn't shy. She'd tackled him his first day on the job because she wanted him. So if she wanted him to stay, she'd fucking ask him, right?

Which obviously meant she didn't want him to stay.

She continued to look anywhere but at him. "No. I think we have a strong, almost animalistic attraction to each other. We're sexually compatible, and we get along. It was a summer fling. Lust. Making the most of an opportunity."

Every word cut him deeper.

Clenching his molars, he nodded. "Sounds about right. We certainly fucked like bunnies."

Her chuckle was weak and forced, but her eyes flared for a moment. "We did do that."

He needed to get the fuck out of there and on the road. Clear his head and move on. She obviously had already moved on in her head. Even if she did love him, she'd clearly resolved that they would never work. He needed to do the same.

Swinging one leg over his bike, he fastened the helmet strap beneath his chin, turned over the ignition, pushed the kickstart, and let it rumble for a moment. "It's been an epic fucking summer, Bianca Dixon. One I won't soon forget. You take care of yourself and those kids, okay, darlin'?"

She nodded and crossed her arms in front of her chest. Her meek smile with trembling lips had him pausing. "Will do."

He revved the engine. Why hadn't he left already?

"Ride safe, Jack."

He checked for traffic, glanced back at her, pushed the choke in on his sled and peeled out onto the road. "Later, darlin'," he called before he gave her some gas and sped off to go home and finish packing and see if he could find Bob. Otherwise, Simon would have to locate her.

He glanced back in his rearview mirror with the hope that she'd be standing there watching him. But when he did, she was gone. Disappeared back into the house and out of his life for good, which was apparently just how she fucking wanted it.

ALMOST TWO HOURS after Jack left, the tears still fell in abandon as Bianca cleaned the unit she was in and started setting up the furniture. She'd done it. She'd let him go without telling him that she loved him. She didn't ask him to stay because that would be selfish. Then she'd also never know if he stayed because *he* wanted to or because he couldn't say no to her.

It was better to just let him go. Let him live his life the way he always did, free and unencumbered by the weight of a needy woman and her three darling but demanding children. He didn't sign up for that life, so it would be foolish for her to think he wanted it now.

Jack and the guys hauled in all the furniture she purchased for the units, including double beds for the rooms, desks, dressers, couches and tables and chairs. The furnishings would be bare bones so the students could make their home their own.

Casey was in the living room washing walls and windows. Over the last month or so, the young woman had put on some weight, which Bianca was happy to see. She'd been skin and bones when she started working, but doing all the yard work and eating right had added some muscle to her arms and more meat on her bones. She had her headphones on as she worked—like she often did—but the tune she was humming felt familiar to Bianca even though she couldn't place it.

That also meant the house was quiet, leaving Bianca to her rampant thoughts, which only caused the tears to continue to flow.

The more time she spent in the silence, trapped in her own mind and the carousel of doubt, the more she wondered if she'd been wrong to hide her feelings from him. Wrong to lie and say she hadn't fallen in love with him. What if she really did never see him again? What if something happened to him in Mexico or on his trip down? Motorcycles were two-wheel death traps, as sexy as they were, and all it would take would be one semi-truck driver coming in the opposite direction to fall asleep behind the wheel and Jack would be gone forever.

"Shut the fuck up," she murmured to herself. When left alone for too long, her brain tended to go off the rails and get quite morbid. He'd been doing this trip for years. He knew the road, knew his route. This was his life, his plan. She couldn't interfere with that. The man had earned his freedom to do as he pleased. She needed to let him be.

With a sigh that rattled the last remaining pieces of her broken heart, she pulled the mattress protector over the mattress and nudged the bedframe back against the wall.

"Casey, I'm hungry. I'm going to pop out and grab something for lunch. You interested?" She spun around, chastising herself for her stupidity in thinking Casey would be able to hear her over the headphones, when she came face-to-face with a man she thought she'd never see again.

20

"CASEY!" Bianca shouted, her eyes darting around the small bedroom for an escape. Rod blocked the door, and she wasn't sure she'd fit through the window. Even if she could, he'd get to her before she could get out.

Rage filled the cold, pale blue eyes of the man who'd tried to ruin her life. His face was a mottled and angry red, and his fists clenched and unclenched at his sides. "Thought you were rid of me, bitch?" he asked with a sneer that showed off his yellowing teeth and cracked lips.

"You need to go," she said, her voice low and as calm as she could muster. Meanwhile, inside, her thoughts immediately went to her children and the possibility of never getting to hold them again.

He clucked his tongue and took a step into the room. "I tried to do this the legal way. The *civil* way. But you had to sic your dogs on me."

"They're not dogs. They're lawyers, and they're family. They did what any *sane* person would do and countersue your ass to get you to withdraw your ridiculous claim." Even through the fear, she wasn't going to let this waste of skin think he had her over a barrel, that she was afraid of him.

She'd let Ashley walk all over her, and she vowed never to let a man do that again.

"Casey!" she called out again, moving to see if she could see the young woman in the living room.

Rod's lip lifted up on one side. "She can't hear you. Those noise-canceling headphones are a dangerous thing. *Anybody* can sneak up on you."

Dread made her limbs turn icy. "What did you do to her?"

He shrugged. "What she deserved, stupid whore."

"Casey!" No longer caring about what happened to her, Bianca charged Rod and tried to break free through the door. He blocked her but not before she saw Casey lying on the living-room floor, not moving.

Was she dead? Unconscious?

She scratched at his arms and face, causing him to cry out in pain and smack her hard across the face. She saw stars and faltered for a moment, giving Rod an opportunity to grab her by the arms, his fingers digging into her flesh enough to leave bruises.

"Stupid cunt." He spun her around, crossed her arms in front of her chest and plastered her back to his front. He guided her over to the bed.

Oh no.

No.

NO!

"Gonna get what's owed to me another way," he said, bending her over the bed with a hard knee to the back of her legs.

She was forced to oblige and bend over.

Tears stung the back of her eyes, and her throat grew tight.

This couldn't be happening.

She bucked her body and kicked behind her in a frantic attempt to break free, but he tightened his hold on her arms, causing pain to shoot up through her shoulders. He released one hand, and a hard smack to the side of her head made her flailing end. Stars burst in the back of her head, and pain sprinted to the base of her spine.

"Don't got your fucking camel jockey here to protect you anymore. Saw that motherfucker leave for good. Know you two were screwin'. You like the brown dick, bitch?"

"Fuck you!" She struggled again, her body jerking side to side, head thrashing. She screamed out for help. Cried rape, rattled the rafters with a holler she was sure they would be able to hear ten blocks away, but all of that was silenced when the cool, sharp blade touched the front of her throat. "Fight me, and I'll cut you."

Try as she might to not show him that he scared her, a whimper burbled up from the depths of her throat, and tears burned the corners of her eyes. Her cheek pressed into the mattress, and she clenched her teeth in anticipation.

The *clang* of a belt being unfastened and the *zip* of a zipper had her tensing, but she kept that image of her children on the back of her eyelids.

He'd taken her power. Was about to take her body, but he couldn't take her mind. He couldn't control what she thought about while he overpowered her.

The blade moved away from her throat, and she sucked in a deep breath that burned her lungs.

"Please don't do this, Rod. I'll get you the money, if that's all this is. I'll pay you the rest of the four grand. Please don't do this." The images of her children began to fade, and salty tears spilled over onto her lips as she choked on a rough sob and blubbered her pleas. "Please don't do this." She heard him rearrange his pants, and *something* pressed against the crease of her ass.

Her pants were next.

"Rod, please ..."

"Shut up!" The tip of the blade pricked the base of her neck. "Stupid fucking cunt. Fucking a raghead Ay-rab. Disgusting."

Bianca trembled and sobbed as she waited for Rod to remove her pants, to *get what she owed him.* "Please ..."

He released her, and his fingers curled into the waistband of her pants, pulling them down, along with her underwear.

"No ..."

"Shut the fuck up!" Out of the corner of her eye, she saw him lift his hand, preparing to hit her again, but it never happened. Rod was flung back into the room and away from her.

Then the sound of fist meeting face echoed into the room, followed by men fighting and Rod grunting in anguish.

Bianca pulled up her pants and spun around just in time to see Jack sitting on top of Rod's belly, pounding the living shit out of him.

"Jack!" She raced over to him and grabbed his arm as he lifted it high into the air, preparing it bring it back down on Rob's bloody, mangled face. "Stop! Don't kill him. Don't!"

Jack's chest heaved, and she could feel it in his muscles that his brain and body were struggling to connect. She bent over and pressed her forehead to the top of his head, squeezing his arm as she did so. "He's not worth the jail time. Don't kill him. Please."

That seemed to knock some sense into him, and he blinked a few times, his body relaxing.

Rod was still breathing, but the man was unconscious. If she'd let Jack continue, he would have been dead by now.

She helped Jack up, then went to tend to Casey, who was just beginning to rouse.

"Wh-what happened?" Casey asked, propping herself up on her elbows and wincing.

"Rod attacked you from behind, then he came after me."

Casey's gray eyes widened. "Oh my God, Bianca, are you okay?" Her gaze drifted up to Jack, who was already on his phone, probably calling the attack in to the cops.

Bianca nodded. "I am, yeah. He hit me a couple of times, but I'll be okay. Are you?" She helped Casey sit up and watched as the young woman rubbed the back of her head.

"I didn't even hear him come in. I had my back to the door, my headphones on, and then I felt a hard slam to the back of my head."

"No more of that, huh? We'll get you a portable speaker, and you can sync it to your phone. Just because Rod had an ax to grind with us doesn't mean it couldn't be a random stranger next time." She helped Casey stand up and rubbed the young woman's back.

Jack stowed his phone in his pocket and turned to them both. "Cops are on their way."

"Just drag him into the bathroom and lock the door," Casey said, stepping over Rod's limp arm toward the bathroom. She flicked on the light and opened the door. "There aren't any windows, so he can't escape."

Jack nodded, shoved his hands under Rod's arms and dragged the dead weight to the bathroom, leaving him on the floor, his cock out and everything. No sense tampering with the evidence.

Casey shut the door and locked it, then dragged a heavy wooden table in front of it for good measure. "This creep needs to go to prison," she said, wiping her hands on her denim shorts.

Bianca and Jack's lips both curled up at how take-charge Casey was. She was really proving to be a huge asset and a wonderful person Bianca was proud to know.

She was also far more astute than her twenty-one years would lead one to believe. With a coy smile, she headed to the open front door. "I'm going to go grab some air, give you two a minute. I'll meet the cops when they get here."

Jack snorted and smiled. "Thanks." Stepping toward her, he shoved his fingers into his hair and shook his head. "Fuck, darlin', if I'd have come just a minute later ..."

She grabbed his hand and turned it around, palm down. "You're injured."

A single-syllable laugh shot from his throat. "Yeah, beating a man's face in will do that."

"We need to get you to the hospital."

His head shook again, and he pulled free from her grasp, cupping her face with the same hand. "I'll be fine. Gotta tell you something."

Bianca glanced up at the man she'd fallen head over heels in love with and blinked through the threatening tears. "Yeah?"

"You're a liar."

Well, that wasn't what she was expecting to hear him say. "Excuse me?" She tried to pull away, but he wouldn't let her.

"You're a liar, Bianca. A big fat one."

"Did you just call me fat?"

His head shook, but the seriousness with which he looked down his long nose at her didn't waver an inch. "Nope. 'Cause you're not *fat*. But you are a big fat liar. You love me, and when I asked you if you did, you said no. That makes you a liar."

"I—"

"You broke your promise."

"Jack—"

"And you acted all weird and distant today because you didn't want me to think you broke your promise. You pushed me away."

Squeezing her eyes shut, she tried to drop her head, but he held her jaw and wouldn't let her.

"I was angry how you treated me today. Like I was nothing more than a booty call. A dick to warm your bed for the summer. But I didn't even get out of my driveway before it all clicked into place. Before I realized that everything I want, everything I need, everything I *love* is here. I—"

"Guys." Casey popped her head around the corner of the door. "Rod has a cat in a live catch trap in the back cab of his truck. Windows and doors are all closed."

Bianca's eyes went wide, and Jack released her, taking off out of the house into the front yard, where Rod's truck was parked.

Casey's pace was brisk, but Jack was nearly in a full-out sprint. He passed her on the sidewalk and got to Rod's truck, peering into the closed window. Bianca and Casey joined him seconds later.

"That's Bob!" Jack yelled.

Bianca's eyes widened. She peered into the window too. "Fuck, he's got her in a closed vehicle in this heat. We've got to get her out of there before she dies."

They all tried the door handles, but the vehicle was locked.

"I can go and get his keys off him," Casey offered, prepared to head back to the house.

Jack grabbed a huge rock from the neighbor's yard and lifted it over his head. "No time. Stand back." He brought the rock down hard into the front passenger window, shattering the glass enough to reach his hand inside and unlock it. Pushing the seat forward, he retrieved the live catch trap and hauled it out, moving over to the shade of a big oak tree before he set it down on the grass. He pulled Bob out. She didn't look good.

"Fuck, we need to get her water. What if he's had her since Friday?"

Right. Jack mentioned that morning that Bob had been missing since Friday. Was this all part of Rod's evil plan?

They moved back into the house just as two police patrol cars pulled up to the curb. Casey went out to greet them while Jack and Bianca took care of Bob.

The cat was breathing, and her eyes were open, but she was lethargic and incredibly hot.

"It's okay, baby," Jack cooed, sitting on the floor, cradling Bob in his arms and rocking her. Bianca brought over a bowl of cold water, but Bob wouldn't drink. It took Jack dipping his fingers into the water and bringing the droplets to the cat's mouth for her to lick for Bob to drink anything.

Casey entered the house first, followed by none other than Isaac and a female cop with a blonde bob. Relief flooded every cell of her body to see a familiar face. Isaac knew the story of Rod and Casey. He would be on their side from the get-go.

Concern flashed hard in his blue eyes as he made his way over to Bianca and Jack. "Fuck, guys, when I got the address, I got here as fast as I could. Did Rod really come back and—"

"Yes," Bianca said. "He knocked Casey unconscious and tried to rape me. Jack intervened. He's locked in the bathroom."

Isaac and his partner nodded then headed toward the bathroom. His partner knocked, announced that they were Seattle PD, and unlocked the door.

From what Bianca could see, Rod was just coming to, but remained hunched over and groggy sitting on the toilet lid. They cuffed Rod and Isaac's partner started to read Rod his Miranda rights.

Isaac made his way back over to where Bianca sat with Jack. He squeezed his eyes shut for a moment before opening them and focusing on Bob. "What happened here?"

"She went missing on Friday. I spent all weekend and all morning looking for her. Found her locked in a live catch trap in Rod's truck. Parked in the sun, no windows down." Jack looked away and pinched the bridge of his long nose as he closed his eyes.

"Fuck," Isaac breathed, reaching down to pet Bob. "Poor baby. You want me to call a vet, see if we can get one to come out?" He jerked his chin toward the other police officer, who was speaking with Casey. "Mel's brother-in-law is a vet. Helped me with my cat. I'm sure he'd come out."

"That'd be nice," Jack said, his words faint as he stared down at Bob, continuing to lift water droplets to her mouth.

Isaac nodded and stood up, indicating Bianca should follow him.

"I'm going to need a full account of what happened here today. I know Rod dropped the civil suit against you. Do you think this has anything to do with that?"

"It has everything to do with it," she said. "He said so. Said he came here to *get what was owed to him* another way, since I sicced my dogs on him and filed a countersuit."

Isaac nodded and breathed out deep through his nose. "Jack beat him?"

She nodded."

"Not enough to kill him, thankfully."

"Not quite. I stopped him before he could."

"Good. I'd hate to have to arrest a friend." Isaac's smile was bleak. "I'm gonna get Mel to help me get Rod out of here, take him down to the station." He glanced at Mel and nodded. She joined him, and the two of them hoisted Rod up off the toilet and escorted him out of the bathroom and house to one of the patrol cars parked along the curb.

Among all the chaos, another police car had arrived and

Bianca saw Casey standing outside on the sidewalk speaking with the female officer.

Thank God Casey was okay. The young woman was resilient and seemed completely unfazed by what had just happened to her. Strength was her middle name.

Rod on the other hand, Bianca couldn't give two shits about. As long as he went away and for a considerable amount of time. She focused on Jack and knelt down beside him and Bob. "How's she doing?"

He glanced up at her, sadness infused in his gaze. "I love you."

A soft but hope-inspiring *meow* emanated from the drowsy Bob. She lapped up water from Jack's cupped hand, and a gentle purr started to rumble from her.

Bianca sighed in relief. "I think she's going to be okay."

He nodded. "I think so too."

Resting her head against Jack's, she scratched behind Bob's ears. "I love you, too. I'm sorry I lied. I'm sorry I broke my promise, and I'm sorry I pushed you away today. I just thought it'd be easier."

"Was it?"

"No." Pretending they were no more than a summer fling had been agony, and the look on his face when she stuck her hand out for a shake would be one she'd struggle to get over for a while to come.

"I'm going to have to go to Mexico at some point to sort things out, but I'm not going to stay for the eight months. Maybe a week, two tops. I need to see if the guy who runs my bar while I'm away for the summer can continue to do it year-round. But I'm staying in Seattle for good. My home, my life, my *family* and everyone and everything I love is here."

Bob seemed to have had enough water and was now purring contentedly in Jack's arms with her eyes closed.

Jack cupped Bianca's jaw and brought her to face him until they were nose to nose.

"So you're staying?" she asked, frustrated that yet more tears were piling up and about to breach the dam.

"On one condition."

She lifted a brow. "And what's that?"

"You promise you won't ever fall *out* of love with me."

Smiling like a lovesick idiot, she let those tears fall. "I think I can agree to those terms, Mr. Savage."

He brought her lips to his and murmured against them. "Jack, darlin'. You really need to call me Jack."

Looping her arms around him, breathing him in, she whispered, "How about I just call you mine?"

EPILOGUE

A week later ...

TURNING AROUND in the front seat of the minivan, Bianca double-checked that all her children were properly strapped in. "Ready?"

The kids tossed their hands into the air and cheered.

Smiling, she turned back around in her seat and waited for Jack to engage the GPS and start driving before she picked up her phone and hit speed dial. It wasn't very long of a drive.

He picked up on the third ring. "Hey, Bianca."

"Hi, Ashley. How's it going?"

Instantly, his tone became skeptical. "Good, and you?"

"Great, actually. You know, I've decided that I *will* fly down with the kids for a week and then fly home with them."

Her ex sputtered. "You will?"

"Yeah, I mean, it's just a week, right?"

Ashley exhaled a sigh, obviously from relief. "Exactly. That's what I've been saying all along. I'm glad you've finally been able to see reason, Bianca. I'm hoping that we can turn this into a more amicable and even friendly relationship between us. I honestly think you and Opal could be friends if you gave her a chance."

Bianca mimicked sticking her finger down her throat and fought the urge to gag.

Yes, because the day she became friends with the woman who destroyed her marriage and family was the day she asked her brothers to commit her to the nuthouse and she demanded the doctors give her a frontal lobotomy.

She pointed for Jack to turn left.

"Well, let's take this slow, shall we, Ashley? She did, after all, sleep with my husband and smile to my face while doing it."

Jack smirked, and she nodded when he asked if they were in the right neighborhood.

"I thought we were turning over a new leaf, Bianca. You're bringing up the past," Opal cut in, her breathy, bimbo voice making Bianca's skin crawl. "We've *all* done things we're not proud of. Even you. People in glass houses really shouldn't be throwing rocks."

"You're right, Moonstone—I mean, *Opal*, we are. New leaves. New branches. Even new trees." Whatever the fuck that meant. "Which is why I'm doing what I'm doing. Flying down with the kids so you can see them for the week and flying home with them. Paying their airfare both ways."

Jack put the van into park and shut off the ignition.

"Someone's here," Opal said, her voice distant on what was obviously speakerphone.

"Listen, Bianca, I'm so happy you've finally come around. Can I call you right back?" Ashley asked.

Bianca unbuckled her seat belt. "Absolutely."

Ashley disconnected the call.

Just as she and Jack were hauling the children out of the van, Opal and Ashley carrying the twins emerged from their cookie-cutter Palm Springs palace on the golf course. Opal and Ashley's eyes were wider than the headlights on Opal's fancy new Mercedes.

"Did I forget to mention I was bringing them *now*?" Bianca asked, setting Charlie down on his feet. "I ended up chatting with your sister randomly over Instagram, and she mentioned that you had this week off. Funny you didn't mention it to me when we spoke last week."

Ashley looked like he was ready to puke. Opal wasn't much better off.

Bianca shrugged and grinned, her attention focused on her ex-husband but not missing the darting eyes of his mistress. "Must have just slipped your mind, huh?"

Hannah and Hayley were already ogling the babies, and Jack was lugging their suitcases from the back of the van. Ashley's eyes landed on Jack, and his whole body stiffened.

"Anyway, we've gotta run. We'll be back in a week to get them. Sound good?" She stepped toward Charlie, pulled her son into her arms for a hug and kissed his cheek.

"You're not *staying* in Palm Springs?" Opal practically shrieked.

Jack actually stuck his finger in his ear, shook it and winced from how high-pitched the homewrecker's voice got.

"Jack's got a place on the Baja. We're going to fly down there and go check it out, stay for a while. We worked like dogs all summer to get that fourplex up and running. Need a vacay before the craziness of back-to-school starts up." She looped her arm around Jack's waist as Charlie took off to go roll around on Ashley's front lawn like a dog. Her son really was a unique little human.

"Who are—" Ashley didn't even have a chance to spit out his question before Jack stepped forward and offered his hand.

"Name's Jack. Jack Savage."

Bianca had to turn her head to hide her smile after seeing

Ashley's face crumple when Jack shook his hand, obviously squeezing much too hard for Ashley's soft, manicured fingers.

Her ex-husband cleared his throat. "I didn't even know you were seeing someone."

Bianca shrugged. "There's a lot you don't know about me, Ashley."

Her ex looked incredibly uncomfortable, which made Bianca really freaking happy.

Ashley's body shook like he'd just jumped into a frozen lake. "You can't just leave—"

"My children with their father? I think I can. In fact, I'm going to." She released Jack, took Hannah and Hayley by the shoulders, hugged them both and kissed them. "We'll be back in a week, okay? You help your dad and Opal with the twins and Charlie. Be the big sisters you were born to be. The big helpers, and I'll bring you back something super special from Mexico."

Their faces turned sad. Charlie had found a random sprinkler that was on in the adjacent yard and was already soaked to the skin.

"We're going to miss you, Mom," Hannah said, moving into Bianca for a bigger hug.

"And I'm going to miss you. But you have the phone. You can call me whenever you need to, okay? Day or night. I bought long-distance minutes. But there is no internet or games on the phone. It's an old flip phone, but it'll work. Keep it charged, and call me if you need to talk, okay?"

Hannah and Hayley nodded.

"Will you even have any fun there without us?" Hayley asked.

"It'll be tough, but I'm going to try." That seemed to ease her daughter's anxiety.

Jack snorted a laugh behind them, which made the girls'

heads pop up. They took off toward him and looped their arms around his waist.

"We're going to miss you, too, Jack," Hannah said with a huge pout.

Hayley squeezed him. "It's up to you to help Mom have fun, okay?"

Ashley made a choking noise in his throat.

"Me too, me too," Charlie called, joining in the group hug between Jack and the girls. "My miss you, Jack. My lub you."

Jack squeezed his eyes shut for a moment before opening them again and hoisting a drenched Charlie up onto his hip. "I'm really going to miss you kids. You have fun with your dad and stepmom, though, okay? We'll be back to pick you up in a week."

He planted a kiss on Charlie's cheek and set him down on the ground. The girls returned to Bianca, looking like they'd just been told the truth about Santa Claus.

"I'll call you when we land, okay?" She said that to her girls, because she didn't give a shit about Ashley or Opal. She couldn't trust either of them to give her the truth, but she could trust her kids. Which was why she got the girls that flip phone.

With the imminent separation from her children hanging like a wad of stale bread in her throat, she sniffled, swallowed and backed up into Jack's arms once again. "You guys are going to have a great time with your dad and Opal. He took the whole week off just to be with you."

Hannah and Hayley didn't seem convinced.

Bianca faced Ashley again. "I packed loads of clothes, books and activities for them. And I ordered a car seat for Charlie and booster seats for the girls online. They should be here this afternoon." Tilting her head toward his Escalade, she smiled. "Seats seven, right?"

Ashley and Opal still hadn't said much. The shock on

their faces and paleness of their normally tanned skin brought Bianca so much joy, she could hardly keep herself from laughing.

But that would only make the situation worse. Instead, she smiled, toned down her happiness just a tad and thought of her children.

Jack squeezed her hip. "Need to get moving, darlin'. Get this rental back and catch our flight."

She grinned up at her man. "Right." Her eyes fell on her children again. "I love you guys, and I'll see you in a week."

A dripping Charlie had joined his sisters on the walkway, and all three children looked like the last thing they wanted to do was spend a week with their dad. Up until they arrived at his house, they'd been excited to see Ashley, but once it set in that Bianca and Jack were leaving, staying with Ashley and Opal didn't look so good anymore.

Jack and Bianca climbed back into the rental van, and Jack started up the engine.

Hannah and Hayley's pouts were probably visible from space, and Charlie's wave was obviously made of limp noodles.

"My lub you, Mama," Charlie called. "Lub you, too, Jack."

Bianca blew her children three kisses, waited for each of them to catch the kiss and press it against their heart.

She waved, rolled down her window and called out as Jack backed out of the driveway, "I'll miss you. Have fun with your dad. Behave. I love you."

Hannah and Hayley glanced up at their father like he was the most boring person in the world, incapable of fun, and their week was going to involve watching paint dry, they just knew it.

But for all his faults, Ashley was a good dad. Sure, he'd fucked up royally banging his secretary and tearing their family to shreds, but when he had his kids, he was a good, hands-on father, and Bianca had zero concerns leaving her children with him. If she did, they'd be at her parents' right now while she flew down to Mexico with her hot handyman.

Jack reached for her hand and kissed the back of it. "Excited or just sad?"

Smiling at him, she linked their fingers together and rested them on the gearshift. "Not sad. Definitely excited. This is just the first time I've been away from my kids for this long. They've spent the night with my parents and brothers but never for more than one or two nights. And they've always been just a fifteen-minute drive away." Her eyes bugged out, but she continued to stare straight ahead, determined to not give in to the sting behind her eyes. "We're leaving the country."

"Say the word, and we'll turn around, grab them and bring them with us." He glanced at her when they came to a red light. "I'm on board with whatever you want."

And that was why she loved this man so freaking much. Because Jack understood her. He got her. He offered her the flexibility and understanding that Ashley never could. But most of all, Jack respected her.

Shaking her head, she squeezed his fingers. "Keep driving. They are with their dad. They're going to be fine. This mama needs a vacation."

"She certainly fucking does."

The light turned green, and he hit the accelerator again, eyes back on the road.

"Thank you, Jack."

His quick head turn and smile had the butterflies in her belly going berserk.

"For everything. For being there when I needed help— not once, not twice, but three times. For being so good with my kids. For loving me. For coming back. For—"

"You don't have to thank me, Bianca."

"But I want to. I—"

"I came back because I *had* to. I mean, I wanted to. But I *had* to. I realized that the reason I would always head off down to Mexico was because I didn't think I needed any sort of stability or constant in my life. That I didn't need love, roots or a place to call *home*. But I found that home, in you, in the kids. I was searching for it without even knowing what I was searching for or that I was even searching. I *had* to come back, because I left my heart with you. And I can't live without a heart. You, the kids, Simon. You're my heart, my home, and there is no place I'd rather be." At this point, he'd actually pulled off to the side of the road and put the hazards on.

Tears ran down her face like a river after the ice melts, and she used the hem of her tank top to blot at her eyes.

Jack unbuckled his seat belt, unbuckled hers and hauled her across the console into his arms. "I didn't mean to make you cry, darlin'."

She shook her head. "They're tears of joy, I swear."

Chuckling, he kissed her forehead. "I figured, but still. Never want to make you cry."

"I love you so much, Jack. You're home to me too. I didn't think I'd ever feel love again, let alone a love like this." Bianca blinked through the tears, cupped his face and kissed him, her salty lips finding solace against his strong, soft ones. The wiry hairs of his beard and mustache were a familiar comfort, something she'd quickly grown to love.

He broke the kiss, pressed his forehead against hers and held on to her. "This is it, baby. You, me, the kids, Simon, Jared and Casey. We're a family. A blended family. But we're a family."

Bianca smiled, looped her arms around his neck and blinked, her lashes damp. "We're a family."

"And I'll do everything in my power to protect my family."

A fierceness burned in his eyes, one she knew came directly from the depths of his soul, and was fueled by his past. "I protect what's mine. I protect my home. I protect my heart."

She moved one hand down and pressed it over his heart, the thin, soft cotton beneath her palm warm from his skin. "And I'll protect you. Because as much as I'm yours, you're mine. Home. Heart. You're it. You're everything."

One year later ...

BIANCA TIPPED her sunglasses down her nose and stared at the dripping wet, tanned Adonis emerging from the water. Like Jason Momoa in *Aquaman* but even better, because he was real and she could touch him.

She put her book down on her lounge chair, entertained by the man exiting the sea far more than the parenting book she was currently reading.

Jack snagged a towel off the end of her chair and dried off his hair and torso, the water droplets on his nipples catching the sunlight and dangling like diamonds.

He'd look hot with pierced nipples.

"You okay, baby?" he asked with a knowing grin. "Kinda look like you've got spontaneous paralysis or something." He sat on the chair and ran his fingers up her shin, then down the inside of her thigh, stopping just before he reached her bathing suit. "Or was it a spontaneous something else?"

The thumb from his other hand reached up and tugged her bottom lip out from between her teeth. She hadn't even been aware she'd been biting it.

"Damn, you're hot," she finally said, swallowing and shifting on the chair so his finger brushed her bathing suit. A rush of pleasure sprinted up from between her legs directly to her nipples when he grazed her clit.

"Not as hot as you, baby," he purred, pushing her bathing suit to the side and running two fingers through her slippery folds.

Bianca glanced around the beach. Normally, the place had a lot of kids and families around, but today it was pretty quiet. They were also off in their own little area, and she had a beach umbrella protecting them from peeping Toms. He pushed two fingers inside her and began to pump, his thumb working her clit over the Lycra bathing suit.

They were turning this end-of-August trip into a tradition. Even though Mexico was hot as hell this time of year, that also meant the tourists weren't piling into town in droves, clogging up the beaches. It also meant that Bianca could leave her children with their father without them missing any school. They did plan to fly back down for Christmas, when the weather was cooler.

But this trip was about her and Jack.

They'd only been there a total of two days, and she'd already lost count of how many orgasms she'd had. Even after over a year together, the man was insatiable. And generous with the orgasms. Boy, was he generous.

Her hips arched and her eyes closed as he brought her closer to climax, the sensation building deep in her belly and between her legs.

"Gonna come for me, Bianca?" he asked.

She snagged her bottom lip between her teeth again and nodded. "Mhmm."

"Gonna come for me, baby, then you're gonna marry me."

What?

Her eyes flew open, and she sat up, struggling to get her elbows beneath her for support. "What?"

His thumb maneuvered its way beneath her bathing suit

and rubbed over her clit. Her leg jerked. "Sorry, darlin'. I should have been more specific. Gonna make you come *here*. Then gonna propose. *Then* gonna go back to our place, eat you out, fuck you. *Then* we'll call your family and tell them the good news. Didn't mean to confuse you."

Her brain was beginning to short-circuit. He was fucking her with his fingers and doing a hell of a good job of it, but he'd also just brought up marriage and proposing. Now he was fucking with her head.

Was this what it felt like right before someone had a stroke?

She didn't smell toast, just Jack's magnificent scent, the sea, the breeze and sunscreen. She hadn't said anything yet, so she wasn't sure if her speech would be slurred.

Not a stroke but just a really intense impending orgasm with a veil of confusion over top?

That was probably more like it.

His thumbnail scratched the hood of her clit, and she detonated. Exploded. Combusted. Like a powder keg dripping in kerosene struck by lightning, she went off.

And off. And off.

If there had been families and children at the beach, they all would have noticed her, convulsing there on the lounger like a fish on the dock. Jack's body shielded most of her and what he was doing to her, but her moans and whimpers of pleasure when the climax took hold of her body couldn't be stopped.

It was like an out-of-body experience. Her soul left her for that brief moment, hovered above in the glare of the sun watching as she came unraveled.

When the orgasm waves finally receded, gathering back in her center, she slumped down in the lounge chair, her limbs heavy, eyes closed, mouth slack.

Jack withdrew his fingers from her, and she could hear him sucking them clean.

"Open your eyes, Bianca."

Lazily, she complied, a big, satisfied smile curling the corners of her mouth. "That was ..."

"Yeah?" he asked, his own smile huge. He hinged forward and pulled something free from his cargo shorts on the sand below her chair. That's when she remembered the *other* thing he'd mentioned. Orgasm amnesia was a real thing, at least when it came to Jack Savage. He could make her come so hard, she often forgot what she was doing or talking about before she came.

Sometimes she never remembered.

But this time she did.

Sitting up straight again, he brought a small, dark brown wooden box in front of her and opened it.

She couldn't hold back her gasp even if she tried. Her hand flew to her mouth, her throat clogged and her eyes burned.

"The girls helped me pick it out."

Which girls? Celeste and Bianca or the twins?

"Both sets of girls." His brows knitted together. "Actually, I had *a lot* of female input. Most of your friends know this is happening. Celeste and Lauren, Richelle and Eva—they all gave their opinions on rings until we picked something that we all knew you'd love. And then, of course, I had to run it past the little divas."

She choked on a sob. How her girls had managed to keep such a secret was beyond her.

"Got Hayley's seal of approval right off the bat—says she likes the halo diamonds around the bigger one and the rose-gold band. Hannah thinks the diamonds on the band need to be bigger and the center pear-shaped diamond should be pink." He rolled his eyes. "That girl's gonna need a man with a lot of patience and a big bank account." He paused. "If she swings that way. Otherwise, she's going to need a woman with a lot of patience and a big bank account."

Bianca snorted a laugh, her eyes now dripping, nose threatening to run.

"Everyone approves of it, of us. I guess I just need to know if you do too? I asked your dad and your brothers. They both welcomed me to the family with open arms. Though Liam murmured a few threats in my ear, which I expected."

She laughed again, her vision growing blurry from all the tears.

"Bianca Dixon, you are my heart, my home, my soft landing. I've never been married before, but you have been, so we can do it as big or small as you want. I don't care about the size or the expense. All I care about is you becoming my wife. Our families officially becoming united and you by my side until death do us part. Your kids, my kids and that big crazy lot you call an extended family, if that's all you want, then I'm good with that. You want to elope, get married down here?"

She lifted a brow. Elope? Really?

His head shook. "No, I'm not good with that. I want our kids there."

That made her smile. *Our kids.*

"But big or small, we'll do it together because together, we're better."

"Together, we're better," she repeated, believing the words so fully in her heart.

"Will you marry me?"

Bianca nodded, threw her arms around his neck and pulled him against her. "Of course, I will. I've never been happier in my entire life than I have been with you, Jack. I want all of it, forever."

He held her tight for a moment before pulling away, wiping her tears with his thumb, then showing her the ring again. He pulled it from its satin bed, and she held out her left hand.

"Perfect fit," he said, sliding it onto her finger.

"Just like us." She held her hand in front of her and blinked back more tears. "My handyman. My husband. My partner. My heart."

He pushed her back to the lounge chair and covered his body with hers, his lips hovering just a hairsbreadth over her mouth. "My home."

Bianca wrapped her arms around Jack's neck and pressed her lips against his. "My home. Forever."

For an extended, EXTRA epilogue go here: whitleycox.com/bonus-material

---

If you haven't read The Single Dads of Seattle, now's the time to start.
Grab Hired by the Single Dad, Book 1 of The Single Dads of Seattle.
BUY IT HERE: mybook.to/hiredbythesingledad

Sign up for my newsletter to hear about all my new releases, sales and giveaways.
GO HERE: http://eepurl.com/ckh5yT

HIRED BY THE SINGLE DAD - SNEAK PEEK
THE SINGLE DADS OF SEATTLE, BOOK 1

Chapter 1

"To divorce!"

"Hear, hear!"

"Good riddance!"

Did somebody groan?

Mark Herron's interest piqued at the numerous cheers of the women behind him. Glasses clinked and giggles echoed around the big booth table at the posh bar, The Ludo Lounge, in downtown Seattle. He didn't dare turn around, at least not yet, but he tuned out the rest of the bar and zeroed in on the intriguing conversation going on just one table over.

Who celebrated divorce?

Certainly not him.

It had been one of the most horrible, gut-wrenching things he'd ever gone through. Not to mention the toll it had taken on Gabe. No, Mark's divorce from Cheyenne had been brutal.

But yet, these women appeared to be in celebration. At least some of them did.

It was certainly the place for it. Dark, big, deep booths, rocking music, a small dance floor and a price tag on even a glass of house wine high enough to keep out the hooligans who came just to get shit-faced and laid. It was a classy bar. But that didn't mean you couldn't have a good time at a classy place, and that's exactly what these women sounded like they were after.

"Come on, Tori, celebrate," one woman encouraged. "He's gone for good."

"Yeah ... " came a breathy, almost hesitant voice. "Gone for good." She didn't sound nearly as enthusiastic as the rest. "We're not *technically* divorced yet. I just filed for separation."

"Well, it's a start!" a third woman cheered.

"After he kicked me out," she murmured.

"Come on, you've got your whole life ahead of you now," came another friend. "Plenty of hot, single men in Seattle."

"That's right. Take life by the balls, chica." This woman sounded incredibly drunk. Mark could just picture her pantomiming grabbing a scrotum that hung precariously over their table. "The world is your oyster ... speaking of, we should get some raw ones brought over to the table. They're an aphrodisiac, and we need to get Tori here *laid!*"

Mark cringed. Whoever this Tori was, his heart went out to her.

"I'm okay, guys, really," the same hesitant voice from earlier affirmed. "No aphrodisiacs needed. Nobody ... at least not me ... is going to be getting laid tonight. I'm taking a break."

"I don't think Ken is taking a break," the obnoxious oyster-loving friend said. "He couldn't even be faithful *during* your marriage. What makes you think he's taking a break now?"

"He's not. I know that he's with Nicole, the dental

hygienist he was cheating on me with. His sister confirmed that Ken moved her in a few months ago."

"See! See! All the more reason for you to jump back on the horse."

"Stallion! Find a stallion this time. Ken was no more than a lame pony with one ball." Oh, that oyster-loving drunk chick was a piece of work. Mark was itching to get a peek at her.

"He had testicular cancer." Her voice was quiet and, although not meek, she definitely didn't sound as enthusiastic or keen on being there as the rest of them. She sounded tired, sad.

"Okay, so he's a half-gelded lame pony. Whatever. Ditch the kiddie saddle and find a stallion you can bareback."

"Can we ditch the equestrian references please? They're creeping me out," Tori said with a groan.

"Look, Tori ... " Oh good, this friend sounded significantly less drunk and far more on the level. "We know Ken did a number on you."

"I filed for separation. I'm the one who called it quits."

"And rightfully so. You worked three jobs to put that bastard through dental school. He promised you once he finished, he'd put you through grad school, only instead he cheated on you with some little hoochie and left you high and dry."

"Yeah ... "

"Yeah?"

"But ... "

But what? Mark fought the urge to spin around. His instinct to protect overwhelmed him. Who on earth did that to a person? To their wife no less? He hadn't even met this woman, and yet the desire to find her ex and give the bastard a real piece of his mind was damn near all-consuming.

"But ... he was my husband. We took vows. For better or worse."

"Yeah, but Ken was beyond *worse*. Ken was despicable. And the shit he pulled is downright unforgivable. You did nothing wrong. Don't beat yourself up, and celebrate instead."

"That's right!" Oh shit, not the drunk friend again. "To divorce!" This cheer again?

Glasses clinked again, and more women cheered.

Call it stupidity, curiosity, and definitely the rye in his system, but before he knew what he was doing, Mark was up and out of his seat. Holy shit, there were more of them than he thought. A quick count said at least six women sat around the table.

He cleared his throat. "Excuse me, ladies, but I couldn't help overhearing—"

"Couldn't help?" The obnoxious one cut him off.

"Shut up, Mercedes, and let the handsome man speak," another woman scolded, slapping *Mercedes* on the shoulder. "Go on ... you were saying?" She flashed Mark a bright white smile, and heavily lashed brown eyes blinked at him.

Fighting not to roll his eyes, Mark offered the women a big smile instead. "Thank you. Yes, well, I was sitting right behind you and couldn't help but overhear that you're celebrating a divorce."

"That's right," Mercedes said with a nod, tossing her poker-straight blonde hair behind her with the kind of attitude you would expect from a moody teenager. "Tori here just separated from Ken, King of the Asswipes, and we are cel-e-brating!" She pointed to the cringing brunette in the corner with bright blue eyes and the color of absolute embarrassment staining her high cheekbones.

"Well, I'd like to offer to buy your table a round of drinks," Mark went on. "I'm no stranger to an ugly separation and divorce and being hurt, and I wish I'd had a group of friends to rally around me like this when it all went down."

Tori's eyes pinned on him. Jesus, she was a stunner. It didn't even look like she was trying, and the woman had the girl-next-door look down pat. Big pouty lips, long feathered lashes and, when she finally bestowed him with a smile, although small and demure, it stole his breath clear from his lungs.

"Ah, fuck. I'll cover your tab for the night. Drinks are on me." Well that came out before he could stop himself. Had the woman in the corner really put that much of a spell on him?

"Wow! Thanks, dude," Mercedes whooped, her light gray-blue eyes sparkling under the muted pot lights above the booth. "I may have judged you a bit too harshly. Thought you were coming over to tell us to be quiet."

"You ... uh ... you want to join us?" another woman offered.

"Mark. Just call me Mark."

"Care to join us for a moment, Mark?" She scooted over. "After all, it's the least we can do since you're covering our tab."

"And what a tab," Mercedes chimed in.

Mark wasn't sure he liked this woman. How did sweet little Tori know this woman? Were they BFFs? He certainly hoped not.

How do you know she's sweet little Tori? She hasn't said a word to you.

Yeah, but that dreamy pout and those big wide doll eyes said a lot.

Mark sat down next to the woman who offered him a seat, but his gaze remained fixed on Tori.

The woman he was sitting next to tapped him on the shoulder. "I have to use the ladies' room. Do you mind?" The club music was pumping, unlike a moment ago where it'd been low enough for him to overhear their booth, so they all had to kind of yell at each other. The new DJ liked it loud.

Just as quickly as he'd sat down, he was back standing up, letting three women (because women never went to the restroom alone) vacate the booth. Thankfully, one of those women was Mercedes.

"I'm going to order us another round on my way to the loo," Mercedes hollered, donning a fake British accent.

That left two more quiet girls on their phones and Tori in the booth. And of course, Mark.

Tori caught his eye. "Thank you."

He took his opening and scooted across the bench seat, leaning in next to her ear so he didn't have to yell. "You're welcome."

"So you're separated too?"

He nodded. "Yeah, divorced. Coming up on a year."

"I'm sorry."

"Yeah, me too. But it's for the best. So I overheard that you put your ex through school only for him to cheat on you with his colleague? Did you get to attend school at all?"

Her big sapphire orbs went wide, and with a single nod, she reached for her drink and finished it. "Yep and nope. All I have is my undergrad. He screwed me over for grad school. The prick."

"Wow. I'm really sorry."

She stifled a belch. "Thanks."

"What were you going to go to school for?"

She glanced at him out of the corner of her eye. "What's your angle here, dude?"

Oh, she had some spunk to her. He liked that.

Holding up his hands in surrender, he shook his head, hoping the look on his face was convincingly innocent. "Nothing. I swear. I was supposed to meet a friend here tonight, but he got called away last minute, so I decided to sit and finish my drink. That's when I overheard your party. To be fair, your friend Mercedes isn't exactly quiet."

Tori rolled her eyes. "We're not that close. She went to college with my younger sister. She's more Iz's friend than mine. And yes, she's extremely loud." She nibbled on her bottom lip for a moment, then spun to face him dead on. Something almost akin to panic graced her beautiful face. "But she's got a big heart. I don't *dislike* her. She showed up on my doorstep with wine, cheese and chocolate the moment I let the breakup cat out of its piss- and fur-filled bag."

Mark chuckled. "As long as her heart is big, I suppose."

"It is big ... " She glanced at the women across the table who were engrossed in their phones. "But so is her mouth. Sorry if she offended you at all."

"Takes a lot to offend me. Don't worry. She's been drinking. I'll give her a bye." His eyes ran over her body. She was wearing a black dress with a deep V that cut down past her cleavage. She wasn't big-chested, which was probably why she could pull off such a dress. She wore no jewelry, and her makeup was minimal. Like a sexy version of the girl next door. Not quite demure, but pure and perfect with just a touch of spice, a touch of dirty.

"Ya done?" she asked, clearing her throat.

Mark's eyes snapped up to her face. "Done what?"

"Checking me out?"

He also didn't embarrass easily. "Yep."

She scoffed and shook her head with a small smile. "I hope you also managed to overhear that I am in no position and have zero interest in *finding a stallion I can ride bareback* at the moment. I'm taking some time for *me*. I need to figure out my life. Figure out work and school."

"Right. I *did* hear that. Sorry, you're very beautiful, but I won't make a move. I promise. I get that things are still raw after your separation. It's never easy. Our hearts aren't made of rubber. They don't bounce back easily."

A small smile drew up the corner of her mouth. "Nice analogy."

"I've been known to come out with some good ones from time to time."

Eyes as crystal blue as Lake Louise glimmered back at him. Even under the weird lights at the club, he could tell they were vibrant and full of life. "I appreciate your understanding. Thank you."

He smiled. They were back in a good place. Excellent. "So, what do you do for work? What are you hoping to go to grad school for?"

"Wow, you really were eavesdropping."

"Your friend ... "

She nodded. "Right. Mercedes. She's volume-challenged."

"So? What do you do for work?"

"Well ... I *used* to wait tables down at The Sunspear Bar and Grill three nights a week. I was also a dog walker three days a week, a cat sitter when needed, and I worked with children on the autism spectrum as an intervention therapist and educational assistant. I have my bachelor's degree in child and youth care, with a special focus on children with special needs and learning disabilities."

Mark nearly spat his rye out but managed to swallow it all down, causing his esophagus to spasm in the process.

Had she noticed?

The look she gave him said she did.

"You okay there, Mark?"

"Yeah, sorry. It's just, well ... I may have a job for you."

One eyebrow slowly slid up her forehead in skepticism. "Yeah?"

The woman was clearly jaded when it came to men, and she'd told him loud and clear that she wasn't interested in anything remotely resembling a relationship or otherwise. He needed to play this one cool. If she thought for one minute that he was only offering her the job to hit on her, she'd be out the door.

His mother, bless her flower-child soul, would call this fate.

Mark needed someone exactly like Tori in his life. And here she was.

"And what kind of a *job* would that be?" Her gaze slid down his body and landed on the crotch of his dress pants.

Wow, she was a ball-buster.

"Not *for* me. I just know of a job. A friend of mine is looking for an intervention therapist for his son. His son is on the spectrum, and they just lost his therapist a little while ago."

Her eyes perked up, and the disbelief faded from her face, though not entirely. "A *friend* of yours, huh? And what does this *friend* do?"

"He's a doctor. He's also divorced, like me. It's just him and his little boy, Gabe. Cute kid, crazy smart."

"How old?"

"Thirty-eight."

Her lip twitched into a sort of smile. "I mean Gabe. How old is Gabe?" She rolled those gorgeous blue eyes and shook her head. "Yes, how old is the dad? Good lord."

Mark chuckled. "Gabe is five. He just started kindergarten in September."

She nodded. "And your friend, what's his name?"

Mark swallowed. "Uh ... Chris. Dr. Chris Herron."

"Chris Herron?"

"Yeah."

"Oookay, let's say I'm interested. How would I go about applying with this *Dr. Herron?*"

"I can set it up. I can give you his phone number. That

way you don't have to give me yours. And you can text him. I will let him know that I found someone who might be interested in the behavior interventionist job, and she'll be contacting him."

"You think texting is professional enough?"

Mark's head bobbed in agreement while the hair on the back of his neck prickled as the little white lie he'd started to spin slowly began to take on a life of its own. "Oh yeah, totally. He's a busy guy. Can't always answer the phone, but always has it on him to text."

"If you say so." She pulled out her phone. "Okay, give me his number."

IF YOU'VE ENJOYED THIS BOOK

If you've enjoyed this book, please consider leaving a review.
It really does make a difference.
Thank you again.
Xoxo
Whitley Cox

ACKNOWLEDGMENTS

There are so many people to thank who help along the way. Publishing a book is definitely not a solo mission, that's for sure. First and foremost, my friend and editor Chris Kridler, you are a blessing, a gem and an all-around terrific person. Thank you for your honesty and hard work.

Thank you, to my critique groups gals, Danielle and Jillian. I love our meetups where we give honest feedback. You two are my bitch-sisters and I wouldn't give you up for anything.

Kathleen Lawless, for just being you and wonderful and always there for me.

Author Jeanne St. James, my alpha reader and sister from another mister, what would I do without you?

Megan J. Parker-Squiers from EmCat Designs, your covers are awesome. Thank you.

My street team, Whitley Cox's Curiously Kinky Reviewers, you are all awesome and I feel so blessed to have found such wonderful fans.

The ladies of Vancouver Island Romance Authors, your

support and insight have been incredibly helpful, and I'm so honored to be a part of a group of such talented writers.

Author Cora Seton, I love our walks, talks and heart-to-hearts, they mean so much to me.

Author Ember Leigh, my newest author bestie, I love our bitch fests—they keep me sane.

Ana Rita Clemente, the first "fan" I ever met in person. Thank you for proofreading this one.

My parents, in-laws and brother, thank you for your unwavering support.

The Small Human and the Tiny Human, you are the beats and beasts of my heart, the reason I breathe and the reason I drink. I love you both to infinity and beyond.

And lastly, of course, the husband. You are my forever, my other half, the one who keeps me grounded and the only person I have honestly never grown sick of even when we did that six-month backpacking trip and spent every single day together. I never tired of you. Never needed a break. You are my person. I love you.

ALSO BY WHITLEY COX

mybook.to/quickandreckless

Book 3, A Quick Billionaires Novel

Silver and Warren

Quick & Dangerous

mybook.to/quickanddangerous

Book 4, A Quick Billionaires Novel

Skyler and Roberto

Hot Dad

mybook.to/hotdad

Harper and Sam

Lust Abroad

mybook.to/lustabroad

Piper and Derrick

Snowed In & Set Up

mybook.to/snowedinandsetup

Amber, Will, Juniper, Hunter, Rowen, Austin

Hard Hart

mybook.to/hard_hart

The Harty Boys, Book 1

Krista and Brock

Hired by the Single Dad

mybook.to/hiredbythesingledad

The Single Dads of Seattle, Book 1

Tori and Mark

Upcoming

Doctor Smug

Mybook.to/doctorsmug

Daisy and Riley

Lost Hart

The Harty Boys, Book 2

Stacey and Chase

Torn Hart

The Harty Boys, Book 3

Dark Hart

The Harty Boys, Book 4

Quick & Snowy

The Quick Billionaires, Book 5

Raw, Fierce and Awakened: Part 1

The Dark and Damaged Hearts Series, Book 9

Raw, Fierce and Awakened: Part 2

The Dark and Damaged Hearts Series, Book 10

ABOUT THE AUTHOR

A Canadian West Coast baby born and raised, Whitley is married to her high school sweetheart, and together they have two beautiful daughters and a fluffy dog. She spends her days making food that gets thrown on the floor, vacuuming Cheerios out from under the couch and making sure that the dog food doesn't end up in the air conditioner. But when nap time comes, and it's not quite wine o'clock, Whitley sits down, avoids the pile of laundry on the couch, and writes.

A lover of all things decadent; wine, cheese, chocolate and spicy erotic romance, Whitley brings the humorous side of sex, the ridiculous side of relationships and the suspense of everyday life into her stories. With single dads, firefighters, Navy SEALs, mommy wars, body issues, threesomes, bondage and role-playing, Whitley's books have all the funny and fabulously filthy words you could hope for.

YOU CAN ALSO FIND ME HERE

Website: WhitleyCox.com
Twitter: @WhitleyCoxBooks
Instagram: @CoxWhitley
Facebook Page: https://www.facebook.com/CoxWhitley/
Blog: https://whitleycox.blogspot.ca/
Multi-Author Blog: https://romancewritersbehavingbadly.
blogspot.com
Exclusive Facebook Reader Group: https://www.facebook.
com/groups/234716323653592/
Booksprout: https://booksprout.co/author/994/whitley-cox
Bookbub: https://www.bookbub.com/authors/whitley-cox

Subscribe to my newsletter here
http://eepurl.com/ckh5yT

JOIN MY STREET TEAM

WHITLEY COX'S CURIOUSLY KINKY REVIEWERS
Hear about giveaways, games, ARC opportunities, new releases, teasers, author news, character and plot development and more!

Facebook Street Team
Join NOW!

DON'T FORGET TO SUBSCRIBE TO MY NEWSLETTER

Be the first to hear about pre-orders, new releases, giveaways, 99 cent deals, and freebies!

Click here to Subscribe
http://eepurl.com/ckh5yT

Made in the USA
Middletown, DE
26 March 2021